Acclaim for the authors of

THE THREE
*Gifts*

### LYNN BULOCK

"A tender story, carefully penned with warmth..."
—*Romantic Times* on GIFTS OF GRACE

"A compelling story of love which
will touch your heart and stir your soul."
—*Rendezvous* on LOOKING FOR MIRACLES

Although Lynn wrote her first book in fourth grade, she
began her career as a broadcast journalist before deciding
to write full-time. Since then, Lynn has written
numerous books and articles.

### IRENE HANNON

"A wonderful, fulfilling read."
—*Romantic Times* on THE WAY HOME

"A poignant, touching story...great!"
—*Rendezvous* on ONE SPECIAL CHRISTMAS

A prolific author of inspirational and
traditional romances, Irene began her writing career
at the age of ten when she won a story contest
in a national children's magazine.

### LENORA WORTH

"A sweet holiday story
to get you into the giving season..."
—*Rendezvous* on
I'LL BE HOME FOR CHRISTMAS

"Truly inspiring and heart warming."
—*Rendezvous* on ONE GOLDEN CHRISTMAS

Since selling her first book in 1993, Lenora has written
over ten titles for Steeple Hill. This talented author has
mastered the talent of pulling inspiration from the people
and events that surround her.

# THE THREE *Gifts*

## LYNN BULOCK

## IRENE HANNON

## LENORA WORTH

Steeple Hill™

Published by Steeple Hill Books™

STEEPLE HILL BOOKS

Steeple
Hill™

ISBN 0-373-87240-2

THE THREE GIFTS

Copyright © 2002 by Harlequin Books S.A.

The publisher acknowledges the copyright holders of the individual works as follows:

GIFTS OF GRACE
Copyright © 1999 by Lynn M. Bulock

ONE SPECIAL CHRISTMAS
Copyright © 1999 by Irene Hannon Gottlieb

I'LL BE HOME FOR CHRISTMAS
Copyright © 1998 by Lenora H. Nazworth

Visit us at www.steeplehill.com

**Printed in U.S.A.**

# CONTENTS

**Books by Lynn Bulock**

Love Inspired

*Looking for Miracles* #97
*Walls of Jericho* #125
*The Prodigal's Return* #144
*Change of the Heart* #181

*LYNN BULOCK*

lives in Thousand Oaks, California, with her husband, two sons, a dog and a cat. She has been telling stories since she could talk and writing them down since fourth grade. She is the author of seventeen contemporary romance novels.

# GIFTS OF GRACE
## Lynn Bulock

To Joe, always,
and
to "little Joe," "Triple J," "Bula"
and "Joey-Joe-Joe"—
I love you all.

# Prologue

"What am I going to do?"

Standing in her cold living room long before dawn, there were no people to keep Grace Mallory company and very little furniture to deaden the echo of her own voice. The battered couch had come with the rental house, although the afghan draped over it was hers, one of her few prized possessions. Feeling a chill, Grace picked up the coverlet and wrapped it around herself.

She needed a hug. She needed a lot more than just one hug, but the soft old coverlet's embrace was as close to that as she was going to get. "Aunt Jo, what am I going to do?" she mused to the woman who had raised her and crocheted the afghan. Grace had no idea where Jo was now, or where she had been for years. She might even be with the Lord she loved so much and had told Grace about so many times.

Wherever she was, Jo would have known what to do. Grace didn't know. She'd been so worried about the children. This was their third Christmas in a row without their father. First he'd been in jail, then last year before the holidays he was killed in an inmates' brawl. Now, her memory of him had faded, but the legacy of pain and poverty he'd left behind was still here: She had nothing to give the children for Christmas.

Her son Matthew had been concerned about that—not for himself, but for little Maria. At age ten, Matt was sure he was too old and tough for Christmas to matter. At bedtime last night he'd stood before her at the kitchen table. "Don't worry about Christmas. I took care of it,'' he'd told her. Grace had been too worried about other things at the time to give the matter much thought.

But at three this morning when she couldn't sleep, something had drawn her downstairs. The wrapped presents under the tree, even if they were few, filled her with dismay. Nobody would hire a ten-year-old to work in town, would they? Could Matthew have stolen these things, and the bright paper to wrap them in?

Grace felt so helpless. She'd done everything she could to try to raise the children right, to keep them from making any of the mistakes she and their father had made. Now her heart told her things were terribly, terribly wrong. ''What do I do?'' she whispered. ''What do I do?'' It had started out as a question for Jo, but by the time she voiced it out loud, it was a prayer.

It had been a long time since Grace had prayed. She still believed in God, but wasn't He just up there someplace watching? Surely He didn't care about her. That was pretty obvious in the downward spiral her life had taken in the last few years.

*Wait. Watch. Pray.* The words were as clear as if someone standing in the room with her had spoken them. Grace stepped back, stunned. Wait, watch and pray? She could do that. The wait-and-watch part, too. She looked out the window, where ancient drapes framed a frosty scene. Outside? Surely it was too cold to sit out on the porch and pray. And what if Maria called her? Grace was sure she was getting sick again.

Still, the porch drew her like a magnet. She went to the kitchen and grabbed a chair. Then, with the afghan still wrapped around her shoulders, she opened the front door and set the chair firmly on the front porch.

The chrome legs of the chair settled into a light dusting of snow. Grace smiled wryly. It really wasn't much colder on the porch than it had been in the living room. ''All right, I'll wait. And watch. And pray,'' she said softly. Maybe God wasn't so far away after all. Grace couldn't help feeling that He was out there, someplace close by. For the first time in a very long while, hope poked into her heart, nudging aside the despair that was her constant companion. She settled in to wait the coming of the dawn, and whatever the day would bring.

# Chapter One

Carl Brenner trudged through the snow, wondering why the house wasn't next door to the store. Not that it mattered most of the time. Most winters in Missouri didn't bring snow this deep before Christmas.

Today it was cold enough that he would have driven the pickup the five blocks between the house and the store. But that would have meant giving up one of the precious parking spaces in front of the store on the Redwing town square, and this time of year they were at a premium. So he and the yellow dog with no real name except Four—for his position in a line of yellow dogs that stretched back twenty-five years—walked in the bitter cold.

Right now, one of those moods had closed in on him again—of wanting something. Except he didn't know what he wanted. He just knew it was out there, intangible and just beyond reach. No amount of prayer and Scripture had brought it closer, either. He was still running a store he didn't care much about in a town that didn't amount to spit. Granted, he never went hungry and he always had a roof over his head. He wasn't in debt. But he wouldn't miss anything in his life if anyone stole it, either. Except Four, and perhaps a pile of papers that would be meaningless to any other human being and didn't amount to enough physically to start a good fire.

The wind had died down once he turned the corner onto Main, where the buildings on the square gave some protection from the bitter breeze. Four perked up, and Carl looked ahead to see why.

The reason was quickly apparent and as quickly unwelcome. A

delegation waited on the sidewalk, and it wasn't customers waiting for him to open the store. This was not the way to start the day.

Twenty minutes later the crowd had filed into the bank and Carl stood with them, shifting uncomfortably from foot to foot, dripping melted snow on the bank floor like everybody else. Like Four, mercifully curled up in a back corner so he wouldn't jump on people, Carl never felt comfortable during official town meetings such as this. He might have agreed to fill the empty seat on the town council, but he still didn't like these meetings.

"You know why we're here," Mayor Larry Trent finally began, looking at Carl. "It happened again yesterday. And I know he came in your place, too. This time you have to do something." The other two merchants nodded, Naomi from the café most emphatically.

Carl just couldn't stir up the same kind of righteous indignation as the rest of the group. "Now, look," Carl warned the shorter, portly man. "I have a store to run, and it's Christmas Eve. I don't see why I should be the one to go out to that farm and tell Grace Mallory she's raising a thief."

Mayor Larry Trent smiled uneasily. A squiff of his mouse-brown hair stood straight up, probably part of that patch he usually combed carefully over the bald spot at the top of his head. It gave him a comic air that belied the empty bank's frigid, formal atmosphere. "We can get somebody to watch the store for you, Carl," he coaxed. "Besides, it just doesn't look right, my going. The bank is the one place the kid doesn't ever take anything from."

"Wish I could say the same," huffed "Doc" Conrad, the town pharmacist. "I lose ten bucks every time that kid comes in the drugstore lately."

Carl huffed. The bank wasn't getting any warmer, and he had plenty to do next door before opening up. "Why don't we get you to do this? Or Ed? I mean, what are we paying him for as police chief, if not for stuff like this?"

"Because Doc would scare her to death. And if we let Ed in on this, it's going to get official," Naomi said, looking like the grandmother she was. "Then we're talking the county juvenile hall for a ten-year-old. He's a thief, but he's not even a good thief. Surely we can handle this ourselves and keep it quiet."

The anger rising in Carl nearly warmed him. "It's not like I'm taking home a lost dog, here. I'm going to have to tell the woman her kid's been stealing the town blind.''

''And you'll do a fine job of it, Carl,'' intoned the mayor in his best professional voice, his plump white hands steepled in front of his white shirt. ''Why don't you give me the key to the store?''

Carl trudged back home to get his truck, thinking very unchristian, un-Christmaslike thoughts about his mission. This time Four didn't stop anyplace along the way, just followed obediently, seemingly aware of his master's mood.

As he and Four got into his truck, Carl hoped he'd recognize the house, and the woman, once he got there. He knew the Mallory family rented the old Krieger place. It had gone to seed so badly after old Mr. Krieger lived there alone. Mrs. Mallory and the two kids had moved in about two years ago.

He tried to remember what Mrs. Mallory looked like, the times he'd seen her. Pale hair, he recalled. A pale, narrow face. Not very tall, and not very wide. Past that, she was a cipher. Carl had guessed that maybe she was afraid of him.

Of course, many people seemed intimidated by his size. Not that Carl enjoyed it much himself. At well over six feet, he was constantly hitting his head on things or having to fold himself up to fit somewhere, like in the overly narrow pews at church.

Carl could vaguely remember the younger Mallory child. He recalled it was a girl, but like her mother she remained a shadow in his mind. The family didn't go to the church in town, so his knowledge of them socially had been nil.

About the time he'd admitted to being hopelessly lost, due to the heavy snowfall the inkling of a path up ahead led away from the road. Carl turned the truck onto the poorly kept track, immediately sliding on the icy gravel beneath the deep snow.

At first the Mallory house was just an outline on the horizon, then it came into focus as a gray heap of lumber ahead. It looked awfully small—even for a family of three. Only the covering of snow smoothed out the uneven stubble of the fields. The barn roof sagged at one corner, and the shack that seemed to pass for a chicken coop looked as if a good wind would blow it over. A widow and two kids left on this rattletrap farm.

''What a Christmas!'' Carl said aloud, expelling a tired breath.

The dog leaned up against him, looking for warmth and comfort, and Carl had little of either to give.

Jake Krieger made a lousy landlord. Why hadn't he painted this place, and done more repairs? Surely he wasn't expecting a single woman as a tenant to do his work for him. Carl knew just enough about Grace to believe she would have fixed the place up if she had the money, but it wasn't her job.

It was coming closer. Grace hadn't really been aware of the truck until it slewed in the gravel as it turned off the main road. She shifted in the chair, marveling that day had already dawned. She had been so numb with grief that turned into anger and confusion that she'd been oblivious to it growing lighter.

Now it was Christmas Eve morning, and instead of the police car pulling in as she'd expected, someone else drove toward her through the snow in a black pickup. She pondered that in her mind, but no explanation came—probably because she was so cold and so tired and so entirely worn-out that no answers to anything were going to come right away.

She didn't recognize the driver even as the truck came closer. It wasn't Ed Dobbins, that much she knew. Relief warmed her stiff body. That meant that what she had been contemplating since before dawn—what she had been steeling herself for—she wouldn't have to do. Not now. Not today, anyway.

If Ed did come to the house, he was going to have to arrest her before he got Matt. That much she had decided in the predawn hours. By morning she'd wavered, picturing her children in separate foster homes if she went to jail. Would that be any better than just letting them take Matt?

She still couldn't figure out the identity of the man up ahead. He was tall sitting in the truck seat, and even as he got out there was a powerful depth to his body.

Someone sat beside him on the seat. Not someone, exactly, Grace saw, as a big yellow dog leapt out of the pickup behind the man.

As the two drew closer and came up to the fence line, Grace found herself more aware of her stiff, cold body. She wondered if she could rise from this chair.

The man was nearly at the porch now. This close she could see who it was, although she couldn't think of his name—the store-keeper from town, the one who always treated her like a real person when she was in his store. Why had they sent him instead of the police?

"Mrs. Mallory? Can I come up?" Carl asked as he stopped at the bottom of the steps. She was as he had remembered her and much more. Her pale hair was a yellow lighter than corn silk, pulled back severely to frame a face that looked much too narrow. Strands of it straggled out of the band that held them. The woman's eyes were dark and clouded like those of a wild animal, and there seemed to be smudges under them. She looked so fragile in her faded jeans that a good puff of wind would probably have knocked her down. This was going to be difficult.

"You're welcome. It's about Matt, isn't it?" She sounded tired. "You're not with the police. Does that mean he's not in trouble?"

The dog whined beside him, and Carl put down a hand to quell him. "No, ma'am, he's still in trouble. Could we go inside?" He started toward the porch steps which were still covered with new snow.

"If you're here to arrest him, I don't want to go inside," Grace Mallory said. Up close she didn't look as wild—just muddled. Looking at the quilt thrown over her faded jeans, though, Carl wondered if she'd spent the entire night in that chair. Her clothes had a frosty look to them.

For a moment he questioned her sanity.

"I don't have the authority to arrest him," Carl told her. "We can just consider this a warning." He went up the steps, which creaked under his weight.

Being on the porch made him more conscious of his size than ever. The roof hovered bare inches above his head, and he towered over the woman, which made him feel like a thug.

"So the things I found... Matt didn't buy them, did he? He doesn't have an after-school job in town."

His task refused to get any easier. "That isn't exactly what happened," Carl replied, shifting his weight uncomfortably. The wind didn't get to them here, but the cold sure did. How could the woman have spent the night here?

She looked up at him, the expression in her dark eyes more focused and alert. "What *is* going on?" she demanded sharply. "If you're not going to arrest him, what's going to happen now?"

Carl took a deep breath. "The boy's been stealing from every store in town—even Miss Naomi's Café. They sent me out here to tell you, and say that it has to stop." As he spoke, Grace Mallory stood straighter for a moment and then her eyes widened and she swayed. Carl readied himself for the female hysterics he expected to follow.

Instead, she came upright again and asked, calmly, "You're really *not* going to try and take him away?" Her eyes were even wider with surprise, and as innocent as those of his dog.

"Hadn't planned on it," Carl confirmed, ready for the protestations of her son's innocence to begin.

"Then we'd better go in and talk to Matt," she said. "He's got an awful lot of explaining to do."

Carl didn't know what took him more by surprise at that moment. At first it was her attitude—totally the opposite of the defending mother he'd expected—and then her actions that startled him. As Grace Mallory turned to swing open the door to the sagging house, the gravity of the situation must have caught up with her, and she lost her balance on the snowy porch. She was fainting or falling— Carl couldn't tell which—and she was headed for the ground if he didn't catch her first.

# Chapter Two

Her body felt very cold and impossibly light, Carl thought, as he caught her. But even as light as she was, Grace Mallory filled his arms so that he couldn't reach the doorknob. He stood in front of the door, flummoxed, with his burden of woman and coverlet in his arms, and the dog whining and winding around his legs. Should he kick on the door and hope those kids were awake and would open up?

Before he could kick, Matthew opened the door. The boy's coltish arms and legs poked out of his shirt and jeans, and his pale hair looked even more disordered than his mother's. As soon as the door was all the way open, the boy's eyes widened as much as Grace's had and he launched himself at Carl. The dog barked at someone charging his master, but Carl called him back and he sat. The boy cried out, still launching himself at his much larger adversary.

"Mom! If you've hurt her..."

"I didn't hurt her. She fainted or something," Carl said, brushing past the boy as gently as he could. "Is there someplace to put her?" How could someone who couldn't be much more than five feet of skin and bones make his arms ache like this?

Matt still looked at him suspiciously. "In the living room." The Mallorys' "living room" was not made for living. It was as cold as the bank lobby and almost as empty. Carl was surprised that the scraggly Christmas tree wasn't decorated with icicles. "Maria. Move, now," the boy said with noticeable gentleness.

A small girl, with even more wild hair than anyone else in the family, slid off the beat-up couch that was the only piece of furniture in the room. As the child stood, she whimpered.

"She's sick," the boy said. "You sure Mom's going to be okay?"

"She'll come around in a minute," Carl said as he deposited his burden and started probing for a pulse in the woman's cool throat to see if he was right. Her even breathing reassured him, but the feverish feel of her skin under her shirt collar worried him.

She murmured something, and then her eyes came open. They were the same shade of brown as both her children's eyes, Carl noted, and they were as confused as a baby's. "What happened?" she asked.

"You passed out or something. Thought you needed to be inside," he explained. "Could you sit up and drink something warm?"

"I can sit up, I think." Her thin hand passed over her hair, all loosened now by Carl's clumsy efforts to get her inside the house. "I doubt there's something warm to drink."

"There's no milk," the boy said, sounding apologetic. "I wrapped Maria in another blanket. But she says she's hungry."

The little girl nodded, and made a noise somewhere between a sob and a mew. She moved toward her mother, flinging thin arms around her neck. She didn't move with a lot of energy. Carl puckered his brow as he looked at her. "The boy says she's sick?"

Grace's eyes clouded even more, then cleared and she stared down at her own lap, putting one arm protectively around the child. "Another ear infection, I suppose. I kept her home from school yesterday, hoping she'd be better."

"But you didn't call the doctor?"

"Don't have one. We go to the county health clinic when we can. I knew there wasn't money for medicine even if I went, so we didn't go," Grace said simply. Her outthrust chin dared him to say anything.

Carl lost his balance in surprise, and went from crouching beside the couch to sitting on the floor. The rug under him felt coarse and cold. "No doctor at all?"

"None. I guess we could get vouchers or something if we went on welfare, but I'm not about to do that, Mr.—"

"Brenner, Carl Brenner. From the store in Redwing."

"The store part I remembered, Mr. Brenner. Just your name escaped me."

Her husky voice had a little bit of the South in it. The boy's voice when he spoke sounded sharper. "Are you sure he didn't hurt you, Mom?"

"Not at all. In fact, Mr. Brenner caught me so I didn't fall out there. Mr. Brenner and his dog, I think. Where did he get to?"

"Still out on the porch. If I'm going to be here a while, could I call him in? He's clean and gentle. He'll stay in a corner."

"Of course," Grace said. "Not even a dog should be out too long in weather like this." She looked at Carl again, communicating much with few words. "Are you sure about what you told me out there?"

"Yes, ma'am. I saw things myself."

She sat up a little straighter and pushed her hair behind her. "Then could I ask you to give me a moment alone with my children? If you could put some water on for tea or something, to thaw us both out…"

Carl nodded. What little he'd seen of Grace Mallory so far told him that she could handle the difficult conversation with her son well—perhaps better if Carl left the room. He whistled Four in off the porch, and shut the door behind him. Going down the narrow hallway, they entered the only other door opening off it besides the living room, and Carl told the dog to lie down. Four found the most out-of-the-way corner and settled in.

The kitchen was a good size, but poorly furnished. There was a dinette set that looked far older than the children, the three chrome chairs around the table matching the one on the porch, and a small array of metal kitchen cabinets. The chipped countertops were clean but empty. There was no microwave, no coffee maker, not even a toaster oven. Judging from the limited range of kitchen appliances, it wasn't fancy cooking that went on here.

There was a battered teakettle on the stove, and he took it to the sink. The water still ran when he turned on the faucet, so at least the county was getting paid basic utilities. Either that, or the place had a well.

He filled the kettle and put it on the stove. The burner turned on with a whoosh when he turned the knob. This far out there would be a propane tank someplace in the backyard. Carl was willing to bet there was precious little in it.

While the water boiled Carl scavenged for tea or instant coffee, and thought about the boy's reaction to him bringing Mrs. Mallory in off the porch.

Carl knew that if his own mother had been alive when he was that age, he would have tried to take anybody apart who hurt her. He remembered what he'd done when he hadn't been much older and somebody had sicced a hunting dog on the original Yellow Dog.

There was scarcely any food in the kitchen. The more Carl looked around the place, the more his opinion of the young mother changed. He'd expected to come out here to find a woman who would deny her son was stealing and get in his face. Instead, a nagging thought was taking hold: Matthew Mallory was stealing to keep his family together, and hiding it from his mother.

This changed the complexion of things a bit. Carl shook his head. There had to be something he could fix for breakfast to go along with the tea. Looking around, he didn't find much. No dry cereal, only half a loaf of bread. Peanut butter in the pantry, and part of a box of oatmeal. Matt had been right; there was no milk except powdered. That would do mixed with water as liquid for oatmeal, Carl reasoned. He started reading the box.

Before he could get oatmeal on the stove, the boy came into the kitchen, backhanding the evidence of tears from his face. "Did you have to tell her?"

"Yeah, I did. You're big enough to know stealing is wrong. You're lucky it's me out here and not the police chief. If it was him, you'd be going to juvenile hall, or a foster home."

The boy tried to look tough. It didn't work very well. "Would you have given me a job if I asked for one?"

Carl stood beside him for a moment, feeling more awkward than usual. The boy looked up, his eyes bright. He seemed to sense Carl's discomfort. "You know I wouldn't. But there are alternatives." Carl put a hand on his shoulder, feeling the prominent bone under his fingers. "There's a whole town about six miles down the road, willing to help if you ask. You don't have to be a full-grown man at—what, eleven?"

"Ten." He said it looking down at the floor, as if ashamed to admit less age than Carl had guessed.

"Ten, then. It's an age to go to school and stay out of trouble. There will be ways for your family to get on. We'll see to it."

The boy's eyes held a challenge Carl could have recognized in himself at the same age. "Yeah, well, it won't be welfare. Mom won't go for that. Or charity from some church, either. That's why we moved here in the first place. Some goofy church adopted us for Christmas when my dad was still alive and in jail. And they wanted to do it again last year once he was dead. Mom wouldn't have it." The boy seemed to run out of words. He looked up at Carl. "Do you play basketball?"

Carl had to laugh. "I'm not that tall. Only about six-three, maybe six-four."

Matt gave a low whistle. "That's still pretty tall. You wouldn't fit inside that henhouse out back."

"Would I want to?" Carl asked. "If there's chickens in there I could scramble eggs for breakfast instead of cooking oatmeal."

"No chickens. We would have eaten them if there were," Matt said with great practicality. "I mean, I'm pretty good, but I couldn't steal chicken feed."

Carl looked at him sharply. "You're not pretty good. You stink as a sneak thief. For which I am very thankful, because if you were good at it you would still be doing it."

"Hey, if I were good at it we'd be having Christmas," Matt challenged. "But I've got one up on you. You don't know how to make oatmeal, do you?"

Carl felt chagrined at being found out by a ten-year-old. "Not a clue. I cook the kind you dump in the microwave. Want to give me a hand, here?"

The boy's thin face split with the first grin Carl had seen from him. "I may stink as a thief, but I can cook oatmeal," he said. "Watch and learn."

The warmth of the kitchen felt welcoming. Carl noticed that the boy's worn sneakers looked awfully small for his tall frame, and narrow, as if perhaps they had belonged to someone else first. Carl was pretty sure he could see sock through a couple of holes.

The boy was at the stove stirring the oatmeal. Carl hoped he knew what he was doing. The kid had been impressed that Carl had thought of using the powdered milk to fortify the stuff. It looked less like wallpaper paste that way. He wished there was some cinnamon to go with the brown sugar in it. Or raisins. Some Christmas Eve breakfast this was for anybody.

Matthew tried to sound nonchalant as he stirred the oatmeal and talked at the same time. "A while ago when you were talking about foster homes? It sounded like you knew something about that."

"I do," Carl said. Nobody else in Redwing knew how much he knew about that particular subject. Redwing's knowledge of Carl began when he was a skinny, gangly young teen, come to live with his mother's brother, Jim. He struggled over how much to tell the boy. "I saw a few foster homes before I was your age. Trust me, you'd rather be here with your mom."

"Yeah, but wouldn't it be easier on her if I weren't?" The pain in the young boy's voice was agonizing for Carl.

"No!" he said sharply—more sharply than he'd intended. He noticed that Matt nearly dropped the spoon. "Take my word on it, your mom would rather have *three* of you getting into trouble all day long right under her nose than give you up." He'd only really met the woman this morning, but that much was evident.

He wished there had been someone to tell him that at age ten. Of course, by then he was an orphan in the third foster-care home he'd been in, with Yellow Dog the only constant in his life and childhood nothing but a vague, troubling memory. Even if someone had told him that, it would not have been the truth. But for Matthew it was, and it seemed to comfort him some. "That stuff ready to put in bowls yet?" Carl asked, trying to do the man-to-man thing and ignore the tears that threatened to engulf the kid again. Besides, he needed time to think himself. He was getting an idea. It was a crazy one, and it needed some working out. And it was the last thing he would have considered while driving out here. But suddenly this crazy idea sounded like exactly the right thing to do.

*He cooked them breakfast.* The wonder of it pushed through the confusion that clouded Grace's thoughts. This strange man, whom she barely knew had come to tell her that she could lose her son if she didn't find a way to get him to stop stealing from every store in town. And then, instead of nodding briefly and leaving her outside on the porch like any normal man, he had stayed around, and had picked her up when she'd fainted.

Since then, he'd done nothing but surprise her. His elegant movements and rough clothing were a contradiction of each other. The black pants and white shirt were certainly not the finest. He looked like someone who didn't care much about quality as long as his clothes fit, which she suspected was a challenge, given his tall, broad frame. His jacket hung oddly, as if he had the habit of shoving his hands and small heavy objects into the sagging pockets. His dark brown hair needed a trim. But despite all that, he looked as genteel as a prince in disguise.

And he cooked them breakfast—steaming tea, and oatmeal as good as anything she could have put together.

He sat at the table watching them eat. When she motioned toward the bowls with a questioning look at him, he shook his head. Grace itched to stroke his unruly, thick dark hair as she would little Matt's. It looked as if it would be springy and alive under her fingers.

Wondering where that thought had come from, she stared down at her bowl in silence. It surprised her that she could eat. Surely everything she had been through lately should have rendered her incapable of eating. But she knew she had two children to raise, alone. It wasn't ever going to get any easier. Matt's disaster here had pointed that out. It was time to move on, take some action.

"Do you need any help in that store of yours in Redwing?"

The question seemed to startle Brenner, whose eyes widened. Grace couldn't tell if he thought she was being rude or just insensitive in front of the children. She hated to tell him that they'd dealt with much harsher realities already in their short lives than planning shoplifting restitution at the breakfast table.

"I don't hire kids. Especially ones not even in their teens." The man didn't seem to have a lot of spare words. That was all right. She wouldn't have known what to do with a talkative man. "Besides, how would any of you get there?"

Grace looked at him. "That junker outside runs. It doesn't look like much, but it does still run most of the time. It ran well enough to get me to and from work on the line at the paper plant in New

Hope until I got laid off before Thanksgiving. I can hold a job. I'm capable.'' She seemed to have surprised Brenner by reading his thoughts. He looked embarrassed. ''Besides, getting there may be a lot shorter trip soon. This place is falling apart over our heads. If the landlord doesn't do something about it, I've told him I'm not signing a new lease next week. What is it, Mr. Brenner?''

''Just trying to figure things out. Right now it seems I came out here to solve one set of problems and got a different one instead.'' Carl looked around the room. ''No phone, right?''

Her nod confirmed what Grace was unwilling to say. She hadn't been able to afford a phone since they'd moved here.

''Still got a county phone book someplace?''

''It's down in the far right drawer,'' Grace said, watching Matt spring up to get it.

''Great. You know what a cellular phone looks like?'' Carl asked Matt.

Grace watched her son as he swallowed the last of his tea and nodded. ''Sure.''

''Good. Mine's on the seat of the truck. Go bring it back in.'' He handed the boy a set of keys.

Matt's eyes widened as big as the mugs they were drinking out of. Grace wondered what he'd say. Brenner was treating him almost like an equal—not a situation the boy was used to with any grown man.

Matt grabbed the keys and headed out the door.

''I can't remember all the numbers I need. We need to get Doc out here with some medicine. He'll make a delivery if we can get somebody from the clinic in New Hope to prescribe something. That child needs something today.''

Grace couldn't have agreed with him more. And just now, she didn't relish being alone with the children. Even after hot tea and a little food she felt strange, as if she might float away if she didn't keep herself firmly tethered.

Matt came in with the phone and the keys. ''All right,'' Carl said, looking up from the thin phone directory. ''And you didn't even lock the keys in the truck. I do that about once a month, myself.''

Matt grinned. ''You're too big to fit through the window, too.''

"You bet. I finally had Ed show me how to use one of those metal jimmy strips to get in. But I'm not gonna show you."

"Good," Grace said tartly. "We don't need to advance his illegal skills any."

Carl shrugged and dialed his phone. He made several calls—a little cryptic, when hearing only his end of the conversation. Finally he made another call, and during the conversation told the other person to hang on. "I need a pencil and paper," he told Matt.

He'd seen that Grace wasn't going to be able to get up and help, because Maria had fallen asleep on her lap. Matt nodded and quickly brought them. "Okay," Carl said into the phone, and listened for a while. Then he put the phone down again.

"If I drew a map to this place, could you ride into town with me and ride back with Doc to help him find the way here?" he asked, looking at the boy.

Matt looked at him, swallowing hard. "I think so."

"Good. Doc does a lot of things real well, but finding new places on unmarked county roads isn't one of them." He spoke into the phone a little more, then hung up. Matt settled down to watch Carl draw the map, putting in comments once in a while.

*He even writes gracefully for such a big man,* Grace thought. She was surprised that Carl could make an act look both masculine and graceful at the same time.

Matt seemed spellbound. While he leaned his elbows on the table to watch the proceedings, Grace shifted Maria a little and coaxed the fitful child to eat more.

She shook her head, pushing away her mother's hand. "Hurts. Don't want anything to eat."

"How will you get strong again if you don't eat, sugar?" her mother coaxed. But Maria wanted nothing more than a lap to cuddle in. Finally giving up, Grace settled the child in even more firmly and sipped the last of her warm tea.

Then she sat back in the chair, bone tired and almost oblivious to anything going on around her except her own thoughts. Because her husband had left her a penniless widow with no place to call her own, Matt had decided to solve that problem now by shoplifting. Grace thought that most women would be in a panic, faced with her situation.

Instead, it gave her the greatest surge of freedom she'd felt in a decade. For things to turn out this well when they had looked as awful as they had before dawn, God had to be watching out for them, after all. Those desperate prayers in the dark had reached someone Grace wasn't sure whether to believe in anymore. Perhaps they were all going to be all right, after all. As she sat wondering, the low, reassuring rumble of Carl Brenner's instructions to Matt lulled Grace to sleep in the warm kitchen.

# Chapter Three

Grace woke up with a start some time later. How had she and Maria both gotten onto the couch? She had a vague memory of having been half led, half carried there by Brenner. Maria, settled in alongside her, was sleeping and felt a little less feverish. They were both nestled under her Aunt Jo's granny-square afghan. Grace was touched that this strange man had tucked them in, even though it was a rather clumsy job, before he'd gone out to fetch medicine.

As Grace grew more alert she was able to figure out what had woken her. There were the sounds of car or truck doors slamming outside and heavy boots stamping off snow. In a moment Matthew opened the front door quietly. "Mom?" he called in softly. "I think she's still asleep," he said, apparently to someone with him.

"No, I'm not." Grace tried to keep her voice down. "But your sister is, so come in quietly."

"Okay." Matt passed the message on, and Grace could hear several pairs of heavy feet in the hall. One of them had to be Brenner's, because no one smaller could thump that loudly while trying to be quiet. She almost giggled, picturing the effort.

In a moment there were three men, all in stocking feet, in her living room. Grace had settled Maria into the nest of covers and got up from the couch. She missed the warmth immediately, feeling slightly dizzy and cold.

"Mrs. Mallory, I'm sure you've met Doc Conrad, who runs the pharmacy in town," Carl said, holding out a hand to the older gentleman of the two strangers with him.

"And my son Tom," the pharmacist said proudly. "First-year resident at Barnes-Jewish Hospital in St. Louis. He's home for Christmas and he can prescribe medicine now. We brought him on his first house call." A father's pride shone in Doc's blue eyes, and Grace looked from one man to the other, feeling helpless.

"You didn't have to do that. I'm so sorry they pulled you away from your break," she apologized.

The young man grinned. "No need to be sorry. Once I'm done training I plan to come down here and be a family-practice doc. I'll be doing this every day. This is kind of neat." He looked over to the couch. "Is that the patient? I hate to say it, ma'am, but you don't look so good yourself."

"My daughter's the patient. And normally I'd thank you to keep your opinions to yourself, but I don't feel any better than I look. Maybe after you get done examining Maria we can talk about me." Grace felt stunned. What was coming out of her mouth? A request for help? For herself? This was a terribly odd day. It had started oddly and it was just getting stranger all around.

It had taken this long to realize that beside the battered sofa, where she could have reached out and touched him from where she'd been lying, was the dog. When she looked at him, his tail thumped, but otherwise he didn't move from his stretched-out position, guarding Maria. "He wouldn't leave when we did," Carl said. "That's unusual for him, but he seems to have decided you and the girl need protecting." Grace liked the kinship she'd seen between the big beast and his owner. And obviously, neither of them planned to let anyone hurt Maria.

Brenner was a pretty resourceful man. Grace wondered if he was married. If he was, there was one fortunate woman in Redwing. He wore no ring, but then her Matt never had, either. They hadn't had money for one nearly twelve years ago. Not that he would have worn it even if they did, Grace reflected. Matt Mallory had never been the kind of man to be tied down with a golden band.

Doc Conrad looked at Grace. "Could you bring a straight chair in here for Tommy? It would be easier to examine the child sitting down, I think."

"I can do my own requests, Dad," the young man said good-naturedly.

"I know, son. After all, you're the doctor now." The older man stood still, hand frozen in a gesture. "I just thought of something awful."

His son looked concerned. "What's that, Dad?"

"You really *are* the doctor now. That means if there's going to be a Doc Conrad around here, it should be you. Folks are going to have to go back to calling me Kermit."

Carl laughed, and Tom Conrad laughed with him. "Oh, no. We can't let you do that. I can be 'Little Doc,' or 'Doc Tommy,' or something. I can't imagine you having to be Kermit again. Mom says you haven't answered to that since before pharmacy college."

"I haven't, either," the older man said. "But it just seems fit—"

"We'll work it out later. For right now I can still be Tommy, Dad. Especially from you. And I would appreciate that chair," Tom added, turning to Grace.

She stood in the doorway, watching the goings-on as if entranced. Did men really relate to each other this way? Fathers and sons like adults, with kindness and concern for each other? It was new to her. She nodded and got the chair.

Coming back to the room with it, she saw the dog was still guarding Maria. She prepared to touch the child's shoulder. Before she did, she stooped down, cupped the large, furry jowls of the animal in her hand. "It's all right," she told him, so he wouldn't think they were going to hurt his new charge.

She sat on the sofa and settled Maria in her lap. The girl still wasn't really awake. Slowly, with Grace coaxing her, she sat up and answered the doctor's questions about pain and how she felt. He opened a very new-looking medical bag, took out an instrument, and peered into her ears.

The whole situation touched Grace just as the morning's events had. The boy had to be in his middle twenties, not much younger than herself. He looked about fourteen. Well, maybe eighteen. But he seemed to know what he was doing, and finally he pushed back the straight chair and sat looking at her.

"You were right on target, Mrs. Mallory."

"Oh, please, call me Grace. It's bad enough these older guys are calling me Mrs. Mallory—"

"But from somebody who looks like he ought to be eating Christmas cookies instead of writing prescriptions, it's a downright insult, isn't it?'' Tom Conrad finished for her. He had a nice grin. It was infectious enough that Maria giggled when he smiled.

''That wasn't what I meant,'' Grace spluttered, feeling flustered.

''Oh?'' Carl was smiling, too. ''I gather from what you said I get classified as one of the 'older guys.' Since when is thirty-one an older guy?''

''Since I can remember you coming over to watch me when I was in grade school,'' Tom Conrad retorted. ''You've got six years on me, old man.''

''Thanks. Thanks loads,'' Carl groused. ''If that's supposed to be my Christmas present...''

''Only one you'll get from me. Now let me get back to diagnosing this kid. I like the sound of that. My first independent diagnosis.''

''Thought you said her mother diagnosed her, Dr. Tommy,'' his father piped up from where he leaned against the wall, smiling.

''Well, yeah, there is that.'' The young man looked a little crestfallen. ''Is she allergic to any drugs?''

''None that I know of,'' Grace said. ''She doesn't usually take much unless she's real sick. I can't take off work and run to New Hope to the clinic unless she is really ill. Or at least I couldn't until Thanksgiving when I got laid off. Since then, I've had all the time in the world.''

''How about yourself? You allergic to any antibiotics? You look like you could use whatever Tom is giving Maria,'' Carl interjected.

Tom Conrad stood, looking more like the man in charge. ''Actually, she probably doesn't. The virus that gave Maria the ear infection to begin with won't respond to antibiotics. And most adults don't react to cold viruses with otitis media.''

''Whatever,'' Carl said, smiling a little. Grace could tell he was tickled by Tom's gravity.

''Is this why I'm out here?'' Doc piped up. ''Not only to witness this auspicious occasion but to make my own house call, as well?''

''You got it, Dad. This prescription isn't going to have to travel far.'' Tom finished writing with a flourish and handed the slip to Grace, who handed it over to his father.

''You can't be a real doctor,'' Doc joked. ''I can still read this.''

After laughter and back pounding worthy of Tom scoring a winning touchdown, Doc went out to the car and brought back a vial of liquid.

"Brought a couple of things just in case," he explained, handing the medicine over to Grace. "No charge for this one. It was worth the couple of bucks to see Tommy in action the first time. Merry Christmas."

"Merry Christmas," she echoed, looking down at the bottle of pink liquid. Yes, it was a very strange day.

*Kayla Trent.* Of all the able-bodied people in town that Larry could get to mind the store all morning, he'd chosen his own daughter. Carl muttered under his breath outside, raising a cloud of steam with his words, so as to let out all of his frustration before he actually had to face Kayla. He was thankful the dog had stayed in the kitchen at home, sleeping as if worn-out from the morning's excursion. Four detested Kayla even more than he did himself. Probably because she always spoke in baby talk to him, and the dog considered himself too intelligent to put up with such nonsense.

She sat on a stool at the counter, one hand pillowing her vacant, peachy face, her other fingers tracing a pattern on the countertop before her. There were goods left on some of the shelves, so she hadn't given the whole place away.

The bell rang overhead when Carl strode through the doorway. "Oh, Mr. Brenner," Kayla said, looking up dreamily. "You're back. Do you want me to stay and help out? This is the first time all morning I've been alone for more than ten minutes."

"I'll bet," Carl muttered to himself. When anybody who still had merchandise on layaway heard that Kayla Trent was minding the store, they gathered like a flock of vultures.

"Any money in the till?" he asked, trying to sound nonchalant.

"Twenty-seven dollars," Kayla said proudly. "Mrs. Green said she still owed you five on that big doll for Hannah, and then Bill Parker came down to get something for his mother. He came by twice," she added with a giggle.

Bill was one of Kayla's more persistent boyfriends, though what anybody would want with the vacuous teenager was beyond Carl.

"Didn't he get what he wanted the first time? I know I had plenty of things he could have gotten his mom for Christmas."

Her eyes got even bigger. "He wanted panty hose for her, and I didn't know which kind to sell him. He didn't know which kind his mother wanted."

"'Which kind'?" Carl felt out of his depth. Kayla had a way of doing that to him, speaking plain English so earnestly but in such a convoluted fashion that he got lost in the conversation.

"Sure. *Which kind.* I mean, there's control top, silk, sandalfoot, regular, and then there's the size thing...." she droned on.

"But you got it straightened out," Carl said, willing himself not to shake his head. It was beginning to hurt.

"Sure did," Kayla said proudly, standing and brushing down the red-and-green baby-doll top she wore over a white long-sleeved T-shirt and jeans. She looked like a Christmas-tree angel, and probably had just as much sense in her blond head.

"Well, I'm glad. I appreciate your helping me out, Kayla. Anybody else come in?"

"Lots of people. I wrote them all down, just like Daddy told me to. He said I should keep a list of everybody who came in so I could tell you."

Carl could have ticked off most of the names without looking. The five people paying him on time for things in the back room. At least Mrs. Green had left him five dollars. The rest had strolled out with their merchandise without leaving a cent. And he would never be able to convince Kayla that she'd done anything wrong by giving them things before they paid them off. It wasn't even worth trying.

"You know, Kayla, I expect you need to get on home," he said, helping her with her coat. When she was almost to the door he spoke to her again, making her turn around. "You tell your dad you did a good job. In fact, tell him I said I think you're ready to help him out in his business. Maybe even work on the books for him some, or be a part-time teller after classes." Let Larry get a taste of his own medicine.

Kayla burbled with laughter as she walked out to the sidewalk and down the snowy street. Carl smiled grimly, picturing her father's florid face when she suggested helping out.

He took off his jacket and went to the back room. At least she'd gotten the heat running. Now, if there was only something to eat. He was starving.

Of course, he'd worked hard all morning. He'd driven back and forth from the farm to town more than he liked to think. At least Tom had pronounced Grace shaken, but basically healthy. "Needs a lot more to eat," he'd added. "And a lot less worry. I don't see how they'll keep that farm."

"There's no way. But I've got an idea or two," Carl had told him. Tom hadn't asked any more questions, and Carl hadn't volunteered any more harebrained ideas.

Carl's growling stomach distracted him again. Cheese and crackers. Not much of a dinner, but close at hand while he kept busy at the store counter. On Christmas Eve he expected a constant stream of customers until he shut the doors in the early-winter darkness. Women still one little gift short for Christmas, and children with new money from Grandma all needed something. Farmers would stop by to buy the wife a little something for tomorrow, and he knew Bill Parker would be back at least once more.

*When you're that young, hope springs eternal,* Carl thought.

*When you're older, hope doesn't spring much at all.* Carl already knew that from his own experience, so it was no surprise that the day flew by and he never got anything else to eat. At five it was dark outside, and he was ready to lock up.

In the long run Kayla hadn't cost him all that much. Most of the folks that had slunk off with their merchandise could be gently persuaded to pay their balance by New Year's. Lottie Green likely wouldn't, but she'd owed less than ten on the doll, and Carl knew it would be her daughter Hannah's pride and joy.

He looked at the one left on the shelves in the dimly lit store. It had pale hair like Maria Mallory, and he could picture it cradled gingerly in her arms. He wondered if she'd ever had a doll.

They would be cold out there at the old Krieger place. Probably hungry and in the dark, too. Suddenly Carl's need to get home and change clothes, eat dinner and go to the carol service at church transformed into a desire to do something as foreign to him as walking into a wall at full speed.

He wanted to give things away. He wanted to go home and get

the truck, then come back here and load the bench seat with bags of candy and a good sturdy wool blanket. Maybe some boots if he could figure out which size would fit the gangly boy. And he wanted to take it all to a lonely farmstead out in the snow where a woman waited—a woman who wouldn't appreciate what she would see as charity.

Even picturing her determination to refuse his gifts didn't stop Carl from putting his jacket back on and going out. He was sure that determination would be followed by disbelief. He'd seen it once today already, when Tom Conrad had absolutely refused payment for his services, just like his dad.

Grace Mallory didn't believe that anybody would do something for nothing. And with a determination even fiercer than hers, Carl Brenner suddenly wanted to prove to her that there were plenty of people in the world willing to help her. It was something he needed to do for reasons that went far beyond Grace Mallory. Reasons that had more to do with the kind of Christmases he'd had as a child, and what—or mainly who—hadn't been there.

# Chapter Four

By seven, Grace wondered why she had wished for company. Grace knew that most folks would be at church now. Without a sick child, she might have gone herself, considering the events of the day. Of course, the walls would probably have fallen in on her, to quote one of Jo's sayings.

Surely sitting alone would have been preferable to entertaining a silent, out-of-place Jake Krieger and his young wife. She didn't know who felt most uncomfortable—her young landlord, or his child bride. He apparently didn't know what to say, and his companion was so hugely swollen with child that she couldn't sit still long enough to say anything.

It was odd to see Jake here, but not totally surprising. She *had* told him she wanted to discuss the lease in detail, and the condition of the house, before she signed anything. Leave it to the clueless young man to come tonight.

So far, all her attempts at conversation had failed miserably, and Grace sat stirring her instant coffee, trying not to ring the spoon like a chime against the chipped cup's rim. The Kriegers had the two that were whole.

When Grace heard the crunch of tires outside, she actually smiled. Someone else was coming. She hurried to the front door to see a man descending from a pickup at the gate, his arms laden with bundles.

It was Carl Brenner. Even though Grace wondered what on earth he was doing out here again, any other human company besides the silent pair would be a relief. "Mr. Brenner. This is a surprise. Please come in."

"No, I can't stay long," he said, faltering to a stop at the front door. "There were just a few things I thought of…for the kids.…"

"I've already got a little Christmas Eve company. Come in and join us," Grace said, trying to sound cheerful. Carl drew back.

"I wouldn't want to horn in on a party. Who else is here?" His expression told her that he was curious. Grace bristled. Who was he to decide how she managed her life?

"My landlord. And I wish you'd come in and join us," Grace said, trying to sound as if she meant it. As he stamped snow off his boots, she couldn't keep her eyes on his troubled face. Something else even stranger caught her attention. "Mr. Brenner? Your coat seems to be…moving."

If there had been more light, Grace expected she would have seen him blushing. The oddest expression flitted across the big man's features. It was entrancing. "Oh, well. That. Guess I'd better come in a minute." Without further explanation, he entered the narrow hallway and made his way into the parlor. "Jake." He gave a curt nod, arms still full. "Good seeing you. Give me a hand, here?"

Krieger leaped up, looking grateful for something to do. Grace realized that the young man wasn't unfriendly, just ill at ease. He probably had no idea what to do with himself inside his grandfather's old house, dealing with her. Given a job to do, he began talking.

As he helped Carl divest himself of various parcels, the younger man answered a volley of questions that Carl put to him. Although Grace hadn't gotten a whole sentence out of him in an hour, in the five minutes it took for Carl Brenner to get himself unwrapped, unwound and sorted out, she learned that the Kriegers might be having twins, and that as soon after the birth as possible, they would finally be going to Oklahoma with the rest of the family.

Brenner's coat came off and was put with the rest in a pile in the hallway. Then Grace could finally see what had been making the gyrations at his front. Out of his vest popped a tiny head, giving a loud caterwaul that rose over the volume of the men's conversation.

"A kitten?" she cried, rising from her perch on the chair. "You brought us a kitten?"

The little animal fit into one of Carl's hands. He looked apologetic. "I started out with a doll. But then I wasn't sure if most girls really played with them anymore. I stopped in town to ask Mrs. Green about it, because she has a girl. She also had a cat with kittens, and when I saw them..." he faltered for a minute. Taking a deep breath, he went on. "When I was five my folks died in a fire. I went to foster care, and I didn't have anybody—except for a yellow pup nobody else wanted. He was the runt of the litter. Couldn't catch birds for anything, but he sure listened good."

"The one you have now?" Maria piped up from the corner. Grace didn't know when she'd come into the room. Usually silent in front of adults, she apparently couldn't resist the lure of the animal. She came closer to see the mewling bit of fur.

"No. That yellow dog was three dogs ago. Guess that made him the great-grandfather of the one I've got now." Carl had telescoped down closer to the floor so he didn't tower over the little girl.

In the shadow of the large man in front of her, Grace could see the five-year-old boy, left suddenly alone. It helped to understand parts of today; why the large, somewhat-aloof man seemed to be drawn to her children. He had been a lonely child himself, once. A lonely child comforted by a yellow dog.

She knew that Maria would love to have a kitten. Her daughter looked up at her in silent question. "You may keep her if you want." Judging from the speed with which Maria settled herself on the floor to make a lap for the tiny animal, she wanted her. Grace watched Carl as he put the kitten in Maria's lap. Her daughter's fingers touched the orange fur, and the little creature quieted down and started curling up for a nap. Removed of his burden, Carl looked a bit awkward again as he straightened. "I brought kitten food, the dry kind. And the kind of litter Lottie's been using for them. It's all she'll need for a little while, that and water."

Grace was touched that he'd thought of everything.

"Would you like a cup of coffee?" she asked. "You must be near frozen, making that trip again, Mr. Brenner."

"I'd take one," he said solemnly, still looking down at Maria and her new friend.

Missy Krieger rose awkwardly from her place on the chair.

"Let me go with you to help make it," she said. Grace was about to refuse her offer of help when she thought of all the time she'd spent, at the end of each pregnancy, just walking around in circles because no other position felt just right. Instead of turning the young woman down, she nodded, and motioned her along the hallway into the kitchen.

Suddenly everything seemed lighter. So she only had eight dollars left from her unemployment check in the whole house, Grace told herself on the way to the kitchen. So they'd had pancakes for supper. Given the prospect of Maria having a real Christmas present of a tiny orange kitten, suddenly tomorrow seemed like a future.

Carl squirmed uncomfortably on the low couch, wondering if Grace had really heard Jake's words. She seemed oblivious to the young man's plans to be with the rest of his family.

Surely she would figure out any minute that she was either going to have to buy the place from Krieger or move. Soon. And from what he'd seen already, Carl knew that Grace Mallory didn't have the kind of money needed to buy this farm. She probably didn't have enough money to buy next week's groceries.

She sat across the room in the rocker and seemed a thousand miles away. She looked less wan than she had this morning, Carl thought. Her hair was once more pinned up into a tidy mass, still scraped back tighter than he would have liked to see it. More of it around her face would have called less attention to the sharp planes and dark hollows there. She was wearing clean jeans and a cream-colored sweater.

Carl found himself wondering what she'd look like in a dress, with her hair arranged in some sort of curls. Grace in a dress? He shook his head, wondering where that little bit of woolgathering had come from.

Fortunately, no one noticed. Krieger still kept on about Oklahoma, with his young wife listening raptly and nodding. Grace's attention had strayed from the young couple to Maria, who sat on the floor about five feet away and crooned to the kitten.

Carl was so glad he'd gotten it. The kitten was worth the trade he'd made with Mrs. Green to settle her debt. Now there were two happy little girls tonight, both with their heart's desire. Not that he would have thought of either of them on his own. Seeing Maria earlier in the day had made him decide that he would go back and give Lottie Gruber the doll for her daughter, but Kayla had beaten him to that. And the woman's gratitude when he'd come to her door in the dark and only wanted to know what she thought a six-year-old girl would want for Christmas had been amazing. She'd been more than happy to part with one of the kittens tumbling on the floor.

Seeing Maria with the kitten brought back so many memories, few of them happy. How many hours had he spent curled up on some narrow mattress with Yellow Dog? Whenever the unfriendly world had threatened to swamp him, the pup had always been there. He'd helped him carry the burdens no little boy of six or seven should have borne; the ugly stares and even uglier whispers of adults who'd never realized he'd heard what they said about his parents.

Animals truly made the best companions, he thought. His dog never reproached him for anything. He was always glad of a kind word and a few scraps. And those liquid brown eyes always understood, no matter what Carl had to say to him.

Why did some cats get so silly and contented when you laid them on their backs? Carl had never wondered about it before. Now, as he became lost in thought, oblivious to what Jake was saying. Watching the little orange puffball seem to smile up at the child made odd sensations crawl through the aching muscles of his chest and arms, tired from the exertion of the day.

The crawling sensations were only partly due to muscle fatigue. Partly, too, they came from looking around the room. It was so empty. Carl knew that the couch and the dinette set in the kitchen had belonged to Jack's grandpa. Nobody had wanted them when the old man had died, so they'd just stayed in the house.

The Christmas tree was tiny, artificial and pathetic. Again, he felt overwhelmed by unfamiliar feelings. These children—the girl on the floor, the boy standing stiffly by his mother's rocker—shouldn't have to sleep in this place tonight. It repelled him to think about them waking up on Christmas morning in the cold of the sparsely furnished rented house for another in what promised to be a series of bleak Christmases. He couldn't let that happen.

Jake had apparently gotten around to breaking the news to Grace while Carl had been watching the children. Because now Grace sputtered a little, quietly, looking hard at her young landlord. "I don't know, Mr. Krieger," Carl could hear her saying. "I know I can't buy the place. That's just out of the question. But I'll need a little time to figure out what I'm going to do next."

"You don't need any time at all," Carl heard himself say. "You can move into my place. I live alone and need help running the store. And there's an apartment in the back of my house, just five blocks from the store in town. We can pack you up tonight if you want."

The room was so still after Brenner's pronouncement that Grace could hear the kettle hissing on the stove in the kitchen. Young Missy Krieger just sat on the hard kitchen chair with her mouth gaping open. Jake fidgeted uncomfortably at one end of the couch, just as silent.

The children didn't even seem to move, as Brenner leaned forward, seeming to wait for an answer. Without thought, Grace knew what her answer should be. Of course she couldn't do that. It would be charity. Scandalous charity, at that.

Her thoughts must have shown in her expression, because Carl was shaking his head, seeming to read her doubts. "There's two rooms on the top floor of the house that don't open onto anything else. They have their own bath, and private stairs down to the kitchen. The folks that built the house originally had money. Planned to have servants all the time, I guess, because the house is built for it.

"Besides, if I want to get down to brass tacks, you owe me money. I figured working in the store could be the way to pay things off, and if you live that close, I know you'll get to work."

Grace wanted to snap her refusal, and quickly. Then she felt the pressure of little Matt's hand on her shoulder. Its strength surprised her. She looked up into the thin face that had looked so young when she'd confronted him this morning.

Since then, he'd been so quiet. He shouldn't be worrying about what they were going to do next, Grace decided. And if she stayed on this farm, he would worry. If they stayed here she wouldn't have the resources to make his dreams come true. And if they stayed here, those dreams couldn't amount to much in the first place.

The man waiting for an answer didn't seem to know just how blunt his statements had sounded. Grace studied the odd figure who'd changed from stranger to protector in the course of one day. He wouldn't be easy to work for—of that she was certain. But he'd be fair and honest. And she knew instinctively that working for him would provide her with a better life than she'd had in a while.

It beat welfare. And she did owe Brenner money for things Matt had stolen. If she was frugal, she could be shed of that debt in less than a month by keeping house for him and helping at the store, even if she worked for minimum wage. Then maybe she could find another place in town and get on with some kind of life—a life that would let her feed and clothe her children, give them a decent home.

She could hardly wait to see the surprise in Carl Brenner's face when she didn't argue with his offer. He seemed every bit as stubborn and proud as Grace knew she was herself. But something was urging her to say yes to this. It felt like the same something—or someone—that had told her to wait and watch before dawn. Was this what she had been waiting and watching for? A strange man to walk into her life and offer to help her out with everything, when he should have arrested her son instead? It was so bizarre that Grace considered it.

She cleared her throat. "Mr. Brenner, I'll take you up on that," she said, waiting for the shock and amazement to cross his face. Of all the aggravating things, why did the man have to smile instead? She needed help in figuring this man out.

# *Chapter Five*

"Like a herd of turtles in a snowstorm!" Grace's pronouncement had the children laughing and Carl regarding her with a questioning look. He might have wondered if she was a little off-kilter before. Now Grace suspected he was certain of the fact.

Shrugging her shoulders, she turned to Carl again. "That's what my aunt always said when we started a trip. She was my great-aunt, really, and she raised me. She had this ancient station wagon the whole time I lived with her, and it always seemed it took us forever to get loaded up and go anywhere. Not that we ever went much of anyplace. But even a trip to the store seemed to be a major endeavor."

It *had* been a major endeavor. Aunt Jo had always had to find something—her wallet or keys, and then a scarf or ball cap that covered her masses of red hair to her satisfaction. Then there was the station wagon—huge, blue and named Alice—which was balky at best. By the time all that was done, the day had always been half over. On good days they had moved as slowly as turtles in a snowstorm.

"We aren't moving much faster," Carl groused as if he'd heard her thoughts. There had been the children's things to pack up, and the tasks of somehow corralling the kitten and settling Maria in with the bags, bundles and a pile of quilts around her and her new Christmas present. The second seat in the pickup wasn't designed to hold so much, but somehow they made it all fit.

Grace felt like singing Christmas carols now. The landscape

zipped by, covered in snow. Thinking about Aunt Jo made her remember the good Christmases of her childhood. Maybe this Christmas would be the start of a new beginning for them.

Carl's home, when she saw it, looked impressive. Even in the dark she could make out a high gabled roof with two broad stories and an attic, as well. The house gleamed in the faint moonlight with a fresh coat of paint. Somehow she could picture him in the cooler autumn days, up there with a paintbrush.

Shaking herself out of her goofy daydream, Grace opened the door and jumped down from the truck. The dog bounded out of the house through a large dog door and ran through the snow until he sat down in front of her, barking once. The noise accomplished what stopping had not, and woke the children in the back seat. "We're here," Grace said, watching Maria's head loll sleepily back onto the quilts piled beside her. "Help me get her down, Matt."

The boy nodded, backhanding sleep out of his eyes and standing in the narrow space between the seats. "C'mon now, Maria. Wake up so Mama can help you down." His sister murmured in her sleep, then sat up slowly and put her arms out to be carried in. She looked dazed and tired. "It will be all right, sugar," Grace told her. "We'll get you inside where it's warm, and in a bed soon. Just help me out, here."

"I'll take her," said Carl beside her, his voice gruff and firm. He leaned into the truck and picked up the child as if she weighed no more than the coverlet around her, and strode up the steps to the house. Somehow he found a way to open the back door and turn on the porch light. The kitchen was still somewhat dark, with only a light over the stove providing a faint glow.

Carl crossed the kitchen and stopped at a closed door. "The apartment. Can you open this for me?"

Grace was right behind him. "Sure." The old-fashioned key turned smoothly in the lock, and the dull brass knob felt cold and heavy in her hand. Opening the door brought cool air smelling of cedar.

"These stairs are a little narrow," Carl said, not turning around as he mounted the flight leading from the kitchen. "But we should be able to get anything you need up or down them."

Naturally the dog had to follow them. They moved slowly. The big dog lumbered up the steps, keeping even with Grace. "He really doesn't have a name?" Grace questioned Carl, stroking the dog's head.

"Just Four." He said it as if it wasn't unusual.

"That's unfair," Grace said.

Carl blew out breath in a puff that was almost a snort. "Unfair to who? I don't mind calling him Four, and he answers to it. Why call him something stupid, like Lord Randall's Conniption or something? He's just an old yellow dog."

"Still, everything ought to have a name."

"He's got enough name to suit both of us," Carl replied, finding a light switch with his elbow. A bulb in an older-looking ceiling fixture illuminated the square room.

"I'm sure it needs cleaning and airing. And the beds aren't made properly," he said, sounding apologetic.

"I got the impression you hired me as the housekeeper as well as working in the store," Grace reminded him. "You're not supposed to have a room ready like in a hotel." What she could see of the room in the dim light impressed her. There was more space here than in the bedrooms of the Krieger farmhouse, and the furniture was in better shape. The plain iron bedstead would be plenty big enough for her and Maria to share. "Is there a trundle someplace I could make up for little Matt?"

"Even better." Carl laid his burden of child and quilt down on the bed. "There's a second room next door. It isn't very big, but it will be good for the boy."

Matt came up behind them, with a bag and the protesting kitten. "My own room?" Matt sounded almost suspicious.

"Not much of a room. There's a bed and a dresser. Nothing fancy," Carl said. He didn't tell the boy it was a small, cramped room. If the boy was as happy with the narrow space under the eaves as he remembered being when it had first been his, he didn't plan to shatter his illusions.

"Come down and help me get your mom's things out of the truck." Matt didn't need asking twice to go back down the stairs. Carl turned to Grace. "There's bedding in that chest over there, I expect. I haven't been up here for a while. If it's not all right to use, tell me and I'll get you some from my side of the house."

"All right," Grace said. She waited for him to turn on more lights. "You're going to go down those stairs in the dark?"

"Done it plenty of times. Besides, if I turn on more lights, won't it wake up the girl?"

"It might. It's kind of you to think of it," Grace said. Listening to him go down the stairs, she crossed to the chest and opened it. The sheets folded on top of the pile of linens smelled sweet, like the cedar lining the chest. They would make a welcoming bed.

Rolling Maria gently from side to side several times, she made the bed without lifting the child out of it. The kitten was more of a challenge, being entranced by all the covers moving up and down. Grace had to fish her out of the wrong side of the sheets and quilts three times before she smoothed the last one down and settled the child—still in jeans and a shirt—under the covers, the kitten on top.

While Carl and Matt were still downstairs, Grace made Matt's bed. As she put sheets on the narrow bed, she could look out the equally narrow window of the small room. Outside she saw a light bobbing between a garage and the house, evidence that they were still moving things into the house.

Back in the main room, Grace sat down on the closed chest and began to get ready for bed. Maria could sleep in her clothes tonight, but she intended to start her new life by putting on a proper night-gown before slipping between the sheets in her new bed. Her muscles protested as she untied her shoes and put them beside the chest.

By the time she'd found her nightgown and laid it out, Matt had stumbled up the stairs, the long day having finally taken its toll. He looked like a little boy again in the soft light. "Turn out that light on your way in, and go to bed. There's enough moonlight for me," she told him, as he went into the small room. She waited to see his light go out under the heavy oak door, and hear his steady breathing before settling down for the night.

For the first time in almost twelve years, there was no litany of her faults and mistakes of the day as her bedtime lullaby. That had been one ritual her pitiful lack of self-esteem had been happy to take over from Matt once he'd gone to prison that final time. What should have been a peaceful, pleasant time of day had always been instead a time for recriminations.

In all the blessed silence, Grace even wondered if she could hear sleigh bells and reindeer hooves. Certainly this peace, just beginning, was a gift from someone.

"What's the matter? Don't you know where you are?" Carl asked, trying to be as gentle as possible. The moonlight filtering through the window illuminated Maria's pale face and hair. Carl felt absolutely helpless. What did he know about little kids—crying or otherwise? Not enough.

Though unable to settle down, Carl had stayed in bed until Four had lifted his head and whined. He never did that at night unless something aggravated him. Usually it meant there was an animal out in the yard. As they'd padded down the stairs, though, the dog had headed toward the front of the house—not his usual post for spotting raccoons and rabbits. Still, Carl followed him and found the little girl in the parlor, her clothes disordered as if slept in, and crying softly.

"He won't know where to go," she said, making the last word nearly a wail. "I can't get my sock off. And even if I got it off, he won't know it's mine."

None of this made any sense to Carl. It seemed he'd spent the entire day at sea, listening to females, and that he was destined to spend the night the same way. None of them, no matter what size, had made perfect sense today. First Grace, then Kayla, and now tiny Maria—none of them spoke the same language he did.

"You don't want your socks off, Maria. Your feet will get too cold up there in bed. Now, how about going back there, all right?"

His touch on her shoulder, which he'd wanted to be comforting and reassuring, was instead the last straw. The wailing began afresh, louder. "No, I can't! If I go back now, he won't know I'm here. Or Matt. He won't come!"

"Who won't come?" Carl asked her, beginning to have the faintest idea.

"Santa. Santa Claus won't come if he doesn't know where I am. Even if I put up my sock."

Relief washed over Carl so strongly that he had to sit down on the floor to control his shaking legs. "Santa Claus? Is that all you're worried about? Of course he'll come. And I guess we *will* need your socks. Both of them, won't we? Because Matt didn't hang one up, either, did he?''

She shook her head, done with her crying now that Carl understood. ''Will you help?''

She looked up with such trust. Carl had never undressed a kid in his life, and he hadn't intended to start tonight. But somehow the two of them found a way to get her socks off and affixed to the mantel. When they finished, he pointed the sleepy child back up the stairs to her room.

Carl wandered into the kitchen then, trying to remember where he'd put the unopened bag he'd brought to Grace's house. He had hard candy in a sack, and plenty of silly little toys for the boy. Surely he could come up with something for Maria, as well. As he stood in the kitchen thinking, soft thumps cascaded down the stairs. The kitten stood in front of him, meaning to be let out.

He scooped up the tiny beast with its prickly little claws and deposited it just outside the kitchen door in the dishpan of sand he usually used to keep the porch free of ice.

''That will do for tonight. In the morning we'll get that box set up. You're an indoor cat.'' Carl shook his head. He was talking to a cat. It might be the first time, but Carl was sure it wouldn't be the last. In a moment he brought the cat inside the house and went in to fill stockings.

Carl knew that he made a decidedly untraditional Santa Claus—in bare feet, a sleeveless undershirt and rumpled black pants, and followed not by eight tiny reindeer, but by a huge yellow dog and a feisty orange kitten.

''He did come! He did! Mr. Carl was right!'' Maria's incredibly shrill voice pierced the pale light of the room. Grace took in her words slowly.

''Who came, baby?'' she asked, not believing what Maria had said.

''Santa. We put my socks out, one for me and one for Matt. And they're full. I can tell. Hurry, Mama. I want to go see again.''

''All right. Let me dress first, and you get your brother up. We'll go down in a while.''

Maria fairly bounced—a sign that the antibiotic must be starting to work. Grace could hear Matt protesting in the next room, and thanked her lucky stars that he wasn't the kind of big brother to tell Maria the truth about her stocking, even when rudely awakened.

Grace rose and stretched. The air didn't feel any colder than it had been in the farmhouse. She couldn't quite bring herself to think of that ramshackle building as "home," even though they'd lived there for almost two years. It was supposed to have been a stopgap, a place to stay until they got on their feet again. The trouble was, they never had.

But still she had to raise these children and keep them out of harm's way. Carl Brenner's attic seemed as good a place to do that as any.

She didn't spend too much time getting dressed, with Maria sitting impatiently on the edge of the bed, urging her to be faster. She'd even infected Matt with her excitement, and he stood at the door of his room, whistling.

Finally Grace was ready except for the heavy shoes it seemed she had taken off only moments before, to go to bed. She made a decision to leave them next to the chest. She wished for delicate, ladylike slippers to wear instead, but she was going to have to make do with her heavy white socks. If she sat down quickly in the parlor, perhaps no one would notice.

"Where's my kitty?" Maria asked, pausing in her jumping for a moment.

"I don't know. Maybe downstairs seeing what Santa brought. Let's go see, shall we?" Grace still couldn't believe that Carl had filled stockings for her children. She intended to pay him back for whatever she found in them, even if it meant working an extra week or two for him.

Once she got down to the kitchen, though, she began to doubt how much she'd be doing. Even this early, Brenner had obviously gotten up before her. A coffee maker bubbled on the countertop, and there seemed to be something in the oven. For someone who claimed to need a housekeeper, he seemed awfully self-sufficient.

In the parlor, a floor vent blew toasty warm air. Grace looked around the room and then back at Matt, who stood wide-eyed near the mantel, looking at the bulging socks. "Please go up the front stairs and knock on Mr. Brenner's door. Ask him if he would like to come down.''

Matt gave the makeshift Christmas stockings one more look, then nodded and pulled himself away. He bounded up the stairs, then the dog barked as Matt knocked on the door. She could hear a hurried conversation between Matt's high voice and a lower one, then he came back down. "He's almost ready. He asked if we would wait."

"Of course." Grace had to keep reminding herself that she had agreed to be the hired help here, not a guest. She ought to see what she could do about breakfast, she thought to herself, heading for the kitchen.

The pan in the oven appeared to contain biscuits. They were the kind that came out of a tube, but there were plenty of them. Grace poked around in the refrigerator to find butter and jelly to go with them. In a day or two, she told herself, she'd know her way around this new kitchen and things would be easier.

As she looked in the cabinets for dishes, Carl came into the room. His hair slicked down with fresh combing and water, he wore a clean blue shirt. "Good morning. I think we're wanted in the other room. You are, at least," he said, dark eyes solemn. "Do you mind if I come, too?"

"It's your house, Mr. Brenner," she reminded him. "You are certainly welcome to do as you like. And I suspect there would be precious little to do if you hadn't gotten up in the middle of the night. I hadn't intended—"

"I know. I figured you hadn't, but those kids shouldn't do without Christmas because of what's happened. If anything, they need it more than ever."

Grace nodded, unable to speak. In the large and serious man before her she saw again the shadow of that boy he'd talked about last night. That boy who knew what her children were going through, and worse. Hadn't he lost both his parents? In that moment Grace wondered what anyone had gotten *him* for Christmas—then or now—or if anyone had even bothered.

She followed him into the parlor and sat on a very nice sofa, which felt as if it had never been sat upon often, given its age. Clearly, Carl didn't do much entertaining.

She only had time to sit before the children began digging things out of their stockings. "Candy...a ball...a yo-yo. Cool!" Matt sounded nearly beside himself. There were oranges in the toes and a handful of nuts. One object looked out of place in Maria's until Grace realized that the small ball of yarn was for the kitten, reminding her daughter of the present that didn't fit in her stocking.

Through all the mayhem the yellow dog sat in the doorway to the parlor, tail thumping. "All right," Carl said after the gifts were all admired, looking at the dog. It seemed to be his signal to enter the room, which he did with as much enthusiasm as the children had earlier.

Maria submitted with good humor to having her face washed by the animal, then turned to look at Carl. "Where's his presents?"

"He doesn't wear socks," Carl said without smiling. Maria seemed to take his explanation at face value. Grace could see under the solemnity a side of Carl Brenner that she hadn't seen before, and wondered in fact how many people ever got to see it. He was actually teasing the child in a friendly sort of way. She could see a glint in his eyes, and he seemed just a flash away from grinning. He was enjoying watching them with their gifts.

And he must have felt her observing him, because he looked across the room at her then. Half a smile lifted one corner of his expressive mouth before he stood. "Can I help put breakfast on?"

"No, indeed. That's the kind of thing you hired me for." Grace got up and started to move briskly.

"Well, the dog needs out, anyway. I'll follow you to the kitchen."

Four's ears pricked up when he figured they were talking about him, and he followed them into the back of the house where full sunlight shone through the windows. "I hope you don't mind. My doing that and all," Carl said. He seemed like a boy again as he apologized, looking out the door after the dog instead of at Grace.

"Not at all, Mr. Brenner. I hope that you'll give me a bill later— for all the things you put in Maria's socks. We'll add that to my debt." Grace tried to sound as businesslike as possible while she set the table.

Carl closed the door firmly, almost slamming it. "I'll do no such thing. Besides, Santa Claus filled those socks. You don't pay back Santa Claus, do you?''

"Not usually," Grace admitted. "What's Santa Claus's favorite kind of pie? Perhaps we could find a way to have one for Christmas dinner.''

"Santa Claus eats any kind of pie on the planet. And today, Santa Claus could probably eat a whole pie by himself," the tall man said as he turned and left the room. This time Grace knew it was no illusion. This time he smiled as broadly as little Matt.

# *Chapter Six*

Carl remained smiling most of the day, which mystified Grace. He definitely smiled through dinner, which he insisted they share at his large dining-room table. Grace could tell the formal dining room didn't get used much. She had to dust the table before laying it with a cloth and plates. His full kitchen was a joy to work in, and Carl seemed impressed when she brought out ham, mashed potatoes, a green-bean casserole and an apple pie.

The children were more than impressed. Grace had to give them several "mother looks" across the table to keep them from falling on the food like wolf cubs. It surprised her to see how resilient they were. Sort of like young wolves in that respect, too, she reflected. But then, healthy children in a better place than they'd ever been before were likely to eat.

After dinner, she went to Carl to talk about the hard things. "We have to go back to the farm. I need to get my car, pack up what little we've still got there."

"I figured you would. Do you want me to stay after I drive you out?"

"It's not much of a way to spend Christmas," Grace replied. "I probably already made you miss church."

Carl shrugged. "They won't miss me much. I didn't even think to ask if you wanted to go someplace."

"Nobody's going to miss me anywhere around here," Grace said. "I haven't been inside a church in years."

"Would you like to change that?" Carl asked softly. "I don't expect you to just follow along where I go, but it would be nice."

"I understand," Grace said, admiring his caution. She still wasn't used to a man who thought things through instead of just lashing out. One who actually asked her opinion seemed too good to be true.

"If you want to talk to the pastor, we could stop in for a minute on our way out to the farm."

"I hate to bother him on Christmas," Grace said. It seemed rude to interrupt someone's holiday.

"He won't mind. He's got four kids, and they've all probably had so much Christmas by now that he's ready for any diversion."

Grace shook her head. "No, really. I couldn't bother anybody on Christmas. I will go meet him. Soon, all right?"

"Fine." Carl stood and stretched, again reminding Grace just how large a man he was. He could have been terribly threatening, and she wondered again why she'd agreed to work in his house with no company but two small children and a dog.

Still, size wasn't everything. Matt hadn't been much bigger than she was, but he'd constantly reminded her how weak, how defenseless, and primarily, how stupid she would always be, compared to him. Carl didn't seem to use his advantages in the same way.

"You want to change clothes or anything?" he asked.

"Just to get my jacket and make sure Maria takes her medicine before we go."

He nodded. "She seems better today."

"I think so. She'd only tell me if it was awful," Grace admitted. "She's a quiet one."

"I can relate to that. It's easier somehow if you are when you're a kid. People don't notice you as much." As he strode away to get ready to go, Grace felt a shiver pass through her. How much of this man's childhood had been spent like that of her children, hoping that no one noticed him? Again she felt the need to reach out to him.

But she instinctively knew the protective layers around that inner child were too thick. Too much man covered up that child, and Grace knew that if she reached out to him she would be too aware of the large man before her to remember the inner child that needed the attention.

The truck took a while to warm up. Grace reflected in the silent interior that she still didn't even know what color Carl Brenner's eyes were, much less the more important things about the man who was now her employer. The few long looks she'd had at his face had revealed plenty, but never the color of his eyes.

She'd seen his concern for her children, and his delight over a warm apple pie. There had been affection for the animals, even the goofy new kitten. But were the eyes that showed all that blue or gray? Some color in between, as fluid as the man himself, Grace decided as they drove off.

When they got to the farm, the place looked shabby to her. She hadn't left it much except to go to work. So she didn't often look at it the way a stranger would. A stranger wouldn't think much of this place. Everything needed paint, and a missing shutter made a gap at one of the upstairs windows. All in all, it looked like a place that belonged to someone who didn't care about it.

Which Grace had to admit, was true. It had been a refuge, a cave, just someplace to hide out and put her life back together again after her marriage and widowhood. She'd moved there because the job in New Hope looked like a fresh start. Raising her kids in the kind of neighborhood she could afford in a bigger city wasn't an option.

The Krieger farm had been the closest available rental to New Hope when she was looking. It wasn't a long drive to the prison where Matt was still alive at the time. She had planned to visit him there, but he wouldn't have her or his children anywhere near the place. That was the only manly decision he had made in over eight years of marriage.

It was still hard to admit that marriage to Matt Mallory had been more difficult than losing him. If she'd known more about what to do, maybe she could have helped him more, Grace told herself. Maybe then, he wouldn't have sunk into his silences that went on for days, broken only when he found more liquor and slunk off to get drunk, after which he'd come back with plenty to say—none of it ever good.

At least most of it had been directed at her. As an adult, she could handle his foul moods and ugly temper. He'd always left the children alone, and Grace had told herself that someday it would all get better.

Except it never would have. She knew now that nothing better had ever been in store for Matthew Mallory. He'd died while serving a prison sentence for petty robbery—the last of several terms in prison he'd had in his lifetime. If Grace was honest with herself she would have to admit that her life was better without him.

She got down from the running board of the truck before Carl could come around and help her. She hefted Maria down as well, and motioned her toward the house.

The front-door lock was balky, as usual. Grace tried to think of anything at all she would miss about this rattletrap farmhouse. She couldn't come up with anything. Once she got the door unlocked, she turned to Carl. "Do you want me to make sure the car will start so that you can go back to town?"

"No." He shrugged. "What would I do there except sit in the house with the dog for company? Surely I can do something around here to help out."

"I imagine you can," she told him. "There's a few plastic crates upstairs in the children's rooms. Why don't you and Matt gather their toys and books and things and pack them in those, all right?"

It wouldn't take long. The milk crates had served as shelves in the bedrooms, and there wasn't much in either room that really belonged to the Mallory family.

"Is there anything in the garage besides the car?"

"Just some boxes. One or two with stuff in them that I never got around to unpacking, and a few empties. I'll need the empty ones in a while," Grace said.

"Good. Hand me your car keys and I'll go out and make sure the car's running. Then I'll bring the boxes in, all right?"

"Fine." Grace concentrated on coaxing the ancient furnace into putting out some heat. "Come in later and get warm. I don't want you catching pneumonia on my account." She fiddled with the thermostat until a groan from the basement told her that the furnace was coming to life. Then she went into the kitchen and started putting things on the table that she'd pack in the boxes Carl brought in.

There wasn't much. She had a sparse set of dishes, the kind collected from the grocery store week by week. Three pots, a tea-kettle and a large cast-iron skillet made up the entire pots-and-pans section.

The skillet was her favorite. It had been Jo's—probably even handed down from her mother or mother-in-law. Grace could remember being taught to cook, standing over this skillet. Jo had insisted that she take it with her after her quick wedding to Matt at seventeen. At least then, they hadn't moved far, and Matt had stayed out of trouble for a while. Jo had seen little Matt several times after his birth. It hurt Grace's heart, knowing that Jo had never seen Maria.

Maybe this move would be a new start in more ways than one, Grace reflected. She could start out fresh with so many things. She could take Carl up on his offer to go to church with him, maybe even talk to the pastor before that. And maybe she would find Jo. She wouldn't be returning to her a success. "More like a miserable failure," Grace said aloud to the half-empty kitchen. But somehow she knew Jo wouldn't mind. Just seeing her and two healthy children would bring a light to the older woman's eyes. Grace began to look forward to seeing that light.

"Thank you. Please add that to my bill." Didn't the woman know any other way to express gratitude? Probably not, Carl reflected as he surveyed himself in the mirror. He'd nicked himself shaving. Naturally, when he was taking Grace and the kids to church for the first time, he'd do that.

Carl was concerned about Grace. She seemed tired and worried all the time, at the end of her rope. It showed in the lines etched in her pale face, and in the shadows under her brown eyes. The tissue-paper-thin skin there looked dark with fatigue.

Surely she couldn't hold in the worry forever. Those feelings had to come out sometime. Probably sometime soon, if she started feeling safe. Carl knew that when she did let go it would be complete for a little while. And from what he'd seen so far of Grace Mallory, it would not be in public. She wasn't a woman to share her emotions.

Not even when he'd insisted, first thing on the twenty-sixth, that she come to the store and they find her a pair of shoes that fit. Carl didn't even have to argue; she'd wordlessly followed him over there, with the children in tow.

It took only about two minutes to find boots that fit Matt. The boy seemed satisfied to know that he'd be working in the store and would earn his new boots. For his mother, it was different. Grace Mallory had narrow, delicate little feet that matched the rest of her body, and again Carl felt this crazy need to get all protective around her.

Finding shoes for Grace really only took a minute or two longer than fitting her son, but Carl's discomfort in doing the job stretched things out in his mind until it seemed like hours. And then all she could say was that, "Thank you. Please add them to my bill." Didn't anything ever rattle the woman? Bring her feelings to the surface?

Her kids, Carl decided. He'd have to watch when she talked about them the next time. Perhaps then he would learn the key to that precious spot—wherever it was—that she had locked up in her heart. It amazed Carl that each day he spent around Grace made him more anxious to find that spot.

Pastor Peterson was nice. Welcoming and friendly—not what Grace expected when she told him before services that it had been nearly a decade since she'd been in a house of worship. "We hope you'll join us here often. And bring the kids to Sunday school," he told her. "They look about the age of a couple of mine, although Maria will be disappointed, because Todd's a boy. When you're six that's not appealing, is it?"

It surprised her that the pastor remembered her name, and the children's, so quickly. She wasn't sure why it surprised her even more that he was a normal person with four rowdy boys who jostled around in the crowded hallway outside his office with a bunch of other kids.

What surprised her still more was that the biggest kid in the hallway seemed to be Carl. Around the children and teenagers he came to life in a way that she hadn't seen before. She wondered if he was active with the youth here. If he wasn't, the church was missing something, Grace thought.

The inside of the church itself was quiet and calm. A huge pine tree filled the stone sanctuary with a light and wonderful green scent. The ornaments on it were different, and all seemed to have some Christian symbolism about them. There weren't many on the tree, and there were large gaping spots where things seemed to have been removed. Grace made a note to ask Carl about it later.

For now she sat quietly, wondering at the pain she suddenly felt. Being in a church—any church—made her think of Matt. It had been his decision that she wasn't to step foot in one—with him or without him—after they were married. Grace had always wondered what had happened that made him so angry with God that he would do anything to avoid Him.

She didn't know much about Matt's life before he'd drifted into hers when he was nineteen. He didn't talk about his family much except to say that he had left for good. From what little he'd said about fatherhood, Grace had thought she knew what his childhood had been like, and she had wanted to make their life together happy.

Still, Grace ached more over the loss of Jo than Matt, and felt Jo's absence from her life far more deeply.

If she had been more self-confident at seventeen, she probably wouldn't have married Matt Mallory. And if Jo had seen more of him before he insisted on running off to get married, Grace knew now that she never would have let the awkward young man ''steal'' her away. She wanted Jo, wanted her fiercely. But Matt had cut off contact with her after they'd moved away. He'd had a fit of anger like no other when he'd come out of jail the first time and had learned that Grace was still writing to her aunt. When Grace had finally summoned the courage and phoned Jo four years ago, the stranger who'd answered had had no idea who Jo Sparks was, much less what had happened to her.

Grace feared that Matt had hidden a final letter—one from one of Jo's neighbors, telling her that her aunt had died. Matt's meanness would have let him keep a letter like that from her and bring it out only long afterward when liquor would have made him evil. Except he'd gone back to jail again and never come out, and Grace was left just not knowing.

That was what started the tears now—thinking of Jo and feeling sure she'd never see her again. The children stared at her, and Carl looked uncomfortable, but Grace couldn't stop crying. She knew it looked odd, surrounded by people singing happy Christmas carols. Let it look odd, she decided. After a few moments, Carl reached into one of his jacket pockets and pulled out a rumpled but clean handkerchief. "And don't tell me to add it to the bill," he growled in a low whisper as he handed it to her. Grace didn't know what made her more embarrassed—crying in church or laughing through her tears at what Carl had said.

After the service the pastor's wife came over and introduced herself. And like her husband, Barb Peterson wouldn't take no for an answer. So Grace found herself and the children having lunch at the parsonage along with Carl and more boys than she knew the Petersons called their own. "It happens this way every week," Barb told her. "The guys all want to bring a friend home after services. I usually plan on at least a dozen for Sunday lunch."

The thought of eating still made Grace's throat close. She fussed over the children—little Matt in his white shirt, looking as if he wanted to tease the collar open, and Maria, solemn and shy, in her one good dress. She looked as if she'd rather be home with her kitten than have people crowded around her. "Soon," Grace whispered to her as she bent to smooth the girl's hair. "We'll go home soon."

How quickly Grace had taken to calling Brenner's house "home." It felt so much more like one than the ramshackle farmhouse ever had. Still, the house screamed out for some attention in ways only a woman would notice. Grace was already itching to open windows and drag curtains outside to the clothesline the first day it got warm enough. Grace wondered what Carl Brenner would do when he saw his curtains on the line.

As if he'd read her mind, he turned and looked at her. Grace found her face warming under his questioning gaze. She glanced down quickly so as not to confront the half scowl he'd turned at her, as if he'd caught her whistling in church. How could he possibly have known her thoughts?

Maybe he hadn't, Grace told herself. Maybe he'd just seen a woman staring at him and, tired of being looked at, he'd stared back. Maybe, like Maria, he just wanted to go home.

Grace took up her plate, where she'd rearranged half a sandwich so that it looked at least nibbled on, and thanked Mrs. Peterson again for the invitation.

Hal Peterson, who'd traded his formal black shirt and clerical collar for a sweater, came over to talk to Matt. "You guys going to walk to school, now that you're living in town? Todd and Josh could always use friends to walk with."

Grace stalled for a minute before looking at Carl. She hadn't discussed this with him yet. "Sure will," he said, getting up. "On days it's warm enough. You folks got a car pool going when it's really nasty out?"

The pastor nodded. "With four, we're almost our own car pool. Of course, this year the older two are both in high school, so the car situation gets touchy once in a while. We'd welcome somebody to trade off with." He leaned over to Maria. "You could be the rose among the thorns."

Grace could feel Maria shrinking beside her. "What does that mean, Mama?" she whispered.

"It means we will have to make all these wild boys behave around you. And it will do them good, Miss Maria," Hal Peterson told her.

"Oh. Good. I don't like thorns. They stick."

Hal Peterson laughed, gently. "All right. Well, we'll see you, then. And Mrs. Mallory? If there's anything else we can do, just let us know." The pastor smiled, extending a hand.

Grace thanked him and left quickly before tears overwhelmed her again. Outside she helped Maria into the back seat, and climbed into the front herself.

Matt climbed into the back next to Maria. "I like Josh. He's in my class. You meant what you said back there, about walking to school with him, and riding, maybe?"

"Every word. And no helping me in the store until the homework is done after school, got that?" Carl said to Matt, swinging around to face him while he backed out of the parsonage driveway.

"Yes, sir." Matt seemed to be as surprised as Grace. His father hadn't been fond of letting the kids have friends. And later, Grace had needed Matt to come home from school to watch his sister while she worked. She could see that living in town, with her working just five blocks from home, was going to open a different world for the boy. "Thank you," she whispered. It was the first prayer she'd said in a long time that hadn't been desperately asking for something, and it felt very, very good.

# Chapter Seven

Surveying the loaded truck bed on Monday morning, Grace told herself that it would take a month of Sundays, going to church each and every one of them, to pay back Barb Peterson for the help in moving. Not only had she brought a Crock-Pot full of soup to Carl's for the evening when everyone would be tired from moving, but she'd also lent them her oldest son, Jon, a strapping sixteen-year-old. He stood in the truck bed, loading furniture as Carl hoisted from the ground.

Grace felt more than ready to move her things by the time Carl had arrived with the truck. At first it had seemed rushed to go in and have everything removed before a new lease would have started on January first, but now Grace realized the wisdom of the plan.

As early as she could get everybody going that Monday, she and the kids had headed out to the farm. They'd worked the whole morning to pack what hadn't been packed before, take apart the two beds that belonged to them, and bundle up the linens.

Not that there was all that much to load. Most of the furniture in the house had belonged to the Kriegers. Grace wouldn't miss any of their things much. None of it had the homey feel of things Grace had owned forever. It was just stuff that someone else had left behind.

What Carl and Jon were putting on the truck would not have been worth much to anybody else, but it was precious just the same. Her rocker, which had held both her children as she'd soothed them to sleep as infants. The beds. One chest of drawers that had been in her bedroom. A family Bible, a couple of other books, and a very few odds and ends rounded out all her worldly goods. The children's clothes and toys were already at Brenner's.

Loaded in the back of a truck it didn't look like much. There should have been more, but Grace had never had the time or money to collect much.

While Carl and Jon loaded the bed frames, Grace went back into the house. There were floors to sweep and vacuum. She set Matt to cleaning the bathroom and let Maria walk around with a spray bottle wiping down the walls for stray fingerprints while she worked in the kitchen with a broom.

When everything was clean, Matt looked like he was ready to wilt, and Maria's hair seemed to indicate she'd been pulled through a fence backward. Grace herded them into the bare kitchen and laid out the sandwiches she'd packed, thankful she had remembered paper plates.

When Carl came in, he had a small cooler with him. "Stopped and bought some cold milk this morning. I even got those plastic quart bottles because I heard from somebody at Jon's house that he drinks from the container when nobody's looking. So I got him his own." ·

The teenager grinned sheepishly, but Grace noticed he didn't deny anything, either. Once more, Grace was struck by how well Carl related to kids. Carl passed the cooler to Jon, who seemed to down half the bottle of milk in one gulp. Grace was relieved that she'd packed double the sandwiches she'd thought they'd need. Carl and Jon, apparently the boy in town most likely to outstrip Carl in height, each put down three without blinking. Maria sat on the floor and looked at Jon with open admiration. "You're big," she told him.

"Naw." Carl leaned on the boy and upset his balance. "He's not that big yet, Miss Maria." She giggled at them roughhousing in front of her. "Why, he isn't all that much bigger than your brother."

Maria giggled again. "Oh, yes, he is. Look at how tall he is."

"Yes, but look at little Matt." Carl's brow furrowed. "We aren't going to be able to call you that much longer, son. That 'little' part is going to have to go."

Matt hadn't looked up from his sandwich until now. Grace ached for him. She couldn't find a way to tell Carl how being made the center of attention affected her shy boy. She knew by the color of the back of Matt's neck under his pale hair that he wished he could vanish beneath the floorboards.

Still Carl persisted, oblivious. "Put your hand out here, Matthew. Look at what I'm talking about." The boy's gaze stayed on the floor, but his hand came out. Carl directed the bulky teenager to spread out his fingers palm to palm with the boy's.

"See, the hands and the feet, they grow first. And Matt isn't that far behind Jon, here. He's going to be one big boy in a couple of years. That's why I'm letting him work in the store," he said, mostly to Jon. "I figure if I train him early, he'll be able to do most of the heavy work by the time he's your age."

Matt went from looking at the floor to looking at his hand. Grace wanted to tell him that Carl was right. His long, bony fingers weren't that much smaller than the hands of the older boy beside him. But she stayed silent, letting her son figure it out for himself.

As he did, his shoulders straightened. "See, Mom. I told you that you should have let me help load the truck."

"Was she the one keeping you back?" Carl demanded. "If I'd known that, I would have said something. When we get to the other end, you get the boxes, all right?"

Matt nodded. "Yes, sir. Next time I will."

"Good. Now, how about putting on your jacket again and helping with those mattresses? They have to be fit in between the other stuff. Then we'll be done, and we can go."

Matt nodded. He watched Jon tip his milk bottle up and take a last swig. The younger boy lifted the jug at him wordlessly, and took one quick swig himself, backhanding a milk mustache from his face in the manner of his new idol. Then Matt, Jon and Carl headed up the stairs. Grace could have sworn she saw an identical swagger in all three backsides.

Later, as she stood outside, with the kids already in the truck and her furniture, such as it was, in the back, Grace looked at the house. "Sure you don't need any more time inside?" Carl asked.

Grace shook her head. "There's nothing here I'm leaving behind." Tears sprang to her eyes as she said it, betraying her feelings.

"No? Then why are you upset?"

"Because now nobody will ever know how to find me. This is the last address anybody has for me. I haven't talked to my family in years, but I've always known we could probably find each other if we had to. Except now I know we can't. I can't be at least."

Carl shook his head. "Moving the five miles or so into town doesn't have to change that. You ever heard of Internet searches for people?"

Grace looked at him, puzzled. "No. What would that do?"

Carl was grinning. And now, looking at him this closely, she could see what she'd wondered about before. His eyes were gray— not a dark, forbidding gray, but a blue-gray with almost the gleam of pewter or silver. Definitely a precious metal. "That, my friend, would find just about anybody in the United States that's alive and has an address or a telephone that's got a listed number."

Grace felt a hope stirring in her that she hadn't felt in a very long time. "Do you know anybody who does that?"

"You're looking at somebody. It's my hobby, you might say."

A stray breeze picked up a strand of Grace's hair and tugged it away from her face. Her spirits lifted with it. She liked this feeling of hope. It was a new feeling, and she definitely liked it.

Grace stared down at her figures, wanting to wince. It was going to take more than a month to pay Carl Brenner back. She should be happy and comfortable. This time of day she had the house almost to herself. Dinner simmered on the stove, Maria and the kitten, which she'd named Fluff, played in a corner while Grace sat at the table looking at a piece of paper covered with numbers. The numbers didn't make her happy.

Even the list she'd added up didn't really compute to what she knew she owed Brenner already. He insisted that even though he was feeding and housing three of them, their board shouldn't count. Carl argued that he was saving more money not driving through fast-food places with Grace cooking all the time. According to him, groceries for four still put him ahead financially. It didn't seem right to Grace, but she'd learned to stop arguing with him unless it really mattered. Even then, it felt like arguing with a wall. So far, she hadn't found a point Carl Brenner was willing to concede in an argument. Maybe she just wasn't used to arguing anymore.

With Aunt Jo, arguing had always been a sport. It had been meant in good humor mostly, as a way to pass the time. Grace suspected it had been a ploy to get her to talk when she was a teenager. If so, it had worked. But arguing hadn't worked with Matt. He'd solved arguments physically.

So Grace had gotten out of practice, which was a shame because Carl Brenner seemed to be a champion arguer. Or at least a champion argument-winner. And not because he threatened to use his larger bulk to make a point, either. He just sat stolidly at the table and said his piece. And Grace let him win.

Of course, he was paying her. So she probably should let him win. But it didn't seem fair to Grace that he fed and housed three people and got precious little in return. She'd worked in the store the hectic week after Christmas for a few hours each day, training. It hadn't been difficult, and Carl professed that it had helped him.

As far as Grace could tell, he didn't really need help in the store that much. She felt more useful keeping house. When school started up again Matthew spent most of his time at school, or doing home-work at the kitchen table, then maybe running back to the store for an hour. Maria didn't have much homework, being in first grade. At six she was starting to be a help, but mostly she sang to the cat. The cat loved it, but that didn't get any housework done.

Grace reveled in Maria's singing. For the first few days after they'd moved to town, she'd continued to say little. She was still getting well, and getting used to a strange place. Then slowly she began to talk more, and one morning Grace stopped in the middle of dusting the parlor when she heard a strange noise. She couldn't quite figure what the high sound was until she went closer to the kitchen and heard the strains of some ballad on the radio being mangled by her daughter.

Since then, the kitten had been treated to every song that Maria knew, plus a few Grace wondered where she'd picked up. Her shrill voice lacked a sense of rhythm, but she sang anyway. If Fluff would listen to that, she could, too.

Maria had her little chores, but they didn't amount to much in the scheme of things. Like any small child, she required as much chasing after and taking care of as she gave back in the way of help. And that was on good days. Still, Carl insisted on bringing home little things from the store or from Doc's for her and little Matt, and got frosted when Grace tactfully tried to tell him that she couldn't afford the treats.

"I didn't ask you to pay for them," he told her repeatedly with a glare that seemed to be more anger at being caught than anything else. He wouldn't have dreamed of giving out free merchandise to his other customers. Why her children? And why did he get so aggravated when they ate in the kitchen instead of the dining room with him?

Still, that arrangement had only lasted for about three days. On the fourth evening Carl had started a parade back into the kitchen with his dishes as quickly as she'd carried things into the dining room. After a third trip, she'd conceded and they'd eaten at the kitchen table together, no one speaking much. When he'd come home the next evening and seen Maria setting four places in the kitchen, the grunt as he'd taken off his boots had seemed to be one of satisfaction. It had been done his way ever since.

So he'd won his arguments. Grace, however, couldn't win much of anything. The paper in front of her told her that by the middle of February she would be at a point where she didn't owe Carl anything. Of course, that was counting on her getting her deposit back from Jake Krieger; and while the young man was honest, he wasn't good with finances.

Her calculations also left out some things Grace had to admit were important, like the cost of starting over anywhere that wasn't partially furnished. And the kids were both growing; last year's spring and summer clothes weren't going to fit.

She was still sitting there, figuring it all out, when Carl came in for dinner. He and little Matt burst in the door together, oblivious to the mud they tracked in until she pointed it out; then neither of them was terribly repentant. "It's warm out there," Carl said. "Spring just around the corner. Of course there's going to be mud."

"There's got to be cleaning, too," Grace replied, trying not to grumble as she got up and gathered her figuring. "Maria, set the table. Matt, take off those boots and then wash your hands."

"Guess that holds for me, too," Carl joshed, coming right behind her and looking straight down. What had gotten into him to make him this cheerful?

"I can't tell you what to do. It's your house." Grace swung by him and went to dish up the potatoes and the steak and gravy that had been stewing for hours. As she ladled the meat and gravy into the bowl, Carl's nose was twitching more than the kitten at her feet. She had to laugh, watching him, obviously in rapture over the smell of plain steak and gravy.

"Who fed you before?"

"Nobody except me. And I never learned to cook quite like that," he said. "There are days when I catch myself almost running home for dinner. Of course, I guess I need to run if I want to beat this one here to the table." He was reaching out to ruffle Matt's hair and seemed to be amazed when the boy scowled and ducked away from him. Grace gave her son a warning look and once again they ate in relative silence, Matt bolting a small portion of food, jamming his boots on and vanishing before Carl could say much of anything.

Maria, sensing the tension, ate quickly and excused herself after clearing her place. Grace knew she would go upstairs to hide under the covers of her bed, just to get away from what she felt down in the kitchen. Only Carl stayed at the table, and he looked stunned.

"What did I do?" His hushed question was full of pain.

"Nothing you shouldn't have."

"That's not true. That boy jumped almost as if I'd shot him." He looked down at his plate, stirring around the remains of his dinner. Getting up, he scraped it into the dog's bowl and whistled for Four. Grace had almost forgotten that the yellow dog had come in with the man and boy earlier, but he seemed happier to see the leftover steak than anyone at the table had been.

Grace tried to find a way to explain Matt. "You didn't do anything wrong, really. It's just that, well, Matt's daddy didn't call attention to him much. And when he did, it meant trouble. So he's not used to friendly teasing. Especially not from someone he admires."

Carl swung around from watching the dog eat and his gray eyes held real pain now. "It's my fault. I don't know how to act around him and the little girl. I didn't exactly have a normal childhood myself, and I've forgotten what it's like to be a kid."

"I don't think so," Grace said softly. "I think you remember all too well."

Carl's face clouded over even more. "Maybe you're right. But I still messed things up." He stormed out of the kitchen, slamming the door shut behind him, leaving the confused dog still standing over his dinner bowl.

He had been angry. As angry as Grace had ever seen Matt. But he didn't swear, and he didn't hit. And he was angry not at her, or little Matt, but at himself, and at the world in general that let little boys go through the pain of growing up. Grace could feel herself trembling—partly in fear and partly in wonder.

The fear came from all the times she'd witnessed anger and borne the brunt of it. The wonder was a new thing, blooming like a flower. Carl showed her real, righteous anger over anybody not caring for a child. He had promised to take care of them all—as easily as Matt would have promised to slap her.

Then, with all that anger racing through him, flushing his face and balling up his fists, Carl walked away. Without hurting anybody. Was this his faith at work? If so, Grace wanted a share of that faith. She could see him outside the window, striding purposefully up the street. In a little while he would catch up with the hurrying smaller figure ahead and amaze him with what Grace already knew he would say.

A sheaf of white on the floor caught her eye. Carl's door slamming had pushed a breeze through the kitchen, blowing Grace's papers with their careful figures into a heap beside the dog still finishing his food.

She picked up the pages of calculations. She could probably use them to light the fireplace later—because suddenly she wasn't worried about overstaying her welcome here. Suddenly she had more important problems to solve, and all of them seemed to require her staying in this house. Here she had a child just learning to sing and one who needed to learn to be teased. And somehow she had realized that no matter how long she worked at paying Carl Brenner back, she would always owe him more than she could ever repay.

# Chapter Eight

Grace had a headache. She seemed to have one perpetually these days. Probably from Kayla's constant chatter. The young woman had taken to coming to Carl's straight from class at the junior college and staying until just before dinner. She'd flit out the door, timing her disappearance to avoid Carl and manage to get home just before her father.

Grace wasn't sure if it was her company or her instruction that Kayla craved. With no mother living, the girl had nobody to teach her how to do things around the house, so she spent as many afternoons as Grace would let her underfoot in Carl's kitchen, hanging about and talking constantly. Today Grace had put her to work, peeling apples for three pies. Grace had thought that would slow down her tongue, but it didn't. Not nearly enough, anyway.

"I think black is my favorite color. Dad says it's not a color at all. If it's not, I guess my favorite is teal. How about you?" For what, Grace had no idea. She'd been too busy trying to triple her piecrust recipe in her head to pay attention.

"I'm sorry. Color for what?"

Kayla giggled. "Anything. I love the sound of the name. Teal. What's your favorite color?"

"Don't have one." Grace measured salt into the cupped palm of her left hand. Too much? Enough? She added a tiny bit more and poured it into the bowl with the flour. Creaming in the shortening, she could hear Kayla sighing. "Now what's the matter?"

"Everybody has a favorite color. How can you not have one?"

"Haven't thought about it in a long time. I've got more to do than wonder what my favorite color is. Besides, what good is it?"

Kayla's perfect brow furrowed and she spluttered. "Well, lots of good. When somebody wants to buy you a new car, they know what color to buy if they know you have a favorite color. Or if you're going to buy yourself a new top…"

"I haven't ever had anybody buy me a car, new or otherwise, Kayla." She tried to say it without sighing. "And when I need clothes I tend to buy them on sale, or at a resale shop. Color doesn't much matter."

"Oh. Well, I still like black. And teal." Kayla went back to peeling the apples.

Grace felt badly about snapping at the girl. She couldn't help sounding so witless. Kayla just loved to talk, and she had nobody at home to talk to. Getting the tiny hand grater, she grated a little nutmeg and cinnamon into the pie dough, then started stirring in cold water until the dough balled up.

"Why did you do that? Stir in the spices, I mean. I thought they just went in the filling."

"Usually they do. But since I have them, I figured why not use them," Grace explained, gathering up the dough to cool for a few minutes in the refrigerator before she rolled it out. She didn't explain to Kayla that cooking in Carl's kitchen felt like heaven. After years of making do with whatever scraps she had on hand, having a widely stocked pantry and time to use it made her feel exuberant. So did having an enthusiastic Carl to feed three times a day.

Besides, she wanted supper tonight to be special. It was the beginning of her plan to pay Carl back for all he'd been doing for her family. She figured his own apple pie would be a start. He'd hinted at Christmas that he could put away one on his own.

"Now, let's put sugar and flour on those apples to draw some juice," she told Kayla, leaning over her. "Then you're going to learn to roll out a crust." Kayla groaned. This should keep her quiet for a few minutes, Grace thought; a tongue poking out of the corner of one's mouth for concentration could not be used for talking.

The house smelled wonderful. Kayla, packed off with her first homemade pie, vowed that she would send her father over to talk to Grace if he didn't believe she'd made it herself. Grace didn't relish talking to Larry Trent, but she would back up his daughter. The girl needed a mother, Grace thought again. A mother would have taught her all the things she was lacking. A mother would also point out to Larry that Bill Parker needed to stay away more or have more supervision when he was at the Trents' house. As it was, Grace figured Larry was probably so happy to have someone else dealing with his chatterbox daughter that those two didn't get the supervision they needed.

It would take more than his own apple pie to get Carl in the mood to listen to a plan to chaperon Kayla and Bill. Even Grace knew not to attempt that. So Grace quietly put supper on the table and stood watching her family settle in.

It was evident by the time Carl and Matt came home for supper that Carl had patched things up with her son. Grace itched to ask him how, but she knew better. Neither of those quiet, prickly males would take kindly to her knowing about their private conversations. She just had to be happy with the fact that they were speaking to each other in a limited way, using the little half bath off the kitchen to wash up together and seeming to get along.

Her traitorous fingers wanted to touch Carl more and more often. He seemed to invite her touch just by his very presence. The way his hair curled softly at the back of his collar made her want to twine her fingers there and stroke. The set expression around his mouth made her want to trace the lines away. The lines would fall away, too, if she just put one finger there and drew it down the side of his face.

Sometimes now it took all her willpower to remind herself that Carl was not for the touching, no matter how tempted she was. She was a widow with two children to support, and Carl was her employer. Nothing more.

Maria pulled on her sleeve, demanding attention. "Mama! You're always telling us to sit down while it's still hot. How come you're still standing?"

Grace felt her cheeks warming. "Just daydreaming, I guess. Your turn to give thanks, sugar." The table talk picked up again the moment Maria finished, and Grace was saved from any more deep thoughts about her predicament by making sure everyone had bread and neither child upset their milk.

* * *

She'd baked him his own pie. Carl was so touched by that little gesture. True, the apples and flour and everything else had come from his grocery shopping. Still, that pie cooling on the countertop with a C cut in the top instead of the usual little chicken-track vent marks moved him—maybe because no one else in Redwing would have thought of it.

*No one else anyplace would have thought of it,* Carl admitted to himself. He probably couldn't come up with the names of five human beings who cared if he lived or died. Larry might miss the convenience of the store, perhaps. And Doc wouldn't have anyone to debate with. But truly miss him? Not likely. Only Four—hunkered in his corner, basking in the reflected warmth of the kitchen, would care. And now, perhaps, Grace and the children. And maybe even that stupid kitten—as far as cats cared, which didn't appear to be much.

With each passing day it got harder not to stare at Grace across the table. Each day, even each meal, she seemed to be more at home in his house. Little things were rearranged here and there to prove that she'd touched them far more than he ever had. Things he hadn't ever thought of cleaning had been scrubbed, polished, waxed or shone.

It had never occurred to Carl that the tops of door frames were objects to dust. He wondered how Grace got that high. Probably dragged a kitchen chair around the house. Over his dinner he envisioned her in his bedroom, standing on that kitchen chair, reaching up to work on the top of the door frame. Her slight figure would be enhanced by her lifting her arms over her head. He imagined her high squeal when he stood behind her and gently clasped his hands around her rib cage, then lifted her down from the chair.

She would be warm in his arms, and smell of roses. He could turn her around in his hands as easily as he could handle the kitten. Knowing Grace, though, she'd probably whop him on the head with whatever she was using to dust that door frame.

Grace spoke and reality washed over him like a cold bucket of water. "Something wrong with dinner?" Grace asked, pushing away his lovely daydream. She had little puckers of concern between her eyebrows. "You feeling all right?"

"Fine." It came out more harshly than Carl had intended. "Just…thinking about the store accounts." What a lame excuse for where his thoughts had been.

Carl wasn't proud of those thoughts. Especially when they concerned a widow with two little kids. She'd shown no indication that she felt anything but gratitude for having a roof over her head and kind treatment. It would be ridiculous to assume anything more just because she'd baked him an apple pie. He glanced over at the dog, searching for something—anything—to bring into the conversation.

When he looked closely at Four, he saw at least one reason for the big animal's expression of bliss. Instead of his normal patch of floor, the dog seemed to be stretched out on a blanket. "Making a bed for the dog now?"

Grace seemed abashed. "I found that blanket in one of the chests, full of moth holes. I couldn't patch it. So I folded it and bound the edges. He looks cold sometimes." Four's heavy tail thumped as if he agreed with her and knew what she'd said.

"All right. But no bows tied around his ears or anything."

"I wouldn't dream of it." There seemed to be a giggle buried just under the surface of her reply. For the life of him, Carl couldn't look at Grace again for the rest of the meal. If he did she'd surely see his embarrassment over thinking he'd been given special treatment, then realizing that even the dog got special treatment around here.

*He ate half the pie.* Grace knew the man had an appetite, but even she was amazed. Her husband had never eaten that much at one meal in his life. She got pure joy now out of watching Carl eat.

In fact, Grace had to admit that she got joy out of watching this man, period. Each day the image of the lonely little boy he'd described receded a little into the background. His large frame and that tiny bit of a scowl that seemed to be a constant part of expression made him seem anything but boyish.

It was good to see him without the scowl as he told little Matt how good his mom's pie tasted. A fact that Matt wasn't disputing, having eaten a second piece himself. Granted, beside what Carl had eaten, his pieces had looked like slivers. For a brief flash Grace could envision the two of them years into the future, both eating like truck drivers. It would be a challenge to feed them.

Maria dropped her fork. The noise shook Grace out of her fantasy. She wouldn't be here in a couple of years. She probably wouldn't be here longer than a few months. By the time the school year finished, she'd be settled somewhere else, away from Carl.

She couldn't stay. Not if she wanted to keep out of trouble. Because as Carl looked less boyish every day, he looked more manly. More in need of her touch. It would be so easy to walk over to where he sat enjoying that pie and run her fingers around his collar at the nape of his strong neck. So easy and yet so dangerous because of the temptation it would stir up.

Carl's voice as he talked to little Matt pulled Grace back to reality. "We going to study after dinner?"

"Yes, sir," Matt said hurriedly, sliding off his seat. "At least I think so. I better go check."

Carl smiled. "And you, Miss Maria. There's a brand-new pencil on my desk in the parlor, and a piece of paper. How about you go practice your letters with that for a while, all right?" Maria nodded and dashed off, as well. Maria never needed any urging to write or draw. Carl seemed to understand that while her shyness around him continued, her natural love of writing and drawing won her over when he encouraged her. Slowly but surely he charmed her to him, one piece of paper at a time.

Grace wondered why he wanted to be alone with her. And wondering pushed her into nervous movement. "More coffee?"

"I'll take one more cup. I'm stuffed as it is, but I still want to sit awhile." He stretched luxuriously, reminding Grace of a large, just barely tame animal. She wondered if anyone else saw him the way she did. To everyone else was he just Carl the storekeeper—one of the many familiar folks in town? Did anyone else sense the restlessness just under his surface calm, see the bunched muscles that took hours to relax when he came home at night?

She poured his coffee, not daring to look into those gray eyes. One look would be all it would take tonight for her to start talking in earnest. Telling him why she'd baked him a pie, and how much she was touched by his caring.

"Could I have a spoon?" His voice was deceptively soft. Grace felt chagrined that she hadn't put spoons on the table. What kind of housekeeper forgot the spoons? How could a man stir his coffee after he added a little cream if he didn't have a spoon? Come to think of it, what had he been doing all through dinner?

Her haste made her clumsy. That and the fact that she still wasn't used to the dimensions of this room, the furniture in it, everything. Her mind still held the contours of that awful kitchen in the farmhouse. There had been so little to trip over that things here remained a hazard, especially the out-splayed legs of Carl's kitchen chairs.

She had been here three weeks, but she still caught herself on them several times a day as she went about the kitchen. This time, her ankle neatly hooked around the chair leg in her haste to get him a spoon. If the chair had been empty, she would have just barked her shin and knocked the chair over. Instead, Carl's solid bulk anchored his chair, which he'd pushed back a little from the table as he lazed over his coffee.

Grace plowed into the chair leg, and momentum kept her moving forward—forward as Carl's eyes widened and he flung up his hands to catch her. He caught her, all right, but the movement she'd already started carried her smack against his chest. The solid thud she made surprised both of them.

"Well, now." Carl's eyes widened in surprise, and he seemed intrigued to have an armful of her.

And being in Carl's arms was marvelous. Grace closed her eyes and leaned her head back, feeling time slip into slow motion.

Then suddenly, a commotion to end all commotions broke loose in the kitchen.

# Chapter Nine

Grace watched as Carl paced the kitchen. She had just managed to soothe Kayla and wipe her teary face after she'd come bursting into the room. "He's gone!" she'd howled between sobs. "Bill's gone! And he didn't even taste my pie." Kayla now sat in the parlor, comforted by both children and the kitten. The dog would have nothing to do with her, and sat on his blanket in the corner, watching Carl pace.

Carl raked a hand through his dark hair, already rumpled in aggravation. "So why is Kayla so upset Bill left town? Is she— Aw, nuts, how do I put this so I don't offend you, or her? Did they—"

Grace tried not to purse her lips. "The only one offended seems to be you, Carl. If you want to know if Kayla is pregnant, the answer is no. Kayla may be young and impulsive, but she's not stupid. In a town this size, with her father the mayor and the banker, the boy would have been marched back to Larry's with a shotgun long ago if that had been the case."

"Well, how could I know? She comes in here wailing like a banshee, and all. And she is young, and very naive and— I repeat, how could I know?"

He looked so upset that Grace almost felt sorry for snapping at him. Almost. The thought that he had just naturally assumed that about Kayla and Bill didn't amuse her. "Why didn't you just figure that she wouldn't go that far with anybody, even Bill?"

He stopped pacing and looked at her with a pained expression. "I should have, shouldn't I? But look at things my way, would you,

Grace? He's a boy, really a young man. And I remember being a young man. If I'd had a girl like Kayla following me around town at his age, I would have tried.''

Grace stood. ''Oh, I expect he tried. But Kayla is smarter than you give her credit for and believes in the biblical promises about purity.''

He flashed her a quick, rueful smile. ''Good. It makes my job a lot easier if I'm going to find the kid if I don't have a seven-month deadline, and a guy who doesn't want to be found to begin with.''

Grace felt a thrill go through her. ''Find him? You sound like you've done this before.''

He shrugged his massive shoulders. ''It's what I do nights when I should be working on the store accounts. I told you before. I find things. Or people. Some alive, some dead.''

Her lips felt wooden as she kept speaking. ''And you…have success at this?''

''Sometimes. Almost all the time, really. When I'm not looking for someone I want to find for myself, that is. The one time I tried it for me, it didn't work. But I learned enough to do it for other folks. One time I found a girl Hal baptized twenty years ago. Her folks were just passing through town, and he always wondered what became of her. She's living in Montana on some ranch, married to a cowboy and the mother of twins. Found them all last year. Hal was pleased as punch.''

''So you can probably find Bill?''

''Oh, sure. Especially because he's only been gone since this afternoon. I've got a couple of ideas, anyway. With the young ones it's easy. Chances are good he's gone off to St. Louis or Memphis to seek his fortune so that he can be a self-made millionaire by Easter and come back and claim his ladylove.''

Grace found herself giggling in spite of herself. Carl had come much closer to her during his last speech, and now they stood together in the middle of the kitchen, him with his hands on her shoulders.

''I like your laugh. Haven't heard enough of it.''

''Not much to laugh about lately, I guess.'' Grace felt tongue-tied. He always had that effect on her when he looked down into her eyes and smiled.

There were words she wanted to say to Carl, here and now. But she didn't know how to ask. "Could you find someone for me? After Bill, I mean. Bill has to come first."

"Why?"

"Because. Kayla needs him to come back right away. She'll be crushed until you find him and get him home again. And I can wait."

"Can you?" His hand was warm on her cheek.

"If I have to." She sensed a current of meaning between them that went far deeper than the surface conversation. "I'm used to waiting."

Carl's brows drew together. "Used to coming last, you mean. I don't intend for it to be that way here, Grace."

She swallowed hard, wanting to lean her forehead against his broad chest and just stay. Instead, she kept looking into those pewter-colored eyes. "I know. And I'm so thankful for it. But Carl, we both have other things to do. I've got to get my children settled again, and you've got a store to run and plenty of other things on your mind. I know you'll find Jo for me when you can."

Carl seemed to deflate a little, losing the masculine teasing arrogance. "This Joe. Would it be someone I'm going to resent the daylights out of once I find him?" His crestfallen look made Grace reach up to him and stroke his cheek, the way she'd caress one of the children.

"No. And it's *her*. Jolene Sparks, my aunt who raised me. I know she's out there somewhere. I'm almost sure of it. If she were dead...I'd know it." There, the most awful words had been said and she still stood.

"You're right. And we'll find her. I'll show you all my secrets for finding people. We can do it together."

"But first you'll find Bill."

Carl sighed and let go of her. "But first I'll find Bill. You are so stubborn, woman, I don't know what to do with you."

Grace headed toward the parlor, looking back over her shoulder to have the last word. "For the present, Carl, that is a relief."

After a little more discussion, Kayla was sent home to calm down and wait—a process Carl doubted she could accomplish. But he decided to give her the benefit of the doubt, and made a mental note to go over and talk to Larry at some length the next day when he hit a slow period at the store.

Grace busied herself tidying the kitchen for the last time that evening. She put out dough to rise for cinnamon rolls while Carl and Matt finally got to their studying together. Maria sat in the corner nearest the stove, close to Four, and rocked and sang to the cat. Kayla's outburst had upset her. Singing to the cat calmed her by the minute. Grace wondered again at her resiliency.

"Go up and lay out your clothes for tomorrow and come back down in your pajamas," Grace told her son. "I'll read to you both tonight before you go to bed." He seemed to be ready to argue for a moment, then squared his shoulders, nodded and went up the stairs while she put a towel over the sweet-roll dough.

"And you, miss," she said, turning to her daughter.

"Not loud. You'll wake Fluff," Maria said solemnly.

"All right." Grace spoke more softly. "Put Fluff down by the dog and go get your nightgown on, too. I'll braid your hair while we're waiting for your brother."

Alone in the kitchen, Grace savored the faint scent of cinnamon in the air. She gave her hands a last swipe with her damp work towel and went to hang it up on the back side of the pantry door.

This big house felt like a dream. She had anything she should need or want to cook or sew, or otherwise provide for her family. Grace wondered again at that part of the change in her life. How had it happened so quickly?

She felt like a bad person. Just as bad as Matt had always said she was. A good wife would be sorrier than this to be a widow and less relieved every morning to wake up alone except for a cat and Maria.

Her gladness still worried her. Surely her marriage hadn't been that different from other people's. Surely she should be as bereft as the young girl who'd left here in tears just because her boyfriend had skipped town. Perhaps if the Matt Mallory who had died had been that boyfriend of hers, so many years ago at Jo Sparks's home, she would have been bereft. Not anymore.

She turned out the kitchen lights, leaving a single bulb on over the stove. Carl still sat in the parlor, and she would go there to read her children a story. Something uplifting with a happy ending so that they would believe in a far different future than the only one she could see ahead of them.

The next morning Grace rose early, stirring before anyone else. She slid into her clothes as quietly as possible and went downstairs to bake the cinnamon rolls. She hoped she would do well with this batch. It had been a while since she'd baked them. At Jo's they had always been reserved for celebration days, and over the last few years there had been so little to celebrate.

Today felt like a celebration day. The silver-blue winter sunlight coming through the kitchen windows making the clean glass sparkle was like a blessing. Grace felt pride looking at that glass. She didn't think too many other people around the town of Redwing had taken advantage of last week's brief thaw to wash windows. Now, with the return of the icy cold, Carl's windows all sparkled.

The rolls had risen just the way she'd wanted. Fifteen minutes later the rolls were in the oven. Somehow she had been drawn back to the Word more often since she'd been in Carl's house. Was that because it seemed like a haven?

Though not the world's fastest reader, Grace didn't have to follow along on the printed page with her finger and sound things out. Instead, she had a good, steady rhythm that she'd forgotten how much she enjoyed. And Aunt Jo had always used this particular method to time her sweet rolls. She said if you left a pan in there long enough to really read a chapter in any of the Gospels, you would get a good brown finish on them, and have done something worthwhile yourself. Her oven timer had never worked, but that had never bothered Jo. She'd always had her backup "Bible timer."

Grace nearly jumped out of her skin when Carl cleared his throat behind her. She'd been so absorbed in the scents of cinnamon and sugar in the warming room and the words in the book before her that she hadn't heard him come in. She knew she probably looked as flighty as Kayla, with one hand pressed to her chest and sitting up poker straight, but she couldn't help it.

"Is this a private party, or can anyone join?" he asked.

"It's your house. How could I possibly exclude you from

anything?'' Grace fought hard to keep a level tone with no hint of a gasp.

Carl shook his head, making little waves of his dark hair bounce. He needed a haircut. "You haven't learned yet, have you, Grace? To go along with teasing. I always feel so mean when I tease you."

"Don't. I'm just not used to it much anymore." She got up from her place at the table. "The coffee should be ready, even if the rolls have a little while to go. Would you like a cup?"

"Sure would," he said, putting a hand on her shoulder. "And I can get it for myself. Even being the housekeeper doesn't call for you waiting on me hand and foot. Especially not when there's something that smells that good in the oven."

Grace felt herself blush. "All right." No sense arguing over things with Carl. So she sat down and went back to her reading. To time the rolls, she needed to finish the chapter.

Carl settled in beside her with his coffee. "Read it out loud, could you? I stayed up awhile after all of you went to bed last night, and I could use something stirring to get me all the way awake this morning."

She traced the tiny lines of print until she found her place again. "I don't know how stirring you'll find this. It isn't exactly a Gospel that will appeal to a storekeeper."

It was fun to watch his bemused expression as he tried to figure out what she meant. The further she read, the more he understood. "Luke, chapter twelve. I'm already about halfway through. Verse twenty-five. 'And which of you with taking thought can add to his stature one cubit? / If ye then be not able to do that thing which is least, why take you thought for the rest? / Consider the lilies how they grow: they toil not, they spin not; and yet I say unto you, that Solomon in all his glory was not arrayed like one of these. / If then God so clothe the grass, which is today in the field, and tomorrow is cast into the oven; how much more *will he clothe* you, O you of little faith?'" By the time she'd finished, Carl was laughing.

"I see what you mean. If my customers took that one to heart, I wouldn't sell much, now would I? And I take it back. You do know what teasing is all about."

"Just rusty, I guess," Grace said, getting up to look at the rolls. Obviously she wasn't going to be able to sit quietly and read to time them. Carl's presence distracted her, made her want to get up and move. When she sat still she looked at him too much, thought about him even more. Neither led to her feeling calm.

The rolls still needed a few more minutes. The aroma filling the kitchen, and wafting up the stairs would draw the children soon. Grace figured they'd be downstairs ready to eat just about the time the rolls came out of the oven.

When he spoke again, it startled Grace so much she nearly slammed the heavy oven door. "Tell me about this aunt of yours. Why'd she raise you, anyway?"

"Because my mother couldn't. Jo was *her* aunt, really. My great-aunt. She'd raised Mama—what raising she got—and then Mama ran off at sixteen. A couple of years later she came back, pregnant and alone.

"Mama said my daddy had been killed in Vietnam, and she didn't know where else to go. Some folks said she didn't even know who my daddy was. Jo stopped that pretty quick. Mama stayed with Jo for a while after I was born. And even after she went back to wherever she'd gone in the first place, I remember her coming back. Until I turned four and she was in a car accident. I remember her being young and pretty, but not much else."

Carl listened intently, nodding and sipping his coffee. It had been so long since anyone had wanted to know. Matt had never referred to her mother, except in an unkind way. He maintained that everybody in their small community had known Grace's mother was just a free-love flower child, and her daughter would follow in her footsteps; and that she should be grateful that he wanted to marry her.

Opening the oven door, she pushed that particular memory aside and pulled the pan out, moving quickly so as not to burn herself. She slid it onto the top of the stove, using folded towels as a cushion against the pan's heat. Working quickly and deftly, she put the sticky rolls on a plate.

"So your aunt—or great-aunt, I guess—how old would she be?"

Grace leaned back on her heels, calculating. "Well past sixty. Probably about sixty-seven or sixty-eight."

Carl looked thoughtful, serious. "Do you have an address for her, someplace you know she's been lately?"

Grace sat down at the table, looking at the fine-grained wood of the surface. "How lately? I haven't seen her since little Matt was two. And the last phone number I had for her doesn't work."

Carl nodded. "Could she have moved?"

"She could have. Or she could have died. Either way, it's pretty hopeless, isn't it?" Grace let her shoulders droop. Carl put his coffee cup down with enough force to spill a little of the brown liquid onto the saucer.

"Don't say that. Not yet. I've found some pretty impossible folks in the last ten years. Maybe we can find your aunt for you, once I find Bill. You did want me to find him first, didn't you?"

"I guess I still do, for Kayla's sake. I can—"

"I know, Grace." He covered her hand with his larger one. "You can wait. But I don't know how much longer I can."

"Awhile, out of necessity, Carl." She withdrew her hand from under his warm, sheltering one. "Those children are coming down for breakfast. I'm not likely to see you alone again all day." The surprise on his face was worth the effort Grace had to put forth to tease him. She might get the hang of this teasing thing yet.

# Chapter Ten

It did not take long for Grace to decide that as much as she liked most of the store work, she despised inventory. She could see the reasons for it, but counting every item in the store was tedious, even with the little ticket scanner that Carl showed her how to use.

There were a lot of small items that weren't ticketed, like baby socks in the children's department, and almost everything in the Boy Scout case. For those, they had to use the old-fashioned method of one person calling out a name or stock number of an item, the other tallying how many there were. It took hours.

With each hour Grace spent in such close proximity to Carl Brenner, she got to know him better. The better she knew Carl, the better she liked him. In fact, she had feelings that were more than just liking the man.

He was big and brash and good-looking—that part she couldn't deny. But that wasn't what drew her to him. It was the open, friendly way he dealt with all his customers, even though Grace could tell that running the store wasn't what he really wanted to do with his life. Even in the middle of inventory he stopped calmly to answer questions for fifteen minutes for one sweet older lady who ended up buying nothing, but now had her checking account straightened out, thanks to Carl's help.

Carl's talent was with people—that much Grace could tell already. And seeing him with all the different people he dealt with, she wondered why he hadn't ever considered the ministry. At the church he seemed to come alive, especially when he was with children and teenagers, who seemed naturally drawn to him.

"So, did you go to school to learn to do this?" Grace asked casually while they were counting Boy Scout items after the older lady had left.

"Sort of. My uncle sent me to college, anyway. I did two years in business, then came back here when he had a heart attack. That pretty much ended my formal education. He needed me to take over, so I did."

"Ever thought of finishing up?" Grace asked. "I know I've always dreamed of just starting college myself."

"You'd be good at it," Carl said, making her shiver when he turned that silvery gaze on her. "Running the store here told me I wasn't going to finish up. Not in business, anyway."

There was something he hadn't said that Grace felt like pursuing. She wanted to know this man's hopes and dreams. But she couldn't bring herself to ask about them yet. It still felt like an intrusion into his life. Everything she'd seen so far had told her that Carl was a very private person, and as much as she cared for him, she couldn't breach that privacy yet.

But she wanted to. So much of this big man's heart was still a mystery, and day by day Grace wanted in on the secrets. What made him smile? What was he thinking when she caught him watching her those several times a day? Who, besides that magnificent dog, did he love and care for?

None of those questions were going to answer themselves. And Grace wouldn't get an answer from Carl on any of them right this moment because they had company in the store.

Grace looked up when the bell over the door rang. Naomi from the café bustled in with a covered plate. "Oatmeal cookies," she said. "I noticed the kids have taken to stopping here on their way home from school, and I thought you might want to have something for them."

"And maybe for Carl?" Grace added, unable to conceal a smile.

Naomi smiled back. "Well, there is that. I know he likes cookies as well as the kids do."

Grace took a deep breath. "And you're grateful for him taking us in and talking to Matt so all the little goodies on your counter stopped disappearing,'' she said.

Naomi colored. ''I never would have said anything. I raised a couple of boys myself, and I know it happens sometimes, even when you're doing all you can.''

''It won't happen again,'' Grace told her, touched by the sympathetic light in Naomi's eyes. The woman could have said all kinds of awful things, but she hadn't. Maybe, Grace thought, she was going to have to revise her personal opinion of several people in town, not just Carl.

The man himself came in from the back room, his nose twitching. ''I heard the bell, but I didn't know it was you, Naomi. Especially not with fresh cookies.''

''You would have been out sooner, I'll bet,'' she said, her eyes bright. Carl nodded, and took a cookie from the plate on the counter.

''You can say that again. Once the schoolkids get in here these will be gone in a flash. I couldn't talk you out of about a quart of milk to go with them, could I?''

Naomi laughed. ''I should have just brought it along and saved myself the trip.''

''I'll go back with you and get it,'' Grace offered. ''It will give us a minute to talk.''

''Don't let her pay for that milk, Naomi,'' Carl called out as they went through the door. ''Put it on my account.''

''You're not going to listen to him, are you?'' Grace asked.

''I'd better. He's my best customer,'' Naomi said. ''Even though he's been eating at home a lot more, lately. You must be doing better in the cooking department than Carl ever did for himself.''

''I try. There aren't too many ways he'll let me pay him back,'' Grace admitted. She felt she could be more open with the older woman.

''He is stubborn and determined that way,'' Naomi agreed. ''Do you know that when Rafe Johnson broke his arm last winter that man insisted on running him a tab at the café every day? For the entire eight weeks he was in a cast? Said if we didn't have Meals-on-Wheels around here it was the least he could do for one of the old-timers. Of course, he didn't say that to Rafe.''

''I'll bet not,'' Grace said. ''Especially the 'old-timer' part.'' She was touched again by the way that Carl gave of himself to people. Maybe it should make her feel less special, that he seemed to do it for a lot of folks. Somehow she couldn't feel less special where Carl was concerned, though.

Grace got her quart of milk—or rather, Carl's quart of milk—and headed back to the store. The bell jingled for her just the way it jingled for anybody else when she came through the door. "Are we almost done with inventory?" she asked. "And even if we're not, do you want to stop for milk and cookies before the kids get here?"

"Yes, we're almost done," Carl said, with a brightness in his eyes. "I swear, this is like doing inventory with Kayla. You really don't like this part, do you?"

"Not at all. It seems like a bunch of busywork," Grace admitted. "I can't see the point to it."

"The point is that we have to know what sold and what didn't of the stuff I ordered last spring. We've got to replace what sold, and reduce the stock on what didn't so that I don't find myself swamped with the wrong stuff about next October," Carl said. "See, in a couple of weeks the reps are going to come in or call me, and I'm going to have to make decisions on next winter's stock."

"Next winter's?" Grace echoed. It made her head swim. "And I always thought it was awful that the stores got Christmas stuff in before Halloween. I didn't think about having to order it before Valentine's Day."

Carl shrugged. "Breaks of the game. You always have to be anticipating on several levels. But then that's just why I think you'd be better at this whole racket than I am."

"You think I anticipate better?" Grace asked, feeling puzzled.

"You have to," Carl said. "You've managed to raise two kids by yourself and keep all three of you going with next to nothing. That takes planning and anticipation no end. That or trusting in the Lord for everything."

"And you've seen enough of my life to know that I'm sorely lacking in the trust department," Grace said ruefully.

Carl's face changed instantly. "I didn't mean it that way, Grace, honest...."

"I know you didn't," she told him, eager to reassure him that her feelings weren't hurt. "But you can look at my life and tell that it's been a while since I've trusted anybody to provide for me, even God. I have you to thank for what trust I've regained."

"Really?" Carl stepped closer, almost close enough to touch her. Grace felt her mouth go dry. "Then we've both got something to be thankful for, I guess. Because I find that you and your kids add a dimension to my life that's been missing for a long time. Maybe it's *never* been there, really."

Grace didn't know what to say. It was a relief when the bell jingled behind her and the kids poured into the store. Carl stepped back, the noise of several voices and several pairs of wet boots filled the area, and life went on as before.

"All right, cookies!" Matt crowed. "Where did you get these?"

"From Miss Naomi. She sent them over just for you," Carl told him.

"You and the rest of the kids, and Carl," Grace added. "So don't wolf them all down at once, okay?"

"Sure. You want one, Maria?"

"Sure," she echoed. Only a step behind him, Maria was taking off her coat and settling her book bag on the floor. Grace knew she should tell her to put her things in the back room right away, out of everyone's path. But it was so nice to watch her happy, glowing child come in from the cold, with cheeks red and a smile on her face. There would be time to correct her in a few minutes.

Maria had taken to wearing Grace's scarf to school with her coat instead of a hat. The big woolly scarf was also a rich, brilliant blue, and Grace knew it satisfied some need in her daughter to wear it. So she used an old hat herself, and knitted gloves. Maria had mittens, and the big woolly scarf, which made her sigh in contentment over its soft envelopment of her small body.

"Did you leave my kitty at home again?" Maria asked as she put part of a cookie in her mouth.

"We've been over this before," Grace replied, trying to sound stern. Leaving Fluff behind, even for a quick trip to town, had become an effort, but Grace had convinced her stubborn daughter that the half-grown cat had no desire to be stuffed into a carrier for the journey. She could just imagine explaining that one to Carl if they were to let the kitten roam around his store.

"All right." Maria took a cookie in each hand from the proffered plate, looking over her shoulder at her mother with a sly grin. No sense, Grace thought, in trying to tell her different. Carl would spoil her yet. She picked up the blue scarf from the floor where her daughter had dropped it. Maria had already headed for the stockroom, cookies in hand.

"Do you indulge in such things?" Carl asked, still holding out the plate.

"I don't know. Are they any good?"

"Probably not as good as yours," Carl said. "But the best around, otherwise."

Grace took a cookie from the plate. Solid and warm, it felt good in her hand. She bit into it, savoring the crisp outside and the soft, brown-sugar-flavored interior.

For a moment, childhood memories flooded back to her at the sharp sweetness. She had probably been no bigger than Maria when she'd come home from school to warm cookies. Jo hadn't ever had much around the place, but she'd found ways to make small treats for a lonely child.

Sometimes it would be cookies waiting after the walk from where the bus let them off; other times a scrap of cloth left over from dressmaking would have been magically transformed into a dress for Katherine, her doll. There were so many happy memories there when Grace chose to let them in.

The bell over Carl's door suddenly jingled again, bringing her back to the present and the rest of the cookie, still in her hand.

It was Tim Peterson, who seemed to be looking for Matthew. "Hey, Spence, want to come over and do that math together?"

"Sure," Matt answered. "You want a cookie before you go?"

"Sure," Tim said. "I'll go home and make sure it's okay with my mom if you come over. I'll call you here in a couple of minutes."

"Great," Matthew replied, watching his friend go out the door munching on a cookie.

"'Spence'? Would you care to explain?" his mother prompted.

"Yeah, well—" He started and stopped. "There are already two

Matthews in sixth grade with me. It's been pretty confusing all year. One of them goes by 'Matt' and the other 'Matthew' so the teachers can keep them straight,'' he said. He paused for a moment and took a breath. "The new semester started, and I'm ready to make a change. At school I'm going to be Spence. Is that all right?''

Grace nodded, not sure she could say anything. Matthew Spencer Mallory had just started the process of making a man out of the boy he would soon leave behind—a man who didn't want to be in the shadow of a father that no one, including himself, remembered too kindly. "That's just fine. Do you want *us* to call you that, too?''

Matt reached for another cookie. Grace could see that he was trying to remain as casual as possible, not to show that it mattered to him one way or another. There would be no keeping important feelings out in the open for this boy. Not yet. "If you would. I kind of like the way it sounds. Spence.''

"Then Spence it is,'' Carl said, ruffling his hair. "Finish that cookie, Spence, then grab a broom. Somebody got crumbs all over the floor, here.''

They grinned at each other at that one, and Grace's heart soared. Somehow their exchange of looks felt like a conspiracy to her, a male bonding in which she played little part. Matt—no, Spence now—hadn't ever had that with a man before. Even though it meant she was letting go of him a little, seeing it happen felt wonderful.

"Do you need anything for supper?'' Carl asked, watching the boy go to the storeroom for the broom.

"I could use a couple more potatoes,'' Grace said. "That is, if you two will want supper after all those cookies.''

Carl's look of scorn made her burst out laughing. That stopped him in his tracks. "You laughed.''

"I've never had someone speak a whole sentence to me before, just by quirking his eyebrow,'' Grace said, still stifling the last of her laughter.

"So, then, what did I say?'' Carl challenged.

"You said, 'As if half-a-dozen measly cookies would keep me from supper, woman.''' Grace's mouth felt dry as he came closer to her.

"You're good at that. That is exactly what I said.'' He tipped her chin up to him, and Grace didn't resist the movement. "Even the 'woman' part, Grace. You are, you know, a woman. And I've noticed. Quite often.''

Carl seemed oblivious to the large plate-glass window not ten feet away from them. For him there were no voices of children coming from the storeroom. So, for a moment, Grace entered his world and let him tip her chin higher; let his face come lower to hers until their lips met.

His kiss held the comfort of childhood—until she remembered her unhappy marriage, and tears sprang up in her eyes. Grace put both hands on his broad chest and pushed until the contact between them broke.

His eyes darkened with concern as he looked down at her. ''What was I thinking?'' he murmured. ''I'm sorry. So sorry.''

''So am I,'' Grace said, willing her voice not to break. ''It won't happen again.'' She called for Maria, and half-blindly she wrapped the child in her scarf and quickly ushered her out the door. The wind tugged at the edges of Grace's sweater, reminding her of the ice she should be wrapping around her heart to keep herself safe.

*What on earth have you done?* Carl stood in the middle of the store, stunned. Grace's laughter had been so delightful and so unexpected. Laughter transformed her from the serious, guarded creature he'd seen since coming up to her porch so many weeks before. Instead, when she laughed she seemed little more than a girl, her cares fallen away and a new animation in her delicate features.

Then he'd gone and ruined the moment by kissing her. He'd wanted to for so long he hadn't been able to resist the urge.

He should have. Now everything felt all wrong. Grace had whisked out of the store more guarded than she'd been since Christmas. Until he'd looked deep into her eyes, when she'd pushed him away, Carl would have said it had been worth it.

She'd been so alive in his arms. Then, in a heartbeat, she'd turned into a small creature trapped and resisting him. The look on her face had been one of sheer panic. What had possessed him to force his attentions on her? He felt as if he'd vastly overstepped his bounds, and Grace probably felt that way about him, too. All because of one beautiful laugh.

Running a hand through his hair in frustration, Carl looked out the window to where Grace hurried Maria away. One beautiful, liquid laugh of pure joy. After the stunt he'd just pulled, it would be a long time, Carl knew, before he'd hear that sound again.

# Chapter Eleven

It was two days before Carl got a civil word out of the woman, and three before she came near him. Even then, Carl felt that things with Grace were strange and stilted. If he'd known one kiss was going to cause that much trouble, he would have restrained himself. It drove him nearly mad to see her hangdog expression as she went about her precious duties. Why had he hired her as a housekeeper, anyway? Certainly not because he wanted a spotless house and food on the table at every opportunity. He wanted her company and that of her children, but once he'd kissed Grace Mallory, he got precious little of either for a long time.

At least the children still talked to him. The boy especially. Spence was blossoming in his new environment. When he'd first started working in the store, Carl had wished he'd smile at him once in a while. As they'd gone about their job together, the boy's silence and dogged persistence with every new task had surprised him. Spence had been all business. Now the boy had gotten to the point where he socialized with most of the customers who came into the store while he hung out there after school.

When Spence and Carl came home from work together, Maria waited at the back door, ready to tell him what they'd done all day and how she'd spent her time. Neither she nor the boy seemed to notice their mother's new reticence.

With so much free time on his hands, Carl could concentrate on finding Bill. It surprised him, though, that he couldn't work up any enthusiasm for the task.

It wasn't that he didn't want to find the young man. Kayla drooped around town like a wet mop. Every day after school she'd come into the store and ask if he'd had any word of Bill. She hadn't gotten a letter or a postcard or even a phone call. The girl was really beginning to worry. That alone should have gotten Carl going on the search.

He knew that once he started really looking for Bill, he'd probably locate him within a couple of days. That was the easy part. What he'd find once he tracked Bill down was what worried Carl. What if Bill had wanted to get away from Kayla and his very ordinary life in Redwing? Carl might not like Kayla all that well, but he didn't want to be the one to break her heart.

If Carl was honest with himself, there was another reason he was reluctant to find Bill. Once he located Bill, he'd have to keep his promise to find Jo Sparks. And Carl knew that as soon as he found Jo, he'd lose Grace and the kids.

He didn't doubt for a moment that when Grace knew where her aunt was, she would go to her. Staying here, keeping house for all of them and putting in a few hours a week in the store wouldn't be an option once Grace had real family. But then Carl would lose the only illusion of family he'd had in years.

He mulled all this over while he made halfhearted searches for Bill on the Internet. The easiest things didn't turn up any leads. The kid didn't have any credit cards in his own name that he could trace a payment schedule on. And no Bill, Billy, William, or even W. Parker had gotten a new listing with the phone company within the last thirty days anyplace in Missouri. It was disheartening.

Carl tried to reason and rationalize with himself. What would *he* do if he decided at nineteen that he was madly in love, that Redwing didn't hold any future worth talking about, and that he had to go make something of himself, right away? Bill was bright, but no rocket scientist. And three semesters of community college didn't lead to any jobs that were challenging. Not legal ones, anyway.

The kid was over eighteen, so legally he could sign himself up for just about anything. That included just about every branch of the armed forces, which was Carl's next place to check out. He knew the recruiters in Cape Girardeau and St. Louis didn't *have* to tell him anything. Still, they'd helped him out before when they could, so he spent one evening sending all of them E-mail. If nothing else, he reasoned, he'd have something to tell Kayla.

For the first time in a while, Carl regretted turning down the post office and the department of motor vehicles when they'd wanted him to run an office out of the store. Either one of them could have provided good solid leads for him, even if those weren't strictly legal. It was better this way, he told himself. Even to find Bill Parker, he wasn't ready to do anything of questionable legality.

The time in the evenings spent on the search meant that Carl was falling behind on ordering, invoices, and general bookkeeping for the store. He thought about asking Grace to man the counter for a couple of days so that he could catch up, but he couldn't do it.

No. Better to write and search the Internet in the silent parlor at night than suffer through a whole day of Grace's scent tantalizing him, Grace's warm body there at arm's length while her mind could have been a continent away. Just contemplating such a day drove him back to his computer screen every night.

Bill's mother wouldn't talk to him. At first she didn't know where he was; then later, when Carl was sure she did, she was upset with Kayla for driving her boy away to do whatever he'd done. When Carl couldn't get an answer out of her, he was pretty sure that Bill had gone into the service. If he'd taken a job in a larger city and leased an apartment there, Bill still could have come home to visit on his days off. Nope, his mother's aggravation spelled "basic training" to Carl.

He redoubled his efforts with the recruiters at night. Finally the army guy in Cape Girardeau gave him the response he'd been looking for. Carl didn't tell anybody he'd hit pay dirt. No sense getting Kayla's hopes up too soon. There was always the chance that Bill had joined the army to get away from Redwing *and* Kayla. If that was the case, Carl would find a way to break it to her as gently as possible—but only after he'd talked to Bill and his mother.

"Nine weeks," Bill's mother told him, her lips pressed tightly shut. "And four of them still to go. Of course I told him he had to use his phone calls home to talk to me, not that little—"

"Now hold on, Mrs. Parker," Carl interrupted, trying to head something ugly off at the pass. ''By the army's definition, Bill's a grown man. If he wanted to join up, you can't blame it on Kayla.''

''I most certainly can.'' Janet Parker looked older than the nearly fifty Carl knew she was. Of course, life in a little town like Redwing, with nobody but your nineteen-year-old son to depend on, couldn't be easy. ''I can blame her plenty. If it wasn't for wanting to 'be somebody' for that girl, Bill would have stayed right here and finished school, kept his part-time job at the gas station out on the highway and done just fine.''

''He might have done all that—'' Carl tried to stay calm ''—but would he have done just fine? You've lived here for most of your life, Janet. What was the boy going to do once he finished school? Go to work at the auto-parts plant in Cape? Stayed pumping gas? Aren't you glad Bill wanted more than that?''

The lines in Janet's thin face softened. ''I am glad he wants more. Guess I just miss him, is all.''

''When's graduation from basic at Fort Leonard Wood?'' Carl knew the answer already, but thought this might be the chance for some bridge building.

''Second weekend in April.'' Janet's expression was sour. ''But that old truck wouldn't make it there without an overhaul. And I don't have anybody to do it anymore, do I?''

''No, I guess you don't. But if you could see your way clear to making a little deal with me, I think we can get you to that graduation.''

Janet's pale, tired eyes narrowed. ''Will *she* be going too, if we make this deal?''

Carl sighed. ''Yes, Kayla will be going, too. But you'd better get used to saying her name, Janet. Sounds like if Bill has his way, you're going to get to know her real well eventually. Maybe even like one of the family.''

Janet huffed out a breath, making her nostrils flare. To Carl she looked more like a Missouri mule than ever, until she finally smiled. ''Oh, all right. I'll even make up with her—I mean Kayla—if it means seeing my boy graduate. What do you propose, Carl?''

''Lousy groundhog.'' Grace was tempted to shake her fist at the nonexistent animal. February had started this gray and dank thanks to him, and was ending the same way. She was ready for spring now. Why was it so long in coming? Grace peered through the darkness at the kitchen window, wishing the dark didn't come so early in the evening. Wishing that Carl was home from his mysterious errand. It had to be important for him to go someplace for the whole day, leaving her to mind the store, but he hadn't said much about where he'd be.

Of course, he hadn't said much to her in the last month, nor had she said much to him. She'd felt frozen since he'd kissed her, willing her feelings into ice so that she could stay under the same roof with him without losing her mind.

She'd wondered how she could face Carl after the kiss and had tried to hide her feelings. But even in her dismay over kissing Carl in broad daylight and showing him just how deeply it affected her, Grace didn't want to forget that kiss. She couldn't repeat it, but she wasn't anywhere near ready to forget it.

If only he'd come down to breakfast the next morning smiling and whistling like before. Then she might have thawed some. Might have spoken more, loosened her hair from the tight knot she knew he despised. Might have made an effort to speak with him to pass the time of day while she cooked his breakfast or served his supper.

Instead, he had been as grim as she had felt herself that morning, and Grace found herself building up an extra shell of ice around herself that hadn't thawed yet. Or at least it hadn't thawed all the way. She couldn't be in the same house with the man—cooking for him every day and doing his laundry, sitting in his parlor at night while he messed with that computer and she helped Spence study or read to Maria—without warming a little.

Still, drawing away from Carl for a while had been a good thing, she decided. She felt changes inside herself, changes she couldn't deny anymore. The quiet time over the last few weeks also meant that he hadn't had to bear the brunt of her anger.

Anger had come out of nowhere following that January kiss and swamped her like river waves over a child's homemade boat. Who did Carl think he was to just kiss her like that in public in the store? And even more troubling, why hadn't any man's kiss ever felt like that before? Could it be possible, Grace asked herself over and over during those long winter weeks, that she hadn't ever really known love between a man and a woman the way it was meant to be?

At first, asking such a question only made her anger and frustration rise. She fought the feelings by plunging herself into hard, physical work every day. The house shone. Every sheet, towel, blanket and tablecloth got ironed, mended and put away in top condition. She found dishes and knickknacks Carl didn't know he had. She straightened closets, beat rugs when the weather cleared enough to do it, and went to bed each night so tired she could barely walk up the stairs.

The physical tiredness didn't keep her from lying awake, staring at the ceiling. She must have remembered every nuance of that one kiss fifty times. Folding each clean shirt reminded her of how Carl smelled and felt wearing it. Just sitting next to him at the dinner table mesmerized her as she watched his mouth move.

She couldn't live this way much longer. Cleaning the house was a poor substitute for talking to Carl. Cooking meals didn't make her want to touch him any less. Something had to change soon, Grace told herself, as she looked out the window into the dark. She was ready for spring. And ready, definitely, for change.

Change came in the door with Carl that dark late February night. Grace heard the truck in the yard, the slam of doors. He messed with something outside until she thought she'd scream. Finally he was on the porch, stomping mud off his boots, using the iron scraper outside the door for what seemed like an interminable time.

Suddenly she couldn't keep her silence, her detachment.

"Well? Where have you been all day? What did you find out? Get those boots off and have some coffee and tell me all about it," she said, as if they hadn't been strangers to each other lately.

Carl looked slightly perplexed, but not totally confused. First he just stood there for a while, his hand on the doorknob. "You're letting in all the cold air," Grace informed him, as if he didn't know that.

He looked outside and broke into a grin. "Guess I am. And we can't have that." He stuck his head out the door and whistled. Four came bounding in after him, dancing in his excitement to see Grace.

"Yes, and I missed you, too," she said, trying not to laugh while large, feather-furred paws climbed nearly to her shoulders and the dog planted a sloppy cold kiss halfway between her chin and cheek.

She pushed him off, gently. "Oh, get down. You're not a long-lost orphan. Besides, you're probably muddy."

Carl tried to sound indignant instead of indulgent and failed. "You have that dog spoiled rotten."

He took off his boots and clumped over to the table stocking-footed. "You have me spoiled rotten, too, Grace. I didn't realize how good I had it around here with you until I left for a day."

Grace's heart thudded so hard she nearly dropped the coffeepot. "Now what can you mean by that?"

"What I can, and do, mean by that is I ate a purely awful lunch in Cape Girardeau, at a table not half so convivial as mine usually is even when you don't talk."

"Cape Girardeau? What on earth were you doing there? And what have you been doing since lunchtime?" She couldn't help it. This time her shaking hand betrayed her and coffee slopped over the rim of the cup as she poured. "I'll clean that up," she said, surprised by the fear that swamped her—fear that had no purpose any longer, but still haunted her when she made what for Matt had been unforgivable mistakes, like spilling the coffee.

"No problem." Carl didn't even seem to notice the puddle under his cup. "Do we have cream?"

"Coming right up." She whisked away the spilled coffee, put the wet rag on the sink top and went for the milk in the refrigerator. She kept her shaking hands under control as she set the jug on the table, and when Carl patted the chair next to him, she pushed away her usual protestations and sat.

"So tell me all about it," she said, bubbling with an excitement she could see mirrored in Carl's tired eyes. "You found Bill?"

"I found Bill. And in early April we're going to take a trip across the state to see him." She listened as he spun the tale of where his search had led, and what he'd done even that day. The dog took advantage of her rapt attention to Carl and nosed his way under her hand, insinuating himself under the table to do so, even though they both knew he wasn't supposed to be there.

Carl was telling her about his conversation with Janet before she realized she was stroking silky ears and there was a large, thumping tail beating time to his words. "All right. Just this once. But beg under the table while we eat and you'll be in disgrace." The large paw that stroked her knee for a moment seemed a promise that Four would be a gentleman.

Carl's coffee cup was empty and his hands were on the table. "How about me, Grace? Am I still in disgrace? Or have I finally redeemed myself by finding the boy?"

He looked so serious, waiting for her answer. Grace couldn't help but get up—so quickly that her chair tipped over. In an instant she was in his arms. It felt so good. She felt so welcome to be there, savoring the warmth of him, the crispness of his hair against her cheek.

"Oh, Carl. You were never in disgrace. It was me. I know I made such a fool of myself when you kissed me. I couldn't let that happen again."

His eyes were bright as he drew her down closer into his embrace. "Well, if you couldn't let that happen again you should have stayed over in that chair, because I sure want to kiss you again."

His words should have stopped her, should have chilled her blood and sent her racing to safety across the room. But instead she came closer, and they kissed.

This kiss was a welcome back. Back to where she should have been while she'd been berating herself instead.

"So I'm forgiven?" he asked.

"Nothing to forgive."

"I think there was. I know I came on too strong, too quick before. I'll take things slower now, I promise." He looked so boyishly earnest that laughter bubbled up in Grace again. He was so different from any man she'd ever known before. So delightful in all his moods, from somber to happy.

"You do that, then. And you'll start looking for Aunt Jo?"

A look flickered over his face, and then was gone. Grace wasn't sure what she'd seen. Was it doubt, or guilt, or something else equally puzzling? It came and went so quickly, she wasn't sure.

"We'll find Jo," Carl said as he got up. "But for now I am nearly dead on my feet. And I've got to go up to bed."

Grace didn't argue, even though she yearned to have him stay.

Better he left than they both had to struggle with the feelings one more kiss had lit in them.

Since she couldn't do anything about the warmth Carl had started in her, she did more practical things instead. She made sure the milk was put away, that the coffeepot was empty and the lights out. Then she went to bed and for a change she fell asleep quickly, still staring at the ceiling but now tracing her lips with one bemused finger, and fighting giggles in the dark so as not to disturb Maria.

# Chapter Twelve

Spring weather hadn't arrived, but it was spring in Grace's heart. The crocuses were blooming amid drifts of late snow. The wind was still as raw and wet as ever, and yet Grace expected to be able to go out in shirtsleeves and gather heaps of daffodils. Surely if she felt this way inside, it must be spring outside the front door, too.

Her good humor seemed to be catching. Carl went off to the store each morning, whistling as loud as Spence. Sometimes, coming home, Grace caught them racing. She suspected that Carl had to rein himself in quite a bit to let the boy win.

During the first week in March, Kayla came bubbling over to the house twice. She had to be almost physically restrained from hugging Carl and the dog, neither of whom wanted the attention. First there had been a letter from Bill and then on Sunday night, a phone call.

"He loves me." She danced around the room, not able to sit still. "He's almost finished with basic training and then he goes to school at Fort Bragg in South Carolina. Then he'll be a specialist, and he'll get leave. When he comes back I think he's going to talk to Dad about getting married. Can you believe it?"

Grace couldn't answer right away. For once, Grace blessed Carl for not moving into town next to the store. Most of the time she felt a little isolated out on the edge of things, but when Kayla had big news like this, it was worthwhile to be the first to hear their awkward plans.

They were so achingly young. Grace wanted to give them all

kinds of cautions. Carl just looked uncomfortable avoiding Kayla's dance around the kitchen while he drank his coffee. Grace wondered if it was Kayla's discovery of her adulthood that made Carl look that antsy, or just worry that he'd drop the cup.

It wasn't long before the half-grown cat batting at her moving shoestrings gave Kayla the giggles and she sat down. Granted, it was on the floor with the cat, but things were calmer that way. The children ate the cookies Grace was taking out of the oven, and Four made little snorts and moans in the doorway for being excluded from what he perceived as a grand party.

Carl seemed relieved when Kayla headed back to Larry's, the kitchen cleared out, and left them alone cleaning up. "Kayla's very happy," Grace said, rinsing a cup.

"I guess." He sounded tentative.

"I know they don't know what they're getting themselves into, but nobody could tell them that. Especially not a girl as young as Kayla."

"No, probably not." Carl dried the cup with exaggerated concern. "But do you think this will all work out?"

"As well as marriage ever works out," Grace said, trying to sound optimistic. "They seem to love each other. That's a good start."

"Wouldn't it be a better start if he had some money? And she had a little more age on her, and some common sense?"

Grace looked into Carl's face. Usually he kept his emotions to himself, but this time he seemed to have revealed a genuine concern for the young couple. "Kayla's got plenty of sense. I know she looks flighty to you, but that's just because you're not used to giggly girls. And Bill's got plenty of money. You don't need much, starting out."

"If you say so. I'd want more than that to offer a woman. As far as that goes, I'd want more than I have right now to offer a woman." He'd put down the next cup, still swathed in a towel, and was facing her now.

"I mean, marriage ought to start out right. A good house, a steady job—all that is fine. But the people need to be worthwhile, too, don't they?"

He was troubled in a way that Grace hadn't seen in him before.

"What are you saying, Carl? I don't think you're talking about Bill and Kayla anymore."

"I'm not. Not just about them, anyway. I guess they'll get by just fine. He'll probably have to put up with a few burned dinners and they'll fight some if his mama comes to live with them, I expect, but they'll get along fine. But Grace, who would ever want me?"

"I would." The words came out so quickly, they surprised her as much as they seemed to surprise Carl. "I would, Carl." She repeated them, just to taste their delicate sweetness on her tongue.

"Would you? There are things you don't know about me. Things that aren't too pleasant. I'm not as good as you think I am, Grace. And there're things most men bring to a marriage that I can't bring."

"Such as?" As long as he was in a talkative mood, Grace thought, might as well get everything out in the open. After being married to Matt Mallory for ten years, she wouldn't start again with that many surprises.

"I have no family. Few friends. No real connections at all. Even the family that's not there anymore isn't one to claim. I never thought that would be fair. To a woman, I mean, and to children." There were little white tracings of the faint lines around his mouth. His admission had cost him dear, and Grace wanted to repay him for the effort he'd expended.

She wiped her hands quickly on her apron. No sense spattering him with dishwater. Smoothing the lines from around his tense mouth, she held his face between her hands. "Is that supposed to matter to me?"

He looked surprised. "You mean you wouldn't care? About not having anybody? You want to find Jo so bad, I figured family would be doubly important to you."

"There're more important things that I worry about," Grace admitted. "I've got two fine children in your parlor. Could you care for another man's child? Or will you just resent them and where they came from?"

His head dipped, and roughly, he kissed her palm. His action told her so much before he even spoke. "I'd already take anybody apart who tried to hurt those two. I can't help it, Grace. I don't care who planted the seed. I'd like to help the tree grow."

There was a fierce joy building in Grace that threatened to burst
out in tears. "It's too soon," she murmured, feeling frustrated and
happy at the same time. "I'm not ready for this. Besides, the whole
town would say scandalous things. Can you wait?"

"I can wait. But not for long, Grace. And not patiently. I'm not
a patient man, no matter what people are going to say."

"I don't much care, either," Grace admitted. "They've been talking about me for the whole time I've lived here, I expect. What's
to matter if they have something new to talk about now? But let's
wait a little while more."

"If that's what you want." He released her hand from its trap
and stared into her eyes, making her shiver.

"It's what I need. For now."

"For now," Carl echoed, his voice taut with unspoken emotion.
The water Grace put her hands back into had grown cold. With a
shiver that had little to do with the cold water, she hurried to freshen
up the dishwater.

It was Kayla who changed Grace's mind about waiting. Kayla in
her innocence, who never knew what she'd said. Despite what she'd
told Carl, Grace did have a few questions about Kayla's ability to
be a good wife to Bill. She was still so young and dreamy that
Grace wondered if she'd get anything done the first few months of
marriage, or just play house a little. Perhaps Bill wouldn't mind if
he got to play, too, Grace told herself.

Thinking of them "playing house" put a smile on her face the
next time Kayla came over for housekeeping lessons and cooking
help. She did seem a little more serious as the morning wore on.
As they worked in the kitchen together there seemed to be a question on the tip of Kayla's kittenish pink tongue. Grace wondered
how to get her to ask it without embarrassing the girl—sure that it
had nothing to do with their activities in the kitchen.

The cuckoo clock in the parlor had chirped eleven before Grace
found a way to prod the girl into speech. "So what does your dad
think about all this?" Grace tried to sound casual.

"He's okay with it, I guess. He wasn't at first, but he is now.
Bill's looking at when he will get another furlough once he's posted
to his first assignment. Bill says he doesn't believe in long engage-

ments, and Dad says we'd better not, anyway," Kayla said, still concentrating on the checkbook balance in front of her.

"Oh? Did he have a reason?" Perhaps this was the source of her questions. The checkbook was hopeless as far as Grace could tell. They were going to have a long talk later about entering things *when* the check was written. Entries marked "Stuff" and "About $20" just didn't cut it for her.

"I thought we could wait for a while, and maybe I could go up to Fort Bragg and help Bill look for a house. He wants to go off base to live. And I expect his mother will come, too. But Dad said no. He said something about all the money Bill would be spending to furnish a house and if I wasn't careful maybe he'd want to take it out in trade, like you and Mr. Brenner."

Kayla looked shocked then, realizing whom she was talking to and what she'd just said. Grace didn't answer at first. With shaking hands she directed Kayla on how to at least halfway balance the checkbook mess.

"Dad didn't mean..." Kayla started.

"I know, Kayla." Grace did know exactly what Larry had meant, but she wasn't going to say that in front of the girl. She might have a terse discussion with Larry later, but she wouldn't take her anger out on Kayla. "I expect he just meant it wouldn't look too good, an unmarried girl like you in a big town like that with Bill, even with his mother along. And it is expensive to furnish a house, Kayla."

"Do you really owe Carl money?"

"Not anymore. He's paying me a salary for keeping house for him. The first few weeks I worked for what I owed him, mainly for Matt's escapades in town." Grace struggled to keep her voice as even as the column of figures growing in the checkbook. It was no mean feat. She could always pretend the column of red ink was Larry Trent and the rest of the sanctimonious old men in town. Leave it to them to figure that Carl had found an arrangement that didn't include money to pay his housekeeper.

Grace wasn't about to tell Kayla how much Carl insisted on paying her. Or that he wouldn't take anything back for board for her and the children. Fortunately Kayla didn't ask any more questions—not about Carl and Grace's situation, anyway. By the time the checkbook was finally balanced, Grace's hands had stopped shaking. And Kayla wanted to know how to starch and iron lace curtains, as if she and Bill could afford any.

Tactfully refraining from pointing out that fact, Grace took the bank statement Kayla had brought over out of its envelope and began to go over it with her so the checkbook mess wouldn't happen again. And all the while most of her mind was elsewhere, wondering how she would break the news to Carl that the whole town was besmirching their good name. *His* good name, probably. Grace didn't think she had much of a good name with anybody in Redwing—a situation that wouldn't change unless she married Carl Brenner, and quickly.

"It just doesn't look right," Larry said. "She's a healthy young woman and you're not exactly some ailing old codger. Having a housekeeper live in at your age is just leading to talk."

"Well, that's all it's leading to. Talk. Don't you people have anything better to do at town-council meetings than run down honest people?" Carl couldn't keep the aggravation out of his voice. Maybe he'd feel differently about things if he were actually doing what Larry was hinting at. At least then, he'd probably have a healthy dose of guilt about his situation instead of the frustration that made Larry's pronouncement even harder to take.

"Look, Carl, I really appreciate what you've done for me. And I've tried to tell the rest of them to hold off on saying anything. I mean, the woman's still a widow and all. I know she needs someplace to live and it's just Christian charity on your part that makes you give her a home."

"No, Larry, it's a sight more than Christian charity." Carl stayed still and just hollered. He could feel his neck getting redder, starting first at the level of his collar, then rising slowly up to his hairline.

"I am not giving Grace Mallory a home out of charity, Christian or otherwise. She's gotten that house cleaner than it's ever been since I've lived in it. Spence is as good a helper around the store as anybody I've hired in five years, and he's not even eleven yet. And she's a fine woman who I intend to make my wife. Couldn't you let me do it in my own time?"

"I would on my own." Larry's tone had become a definite whine now. "But that girl of mine is going in and out of your house all the time. She's probably got enough ideas about how things are supposed to go with that Parker kid already. All she needs to see is the two of you—"

That was it. Carl's fist came down on the counter that separated the two of them with a violence that rattled the light fixtures. "What on earth do you think she's seeing, Larry? The woman is my housekeeper."

"Try telling that to the women. I don't have a wife at home to contend with, but the other three do. And they're all convinced that two young, healthy people under the same roof with nobody for company but two little kids are bound to get into trouble. And they want it stopped."

"Great. So the town biddies have decided that I can either throw out the best housekeeper I've ever had, or ask her to marry me. Which, this close to her moving in, will probably make her so mad at me she'll leave."

Larry looked a little wan. "I guess that's about the size of it. I didn't think of it your way before I came over here, Carl. And if I had, maybe I would have tried harder to talk to the rest of them about this. But Fred says he hasn't had any peace for weeks at home, and Pete has that snippy little daughter who's going to school with Spence. I wanted to say something to you before that kid gets it into her head to spread nasty rumors she's heard from her mother."

Carl's heart sank. "I think you're too late for that one. Thanks for warning me, at least." He leaned on the counter, trying to ease the tension out of his taut shoulders and back. It would have felt so much better just to punch Larry and get it over with. But it wouldn't solve his problems, no matter how good it would make him feel. Better to talk it out today. "I'll speak to Grace. And Spence. And we'll find some way to shut up the gossips. But this better not foul up my chances of marrying this woman later."

Larry actually blanched. "I keep trying to tell you it's not my fault, Carl. Go blame the rest of them."

"Oh, no, Larry," Carl growled. "You're the mayor. You're in charge. I'm holding you responsible if this falls apart because of the 'good women' of Redwing and their objections."

The mayor left quickly after that. For his own part, Carl just lowered himself to his high stool and traced patterns on the scarred surface of the countertop before him, mulling over how to break the news to Grace.

The talk with Grace was going to be rough. But at least Carl had an idea of what to say. He figured there would be a lot of recriminations from the proud woman in his kitchen. She wasn't going to take kindly to the thought of marrying him just because a flock of old hens was clucking about the two of them.

Worse would be the talk he was going to have with Spencer. He had no idea how to begin that one—especially when he remembered the shiner the boy had come in with the day before. Spence had glossed over the bruise high on his cheekbone, claiming it was due to some roughhousing at lunchtime. Now, Carl had a suspicion it was part of something else altogether.

All too soon the bell over the door jingled to herald the boy's arrival. He wasn't bouncing into the place as usual, and Carl remembered that he'd walked like this the day before, too. Stiff-legged and slow, as if he had to make himself come in, instead of with his normal enthusiasm.

Carl let him go into the back room to put away his things. Then he pulled out the little sign to close the shop; he had more important business to tend to for a while. Mounting the sign on the door, Carl locked it and went back to face the boy.

It wouldn't be easy. He didn't want to offend the kid, not now. The last thing Grace's son probably wanted was somebody to take the place of a father he hadn't been all that fond of, judging by what he *hadn't* said.

The boy looked up in surprise as Carl entered the back room. "I made sure it's just the two of us for a few minutes, Spence. Man to man. And I think I know how you got that shiner. Why don't you tell me about it."

Kids could be so ugly, Carl thought to himself. He'd willed himself not to wince while the boy poured out his story about Pete's daughter and her comment. "And I couldn't hit her. She's a girl. Mom would have my hide if I ever hit a girl. And her brother's in the eighth grade."

"But you hit him anyway," Carl said, knowing the answer from the scrapes on the boy's knuckles that he'd missed seeing the day before.

Spence nodded. "And got pounded. And then got in trouble with the pastor when he picked us up for car pool, for fighting at school. He wanted to talk to Mom, but once the kids told him what the fight was all about, he changed his mind about that. At least none of the teachers saw it."

"You'd be in worse trouble, then."

Spence nodded. "Yeah, suspended. But so would Jessica's big brother." The last was delivered with a grim satisfaction that belied a spirit older than his ten years, and far more bitter than Carl wanted any ten-year-old to be.

"You know they're not right."

"Sure. But there's no way I'm going to convince them of that. Anything I say or do is just going to make it all worse."

He looked so dejected, Carl couldn't resist putting a hand on his narrow shoulder. "What would you say if your mother and I got married? Not right away. And not to shut up those old hens in town."

Straightening, the boy looked startled. "Would that make me a Brenner? Because—"

"No, it would only make your mother a Brenner. If she'd even have me. You'd stay a Mallory for as long as you wanted to." Carl expected to see relief on the boy's face, and felt confused when his expression seemed to mirror more disappointment than solace.

"So you don't want us."

The flat statement delivered with such matter-of-factness drove Carl to his knees, both physically and mentally. "Never say that. It isn't true. I just figured you had a father already, and I don't want to try and take his place."

"You've already done more than take his place. I'm going to school. Nobody makes Mom cry and worry. I've stopped having nightmares." There were tears in the boy's eyes. "I just figured it was too good to last."

"It's not good *enough,* Spence. There's so much more I'd like to do for all three of you. And it would be a package deal, boy. I wouldn't marry your mother without figuring that all three of you came together." He hugged the boy fiercely for a moment.

"I'll never intentionally hurt her. Or you or Maria, either. I had too much of that as a kid and I know what it feels like. You'll always have a roof over your head and a real family. As much education as I can afford to give you both. And if you want to take my name, I'd be proud. But I don't feel like it's much of a name."

Carl stood and backed off, giving the boy time to compose himself. "If you want to marry Mom, I'd like that. A lot. And we'll see about the name business. I'm still getting used to being Spence Mallory."

"Spence Brenner sounds kinda funny, doesn't it?" Carl said, trying it out on his tongue. The boy nodded solemnly. "Well, we'll work on it. Before that, we've got something bigger to work on. How am I going to convince your mom that she ought to marry me?"

Spence shrugged. "Don't look at me. I can't even get her to let me stay up half an hour later on school nights." The tension in Carl exploded in laughter at the boy's blunt statement. He was right. This was a problem Carl was going to have to solve for himself. Maybe going over to Naomi's for pie with the boy would give him an idea or two. At least they'd both be less hungry. He clapped his arm around Spencer's shoulder, and they went out to tend to business.

# *Chapter Thirteen*

All the way home, Carl rehearsed different speeches in his head. None of them sounded right. Reasons for getting married should be romantic, shouldn't they? His real reasons were romantic. Or at least, better than "Larry and the town council think we're living in sin." He couldn't very well tell her that.

He couldn't tell her the way he felt right away either. That he could hardly stand being next to her so much of the day without touching her. That wanting her kept him awake nights and made him mess up the bookkeeping in the store. If this burning kept on much longer without relief he was going to go broke from his own mistakes. And hadn't Saint Paul said that it was better to marry than to burn? Grace probably wasn't going to see it Saint Paul's way.

When he got home, the first few minutes of bedlam didn't give him any room for a serious discussion. Maria, the cat and Four all tangled in a happy melee around him as soon as he got in the door. It did his heart good to see the little girl strong and boisterous. She had looked pretty sick for a while, but Tom Conrad had recently pronounced her in perfect health. Still, he worried. Probably not the way her mother did, but it gave him a taste of what parenthood must be like.

He swung her around, delighting in her hair smelling faintly of baby shampoo and her delicious chuckles at being tossed in the air. "Don't throw her too high," her mother cautioned. "She had a cookie while we waited for you two to get home. I don't want it to come back."

"Yes, ma'am," Carl said in mock contrition, swinging the child back to the ground. Then it was the dog's turn for a little wrestling.

"Now go wash your hands. I don't want you sitting down to supper with dog hair all over you," Grace chided. Carl looked at her, wondering at the sharpness of her tone. Her face was pale, looking pinched in a way he hadn't seen it since just after Christmas. With a rush of anger, he wondered if Larry had come and talked to her, too. If he had, Carl resolved to boot him into the next county.

"Any visitors today?" He tried to keep his tone casual for the children. No sense in getting them upset ahead of time.

"Just Kayla," Grace said, which made him relax a little. Still, there was something wrong. His sense of that didn't dissipate any during supper, when Grace pushed around a bowl of stew without ever really eating any of it. She didn't even pretend to want any of the cherry pie she gave everybody else.

Grace seemed to want to talk to him alone as much as he wanted to talk to her. For a change she dispatched both children to the parlor after supper, insisting that it was Carl's turn to help her with the dishes. It was never Carl's turn to help with the dishes.

. Still, nobody argued with her. Spence, who'd already finished his homework at the store, took Maria into the parlor to read to her, and even the dog trooped in after them. Carl figured there must be serious discussion afoot for the dog to sense it in the air and slink out. For a moment he wished he could join them.

"Are you sure Larry didn't come by here this afternoon?"

"Positive. I take it he came by the store," Grace said. Her expression told him what she thought of Larry's visit, even though she hadn't had one herself.

"He did. But Larry didn't sound like Larry. He sounded like some meddling old busybody. He thinks we ought to get married. Or you ought to move out. According to him, it just doesn't look right, our being young and healthy and under the same roof."

"He's right—it's not his business. But he *is* right, Carl." Her voice was so soft, with an edge that betrayed a broken heart. "Kayla's been hearing things—not just from him but from other places, too. People are talking."

She silently scrubbed a couple more dishes, rinsed them in a pan of clear water and stacked them for Carl to dry. "Would you rather move out?" Carl finally asked, hating to voice his suspicions. He couldn't imagine Grace wanting to marry him. Not now, at least. They'd just started talking about maybe. Someday.

She put down the mug she was washing and looked straight at him. Her look of consternation made his heart soar. "Move out? I just moved in! But if that's what you think is best, I guess we could. Maybe..."

Carl's heart was pounding as fast as if he'd run all the way home from the store. He grabbed Grace before she could get any further on this train of thought. "No. Whoa, slow down, here. We're both making assumptions about what the other one wants to do. Let me start over."

Saying anything more was going to be so hard while he held her. But there couldn't be any other way. If he let go, Grace would withdraw. She'd start packing those boxes, first mentally, and then for real. If that happened, he'd never get a chance to have any kind of life with her.

Carl took a deep breath and loosened his grip on her shoulders, so that it felt more like a caress than a restraint. "Okay, Grace, here goes. I'm not good at this kind of stuff, and this is a lousy situation, but I want to make the best of it. And stop wriggling." He tried to sound stern. It must have succeeded, because her brown eyes widened and she stood still in his arms. "I want you to marry me. I don't want you to move out, and I'm not happy with Larry and the town council for pushing us into this before you're ready.

"But at the same time I could kiss them all for doing it, because I don't know when I would have gotten up the courage to ask without a little push. Grace, I want you to marry me. And not because some old biddies in town are talking about us. I'll take care of you, and your kids, as long as I live. You'll never go hungry or without anything."

Her nose wrinkled. "You're right. That's the most unromantic proposal I've ever heard. But at least you're honest. You seem to be a fine man, Carl. Honest and a good provider. When I was seventeen, those weren't the reasons I thought I'd get married. But now, at twenty-eight with two kids, there are a whole lot of worse reasons."

Her arms came up to join his embrace. Carl pulled her to him. "Of course, if we get married now, it will just give them something else to talk about."

"I know." Her words were a little muffled in his shirt front, but still sounded tart. "I can either be labeled a brazen hussy for being your housekeeper and giving you the milk for free instead of making you buy the cow, or I can be labeled a brazen hussy for marrying you after only knowing you a couple of months." She pulled back from him, and Carl was delighted to see the glow of suppressed laughter in her eyes instead of tears. "I think I'd rather be a *married* brazen hussy, if it's all right with you. Or at least an *engaged* one, so they'll stop talking."

"It's just what I had in mind." And finally he bent down and kissed her, promising her all the protection he could give her within the circle of his arms.

"I do have one or two conditions." Here it came. The reasons she was looking up at him like this.

Carl sighed. "Go ahead. Tell me what they are."

"No great big rock. We'll go over to the discount store in Jackson and get a ring, and that will be it. And I'll marry you, Carl Brenner, when my Aunt Jo can give me away."

Carl felt his heart plummet to his shoes. The first condition was easy. The second one felt impossible. Still, he couldn't let on to Grace that that was the way he felt. "Agreed." He could barely choke the word out and still smile, but he did it. It almost killed him, but he got it done.

Grace looked down at her finger, bemused. She was really engaged to Carl Brenner. It was amazing that a tiny circle of gold and a couple of diamond chips went so far toward shutting everybody up. At least the wedding planning and the finding Jo would carry them past Easter and right into spring. Somehow she couldn't face being married again in the same season they'd buried Matt. This marriage, when it happened, would have nothing of winter in it.

What she'd had with Matt had stopped feeling like a marriage long before it had ended, if it ever had been one. Looking at other couples in a new light, she wondered if theirs had ever been a marriage in the true sense of the word. It certainly had never felt the way to her, from the inside, that other marriages looked from the outside. Doc Conrad walked up to the cemetery with flowers or a card or something every Sunday. He didn't go to church, but he visited his wife's grave. Watching him from a distance, Grace suspected he still talked over the difficult times with her. She was surprised when she'd gone into the cemetery herself to see that Mrs. Conrad had died nearly ten years ago. And her husband still came every Sunday to pass the time.

Even Bill and Kayla seemed to be looking forward to marriage in a way that surprised Grace. Every other Saturday Bill used his one phone call to talk to Kayla, and the next week he called his mother. The women got friendly enough to trade information, so that nobody went without for very long. And everybody was looking forward to going to Bill's graduation.

Grace tried to view her own impending marriage in a practical way. She spent most of her time talking to Maria, preparing her for the somewhat-confusing changes that would take place in her life. Spence seemed to be handling it well. Grace suspected that he and Carl had come to some tacit agreement at the store, because he showed no surprise when Grace broached the subject to him.

The biggest changes—the ones she wasn't anywhere near ready to contemplate—were the domestic ones. Grace found herself going into Carl's room just to convince herself that she had actually agreed to marry this man and sleep here with him.

It was a nice room. Big windows let in plenty of air and sunshine. The bed itself looked huge, taking up the middle of the room on a bright rag rug. There would be plenty of space in it for the two of them never to run into each other, Grace suspected.

Even more surprising to her was that Carl had insisted that the two vacant bedrooms on the same floor of the house—long locked and echoing with emptiness—be fixed up for the children, including new bedspreads and curtains for each room. "You can make a day of it, go to the mall in Cape Girardeau with Kayla. You both need new clothes for the graduation anyway, don't you?"

"I suppose." Grace knew she'd sounded dubious. She hadn't given the subject much thought. Her everyday jeans wouldn't do, though, and even she was getting tired of her one good dress.

* * *

Kayla was more than happy to take the day off from school the following Monday for a shopping expedition.

"I should probably give you my purse, and Daddy's credit cards," Kayla teased as they walked into the mall. "You're supposed to keep me in line, remember?"

"That's only when we're spending money." As Grace looked around at all the stores, she felt like a teenager herself. It was a wonderful, heady feeling, and she intended to keep it for the entire day if she could.

They hit every department store in the mall, which wasn't hard since it only had three. Going through most of the ladies' specialty stores was fun, too, Grace discovered. Had she ever shopped like this with anyone else? Jo had never been a shopper, and Grace just figured she was missing the gene herself. But this was fun, even when she wasn't spending much.

They had lunch at the food court to fortify themselves for the shopping ahead. Grace hadn't eaten a meal in a restaurant without the kids in years. Here, among the ladies who 'lunched,' she felt almost elegant. So elegant that she insisted on treating Kayla to the meal, including ice cream for dessert. "Can you afford that?" Kayla asked, continuing her role of shepherding Grace around.

"Of course. I'm a woman of means, remember?" It was true, after a fashion. Carl had insisted on paying her in cash for the past month, and was adamant that he wanted her to spend her wages on herself and the children.

Most of the money she'd already spent in Carl's store, making sure that Spence had a coat that fit and Maria a cute new outfit for school. But standing in the mall now, Grace felt reluctant to spend the remainder. It was the first time in years she'd had this much cash in hand. "I feel strange spending this much money on myself," she said to Kayla.

"But you're getting married!" Kayla exclaimed. "I've got that much to spend on myself, too. That's why we're here, remember? I can't spend anything knowing you're holding back, Mrs. Mallory. It would make me feel too awful."

Grace looked at the girl. It *would* make her feel bad. Under her flighty exterior, Kayla had a soft heart that went out to anything and anybody, from orphaned baby birds on up. There was no sense in confessing all her worries to someone so excited about life.

Still, the girlishness that had been building in Grace all day bubbled to the surface in giggles. She was twenty-eight years old and she'd never had a chance to be a carefree girl like Kayla. Her first wedding had been a hurried affair to a dour man. And yet she was still young, had her health and a fine man ready to marry her. And money in her pocket.

"But I'm supposed to be the good influence on you here," Grace said, dismayed.

Kayla made a face. "The last thing I want today is a good influence, Mrs. Mallory."

"Then let's get to it, Kayla," she replied.

The trip to Fort Leonard Wood for Bill's graduation started off uncomfortably. Carl silently cursed himself for not having considered seating arrangements in the truck. He should have realized that Janet Parker wouldn't want to sit next to Kayla in the back seat for so long. So it ended with Kayla and Grace in the back, and him up front with Janet.

Carl was surprised they made the whole three-hour trip without Grace wanting to call home. He knew that the kids would be fine with Barb and Hal Peterson, and that they'd remember to look in on the animals often. But he was thankful that Grace had decided everything was all right that way too.

Nor did their stop for coffee in a roadside fast-food outlet loosen anybody up much. Carl tried to make small talk, most of which fell flat. He decided things had to get better once they got to Bill's graduation.

When they all stood in line after the ceremonies, Carl watched Grace. She was quiet, even had her eyes closed some. "What are you thinking?" he asked softly. Kayla and Janet had finally paired up ahead of them and he wasn't about to disturb them.

Grace opened her eyes and smiled. She didn't look any older than Kayla today—well, maybe a little, but only in the most attractive way. Grace could still pass for twenty, especially in the nice sweater and tailored pants she had bought for the occasion. He was sorely tempted to lean down and kiss her.

"I'm sorry, what was the question?" Grace asked. So maybe she wasn't all that solid after all.

"Just wondered what was going on in there," Carl said, tapping her softly waved blond hair.

Her brow creased in a tiny frown. "If you must know, I was praying."

Of all the answers Carl had expected, this wasn't one of them. "'Praying'?"

"Yes. You didn't know I did that, did you?" Grace actually stuck her tongue out at him. Seeing her do that shot an electrified thrill through Carl. This woman would be the death of him, or at least his common sense, yet.

"What were you praying about, Grace?"

"Everything, I guess. Asking God to be as good to Kayla and Bill, and Janet, as he's been to me. To smooth the way before them. It can't be very easy, you know, Carl."

"We all know that." Carl could feel himself shutting down emotionally. He knew that Grace's admission should have had the opposite effect on him. He should be jubilant that she was finding her way clear to walk with God. Instead, why did this make him feel jealous of the very God they both loved?

He was so shaky he could barely look at Grace. Until she squeezed both his hands and he looked directly at her instead of into the sunshine with its drifting dust motes. Her eyes held the same dancing golden flecks—and a promise that everything would be all right. Standing there, holding her warm hands, turning the thin gold band on her left ring finger, Carl felt his fears ease. He didn't know how long that comfort would hold up in the face of everyday life once they left this place, but for now he believed that the Lord would provide for them both. And for now, it was enough.

# Chapter Fourteen

"**Y**ou gave away our rooms?" Carl stood staring at the motel clerk. "But I reserved them in advance. With my credit card."

It was ten o'clock at night. Too late to go anyplace else. Nobody was in any shape to drive the three hours home. He wouldn't trust Kayla or Janet with his truck, no matter what. Grace looked as tired as he felt. Now what did they do?

"Well, not all of them, exactly," the desk clerk admitted.

"So what, exactly, do we have?" Carl didn't shout. He was very calm, under the circumstances.

"Uh, one room. It *does* have two double beds." The clerk brightened.

"Great. We'll take it. The girls can share somehow, and I'll sleep in the truck." Carl put his credit card down on the counter, signed in and went to break the news to the ladies.

The ladies took it better than he'd expected. Even after he'd escorted them to the room and they'd looked at its small confines, nobody complained.

"Hey, it will be like a giant slumber party. No problem." Of course Kayla was used to giant slumber parties. "And it's too cold for you to sleep out in the truck, Mr. Brenner. I mean, can't we get a foldout bed or something?"

Grace called the front desk. "No rollaways. But I agree with Kayla, it's too cold to sleep out in the truck. Besides, you're the one paying for the room. You should at least get to sleep in it." She sounded braver than she looked.

Grace's voice was firm with conviction, but her eyes told Carl how much trepidation she had about sleeping in the same room with him, under any circumstances.

It was Janet who surprised them all. "This is ridiculous. We're four adults here, and we all need a good night's sleep. Kayla and I will take one bed, and you two can sort things out with the other one. I don't care if you share it, or sleep on the floor or whatever. I do know it's been a long day and I want to get out of these dress shoes and into my sweats and fuzzy socks. And honestly, I'm too tired to care about what everybody else does tonight."

Carl looked at Bill's mother from a new vantage point. Maybe she wasn't the dried-up old prune he'd figured her for. Janet was actually being practical and sensible. And it had been a very long day.

After the involved graduation ceremony and a reception, Bill had shown them around the base. Bill had held Kayla's hand in his almost the entire afternoon and evening and he looked, well, like a man now in his military haircut and dress uniform. Maybe that is what Janet had seen too. That this was a time to move on with life and she better get going.

But regardless of the day's events, Carl was still in a strange situation. Sharing a motel room with three women was beyond his realm of experience. As far as that went, sharing a motel room with *one* woman was beyond his experience. What a way to start.

Now that the situation was settled to their satisfaction, the three women were bustling around the room, kicking off heels and working out a bathroom schedule so they could all take turns at bubble baths and makeup removal or whatever. Carl found himself just watching. It was Grace, of course, who caught his eye. She could apparently feel his gaze on her, because she stopped padding across the room's lush carpet and looked over her shoulder at him.

"I'll take the floor. Surely there are enough blankets to make some kind of bed with."

"Oh, come on, Grace. You know what that's going to do to your back." Kayla sounded more like her older sister than a teenager. "Besides, like Janet says, we're all adults. We know nothing's going to happen here except sleep. And I don't know about anybody else, but I'm sure ready for that."

Grace had a strange expression on her face. Carl thought it probably mirrored his own. She looked as if she wanted to argue with Kayla, but was too embarrassed somehow. In the end she shrugged and started rooting through her overnight case. "Fine. I expect we can share a double bed during a giant slumber party, huh, Carl?" She challenged him to say anything to the contrary.

"Sure. Right. We're all adults." Carl really hoped his voice didn't crack. "Hey, if we both take a blanket and a couple of pillows, we probably won't even know we're sharing the bed."

*Right.* Grace's silent look told him everything. She knew that at home he had a queen-size mattress all to himself. This was going to be a long night and an interesting one. How early did it get light at this time of year? Carl groaned inwardly, then went to his suitcase for the flannel pants and T-shirt he'd packed to hang out in. It had been bad enough when he'd figured he was sharing an adjoining room with the three women all next door. This was going to be sheer torture.

She was going to die, or go crazy or something before she went to sleep.

Grace lay on her right side, facing out toward the cool air in the room, willing herself to go to sleep. But all she could do instead was concentrate on Carl's hand. Spread out over her entire side, it spanned her body protectively. And even through the layers of T-shirt and blanket that separated them, it was a very warm hand.

Just the warm, even pressure of his thumb under her shoulder blade, those fingers splayed out against her ribs, the smallest finger somewhere down by her hipbone, was going to drive her mad.

It was so quiet she could scarcely hear Kayla or Janet breathe. Why couldn't either of them snore for distraction? Instead, they'd both put on sweats and slipped under the covers quickly, leaving Grace her turn in the bathroom. She'd come out, switched off the remaining light, and announced she was going up to bed, feeling flighty and awkward.

Now she tried to distract herself with thoughts of anything but the room and its occupants. How were the animals doing at home? Had Larry remembered to come over and feed them, and let the dog out? She suspected that when they got home she'd find both animals curled up together in the kitchen for warmth.

Warmth wasn't something she herself needed more of right now. It was hard not to fling off the covers and suck in the cool night air. The man was a living blast furnace. Carl positively radiated warmth, had it coming out the tips of his fingers to trace patterns on her already-fevered skin.

How on earth did she expect to sleep in the same bed with this man and not make an absolute fool of herself? Maybe if she tried to match her breathing to his, steady and calm behind her, she could go to sleep instead of lying here, rigid and alert, with Carl's hand reminding her just what she was missing.

*Was he totally without feelings?* Grace was still willing herself not to gasp or scream with each small movement of the bed under them, or of the man beside her—and he was asleep. She just couldn't see how anybody could drop off that quickly and uneventfully in a roomful of people. She knew that she herself would still be awake at dawn, counting the stars as they paled, then listening for the cry of a rooster in the distance.

If nothing else, the warm, sweet breath on the back of her neck was going to drive her to distraction. She felt so safe in Carl's arms. Safe from the world, at least—not safe from Carl. Except that she was probably safe there, too, given the speed with which he'd fallen asleep.

Or at least she thought he was asleep. Surely nobody that still, with breathing so regular, could be awake. Or could Carl be doing just what she was doing—willing himself to go to sleep so that he didn't pounce on her as willingly as she wanted to roll into his pounce? She shifted ever so slightly against the even pressure of the hand on her rib cage. It closed in almost convulsively, drawing her closer to his warm body. Feeling oddly gratified by his response to her sharing his bed, Grace snuggled her protesting body even closer to his large, warm, welcoming frame. Carl groaned softly. His whisper was so low, only she could hear. "I'm gonna die from this, you know, Grace. The waiting will kill me."

"At least we'll both die happy, Carl," she told him. "Because if the waiting doesn't kill you, I may wear you to the bone once we stop waiting."

It was the growl low in his throat that warned Grace, but not quickly enough to escape the hand that covered her side. She wondered which of the children had told Carl she was ticklish. One of them had, and she would find the culprit when they got home tomorrow and wring his or her sweet neck. Because he knew unerringly which spot to tickle to make her a helpless mass next to him.

"We will wait. It may kill both of us, but we will wait, Grace," he whispered in her ear a moment later while he still had her in a tight embrace. "I don't want to give anybody in Redwing the satisfaction of thinking we had to get married for the sake of a child."

"I'll agree with you on that one. And I'll agree with you on the other part, too, Carl."

"Which part would that be?" he asked, insinuating himself even closer to her.

"The part that's going to die if we wait too long. Thank heavens this is only for one night. Another night or two of this would kill me." How she ever fell asleep that way, with the dratted man behind her chuckling softly every once in a while, Grace couldn't imagine. She only knew that once morning came and she woke up, they were still joined together in a warm embrace. And both of them seemed to wake up smiling.

"Can I come out yet?" Carl sounded like a little kid kept out of a party. He sent all of them into fits of giggles, Grace the most.

"Not yet." Kayla sat down on her bed. "I'm still putting on my socks."

"And I'm still fastening—"

"Too much information, Janet." His strained voice through the bathroom door made them all giggle again.

"Just hold your horses." Grace looked in the mirror, checking to be sure everything was in place. It had made more sense for the three of them to change clothes together in the room while Carl hid out in the bathroom, but he was getting antsy in there. "You don't want to see us without our faces on, do you?"

"I've already seen you without your faces." Carl made a sound that might have been a snort. "Now, if you're down to a point where there are no other surprises there, I'm coming out."

"Then come on out." Kayla caught her hair up in a stretch band and made a ponytail. "There's nothing to see anyway."

The door opened. Carl came out looking like a rooster with his feathers ruffled. "I knew that before."

"Are you hungry?" Grace was trying so hard not to let her laughter escape while she changed the subject. She couldn't look at him. If she did, she wasn't going to be able to hold in this traitorous giggle. "I'm hungry. In fact I'm starved. I think I'll go down and see what there is for breakfast." She left the room quickly, leaning on the wall down the stairwell for support. She mustn't laugh. She mustn't.

When strong arms grabbed her from behind, she was so startled she shrieked instead. "It's all right. Laugh," Carl said, before burying her in a moist kiss. "I tell you, woman, I'm going to die of wanting you." And there on the stairwell he proved with a kiss that took her breath away that he wasn't as near death as he'd claimed.

The day stretched on like a desert. There wasn't another moment that Grace was alone with Carl until they'd deposited Janet and Kayla at home, picked up the kids from the Petersons', fed everyone dinner and made over the animals. Even then, the evening was full of reading to Maria, running over Spence's spelling words, making sure everybody had the right clean clothes for school the next morning. They had lost their normal "family" weekend. *How had this happened so quickly?* It wasn't losing the weekend that mystified Grace. It was the speed with which she and Carl and the children had become a family to each other.

Finally Spence went up to bed and Grace sat with a cup of tea. Carl took the dog out for a short walk in the brisk night air. When he came back his hair was rumpled. He sat down heavily in the armchair facing Grace.

"I don't know about you, but I regret giving in to peer pressure this weekend." His face was completely somber and serious.

Grace didn't know whether to believe him or not. "I should have slept on the floor."

"No, like Kayla said, that would have been bad for your back. But Grace, I don't think those two had any idea what they were doing to us."

"I didn't have any idea what I was doing to us until it was two in the morning." Suddenly it was more comfortable to look at the curtains or the white mug that held her tea—anywhere but Carl's flushed face.

"Yeah, well, me neither. At least we don't have to worry about compatibility." His voice held laughter. "So are you still serious about finding your Aunt Jo before we get married?"

"Yes, I am."

"Then we'd better do it quickly. Is there anything you haven't told me that might be of help finding her? So far, the easy stuff hasn't worked."

"Well, she moved around a lot when she was a girl. She always said her dad never liked being near his neighbors. So they went different places. When she married Mr. Sparks, she settled down for a while. Said it felt strange." Grace could see Jo, sitting in the rocker that now nestled in the corner of Carl's bedroom, telling her stories.

"Where was she the happiest, do you think?"

"Maybe near a place called Kingdom City. She always said the house they had there was the prettiest thing she ever saw." Casting her mind back to Jo and her stories, Grace could almost hear her aunt's homey laughter.

"Yes, probably Kingdom City or around there. I don't know why that was the best place for her, because my uncle was a trucker, always in and out, and they never had two nickels to rub together. Maybe it was because that's where he's buried. When Mama came back with me, or just about to have me, they moved again because it was a tiny little place. At the time Aunt Jo had her mother-in-law with her. She figured with three women and a new baby, they needed someplace bigger. Then, after they moved, the old Mrs. Sparks died and Mama didn't stay long, so there was Aunt Jo, with me alone in this big old place out in the country. Oh, if I had a nickel for every time she said she wished she'd never moved…"

The tears came then, but not for the reasons Carl probably suspected. Jo had always wished they'd stayed put so that Matt Mallory wouldn't have wandered into their lives. She had never liked him and his stealing of her girl. And it hadn't taken long for Grace to agree with her, even though she and Jo had never admitted that to each other.

Carl leaned between their chairs and gently wiped her tears away. "I was afraid of this. I'm really sorry I can't find any more. But nothing in that whole mess had a return address on it except the last letter you had. And when I found a postmaster there, he was somebody who had taken over after your aunt moved, and he didn't know."

Carl caressed her face. It felt so good to lean her cheek into his warm, callused palm. "Can you think of the name of the place?"

Grace shook her head, dismayed that it all came down to this. "There wasn't one, exactly. It was just a little settlement of a few houses and not much else in Southern Missouri. Not a town, really. There were towns you could walk to, seven or eight miles away. Valle Mines, I think. And there was another one."

Carl's hand moved convulsively beneath her cheek. His skin was pale when she looked at him, and his eyes had a faraway unfocused look. "Big Springs, maybe?"

"That sounds right."

"Then that's where we'll try first. But don't get your hopes too far up."

"I won't. I really appreciate what you've done already. It's a wonderful gift," she told him.

He moved his hand and shook his head briefly, the way Four did when he lost the track on a rabbit. "Well, it's good so far. But I can't make any more promises. Big Springs, of all places." With that, he went to the computer, where he buried himself for the evening. Grace finished her cold tea while she watched him. She wanted to ask what was so unusual about Big Springs, but she didn't. When Carl was ready to tell her, he would. Wouldn't he?

# Chapter Fifteen

*Four days.* That was all it took him to find her. Carl stared at the screen in front of him, unable to move or speak. How could this be? When he'd done searches for himself, nothing this good had *ever* come up. It just wasn't fair.

The blinking arrow of the cursor on his screen mocked him. Four days. And not even whole days at that—just time snatched here and there between jobs at the store. He was almost too busy selling new summer clothes for every kid in town to do this at all. And yet he'd found Jo Sparks.

There was a bitter taste in his mouth, like coffee that had been on the burner way too long. After twenty years of trying, he still couldn't find Danny. But he could find Grace's aunt in less than a week. Carl moved the cursor over to the Print Screen button. The printer hummed for a moment, then a sheet with the name and address and phone number he'd found curled out of the machine. He made a second copy. This way if he gave in to the temptation to burn the first one and not tell Grace anything, he would still be okay.

What was he thinking? Nothing was okay. This was the beginning of the end of his calm, peaceful life with a family. *It had been good while it lasted.*

Carl grabbed the papers from the printer tray. Time to get this over with, quick, before he lost his nerve.

He appeared in the kitchen like a ghost, silent and grim. The coffee mug she was washing slipped out of Grace's fingers and hit the sink mat with a thump. "Bad news?" Her mouth was so dry she could barely get out the words.

His gray eyes were flat, expressionless. "Not exactly. But what would you say if I asked you to marry me now?"

*He had found Jo, but she was dead.* It was all Grace could think. "I'd say it was still too soon. And I'd say I still want you to find Jo first. Unless you already have, and she's...dead."

Tears hotter than the dishwater under her fingers sprang up to burn Grace's eyes. That was it, she was sure of it. Jo was dead and Carl wanted to marry her to take her mind off it.

"No, Grace, she's not dead. At least I don't think so. If she is, she died after she paid last month's phone bill and electric service."

Grace wanted to leap, to dance. "So you did find her? Then why didn't you just tell me?"

Carl shrugged. "Because I know what's going to happen now."

Grace wiped her hands on the towel next to the sink. "Oh, do you? What's going to happen now, Carl?"

"Now you leave. I've found your aunt, and she's your family. Not like me. Let's face it, Grace, you may be wearing my ring, but basically we're still strangers. And blood is thicker than water."

Her hands were still damp. Grace ran them down the sides of her jeans, trying not to show all the aggravation she felt. "You don't think much of me, do you?"

He couldn't meet her gaze. "It's what *I* would do."

"Well, it's not what I would do. Not now, not later."

"Maybe. There's a lot you don't know about me."

Anger flared in Grace. "If there's so much I don't know about you, why should I marry you to begin with? When were you going to tell me all these secrets, anyway, after we got married?"

"That wouldn't be fair. But I'm afraid, Grace." In Carl's expression, she could see the lonely boy again that had haunted her at Christmastime.

Grace sighed. "Afraid of what?"

"That once you really know me, all about me, you won't want to stay—no matter what. That marrying me would be out of the question."

Grace turned back to the sink. "For once, let me be the judge of that. Maybe I'm a more forgiving person than you think I am. Even if I'm not, maybe this God you've led me back to will give me the strength to be one.

"I'm making a pot of coffee. Then we're going to sit in the living room until I know everything there is to tell about you, even if it takes all night."

Carl enveloped her in a wordless hug, wrapping his arms around her spine. She leaned her head back, resting against his shoulder.

He was warm and so gentle. Grace couldn't imagine anything he could tell her that would drive her away. But then, Matt Mallory had looked like a nice young man at first. Maybe she was just a lousy judge of character— *No!* Living those years with Matt had made her an excellent judge of character. Carl might not be perfect, but who was? Grace filled the coffee carafe with water. Better make a full pot. This promised to be a rough talk.

Grace finished half a cup of coffee before the silence got to her. "Okay, let's start with the basics. Ever been in prison?"

"No."

"Killed anybody? Been divorced? Have illegitimate children in four counties?"

"Lord, Grace, *no* to all of the above."

She put down her coffee mug and moved herself face-to-face with Carl on the couch. Grace took both his hands, marveling again at the way they enveloped hers. "What is so awful that you can't tell me, then?"

He couldn't meet her gaze. Grace felt fingers of panic grip her insides. What sins had she missed in her litany?

"You know how I told you my family died in a fire?"

"When you were five," Grace prompted. "I remember."

"Well, they didn't all die in the fire."

She felt lost. "Okay, explain that. Do you mean that you still have family someplace, or that the family you lost didn't really die in a fire?"

Carl sighed. "Both, I guess. But how they died is the important part. As far as wanting to marry me is concerned, for sure. Danny's just a reason for not marrying you at all."

Grace felt a pain in the middle of her forehead. She was wrinkling her brow together so hard that it hurt in an effort to concentrate on making sense of what Carl was saying. "Let's start at the beginning, Carl. Who's Danny? And how did your parents die?"

He ignored her first question. "We lived out in the country. Big Springs was the closest town. My father shot my mother." His voice was wooden, mechanical. "Then he set fire to the house, and shot himself. He didn't expect us to get out, I don't think."

Grace felt as if she had a clue now. "Us being…"

"Me and my brother, Danny. I was five, he was two. I lost him, Grace. I was supposed to take care of him, but I lost him."

Carl's tears devastated her. She was too small to take him totally in her arms and make his pain go away. Grace did what she could, wrapping herself around him for comfort. What should she do now?

*Wait. Watch. Pray. And love.* Holding Carl in her arms, Grace felt hot tears course down her face. She'd cried more since meeting Carl than she had in her whole life. But they were mostly healing tears.

Something inside her was letting go as she wept. With each step she took toward Carl, she felt closer to God, as well. And as she accepted God back into her life more and more, it was easier to put her burdens on Him. Carl's problems didn't sound earth-shattering when she had Jesus to lean on.

She held on to Carl, stroking his hair. Aunt Jo had always said there were no coincidences in God's world. *Maybe everything that had happened was for a reason.* Was this what it was for? All the suffering she'd gone through? Was there really a purpose to all that pain, after all? If this was the reason for that pain, it was worth it.

"Nothing you've said so far makes me love you any less, Carl." Her words were soft and shaky, but Grace managed to choke them out.

Carl's eyes sparkled with unshed tears. "How can you say that? I just told you my father was a murderer. That's the kind of background I come from. And the one thing I could have done to make things right—*the one thing*—I failed at. I couldn't even keep track of my own brother. Grace, he's twenty-eight years old, and I haven't seen him in twenty-six years!"

Grace felt understanding dawning in her. "Is that why you didn't want to tell me about Jo? You were jealous about Danny?"

"She was so easy to find. Everybody for someone else is always so easy to find." There was a note of childlike pain in his voice. "Why can't I find Danny? Why can't I have a family?"

"Like everybody else. Like me." Grace smoothed his hair and pulled him closer, as she would Spence. "Ah, Carl, you need to keep talking. This time, start at the beginning and tell me the whole story."

But where did the whole story start? Carl stayed in Grace's arms, struggling to collect his thoughts. "We have some things in common. My dad was in Vietnam, too. I don't remember him being around much when I was small. My mom raised me, and it was peaceful that way. He must have come back at least once, because there was Danny."

This was hard. Carl pulled back to his own end of the couch. He couldn't move far enough to escape the old pain. "Dad didn't come back the same guy who left."

"A lot didn't."

"Yeah, well, he was one of them. Even at age four I knew things weren't right. Mom tried to protect us from him as much as possible." He could still remember hiding in a darkened room. Danny was in the crib; he was scrunched under it. The noises outside the room were ugly.

"What happened?" Grace reached over and grabbed his hand again. Carl took it like a lifeline.

"He wasn't in his right mind anymore. And he drank, I know. One night they got into it. The next thing I knew, I heard a bang. I knew somehow that we had to get out of there. The neighbors found us out in the snow, watching the trailer burn."

"What happened to Danny?"

"We went to the same foster home at first in Big Springs. But I was bad, disruptive. The people didn't want to keep me. They split us up. Then I kept running away, trying to find the first place we'd stayed together."

Grace sat up sharply. "How old were you?"

"Six."

"And they didn't give you counseling?"

"Nope. For a while they put me in some kind of juvenile home, but that was about the extent of any treatment I got." Carl let go of her hand.

"One day when I was older than Spence, I had a visitor. It was my Uncle Jim, my mother's brother. He apologized for not getting there sooner, not knowing what we'd gone through."

"Where had he been?"

"Overseas. Stationed in Germany with the army. He hadn't been allowed to come back for the funeral, and had gotten the impression somehow that my dad had killed us all. When he came back to the States and found out that wasn't true, he came to find me."

"Wow. Did he take you away from the foster home then?"

"Not that day. There was legal stuff he had to work through. As soon as he could, though, he did. We came here to Redwing, where he'd bought the store."

"But he didn't find Danny?"

"Not a trace. It's like the kid vanished, Grace. I've looked every way I know how to. Once I left that first foster home, it's as if he fell off the face of the earth."

Grace pulled him into her arms again. Carl didn't resist. "Does this mean you gave up?"

"Not really. I still try once in a while. Every time I find somebody for someone else, it makes me look again. But I'll never find him, Grace."

Her eyes blazed. "How do you know? How can you say that?"

"Because God doesn't want me to. I mean, I've asked Him, more times than I care to count. Let me find him. Let me have a family. And here I am." It tore him up to admit that much to her, but it was the truth.

"I don't believe that."

"What? That God doesn't answer every prayer? That sometimes we just ask too much and he says no?"

Grace pounded a fist into her open palm in frustration. "That is not the God you've shown me, Carl. It's definitely not the God that my aunt always talked about."

"So explain what wonderful reason God has for keeping me apart from the only family I have."

Grace's expression was blank. "I don't have any idea. Maybe so you could give me a family again. You know that's what you've done. Given me a family.''

Her face became more animated. "When you came to my house, things could have gone a whole different way. You should have been coming to take Matt—I mean Spence—to one of those juvenile halls you remember.''

"I couldn't do that, just because I remember them too well.''

"So instead we have a home now, and a stable situation. And you found Jo for me, when I didn't know how.'' She took his hands again. Her face was as earnest as a child's. "If you give me the chance, I will be your family. I know that won't replace the one you've lost. But I want to be with you through whatever happens next.''

He pulled her into a tight embrace. The woman had such tiny bones, it felt like holding a bird. Yet, like a bird's, those bones had the strength of steel. Grace was strong enough to stand up to this crisis and any other. "Maybe you're right about God, after all.'' Carl knew his words were muffled, spoken into her soft hair as he crushed her to him.

He had knocked over one of their coffee cups. The liquid was running across the hardwood floor. Carl moved quickly, grabbing a throw rug to soak up the mess. As he did, the flash of white paper caught his eye.

"I never did give you this, did I?'' He held out the crumpled sheet to Grace. "That's the address I found, and the phone number.''

Grace took it with shaking hands. "How could anyone but God make things like this possible, Carl? And how could He not make all things possible in time? We'll find Danny. Maybe we were just supposed to do it together.''

Carl felt small in the face of her optimism. He wished he could share it. "Go call her. I'll finish with the floor.''

Grace seemed to be in a daze. She held the paper as if it were gold-plated. "I think I will. Now.'' She got up and walked out of the room. Carl stayed and wadded up the sodden throw rug. The mug he picked up struck the arm of the couch. Heavy china, it didn't chip, just rang with a hollow sound. *Just the way you feel.*

# Chapter Sixteen

Her hands were still shaking. Grace put the phone down, took a deep breath. It was all she could do to pick it up again, punch in the numbers.

It startled her when the phone rang on the other end. Surely any moment now she'd hear that grating tone instead, and the too-smooth voice of the operator, telling her she's dialed a no-longer-in-service number.

Three rings. Four. A pause and then a sound so incredibly sweet, Grace was nearly in tears again. "This is Jo, except it's this danged machine instead. You probably know how it works better than I do, so leave your name and number. Unless you want to sell me something. Then just hang up."

Jo was still her old feisty self. Grace waited for the end of the series of clicks and beeps that meant she should leave her message. "Aunt Jo? It's me, Grace." She probably didn't have much more time. She repeated Carl's phone number into the machine. "Call me. Hurry." Her hands were still trembling when she hung up the phone.

Grace stayed there and slept in the kitchen chair, slumped over the table. When she woke in the morning, stiff and sore, she resolved to get Carl a cordless phone. That way she could take the handset to bed with her if the call didn't come this morning.

Who was she kidding? If the call didn't come before noon, she'd need more than just a cordless phone to hold on to her sanity. Grace looked out the window at the pale spring dawn. "Keep her in Your care, God, wherever she is. And please, let her call back soon.'' It was all she could do. Only God could do the rest.

''What's wrong with Mom?'' Only Carl was supposed to hear Spence's comment at the breakfast table, Grace was sure. When she turned around from the stove and looked at her son, he ducked his head.

''Mom is waiting on a phone call. And she's nervous. Carl found Aunt Jo, but she wasn't home last night when I called. And she hasn't called me back.''

''And it's driving you nuts, huh, Mom?'' Spencer's expression was serious. ''Are we really going to get to see her again?''

''That's what I want. If I knew she was home, I'd get out my maps and be on the road.''

Carl shook his head. ''In that car? I wouldn't trust that thing to the county line. When you go, Grace, take the truck. Or I'll go with you and we'll all take the truck.''

''You just want to make sure I come back.'' Grace wished she could have taken back the words the moment she spoke. Carl looked as if she had slapped him.

''I'm sorry. I shouldn't have said that.'' She turned off the burner on the stove and hurried to his place at the table.

Both kids were goggle-eyed. Grace could see their silent question to each other. What was going to happen now? But unlike what they'd witnessed before with Matt, with Carl she could use humor to ease the tension.

She leaned down and kissed Carl on the forehead. It put her face nearly upside down in front of his to kiss him there. While she was at a disadvantage he reached up and grabbed her in a cockeyed bear hug of his own.

''You're right. Halfway, at least. I don't *just* want you back, but it is a good observation on your part. I would also worry about you less if you took the truck. It won't break down in the hundred miles or so between here and Big Springs, unlike that car. I'd still rather you made sure Jo was home first.''

This was it? This was how mature, rational folks resolved their differences? Grace felt elation. Or was it just the effect of being upside down? ''Okay, let go of me. All the blood is rushing to my head.'' Grace moved her head so that her hair, which now curtained both their faces, had to tickle Carl. ''Come on, I mean it. I promise I won't take off in that old car. And I'll make sure Jo is home first.''

Maria was giggling. Spence obviously didn't know what to do. Adults who horsed around in the kitchen in a friendly manner were new to him. ''Mom, your face is really red.''

''Yeah, well, have this lummox hold you upside down for a while and see what color your face is.'' Grace tried to sound grumpy.

''Cool. Can I?'' Carl lunged for Spence, who zipped around the table, laughing to avoid his grasp.

''Anybody who knocks over milk or syrup is scrubbing this kitchen. With no help from me, I might add.'' That didn't stop the chase around the table, but it slowed it down. Only after things calmed down and the kids were out the door did Grace realize what Carl had done. When Carl came back to the kitchen, ready to go to the store, she had to compliment him.

''Good job.''

He stopped in the middle of the room, still in the act of tying the hated tie on his way out the door. ''What do you mean?''

''We scared the kids there for a minute. Nice way to defuse things.''

Carl shrugged. ''You didn't get to have much of an opinion, uh, before, did you?''

''Not exactly. I was always too busy to have one if Matt wasn't there, and leery of voicing it if he was. It's taken some getting used to, being opinionated again.''

''I think you're picking it up okay. Want to call Big Springs again?''

Grace looked away from him. His generosity continued to amaze her. ''Yes. No. I don't know, Carl. What if she's just not picking up the phone? If she's just...given up on me after this long.''

''I don't think so. From what little you've told me about your aunt, she wouldn't ever give up on you. I can call if you like.''

''No, I'll do it.'' Grace used the kitchen phone, but she reached the machine again. Grace held on and left another message.

''I don't suppose there's any way I could talk you into coming to the store? I hate to think about you pacing the house all day, waiting for that phone to ring.''

"Not unless the telephone company around here has been modernized while I wasn't looking, and you can get this thing to do call forwarding." Grace glared at the silent instrument on the wall.

"If I could get them to do it just for you, Grace, you know I would."

Grace looked into his silvery eyes. "You would, wouldn't you? You're a good man that way, Carl. Good in most ways. So go to work. If she hasn't called by the time school lets out, I'll come over and scream."

"And if she does call, I'll probably be able to hear you scream from the store."

The urge to stick her tongue out at Carl was overpowering. He brought out the child in her, in good ways and bad. But Grace had to admit he was right. If Jo called, everybody in about a mile radius would know once Grace got off the phone. It thrilled her that in this short a time, Carl knew that about her, and so much more.

"Mr. Brenner? I don't think this is right." Kayla held out a handful of bills. "I think you just gave me back in change what I should have paid for that shirt."

Carl looked at the cash register, then at the change in her hand. "You're right. Thanks for catching me on it."

"No problem. It's kind of cool. I never thought I'd have better math skills than you."

"Yeah, well, enjoy it, because it probably won't ever happen again."

Kayla smiled. "I bet you're right. I hope it gets better, whatever it is."

Carl's brow furrowed. "What do you mean?"

"Well, something has to have you awful spaced out to miss a simple sale like that. I figure you're either sick, or you and Grace had a fight or something."

"More like 'or something.'" Carl had no idea how to explain Jo Sparks and her phone call, or lack of it, to Kayla, who shrugged now as she headed out.

For that matter it was hard to explain to himself. He should be thrilled that Jo wasn't calling back. The longer this wore on, the longer he had Grace. No matter what she said, it was hard to believe that Grace would really choose Carl over her own family.

If somebody walked in here, today, and offered to trade him the whole store for finding Danny, Carl knew he'd give the store away. *What about Grace?* That was a tougher choice. If the only way to find Danny was to give up Grace and the kids, and what they had going for them, would he do it?

*Maybe.* Fortunately, nobody was asking him to make that choice. Nobody ever would, because he was never going to find Danny. He was, however, going to have to get used to the idea of giving up Grace and the kids. Because sooner or later Jo would call, or Grace would call and find her at home. Then this illusion of a family would be gone for good.

The bell over the door jingled. Spence and Maria were done with school. "Did Mom hear anything?" Spence had been running; it showed in his cheeks.

"Good afternoon to you, too. I'm fine. No cookies or anything from Miss Naomi, but it's been a pretty good afternoon—"

"Okay, already. Hi, Carl. How was your day? Mine was okay. I got an A-minus on my math test. Jennifer Brown got higher." Spence fairly wiggled with impatience. "Now, did Mom hear anything?"

"No, not yet." Before Carl could run Maria through the same drill, the phone rang. "Redwing Mercantile," he answered.

"I'm looking for Grace Mallory." The voice was soft, tentative. Just listening to it, Carl could picture an older woman. "Do I have the right number?"

"Yes and no," Carl said. "This is the store, and she's at the house. Can I give you that number?" He could hear a strange buzzing in the back of his head. Why didn't he just hang up, pretend this was a wrong number—anything?

"I think I already have it." The woman on the other end of the phone read back a number. "That's what I heard on the machine, anyway."

"Well, ma'am, I don't know if the machine is a little off or what, but you're not quite right on that number." Carl told her the right one, just one digit off from where she was to begin with. "Would this be Mrs. Sparks?"

"It is. Is there something the matter with my girl?"

"Not yet. But I may have to catch her when she picks up that phone at the house and hears your voice."

"Well, I hope it isn't far from the store to the house, because you're going to have some fast catching to do. And thank you, Mr., uh, I don't expect it's Redwing, is it?" There was laughter in her voice. Carl liked this woman in spite of himself.

"Nope. Not Mercantile, either." The cheerful voice on the other end of the line made Carl giddy instead of depressed. Grace would be so happy. "It's Brenner, Carl Brenner. And there's somebody here who wants to say hello before we hang up."

Spencer all but snatched the phone out of his hand. "Aunt Jo? That really you? Hey. No, not anymore. Mostly everybody calls me Spence. Right, I'm ten." He paused to listen, and Carl could guess what Jo was asking him. Something about Matt Mallory, from the way the kid's expression darkened. "I better let Mom tell you about that. Love you, too. Yeah, I better race Carl home. Bye."

"Are we going to?" Spence asked after he hung up. "Race home? Mom's gonna be a mess once she talks to Aunt Jo. I bet when we get there she's sitting in the middle of the kitchen floor. Probably bawling."

"No bet on that one, bud. Flip over the sign on the front door to Closed for me. Maria, don't take off that coat, sweetheart. Where's your book bag?"

"Here. On the floor. Will we really have to catch her?" Maria asked, looking somber.

"What, your mom? No, I don't think so. But I do want to be there pretty quick." Carl hoisted her up into his arms, and boosted her onto his back. "Piggyback okay with you? I don't want to leave you behind."

Spence was already out the door, the bell jingling madly in his rush. "Cool." Maria giggled from her perch atop Carl. "Let's go. Spencer's going to win."

No, Grace was going to win. And suddenly Carl was glad for her, even if it meant letting go. He wanted nothing but the best for her, and if this was it, so be it. Maria was a sweet weight on his back. "Duck through the doorway. I don't want to take off any important body parts, like your head."

Her laugh was wonderful. Carl prayed it wasn't the last time he heard it. *Let me keep them, God.* It was his prayer all the way home, with the child bouncing in rhythm to his strides.

"See, I told you I wouldn't take a bet on that one." Carl put Maria down just inside the kitchen door. Spence already stood there, watching his mother. She sat on the floor. She was, as the kid had inelegantly put it, bawling. Wiping her wet face with one hand, she held the phone with the other.

Carl could only do one thing. He sat down on the floor with her, his back up against the kitchen cabinets. There was even a handle poking his spine in one place. Splaying out his legs, and wrapping his arms around Grace, he brought her body in close to his. Sitting there, without saying a word, he gave her the comfort he knew she needed as she talked to Jo.

Her body trembled. Carl leaned his forehead against her soft hair. He wanted her to know, in the most basic of ways, that he was there for her.

Apparently he wasn't the only one. Four sat in front of her. He kept offering Grace a large front paw, plopping it down on her knees. Without looking at him, Grace eased him off every time. She was concentrating on one thing only: the woman on the other end of that phone line.

"What? Of course we'll come. I have to talk to Carl first. He owns a store here, and he doesn't have any help at the moment but me. Yes, it would be hard to keep things open with both of us gone. We might be able to train Four to run the register, but he'll want to come meet you, too." Her laughter warmed Carl. "No, he's not a weird kid. He's a dog. A big yellow one. You'll love him."

The conversation went on. Carl tried to think about how to keep the store open if he took Grace to see Jo for a couple of days. Nuts. If he left Kayla in charge that long, the vultures would clean him out to the bare walls.

Maybe if they went on a weekend they'd be okay. At least he wasn't open on Sunday, so that would only give her Friday afternoon and Saturday to mess up the bookkeeping. Carl sat up straighter. Janet could help out on Saturday, too. She wasn't well trained in retailing, but she did have a lot more common sense than Kayla did. The two of them together might do okay. And hadn't Janet said she owed him one for the trip to Fort Leonard Wood? He'd better collect on the favor quickly while she still felt that way.

Grace was making her goodbyes now. Carl heard her click off the phone, and she leaned into him.

"We're going. We're actually going."

"Soon, I hope. Because you'll be a basket case until we do."

"You're right. If there wasn't life to take care of, I felt like telling Jo we'd be there tonight. It's only a couple of hours away."

Something inside Carl tilted crazily. "So let's do it. If the kids miss a couple of days of school, so what? We can get Kayla to feed the cat, and I'll ask her and Janet to take over the store."

Grace's mouth hung open. She looked like a fish gasping for air. "Are you serious?"

"Yeah, I am. Better catch me quick while I still feel this way. You never know how soon I might decide this is a lousy idea after all."

Grace scrabbled around and hugged him, hard. "It's a wonderful idea. And you're a good man just for thinking it, Carl."

*Just for that? Would she still consider you so decent if you didn't have these crazy ideas?* Carl pushed away the questions. Nothing had been quite sane or normal since Grace Mallory had come into his life. Nothing at all lived up to his previous expectations anymore.

Sitting there, with Grace in his arms, he made a surprising discovery: he didn't want anything else. That vague feeling of yearning wasn't constantly with him anymore.

He still missed Danny. And life running a store in Redwing, Missouri, wasn't all it could be. But with Grace in his arms those things didn't gnaw at him in the same way.

It was crazy, really. Having Grace here, so vibrantly here with her arms around him, making a bony, uncomfortable weight in his lap, was bliss. And he had just suggested that they get straight up off the kitchen floor and do the one thing that would take her out of his arms permanently—just because it made her happy.

He should have his head examined. Carl decided he'd do just that when he came home from Big Springs. He'd have plenty of time, anyway. Because he was still pretty sure he'd be coming back alone.

# *Chapter Seventeen*

Grace's stomach fluttered. Why had she let Carl talk her into eating dinner? Even the one single hamburger she'd nibbled on sat in her stomach like a rock.

He and the kids hadn't had any problems eating. Neither had Four, blissfully chowing down a double burger with bacon and cheese in his crate in the back of the truck.

Nobody else was as nervous as she was. Of course, the dog never got nervous. Spencer was too excited about seeing Jo again to be upset about anything, and Maria sensed his excitement, not her mother's nerves.

Carl, driving the truck, had been very quiet. Was he still concerned that she would leave him to stay with Jo? Grace couldn't think of a way to bring the subject up. It was hard for her to imagine that he'd think that way.

Carl's signaling to turn off the highway pulled her out of her thoughts. "We're not there yet, are we?"

"Just to a rest stop. But we're close. Big Springs can't be more than five miles ahead, and Jo's directions put her place about two miles past that." Carl looked at her and Grace felt shock waves jolt through her from the reflection of feelings she saw in his eyes.

"So you want me to drive the last bit?"

Carl nodded. "If you could. For whatever reason, I don't feel up to it."

Grace knew it cost him to admit that. "No problem. Any detours you want me to make?"

Carl shook his head. "Not in the dark. Tomorrow in the light I will need to go exploring." He swung down out of the truck, leaving her to slide over the bench into the driver's seat.

He stretched as he followed the path around the truck, lit by headlights. Grace longed to hug him for comfort. But they were only seven miles from Jo! It was hard to imagine.

Carl got back into the truck. Impulsively Grace leaned over and kissed him, raising a flutter of giggles from the back seat. "Oh, stop, you two." She didn't even bother turning around to look at the kids.

"But it's so mushy up there."

Carl laughed. "You aren't going to believe me, but someday, my friend, you are going to want to be the guy in the front seat."

Spence didn't sound convinced. "No way."

Carl winked at Grace. It lifted her heart. "I know it will be a while, but someday that will happen. Not soon, I hope, but someday."

Spence made a sound like the cat coughing up a hairball. "I hope not soon, either. I mean, I'll kiss Aunt Jo when we get there, but kissing girls? No way."

"No girl would kiss you anyhow," Maria piped up.

That started Grace giggling in the front seat as she pulled back onto the highway. Seven miles and counting. It felt like seventy miles instead. She resisted the impulse to smash down on the gas pedal. If she got a speeding ticket right outside Big Springs, she'd never hear the end of it.

Spence sighed. "Why does Maria have to pick on me?"

"Because she's your kid sister. It's her job," Carl explained, and Grace could hear a thread of pain in his voice. "Heck, I'd give anything if I could have my kid brother back to rat on me."

It was all Grace could do to keep her eyes on the road. Carl was so natural with the kids, and took them into his confidence so readily.

"You have a brother? Cool."

"It would be cooler if I'd seen him growing up. I haven't seen him since I was younger than Maria."

"That's rough." Spence's voice held real compassion and Grace was proud of her son. "At least you had a brother for a while. Do you know what it's like to be the only guy in the house?''

"Yes, I do. And I'm glad I'm not anymore, and I'm glad you're not anymore. We've got to stick together, huh, Spencer?''

"For sure. I figure if you stick around long enough we can talk Mom into getting married. Then maybe we can get the majority around here.''

Grace nearly swerved off the road listening to her son's logic. "Hey, I just thought of something,'' the boy added. If you count Four, we already have the majority.''

Grace laughed. "Not for long. The score is about to be tied. About a mile up the road is Aunt Jo's house, and even counting the dog, we'll be tied again.''

"That's okay. Aunt Jo's on my side anyway. I remember her spoiling me rotten when I was a little kid.''

"And you can hardly wait for her to start doing it again.'' Grace felt a kinship with her son. As she got closer to Jo's door, she was a child again, too. And oh, how she was ready to be spoiled rotten.

Organized chaos? Controlled pandemonium? Carl wasn't sure how to describe the scene in front of him. He and the dog stood on Jo's gravel driveway just far enough from the melee not to get squashed.

Jo was a substantial lady. Her red hair, streaked with white, didn't seem to owe anything to store-bought coloring. Maria had already launched herself into Jo's arms—a sure sign that she must be okay. The child looked natural there, clinging to the woman who was as close to a grandmother as she was likely to get on this earth. After Jo planted a resounding kiss on her cheek, Maria shimmied down to the gravel again, jumping up and down beside her.

Grace and Jo couldn't stop chattering, hugging, separating and starting the whole process over again. Maria and Spence were right in the middle of it. Four wished he were, too. Carl could tell by the way he whined and pulled at the hand on his collar.

"I don't think so. Any more weight and that pile is likely to bowl right over.'' Carl tried to imagine adding an eighty-pound dog to the clump of people in front of him. It wasn't a pretty sight.

"Ah, he's feeling left out. Well, come on over.'' Jo bent down and patted her knees. Her studded-denim skirt pooled around her as she coaxed the dog. "C'mon. A little dog slobber never hurt anybody."

Four understood her tone, if not her words. He bounded over, his entire back end wagging. When he knocked Jo over onto her rear in the gravel, everyone laughed but Carl.

"Now don't you fuss at him." Both of Jo's hands, with their glossy red nails, twined in the dog's fur at ear level. The animal appeared to be laughing with the people. "I asked him over here."

"I know. But he knows better." Carl came closer and Four sat without being told. Jo let go of his feathery ears and extended a hand to Carl.

"If you want to apologize, just help me up off the pavement. Then we'll get you all inside instead of standing out here in the dark and the cold."

Carl helped her up. Jo's eyes glittered with happiness. "I didn't mean to get a hug from the dog before I got one from you."

"That's okay. He's friendlier with strangers." Carl winced at how his own words came out.

"You're no stranger. You brought me back my girl!" Jo's embrace was strong, and she smelled of one of the sweet perfumes on Doc's counter. "Now come inside before we all get chilled."

Carl couldn't imagine anybody being chilled around the warmth of Jo Sparks. But with her hand on his sleeve he wasn't going to argue. He let himself be led into her front room.

Lamps glowed golden, making a place of welcome trimmed with homemade afghans and friendly knickknacks. In the daylight the room might look worn around the edges, but tonight it looked like home. Carl could tell it looked that way to Grace. She sank down in an armchair upholstered in rose plush.

"You're home," Carl said. The words came out sounding more cheerful than he'd expected they would.

Grace leaned back in the chair. "I am. For the first time in six or seven years. But I think I could say that about anyplace this particular chair, and Aunt Jo, were. Think it would fit in your parlor?"

Carl felt an overwhelming wave of feelings. This wasn't a plan he'd considered. "Sure. Do we have to keep it pink?"

"Old Rose," Grace corrected, settling deeper into the chair. "And yes, we do."

"Oh, no, we don't," Jo chimed in. "I've been waiting for eight years to have that chair reupholstered, young lady. Now that you've seen that I kept it that way for you, it goes into the shop pronto. It's a disgrace as is."

Grace stood. "But you kept my favorite chair just the way I remembered it, just for me."

Jo nodded. "I knew you'd be back. I waited and prayed on it, and keeping that chair just the way it was seemed to be the way to tell myself I believed you'd be back. But Grace, honey, that plush has to go."

They fell into each other's arms again, tears and laughter mixing. "Does this mean that there are twin beds with chenille spreads in the guest room?"

"It sure does. I drew the line at keeping the throw rugs. But your bed is still in the spare bedroom. *And* that couch over there makes into a daybed, with a trundle that pops out."

"Let's put the kids in the guest room and Carl in your room, Grace said. "Then we can take the couch and the pop-up and talk all night without disturbing anybody."

"Don't I get any say in this?" Carl asked. "I don't want to put Jo out of her own bed." The identical expressions on the two women's faces told him all he needed to know.

"Well, Aunt Jo, show me to your bedroom and let me unpack my suitcase. No sense in keeping you ladies from your chat."

"You can stay up and talk with us as long as you like," Grace said magnanimously. "However, there are two people here that need to put on pajamas and brush teeth and head for those beds in the guest room."

Her statement was met with groans and protests from both sides.

"I'll get the suitcases," Carl offered. "Maybe we can compromise here. You guys put on your pajamas first, and then come back out to visit. That okay?"

"Sure. If we can go to the creek sometime tomorrow when it gets light. Aunt Jo says there are tadpoles." Spencer grinned.

"Once it gets light. And only if they stay outside. I am not sharing anybody's house with a tadpole." Grace shivered slightly.

"Aw, you never let them have any fun. Besides, it's my house. Don't I get a say as to who, or what, comes in it?"

"Not tadpoles. Please, not tadpoles."

Jo grinned, a sight that made her look a whole bunch like Grace. "Just for you, we'll keep the tadpoles outside. The dog can come in, can't he?"

"He's real well trained. Carl can tell him to go sit down anyplace and he'll do it."

"As long as you don't tell him otherwise. I have this sneaking suspicion that when I'm not home he sits on the sofa and keeps Grace's feet warm."

"He is very warm. But I don't usually let him up on the furniture, because I know you don't like it."

Jo laughed. "Neither of us have changed much, have we? You are still a sucker for any animal that has feet and fur, and I'm still taking in everybody."

"Including animals without feet and fur. Thanks for keeping the tadpoles outside." Grace stood up and clapped her hands. It got the dog's attention, if nothing else. "Now, let's get everybody going," Grace said. "Carl, let out the dog while you bring in the bags. Kids, go with Aunt Jo to the kitchen for cookies."

Yes, Grace was home already. And like at any other time, once she'd made herself at home there was no lounging around for anyone. Carl headed for the door, with Four on his heels. "You can help me bring in the suitcases. There're enough for you to carry, too."

He knew that would earn him some remark from Grace. What surprised him was the fringed cushion that zinged past his head, hitting the door with a plop. "Hasn't she told you about her softball career?" There was laughter in Jo's voice. "I've still got the trophy her team won in the county finals the year she was fourteen."

Carl hurried outside before anything else followed the pillow. Four looked at him with questions in his dark eyes. Carl reached down and patted the silky head. "Don't ask me what's going on. I'm only an observer." And tonight there would be plenty to observe.

\* \* \*

Grace didn't know what it was about Jo that put Carl so at ease. Whatever it was, she thanked God that Carl felt it. He sat in Jo's front room, sock-footed and wearing the old sweats and T-shirt he put on when the kids got into their pajamas. Her favorite pink chair looked tiny with him sitting in it.

It looked shabby, too. Jo was right about re-covering it. That was okay, really. It was Jo's chair, even though Grace had always thought of it as her own personal throne. And no matter what color or print they put on the outside of the chair, it would still be that haven of love.

True to her word, Jo set up the daybed and the pop-up unit with help from the kids. They looked on this whole night as a giant slumber party. It would certainly be more fun than the last one Grace had attended. She felt herself blushing, thinking about that night in the motel. Well, maybe not more fun, but definitely more comfortable.

"Maria's wonderful," Jo said, bringing Grace back to the present. "I'm so glad I got to meet her while she's still young enough to say anything."

Grace wrinkled her nose. "That may work against me once in a while."

Jo laughed. "Probably. But think of how much fun I'll have."

Carl squirmed in his chair and leaned forward, thrusting his long legs out into the room. "How can you do it?"

Grace could tell by the look on her face that Jo didn't understand his question, either. "Do what?"

"Just sit there and laugh and talk. You missed eight years of each other's lives. Those years are gone. They'll never be back. Aren't you angry?"

Jo shook her head. Grace loved watching her do that, seeing those auburn-and-white curls bounce. It made her want to reach over and pat Jo's hair, the way she did when she was a child. "No satisfaction in that for me. My satisfaction is here under this af-ghan." Jo reached out a worn hand to Grace's knee. "When Grace and Matt disappeared on me, I was mad. So angry for a while that I couldn't see straight. But I put them in God's care. I knew that way that they would be safe."

"Even if you never saw them again?"

Jo's voice, when she answered, was choked with tears. "Even if I never saw them again. And I had to deal with that part of it. But no matter where they were, I knew they were safe in the hands of the Lord. And someday I'd see them again."

"But that someday might not have been in this lifetime. How did you deal with that?" Carl asked.

Jo just looked at Carl for the longest time. "Who have you lost? Who are you so angry with? That question didn't just come out of the blue."

"No, ma'am, it didn't." In tortured bits, he told his story. It brought tears to Grace's eyes again, hearing it for the second time.

After he'd finished, Jo sat silently again for a while. When she finally spoke, she was slow and deliberate. "What if you never find him?"

"I don't know. I've got to."

Jo looked as if she wanted to say something, then changed her mind. When her question came, Grace was pretty sure it wasn't what she'd first intended to say. "How old did you say Danny was? About Grace's age, right?"

"Right."

"What if you couldn't find him because he had no idea anyone was looking?"

Carl's brow furrowed. "How could that be? He was almost three when we lost track of each other. He's twenty-eight now. He's got to know he's adopted."

Jo shook her head. "Not necessarily. The whole time you were telling me about looking for your brother, something played through my mind. Now, I'm not saying the little boy I saw was your brother, Danny. But the same thing could have happened to him."

Carl's face was grim. "Tell me."

Jo looked down at her hands in her lap. "Grace always knew we weren't her parents. She was old enough when her mama died to remember her some. But soon after that, Eddie and I wanted to adopt her. We wanted to make sure she knew how much we wanted to keep her. And that was the best way to show her, we thought."

"Sure." Grace could tell Carl couldn't imagine where this was going. *She* couldn't, either.

"I still remember sitting in the waiting room of a little law office in the next town over from where we lived. We'd scraped up the money to do all the paperwork, and folks told us this man was the best for the money. So I sat in there, waiting, with Grace on the floor playing with toys I'd brought.

"Eddie couldn't take off until we went to court. There weren't any other men waiting that day either. But there was another woman. She looked as old as I did. And she had a beautiful little boy with her.

"We had to wait awhile, so naturally, we talked. It turned out we were there for the same thing. But where we wanted to do this to show Grace how much we wanted her, this lady said her little Michael wasn't ever going to know he was adopted."

"Could she do that?"

"I imagine so. With enough money in a small town, you can do just about anything. The lady looked like money was no problem. And she loved the child. It showed in everything—the way she touched him, how he was dressed and the tone of her voice. But that boy probably doesn't know to this day that he's adopted."

Jo stopped then and looked first at Grace, then at Carl. "Could you live with that, if the same thing had happened to Danny? Could you let go of him, knowing he was safe, well and loved, but would never know you existed?"

Carl exhaled a long, low sigh. "I don't know. I honestly don't know."

Jo stood and walked over to his chair. "It must be heavy."

"What?"

"Bearing that burden all by yourself."

Without a word, without a sound, tears made tracks down Carl's face. Jo knelt down beside him. Grace stayed still, seeing something between them that needed to happen without her. "When it gets light, let's all go out together. I want to see where you lived near here. And maybe there, we can find a way to lay that burden down."

"Okay. It isn't that much longer, is it? Until it gets light."

"Only a couple of hours," Jo said. "We've been up most of

the night.'' Grace was shocked when she looked at the clock on the mantel. Had they all really talked that long?

"Weeping may last the night," Jo said softly. "But joy comes in the morning. Morning's coming, kids. Let's get some rest before it gets here."

# Chapter Eighteen

Grace figured they'd have to drive around for a while. She couldn't imagine having been away from someplace as long as Carl had been gone from Big Springs and being able to find what he was looking for right off the bat. Jo seemed to think otherwise. "You know where you're going?"

"Without using a map, once I get this close. I've come back in between times. Gotten as far as the highway, but couldn't bring myself to go down the road past that."

Grace reached out and squeezed his leg above the knee. "We'll all go together."

"We sure will. And we'll stay on the road if you don't hold on to my knee." The kids giggled in the back of the truck.

"Last time I try to reassure you."

"If you want to reassure me, hold on to my arm. But for now don't hold on to anything, because I think I see the turn coming up."

Woods and an occasional small house fronted the two-lane asphalt road. A couple of miles from the highway a narrow entrance led into a grid of small streets flanked by mobile homes. "People still live here," Grace said in surprise. She'd expected to find a burned-out shell, if anything, surrounded by woods.

"Yeah, about six generations of people removed from the folks that were here when we were. I know, because that was the first thing I checked when I was a teenager trying to find out what happened to my family."

"Your uncle wasn't any help?" Jo asked.

Carl shook his head. "He said everything was over and done. He didn't want my dad's name mentioned around him. I guess he thought I'd be better-off if I forgot."

"You weren't, though. Better-off, or even able to forget."

"Not for a moment," Carl said, sounding incredibly tired. They'd passed through the small area of streets and courts that made up the mobile-home park. On the far edge of the development, away from the main road, there was a spot where no one lived anymore.

Here was the emptiness Grace had expected to see. Carl stopped the truck in what would have been the original parking space. Past it, there was only worn, blackened concrete, pitted with age. Woods and scrub surrounded a small clearing behind the concrete pad.

"This is it." Carl opened the door, slid out of the truck. On the other side of her, Jo did the same. Grace opened the front-facing door to the back of the cab so that the kids and dog could climb out, too.

"Now don't get into any poison ivy," she warned. "And don't get anywhere near other dogs."

"We won't." Spence snapped the leash securely on Four.

"Stay out of any creeks back there. And stay within shouting distance," Carl said.

"Your shouting distance or Mom's?" Spence asked.

"Mom's." Carl's answer was quick and firm.

"Nuts. Okay. C'mon, Maria, before they think of any more rules." Spence and the dog headed off into the sparse woods, with Maria following.

Carl stood on the concrete. Grace tried to see whatever it was he saw with that glazed look. It had to be so horrible. When she was five she had a loving family, a home; everything was fine. What was it like to have had none of that?

"Do you want us to leave you for a few minutes?"

"Don't go far. But yes, I want to be alone for a little bit."

"We'll leave. But you won't be alone." Jo came up and put a hand on his shoulder. "Call if you need us. We'll stay in shouting range, like the kids."

She took Grace by the arm, and they walked down the asphalt road. It was half a city block before there were any home sites. "I wonder if people thought it was haunted,'' Jo said softly. ''Folks are funny that way, after a tragedy.''

''Not everybody. You never were,'' Grace replied. ''You always pitched in when anybody needed something.''

''I know. But most people just can't do that. I figured I didn't have much, but God gave me whatever I had for a reason, and it wasn't to sit on it like a chicken hatching eggs.''

They walked down the lane a little farther. ''You love him, don't you?'' A breeze teased Jo's curls as she turned to look at Grace.

''I do. But I don't know what to do for him right now.''

''Looks like you're doing all right. He didn't want to bring you here at first, did he?''

Jo always cut to the heart of the matter. ''No,'' Grace admitted. ''He's afraid I'll stay here with you. I told him that once I found you again, I'd marry him.''

''Good. You need each other.''

Grace wrinkled her nose. ''*I* need *him*. But I'm not sure Carl needs anybody. It seems so much like he's done all of the giving and none of the taking in our relationship. What do I do, Aunt Jo?''

''Just what you're doing. We walk a little farther, then we turn around. You try and give all this into the Lord's keeping, just like I asked Carl to do. Let Him sort it all out, Gracie. He's better at it than the rest of us.''

''I hope so. Because I feel really bad at it. Let's turn around and go back.''

Carl was leaning against the truck. His eyes were rimmed with red when Grace got close to him. She walked into his arms, and he wrapped them around her silently. He felt different somehow, as if there were barriers missing.

''Can you make your peace with this?'' Jo asked him.

''Not alone. But with God's help, and a good woman, I think I can.''

''Well, it looks like you've got both. And there's nothing that says you won't find that brother of yours yet. I imagine you'll still keep looking.''

Grace felt Carl's voice rumbling in his chest. ''You know I will.''

Jo tilted her head back at them. It seemed like another serious question was coming. "Is Redwing a decent place to live?"

Carl shrugged. Still buried in his embrace, Grace could feel his shoulders move up and down. He was not about to let her go. "It's okay. Why?"

"Because I gave this girl up once, and I'm not going to do it again. If I come for a wedding, I'm staying. There anyplace in town for an old lady to rent?"

Carl almost let go of her. "Probably. But if you come to Redwing you'll live with us. I'll remodel the rooms where Grace and the kids have been living so you can have your own place if you want."

"We'll talk about that later. Right now I'm going to go look for those kids and that dog. I know there's a little branch of a creek in these woods not too far back, and I can't imagine all three of them staying out of it."

Grace blessed her aunt for knowing what to say, and for knowing when to go. She looked up, still in the circle of Carl's arms. "You meant what you said?"

"Which part? About letting go of Danny? I need to, Grace. Your aunt is so right. It's a burden I shouldn't be bearing by myself. Ever since you came into my life I've been letting go of things."

"Right. Your house, your money, your sanity…"

He leaned his forehead against hers. "More like my troubles, my loneliness, my problems. You're always there for me, Grace. If I ask you, will you stay?"

"Of course." She could feel his hands grip her back. "So ask."

"You want it all out loud, don't you? Okay, here goes. Grace Mallory, I love you. Can we set a date, soon, for a real wedding?"

"Yes. As soon as we can get back to Redwing and arrange it all. Hal will have fun with this, won't he?"

"Definitely. I get the feeling he and Barb and Jo will all be busy for a while, plotting and planning for us. Think we could get Naomi to cater a reception?"

"Sure. We'll have to have cookies, the way you and the kids go through them."

"We'll have anything you want." He kissed her joyfully.

"Wow. There you go, giving things away again."

Carl picked her up and spun her around. Grace shrieked while he laughed. "You still don't get it, do you? Anything I've given away since I met you, I've gotten back tenfold." He set her down on the pavement. "Can I give away one more thing?"

"I guess. As long as it's yours to give."

"Great. I want to give you the store. Hire Jo to help you run it, or Janet, or both. But since you've come into my life, it's so plain that working in that store isn't where I'm meant to be. God has given me this talent for finding people, for helping them. I want to give that talent back to Him and see what we can do with it together." His eyes shone silver-gray.

"Carl, that's wonderful. Sure, I'll take the store. And you can find people. I wonder where it will lead."

"To good things, I'm sure. Knowing you has led to more good things than I could imagine. How can sharing the rest of my life with you lead to anything but more good things?"

Suddenly Four burst out of the woods, followed by two muddy kids and Jo. "Mama? Guess what? There's tadpoles in that creek back there. Do we have a jar in the truck? Can we bring some to Aunt Jo's?"

One of Four's muddy front paws was planted on Carl's jacket, the other on Grace's. Carl laughed at her reaction to the whole melee. "Tadpoles on top of everything else. How can this day possibly get any better?"

"It couldn't, Carl. Unless you kissed me again."

And he did, with the dog and kids and Jo looking on. And there in his arms, with mud on one cheek and wind pulling at her hair, Grace felt exultant, more blessed than ever before. "Thank you," she whispered.

To Carl or to God? Perhaps to both, because together they had given her more than she deserved, more than she had ever expected. These were truly gifts of grace. They filled her heart to overflowing.

*     *     *     *     *

Dear Reader,

What's your favorite gift? I'm not talking about the ones that have appeared under your Christmas tree, or even that special "Oh, you shouldn't have" kind of something that someone special may have given you at one time or another. But what's your favorite gift that God has given you, and how do you share it with the world? Carl and Grace's story is all about the gifts that God has given them, which neither of them really recognize until they "give them away" to each other in the form of the love they share and the special things that only those two individuals could bring to their relationship.

So what's your favorite gift? Mine definitely has to be the wonderful blessing God has given me to be able to tell stories. The fact that fantastic publishers like Steeple Hill allow me to continue to reach people with these stories is an amazing thing, as far as I'm concerned, and I'm thrilled to be able to do so.

Everyone has some special gifts from God to share. Maybe yours is as profound as teaching the Word to someone who would never have heard it otherwise, or as simple as providing a caring hand to a friend or neighbor in need. In either case, I hope you find a way to share your wonderful, unique gift with the world. You can be sure that someone out there is just waiting for you to pass on that gift you've already been given.

Blessings,

Lynn Bulock

**Books by Irene Hannon**

Love Inspired

*_Home for the Holidays_ #6
*_A Groom of Her Own_ #16
*_A Family To Call Her Own_ #25
_It Had To Be You_ #58
_The Way Home_ #112
_Never Say Goodbye_ #175

*Vows

**_IRENE HANNON_**

has been a writer for as long as she can remember. This prolific author of romance novels for both the inspirational and traditional markets began her career at age ten, when she won a story contest conducted by a national children's magazine. Today, in addition to penning her heartwarming stories of love and faith, Irene keeps quite busy with her "day job" in corporate communications. In her "spare" time, she enjoys performing in community musical theater productions.

Irene and her husband, Tom—whom she describes as "my own romantic hero"—make their home in St. Louis, Missouri.

# ONE SPECIAL CHRISTMAS
## Irene Hannon

To my brother, Jim,
and his lovely bride, Teresa—
May all your happily-ever-after dreams come true.

# *Prologue*

It was over in moments, yet it seemed to happen in slow motion.

The car swerved suddenly, fishtailed wildly as the driver struggled for control on the icy road. Then it skidded sideways off the steep shoulder, rolling over once before coming to rest, upright, at the bottom of the embankment.

Eric Carlson watched in horror, his hands tightening instinctively on the wheel as the accident unfolded a few hundred feet in front of him. Though he didn't doubt his eyes, the terrible scene had an odd air of unreality about it, seeming to happen in utter quiet, like an old silent movie. The sleet hitting his car roof, combined with the volume of the radio that Cindy had just cranked up, must have masked the grating sound of metal being crushed, the high-pitched crackle of shattering glass—and the inevitable screams that would accompany such a traumatic crash. But Eric could imagine them, and he swallowed convulsively as his breath lodged in his throat.

*Dear God,* he prayed as the full impact of what he'd just witnessed slammed home. He slowed his car as quickly as the icy road would allow and eased it over to the shoulder.

"What are you doing?" Cindy demanded stridently.

He set the brake and reached into the back for his bag. "Exactly what you think I'm doing," he replied tersely.

"Oh, for heaven's sake, Eric, we're going to be late for the party! They're serving dinner at eight. Let's just call 911 and get out of here. Those other Good Samaritans can help," she said impatiently, gesturing toward two other cars that had also stopped.

He turned to his wife, and as he looked at her petulant expression he wondered what had drawn him to her a dozen years ago. Her blond beauty had attracted him, certainly. And he'd been flattered that someone so sophisticated had found him appealing. But surely there had been more. Hadn't her heart once been kind and caring? Hadn't the smiles she'd given him in those early days been tender and warm? Or had he seen only what he'd wanted to see, imagined what had never been there at all?

As the years had passed and the chasm between them had widened, he'd been forced to admit that perhaps it was his perception—not Cindy—that had changed. Or perhaps she had simply become more of what she had always been as she grew disillusioned with him and disenchanted with the demands of his profession—the "doctor stuff," as she demeaningly termed it. He was well aware that his dedication to his work grated on her, that she felt his devotion to his patients diminished his devotion to her. And perhaps it did. Perhaps if he had been able to give her the kind of attention she needed, their relationship wouldn't be disintegrating. Yet how could he give anything less than one hundred percent to his profession? It was a dilemma he wrestled with constantly, but always the answers eluded him. All he knew was that both of them were unhappy in their marriage.

But it was too late now to alter their status, Eric reminded himself grimly. He had meant the vows they'd made on their wedding day, including "For better, for worse." After all, as his old maiden aunt used to say, he and Cindy had made their bed. Now they had to lie in it.

Eric knew they couldn't go on like this. But his repeated suggestions that they seek counseling were always met with cold sarcasm—and a cold shoulder. As he looked at her now, in the shadowy light of the car, she seemed almost like a stranger.

Cindy shifted uncomfortably under her husband's scrutiny, and when she spoke again her tone was more conciliatory. "Look, those other people will do whatever they can until help arrives, Eric. They don't need you."

"I'm a doctor, Cindy."

"You're a pediatrician."

She didn't say "just," but the implication was there in her disparaging tone. A muscle in his jaw clenched as he handed her the cell phone. "Call 911." Then he stepped out into the darkness, turning up his collar as he strode toward the embankment, sleet stinging his face much as the familiar gibe always stung his heart.

By the time he made it down to the smashed car, slipping and sliding all the way, the other two motorists were already there. Both had flashlights and were peering into the vehicle. They glanced up when Eric approached.

"How many inside?" he asked.

"Looks like just two. A man and a woman," one replied. He eyed Eric's bag. "Are you a doctor?"

"Yes."

"Well, the woman's conscious but the man doesn't look too good," the other passerby reported dubiously.

Eric strode around to the passenger's side of the car, and with some effort the three of them were able to force open the jammed door.

"One of you give me some light," he instructed as he leaned down to look in, noting with relief that the woman's seat belt was securely in place. He touched her shoulder gently, and she turned to him, her eyes wide and dazed.

For just a moment, Eric simply stared at her. Even in the harsh beam of the flashlight, she had the face of a Madonna—a perfect oval, with dark hair and even darker eyes. She was like something out of a Raphael painting, he thought numbly, momentarily taken aback by her beauty. Her looks were classic, timeless—and marred by a nasty bump that was rising rapidly on her left temple. Abruptly he shifted his focus from her physical attributes to her physical condition.

"I'm a doctor. Can you hear me?" He spoke slowly, enunciating each word carefully.

She nodded jerkily. "I—I'm all right. Please…please take care of my husband," she pleaded.

He looked past her, noting the unnatural position of the male driver, who lay crumpled behind the steering wheel, as well as the blood seeping from the corner of his mouth. "All right. Try not to move. An ambulance is on the way."

"Can I do anything to help?" the flashlight holder asked as Eric straightened.

"The two of you can give me some light on the other side," he said over his shoulder. The other motorist had managed to get the driver's door open, and the two men focused the beams of their lights on the injured man as Eric bent down to examine him.

He wasn't wearing a seat belt, Eric noted. Right off the bat, that was a major strike against him. And the car was an older-model compact, without air bags. Strike two. Eric felt for the man's pulse. Shallow. And his respiration was uneven. He showed signs of major trauma, including head-and-neck injuries—which meant possible spinal damage, Eric noted after a quick visual scan.

Frowning, he glanced up and his gaze met that of the woman passenger. She stared at him, and he saw the fear in her eyes suddenly mushroom at his grim expression.

"He's going to be all right, isn't he?" she pleaded desperately, the stricken look on her face making his gut twist painfully. "This can't be happening! Not tonight! Not now!" She let out a strangled sob and turned her attention to her husband, reaching over to touch his face. "You'll be all right, Jack. I know you will. You have to be!" she said fiercely.

The man's breathing suddenly grew more erratic, and Eric snapped open his bag and deftly withdrew his stethoscope. As he listened to the man's fading pulse, his own heart ratcheted into double time. *God, please let the paramedics arrive soon!* he prayed.

But within seconds it became clear that they weren't going to arrive soon enough. The man's breathing grew more labored with each breath, and obviously he was fighting a losing battle to suck air into his lungs. Eric reached for his bag again. In all his years of medical training, in all his years of trauma work, he'd never had to open an airway in the field, let alone with makeshift lighting and icy sleet pricking the back of his neck. But as the seconds ticked by, it was obvious that if he didn't, this man was going to die. He couldn't let that happen—especially after seeing the anguished look in the woman's eyes.

Eric drew in a steadying breath. Then, without further hesitation, he deftly performed the procedure, aware of, but steeling himself against, the woman's startled gasp. Only when he'd finished did he glance up, noting with alarm the pallor of her face and the glazed look in her eyes. She was starting to turn shocky, Eric realized. And he couldn't handle two trauma cases at once.

Just as he began to panic, the welcome sound of approaching sirens pierced the night air. He closed his eyes and slowly he let out his breath as relief washed over him. Thank God! He needed all the help he could get—and the sooner the better.

Within moments the paramedics joined him, and he explained the situation in clipped phrases, the economy of his language honed during years of emergency-room work where every second counted. As one paramedic temporarily distracted the woman, he spoke softly to the other two.

"Probable severe neck-and-head trauma. I opened an airway, but he's still very unstable. Handle him with kid gloves."

"No problem. We've worked cases like this before," one of them assured him.

"Do you need me to stay and help?"

"We've got it covered. But thanks for stopping. Immediate medical attention can make all the difference, as you know."

Eric nodded, then straightened. He spoke briefly to the policeman on the scene, then made his way up the embankment.

As he crested the rise and stepped onto the pavement, he glanced back once more toward the accident scene, surrealistically illuminated by the police-car headlights and the rotating red-and-white beacon on the ambulance. The woman was standing now, her arms wrapped tightly around her, and though it was clear the paramedic was urging her to sit in one of the vehicles, she was adamantly shaking her head. Her gaze was locked on the two men who were carefully extricating her husband from the battered car. Eric could feel her panic, could sense her almost-palpable fear even from this distance.

Would Cindy look like that if something ever happened to him? he wondered. But even before the question formed, he knew the disheartening answer. Any love they had once shared had died long ago.

For just a moment, despite the man's severe injuries, Eric almost envied him. His wife's deep, abiding love was evident in her eyes, her expression, her very body language. Her husband was obviously the center of her world. And Eric knew intuitively that she was the center of his. Which was as it should be in a good marriage.

Finally, unable to look at the heartrending scene any longer, he turned away, his gut twisting painfully. He was reasonably certain he'd saved the man's life. But as he reached his car and slipped back inside, he wondered for just a moment if he'd done anyone a favor. Eric suspected that the road ahead would not be an easy one—for either him or his wife. That tonight was only the beginning of their trauma.

Maybe Cindy had been right, after all. Maybe he just should have driven on.

# Chapter One

*Five years later*

"Mrs. Nolan, the doctor will see Sarah now."

Kate glanced up from the book she was reading to her daughter and smiled. "All right. Thanks." She slung her purse over her shoulder and stood, reaching down to take Sarah's hand. "Come on, honey. It's time to go in."

"Do I have to?"

Kate gazed down into the large, dark eyes—a mirror image of her own—and with an apologetic glance at the nurse, sat back down. She pulled Sarah close and spoke gently. "You don't want to have those nasty tummyaches anymore, do you, honey? The doctor can help make them go away. And I'll stay with you the whole time. I promise."

Sarah's eyes welled with tears and she sniffed. "I don't like doctors."

"You used to like Dr. Davis, remember? And this doctor is a friend of his. So I'm sure you'll like him, too."

"He's not going to give me a shot, is he?"

"I don't think so. Not today."

Sarah's lower lip quivered. "Promise you'll stay with me?" she pleaded tremulously.

"Of course I will, honey."

She gave her daughter a quick, reassuring hug and stood again, her heart contracting as Sarah's small, trusting hand reached for hers. She couldn't even bear the thought that something serious might be wrong with her. Sarah was the only thing that gave her life any meaning or joy. Though she'd tried not to worry during the past week as she'd waited for this appointment, she'd met with little success. Nights were the worst. She kept waking up in a cold sweat as increasingly frightening scenarios played themselves out in her dreams. Sarah was all she had now, and she would do anything—anything—to keep her well and safe and happy.

She tightened her grip encouragingly and smiled down at her daughter, trying futilely to control the almost painful thumping of her heart as they followed the nurse inside. Everything would turn out fine, she told herself resolutely. It had to. Except she knew from experience that that was a lie. Everything didn't *have* to turn out fine. There were lots of times when it didn't—no matter how hard you wished for it or wanted it or prayed for it.

The nurse stopped at the door of an examining room and ushered them inside.

"The doctor will be with you in just a few minutes," she promised.

"Shall I undress Sarah?" Kate asked.

The woman glanced at Sarah's shorts and crop top, noted how tenaciously the little girl clung to her mother, and smiled as she shook her head. "I don't think so. The doctor should be able to check everything out just like that. If not, he'll let you know."

Kate watched the woman leave, then forced her lips into what she hoped was a cheery smile. "Shall we finish our story?" She held up the book she'd brought with her from the waiting room.

Sarah nodded, and as Kate sat down the youngster climbed onto her lap. Though her daughter quickly became engrossed in the story, Kate couldn't so easily forget where they were. Or why. Even when Sarah got the sniffles she worried excessively, and this mysterious ache in her daughter's stomach was making Kate's own stomach clench painfully.

When a brief knock interrupted her reading a few minutes later, she jerked involuntarily, then glanced up with a troubled gaze as the door swung open.

Eric stopped abruptly on the threshold as he stared at the woman whose face had been indelibly etched into his mind on that cold, tragic evening five years before. It was a night memorable in many ways—none of them pleasant. It had begun with the terrible accident, and had ended with his wife's announcement that she wanted a divorce. For years he'd tried to put the events of that dismal evening behind him. But the one thing he'd never been able to forget was this woman's stunning face and the desperate love he'd seen reflected in her expressive eyes.

Her face was still stunning, he noted. But her beauty was tempered now with worry and fatigue, the fine lines at the corners of her eyes and the dark smudges beneath them giving mute testimony to a life filled with unrelenting strain. Nor had her eyes lost their expressiveness—except that now they reflected disillusion and sadness instead of the love he remembered from that fateful night. Whatever burden she had carried for the past five years had clearly taken a tremendous toll on her, he concluded. She looked fragile. And achingly vulnerable. And very much alone. She seemed like a woman desperately in need of a shoulder to cry on or just a comforting hand to hold, he reflected, surprised—and disconcerted—by the unexpected surge of protectiveness that coursed through him.

Kate returned the doctor's stare, held by his compelling eyes. His gaze wasn't invasive or unfriendly—more like…unsettling. As if he knew something she didn't. Which was odd. They'd never met before, had they? she wondered, frowning slightly. Yet there *was* something familiar about him. But surely she would remember hair the color of sun-ripened wheat and eyes so intensely blue. Perhaps he just reminded her of someone from her past.

Eric realized that she didn't recognize him. Which wasn't surprising, in light of their traumatic ''meeting''—if it could even be called that. And maybe it was just as well, considering his odd reaction on seeing her again. She drew him in a strangely powerful, inexplicable way; and that scared him. His divorce from Cindy four and half years before had taught him very clearly that marriage and medicine didn't mix. Since then he'd steered clear of serious relationships. It was a rule he'd never broken. And he wasn't going to start now—with *any* woman. So, with an effort, he put his professional smile in place and held out his hand.

''Mrs. Nolan? I'm Eric Carlson.''

Kate found her fingers engulfed in a firm grip that somehow felt both capable and caring. "Hello, Doctor."

"And this must be Sarah." He squatted down beside the wary little girl, who was watching him solemnly, her eyes wide, as she clung to her mother. "Hello, Sarah. I'm Dr. Eric." When she didn't respond, he tried again. "You know, I have something in my office you might like to see when we're all finished. A big tank full of beautiful fish. What's your favorite color?"

"Pink."

"Well, I have a pink fish that has a bright blue tail. Would you like to see it later?"

Sarah studied him silently for a moment. "Are you going to give me a shot?"

Eric chuckled and glanced at Kate. "Nothing like cutting to the chase, is there?" Then he transferred his attention back to Sarah and shook his head. "Nope. No shots today. I promise. So how about letting me look in your ears and peek at your tonsils? And I'll let you listen to my heart if you let me listen to yours."

Sarah tipped her head and studied him for a moment before loosening her grip on Kate. "Okay."

"That's a girl." Eric reached over and picked her up, then settled her on the end of the table. From that point on, the exam proceeded smoothly. Eric even managed to elicit a giggle or two.

Kate watched in amazement, and her respect for Eric grew exponentially from minute to minute. He had a knack for putting children at ease, for making an exam fun, and she suspected that even on those occasions when he did have to give shots, he drew little protest from his patients. He had certainly befriended Sarah, Kate conceded. Her usually shy, reserved little girl was completely relaxed.

As he worked, Eric casually asked Kate a few astute, specific questions, never shifting his focus from Sarah. When he finished, he straightened and smiled down at his patient. "Now, that wasn't so bad, was it?"

Sarah shook her head. "It didn't hurt at all. I like you. He's nice, isn't he, Mommy?" she declared, looking over at Kate.

Kate cast an admiring glance at Eric. "Yes, honey, he sure is."

Eric felt his neck grow red at Kate's praise. Which was both odd and extremely unsettling. He never lost his cool with patients—or their mommies. To buy himself a moment to regain his composure, he lifted Sarah to the floor, then bent down to retrieve a wayward cotton ball.

Kate didn't know exactly what triggered the sudden flash of memory. Maybe it was Eric's motion of leaning so close to her, or the position of his body in conjunction with hers, or the way the overhead lighting suddenly drew out the burnished gold in his hair. But abruptly and with startling clarity she recalled another time, five years before, when this man had leaned over in exactly the same way as he'd worked on her critically injured husband in an icy wrecked car.

Her sudden gasp of recognition made Eric quickly straighten, and as their gazes met he realized that the odd link they shared was no longer a mystery to her. Her face had gone a shade paler, and he noted the sudden trembling of her fingers as her hand went to her throat.

Eric forced his gaze from hers and smiled at Sarah. "Are you ready to see that pink fish now?"

Oblivious to the sudden undertones in the room, the little girl nodded eagerly and turned to Kate. "It's all right, isn't it, Mommy?"

Somehow Kate found her voice. "Yes."

Eric took Sarah's hand and looked over at Kate discerningly. "I'll be back in a moment. Will you be okay?"

She nodded mutely, still trying to process the bizarre coincidence of today's encounter. When her own pediatrician had retired a few weeks ago, she'd simply selected the most conveniently located replacement from the list he'd provided. Eric Carlson—the man who'd saved Jack's life.

Kate had always meant to find out the name of the doctor who had stopped that night to help, intending to write him a heartfelt letter of thanks. But as the months had gone by she'd been so overwhelmed by all the other demands in her life that she had never followed through. And especially in light of the outcome, which had left her in a deep depression for almost a year. It had been all she could do after that, simply to cope. There were days even now when that was all she did—cope. But that was no excuse. This man deserved better from her, and the guilt had nagged at her for years.

Eric slipped back into the room then and shut the door before taking a seat across from Kate.

"I left Sarah in my office with one of my assistants. She'll keep her occupied until we're finished."

"You were the doctor at the accident, weren't you?" Kate said without preamble.

Eric seemed momentarily taken aback by her abrupt words, then he slowly nodded. "Yes. I recognized you the minute I came in the door."

"I never thanked you. I meant to."

He shrugged. "No thanks were necessary. I'm a doctor. That's my job."

She shook her head vehemently. "No. You didn't even have to stop, especially considering the weather. I don't remember much about that night. I had a slight concussion, and everything has always been a blur. But they told me you saved Jack's life. I always intended to find out your name and let you know I appreciated what you did."

He made a dismissive gesture. "I just opened an airway. It was enough to give him a fighting chance until he got to the hospital." He glanced briefly at her left hand, noted the ring, then proceeded carefully. "Your husband seemed to be badly hurt, Mrs. Nolan."

She swallowed and gave a brief nod of confirmation. "Yes. Two vertebrae in his neck were crushed and he had severe head injuries. At first they weren't sure if he'd even make it through the night. He was in a coma and I just lived hour by hour. But he held on somehow. And with every day that passed I grew more hopeful, despite the fact that the doctors didn't offer much encouragement. They said even if he came out of the coma, he would be paralyzed. That he'd never be the way he was before. But I was sure they were wrong. I had great faith in those days." There was an unmistakable trace of bitterness in her voice, but it was replaced by bleakness when she continued. "We never had a chance to find out, though. He died seven months later without ever regaining consciousness."

It was what Eric had feared. The desolate look in Kate's eyes, the slump of her shoulders, the catch in her voice, made his heart ache. "I'm sorry," he said helplessly, wishing he could take away her pain, offer some words of comfort. But he'd been through this before with other survivors, and he knew words did little to ease the burden of grief or the devastating sense of emptiness and loss that accompanied the death of a loved one. There was no way to make the absolute finality of that parting any less painful.

She blinked rapidly, and he saw the sheen of tears in her eyes. "Thank you. You'd think after four years I'd be able to handle it better than this, but...well, Jack and Sarah were my whole world. Sarah was only six weeks old when it happened, and we had so many plans, so much to look forward to...." Her voice trailed off and she sniffed, struggling for composure. At last she drew a shaky breath, and when she spoke her voice was choked and barely audible. "Everyone said I'd get over it. That life would go on and in time I'd feel back to normal. But you know, I don't think you ever get over it. You just get on with it."

Eric felt his throat tighten at the abject misery in Kate's eyes. "It takes a lot of courage just to do that," he told her gently, his own voice uneven.

She gave him a sad smile and shook her head. "It's kind of you to say that, Doctor. But it doesn't take courage to simply do what you have to do. Sarah needs me. Period. And I love her with all my heart. That's why these mysterious stomach pains have me so worried."

Eric couldn't change the tragedy that had brought Kate more than her share of heartache, but at least he could set her mind at ease about Sarah.

"Well, I don't think you need to worry, Mrs. Nolan. I can't find a thing wrong. She seems like a very healthy little girl."

"Then what's the problem?"

He toyed with his pencil for a moment, his face pensive. "Has there been any sort of trauma in her life recently?"

Kate nodded slowly as fresh tears sprang to her eyes. "Yes. My...my mother died very suddenly a month ago. She and Sarah were very close. We all were, actually. Sort of like The Three Musketeers."

Her voice quavered, and Eric's heart went out to her. She'd had so much loss. It didn't seem fair. He longed to ease her pain, but knew there was nothing he could do. Except listen.

Kate took a deep, shaky breath. "Anyway, Mom lived with us and watched Sarah for me during the school year while I was teaching. I had to find other day care for Sarah at the last minute, and she started a couple of weeks ago, right before I went back to school. It's been a big adjustment for her. For both of us, actually. You see, I always wanted to be home until she went to school. Jack and I had agreed on that. But of course things changed when he died. Having Mom watch her was the next best thing. Now… Well, I hate leaving her with strangers. Sarah is shy, and I'm afraid she may not be mixing well with the other children." Kate bit her lip, clearly distraught.

"You know, it sounds to me like her pains may be emotionally rather than physically triggered," Eric observed. "Coping with the loss of her grandmother was probably hard enough. Coupled with being thrust into a traditional day-care situation—well, it's a big adjustment. Are there any other options?"

Kate frowned and shook her head, her eyes deeply troubled. "This was the best I could do at the last minute. Most of the really good places are booked solid and have waiting lists a mile long." She dropped her head into her hands and drew a shuddering breath. "This isn't at all what I wanted for Sarah!"

Eric's throat tightened. For a brief moment he was overcome by a powerful urge to reach over and take her hand, to give her the reassurance of a caring touch that she seemed to need so desperately. He knew that she was stressed to the limit, torn between want and necessity. At this point he was actually more worried about *her* physical and emotional state than he was about Sarah's. Children had a way of adjusting. And Sarah had the security of Kate's love. But Kate was alone, with no one to share her burdens. Though his heart told him to reach out to her, in the end professional decorum prevailed and he refrained—with great effort.

"You're doing the best you can, Mrs. Nolan, under very difficult circumstances," he reassured her gently, his voice unusually husky. "Don't be too hard on yourself."

Kate looked into his eyes, and she felt strangely comforted by the kindness and compassion she saw there. She *was* trying to do her best, and it lifted her spirits ever-so-slightly to have someone recognize that.

"Thank you. But it's obviously not good enough. I want what's best for Sarah, Doctor. There has to be a better solution than this." She sighed and wearily ran her fingers through her shoulder-length hair. "I guess I'll just have to keep looking."

Eric stared at her bowed head, his face growing thoughtful as an idea suddenly took shape his mind. If he could pull it off, several problems would be solved, he realized. Sarah would have a more personal day-care situation. Kate's guilt would be eased. And Eric's mind would be relieved of a constant worry. It was a long shot, of course. And he didn't want to raise any expectations until he had a commitment. But it just might work.

"I'm sure you'll find the answer, Mrs. Nolan. And in the meantime, remember that children are more resilient than we think. You're clearly a caring, conscientious parent, and children know intuitively when they're loved. That makes a huge difference."

Kate looked at Eric, essentially a stranger to her despite their brief, traumatic encounter five years before. Yet he seemed to know exactly the right thing to say to relieve her mind. Maybe it was a knack he had with all worried mothers. But the caring in his eyes seemed genuine—and somehow personal. Which was silly, of course. She was just another case to him. But she appreciated his kindness nonetheless.

"You have a great bedside manner, Doctor. Even if I'm not the patient," she told him with a tremulous smile. "I feel much better."

He returned the smile, and she liked the way his eyes crinkled at the corners. "I'm glad. And let me know if Sarah is still having problems in a week or so. But I think she'll adjust, given time."

"I just wish there was another option," Kate said with a sigh.

Eric didn't comment as he stood and ushered her to the door. But he had a plan. And if everything went as he hoped, Kate's wish just might come true.

Anna Carlson's hand froze, the glass of orange juice halfway to her mouth, as she stared at her son over the plate of scrambled eggs.

"You want me to do what?"

Eric had known it wasn't going to be an easy sell. Ever since his father had died six months before, his mother had shut herself off from the world, struggling not only with grief over the passing of her lifelong companion but also with a sense of uselessness. A nurturer by disposition, she had found her meaning in life by caring for the men she loved—Eric when he was younger, and in recent years her husband, as failing health made him increasingly dependent. In fact, their already strong mutual devotion had seemed to intensify as Walter's physical condition weakened.

While some women would resent the demands of living with an ill spouse, Anna had never complained. As she'd told her son on more than one occasion, "Walter took care of us for a lot of years, Eric. He worked three jobs at once when you were a baby just to make ends meet. Nothing was too much trouble if it made life easier for the people he loved. How can I do any less now, when he needs me?"

Now, with his father gone and the demands of his practice keeping him too busy to give his mother as much time as he'd like, she was adrift. The inspired idea he'd had in the office a couple of days before had seemed like the perfect solution for everyone. His mother needed someone to take care of. Sarah needed someone to do just that. Kate needed the peace of mind that a good caregiver would provide. And he wanted to help his mother find new purpose in life. It was an ideal arrangement.

But from the way she was staring at him, one would think he'd suggested she take up skydiving.

"I'd like you to consider watching one of my patients five days a week during school hours while her mother teaches," he repeated evenly.

His mother set her glass down and continued to stare at him. "Why on earth would I what to do that?"

Eric mulled over his response while the server poured him a fresh cup of coffee and decided on the direct approach.

"She needs help, Mom."

Anna frowned at him. "Who? The mother or the little girl?"

"Both."

Even if she wasn't exactly receptive, he'd at least aroused her curiosity, Eric thought. His mother hadn't looked this interested in anything since before his father had died. Their after-church Sunday-morning breakfasts had become a ritual during the last six months. It was a time he reserved exclusively for her, but usually she was subdued and barely picked at her food. Today he'd managed to snap her out of her apathy, if only for a few moments.

In fact, as she studied him now, he began to grow slightly uncomfortable. He knew that look. It was one he remembered well from his growing-up years, when she was trying to figure out what was going on in his mind, what his motivation was. Her next question confirmed it.

"Eric, in all the years you've been a doctor, I've never seen you take such a personal interest in a patient. Is there something you're not telling me about this situation?"

He had to give her credit. She was as sharp and insightful as ever. He'd never told her about the accident, but he did so now, as briefly as possible and characteristically downplaying his role. She listened with interest, and when he'd finished she looked at him shrewdly.

"And your paths just suddenly crossed again two days ago?"

"Yes."

She pondered that for a moment. "It seems odd, doesn't it?"

"Very."

"Even so, there's really no reason for you to get involved in this woman's life, is there? You must meet a lot of parents who are facing similar dilemmas."

He couldn't argue with that. Broken families, single-parent households, stepchildren—and the many problems they entailed—he'd seen it all. And he'd never before been tempted to intervene personally. At least not to this extent. His mother was right. There wasn't any reason to get involved in Kate Nolan's life. Except maybe one: he wanted to. And at the moment he wasn't inclined to analyze his motivation.

"Let's just say that I think it would be the Christian thing to do," he replied noncommittally. "You have the time. She has the need. It's the right combination of circumstances at the right time. There's nothing more to it than that."

His mother looked skeptical, but she didn't belabor the point. Instead she glanced down at her plate and poked at her scrambled eggs, a thoughtful frown on her face. Eric waited quietly, praying that she'd at least give this a chance. It would be as good for her as it would be for Kate and Sarah.

When at last she met his gaze, her own was still uncertain. "I don't know, Eric. It's a big responsibility. And they're strangers to me. What if we don't even like each other?"

"You'll like them, Mom. I guarantee it. And they'll love you. Sarah misses her grandmother, and I can't think of a better surrogate. You were made for that role."

And this was the only chance she would have to play it. The unspoken words hung in the air between them. Eric's marriage had produced no children, much to his regret. And there wouldn't be another. He had made his peace with that. Anna never had. She thought he needed a wife, and she occasionally dropped broad hints to that effect when the opportunity presented itself. As she did now.

"I haven't given up on having a real grandchild, you know," she said pointedly.

"It's time you did."

"You're only thirty-eight, Eric. It's not too late to have a family."

"Mom." There was a warning note in his voice, which Anna ignored.

"Of course, you'd need a wife first."

"I have a wife."

"You've been divorced for almost five years, Eric."

"You know how I feel about that."

Anna sighed and glanced at the wedding band on his left hand. "Yes, I guess I do."

Eric knew that most people considered divorce a perfectly acceptable solution for a troubled union, that they found his attitude archaic. As did even his mother, who didn't take divorce lightly. But he believed in the sanctity of marriage; believed that the vows so solemnly taken were for life. He and Cindy might be divorced on paper, but in the eyes of God he believed they were still man and wife. Even Cindy's remarriage three years before hadn't convinced him otherwise. He wasn't going to judge her. He left that to the Lord. But it wasn't the right thing for him. Besides, his dedication to his career had ruined one marriage. He wasn't about to inflict that burden on another woman. In the meantime, they'd wandered far from the subject at hand.

"None of this has any bearing on our discussion, Mom," he pointed out. "If you're worried about whether you'll all get along, then how about this—I'll call Kate Nolan, and if she's interested I'll arrange for her to stop by and visit you. That way, the two of you can size each other up and you can meet Sarah. How does that sound?"

Anna nodded slowly. "I suppose I could consider it. But I'm not making any promises, Eric."

"I don't expect you to."

"I do feel sorry for her, though. So many burdens on someone so young. How old did you say Sarah was when the accident happened?"

"Six weeks."

His mother shook her head. "I can't even imagine. It's enough of a challenge for two people to raise a child. But for a single working mother... And then to lose her own mother so recently. She really does sound like she needs help, Eric."

"She does. She's been living under tremendous strain for years. I'd say she's approaching the danger level on the stress scale."

"Well, I suppose I could meet her, at least. Maybe help her out until she finds someone to take over permanently."

Eric felt the tension in his shoulders ease. "I know she'd appreciate it, Mom."

"This is all contingent on whether we get along, though," his mother cautioned.

"You'll get along fine."

"How can you be so sure?"

"Because I know you."

"But you don't know Kate Nolan. You just met her."

"Let's just call it intuition."

Eric was relieved that his mother seemed to accept that response. Even it if wasn't quite true. Because, odd as it seemed, he felt as if he *did* know Kate Nolan. But he couldn't very well tell his mother that. She would jump to all sorts of conclusions—all of them wrong, of course.

Weren't they?

# Chapter Two

Kate pulled to a stop in front of the small, tidy brick bungalow and took a slow, steadying breath. She still wasn't sure how all this had come about.

Two days ago, when Eric Carlson had called to check on Sarah, Kate had been impressed by his conscientiousness. No doctor she'd seen before had ever personally followed up with a phone call after an office visit. She'd hardly recovered from that pleasant surprise when he'd gone on to say that he might have a solution to her day-care problem. To put it mildly, she'd been overwhelmed.

Even now, it was difficult to believe that he had gone to so much trouble, especially for a new patient. And by enlisting the aid of his own mother, no less! Of course, the way he'd carefully explained it to Kate, she'd be doing *him* a favor if this all worked out. Apparently his mother had been quite despondent since the death of Eric's father, and he was convinced that if she had someone to nurture—namely Sarah—she'd regain some sense of purpose in life.

He might be right, Kate mused. Feeling needed did wonders to help one through the day. But as far as she was concerned, *she* was the one who had the most to gain from this arrangement. Of course, Kate had to feel comfortable with Eric's mother. That was imperative. But almost anything would be an improvement over her current arrangement. Besides, she was sure the woman's character would be impeccable. If she had raised a man as fine as Eric seemed to be, how could she be anything less than stellar?

The stifling heat and humidity of the St. Louis summer slammed against Kate with a force that almost took her breath away as she stepped out of the car. It was a bit late in the season for such sauna-like conditions, but then again, in St. Louis you never knew. It was too bad the weather had decided to act up today, though. The class-rooms at the school where she taught weren't air-conditioned, and she felt totally wilted and drained. On top of everything else, Sarah was cranky after another obviously unpleasant day at the day-care center—not the best time to make a good first impression, Kate thought ruefully. But it was too late to change the appointment now.

"Come on, honey, it will be cool in the house," she told Sarah encouragingly as she unbuckled her daughter's seat belt, then reached for her hand.

"I want to go home," Sarah whimpered, holding back.

"I know, honey. So do I. But I promised Dr. Eric we'd stop and visit his mommy. She's lonesome here all by herself. And we wouldn't want to break our promise to Dr. Eric, would we?"

Sarah wasn't in the mood for logic—or guilt trips.

"I don't want to," she declared stubbornly.

Kate's head began to pound. "We won't stay long. But I promised Dr. Eric. We have to go in," she told Sarah, struggling to keep her voice calm as she gently but firmly pulled her protesting daughter from the car.

"I don't want to!" Sarah wailed, resisting Kate's efforts.

"Sarah! Stop whining!" she ordered sharply, her patience evaporating. "We're going to go in. Now. And we'll be done a lot faster if you cooperate."

Sarah was still whimpering miserably as they made their way up the brick walkway. Despite her terse tone of moments before, Kate could empathize. She was so wrung out from the heat and the stress of the last few weeks that she felt like doing exactly the same thing. Instead, she forced herself to pay attention to her surroundings. She noted the large trees and fenced backyard—a perfect place for a child, she reflected appreciatively. Lots of shade and plenty of room to run and play. And Eric's mother lived just ten minutes away from her apartment. If only things would work out! She needed a few breaks—desperately. So did Sarah.

As a result, for the first time in a very long while, Kate made a request of the Lord. For Sarah's sake. She'd stopped praying for herself long ago, when He'd ignored her entreaties and abandoned her. But maybe He'd listen on behalf of a child. *Let this work out,* she pleaded silently. *I want what's best for Sarah, and I don't know where else to turn.*

As Kate pressed the doorbell, she glanced down at her daughter. Sarah still looked hot and unhappy and ill-tempered. Kate just hoped that once inside, where it was cool, she'd settle down and give Eric's mother a glimpse of the charming little girl she usually was.

The door was pulled open almost immediately, leaving Kate to wonder if the older woman had been hovering on the inside of the door as anxiously as she was standing on the outside. For a moment they looked at each other, each rapidly taking inventory. Eric looked nothing like his mother, Kate noted immediately. This woman's hair was mostly gray, though traces of faded auburn revealed its original color—a contrast to Eric's gold blond. While Eric was tall—at least six feet—his mother was of moderate height. Five-five at the most, in heels, Kate estimated. And Eric had a trim, athletic build, while his mother was softly rounded. But she had a nice face, Kate decided. And her eyes were kind.

"You must be Kate," Anna said at last, her initial polite smile softening into true warmth.

"Yes. And this is Sarah."

Anna looked down at the little girl who eyed her warily.

"My! You're much more grown-up than I expected. I'm so glad you and your mommy decided to visit me today. It's always nice to make new friends, isn't it? Why don't you both come in before you melt and we'll have something cold to drink."

She moved aside, and Kate stepped into the welcome coolness.

"Oh, it feels wonderful in here!" she exclaimed with a sigh.

"It sure is a hot one out there today," Anna commiserated as she led the way into the living room. "Eric tells me you teach. I certainly hope the school is air-conditioned."

Kate made a wry face. "No such luck. But I'll survive. This heat can't last forever."

"Well, let me get you both something to perk you up." She looked at Sarah, who sat quietly close beside Kate on the couch. "Now, I'll just bet you're the kind of girl who likes ice cream. Am

I right?'' Sarah nodded. ''That's what I thought. Let me see—chocolate chip, that would be my guess.''

Sarah's eyes grew wide. ''That's my favorite.''

''Mine, too. How about a nice big bowl to help you cool off? That is, if it's okay with your mother.'' She glanced at Kate, who smiled and nodded. ''Good. I'll just run out to the kitchen and get it ready. Would you like to come, too? I have a parakeet you might like to meet.''

Sarah looked at her curiously. ''What's a para—parakeet?''

''Why, it's the most beautiful bird! Sometimes he even talks. His name is George. Would you like to see him?'' Sarah nodded, and when Anna held out her hand the little girl took it shyly. The older woman looked over at Kate. ''I'll get Sarah settled in the kitchen with her ice cream, and then we can have a little chat. Would you like some iced tea?''

''I'd love some,'' Kate replied gratefully. ''Thank you.''

Kate watched them leave. It must run in the family, this ability to make friends so easily with children, she marveled. Eric certainly had the gift. And now she knew where he got it. She listened to the animated chatter coming from the kitchen, and took a moment to look around the living room. It was a cozy space, neat as a pin but not too fussy. The furniture was comfortable and overstuffed—made for sitting in, not just looking at. Fresh flowers stood in a vase on the coffee table, and family photos were artfully arranged on the mantel.

Kate's gaze lingered on the pictures, and she rose and moved closer to examine them. She started at one end, with a black-and-white wedding photo—probably Anna and her husband, Kate speculated. Then came a picture of the same couple cutting a twenty-fifth-anniversary cake. Eric's father looked like a nice man, Kate reflected. And it was clear now where Eric got his looks. His father was tall, dignified, blond and blue-eyed—in other words, an older version of Eric.

But it wasn't photos of Anna and her husband that dominated the mantel. It was pictures of their son. Eric as a baby. Eric in a cub-scout uniform. Eric in a cap and gown, flanked by his proud parents. Eric with his parents again, in a shot of more recent vintage, taken on the deck of a cruise ship. And on the wall next to the mantel, a framed newspaper clipping about Eric having been named Man of the Year by a local charitable organization. Clearly, he was his parents' pride and joy.

But there was something missing from this gallery, Kate suddenly realized. Eric wore a wedding band. She remembered noticing it in the office, when he'd been playing with his pen. But there was nothing here to indicate that he had a wife, or a family. Or that he ever had. Curious.

Just then Anna returned, and Kate turned guiltily from the mantel, her face flushed. "I hope you don't mind. I was admiring your pictures."

"Not at all," Anna assured her as she deposited a tray holding iced tea and a plate of cookies on the coffee table. "That's what they're there for. Now, I think we can relax and have a chat. Sarah is trying to get George to talk, and I also left her with some crayons and paper and asked her to draw me some pictures of him. That should keep her busy for a few minutes, anyway."

"You and your son both have a way with children," Kate said as a compliment to her as she returned to her seat.

"Well, it's not hard with a lovely little girl like that."

Kate grinned. "She wasn't so lovely a few minutes ago. I practically had to drag her in here. I figured you'd take one look and say, 'No way.' I think she had a rough day at day care." Her smile quickly faded.

"I guess that's what we're here to talk about," Anna replied. "Eric tells me that your mother used to watch her, until she passed away a month ago. I'm so very sorry about that, my dear. The loss of a mother is one of life's greatest trials."

The sincere sympathy in the older woman's voice brought a lump to Kate's throat, and she struggled to contain her tears. With all the turmoil since her mother's death—the disruption in the placid routine of their days, her worry about how Sarah was handling the death, and the necessity of making last-minute arrangements for her daughter's care—she'd had little time to grieve. But the ache of loss was heavy in her heart.

"Thank you. Mom and I were always close, but during these last few years since she came to live with us we forged an even stronger bond. My dad died about eight years ago, and Mom sold the farm in Ohio where we grew up and moved to an apartment in Cincinnati. She came to help out while Jack—my husband—was in the hospital, and when he died, she just stayed on. It was the best possible arrangement for all of us under the circumstances.''

"You must miss her very much."

Kate nodded. The loneliness of her life had been thrown into stark relief by the death of her mother. Even her weekly phone calls to her sister didn't ease her sense of isolation.

"It was hard enough when Jack died. But Mom was there for me to lean on. Now... Well, it's just me. And Sarah, of course. She's such a joy to me. A lifeline, really. Even more precious because we never thought she'd happen. My husband and I tried for five years before we had her. We'd almost given up when we discovered I was pregnant. And we both agreed that I'd stay home at least until she went to school. We were firm believers that mothering is a full-time job.''

Anna nodded approvingly. "I often think young mothers today make a mistake when they try to have it all. Not that you can't, of course. I just don't think you can have it all at the same time. 'To everything there is a season.' And children need full-time mothers, unless there are extraordinary circumstances.''

"I agree completely. But as it turned out, I was faced with those extraordinary circumstances. I guess Eric told you what happened."

"He filled me in on the basics. I understand you lost your husband shortly after Sarah was born.''

Kate nodded. "It was a nightmare. The accident happened on our first night out together since Sarah was born. We'd had an early dinner to celebrate our sixth anniversary.''

"Oh, my dear! I had no idea. How awful!'' Anna's face registered shock and sympathy.

"Unfortunately, the worst was still to come,'' Kate continued, her voice flat and lifeless. "Jack lived for seven months, but he never regained consciousness. By the time he died our finances were pretty much depleted. Long-term care is very expensive, and insurance doesn't cover everything. So I went back to teaching, sold our house and moved into an apartment. We've coped till now, but when Mom died, everything just fell apart again.'' Her voice caught on the last word, and she paused to take a deep breath, struggling to keep her tears at bay. Her voice was shaky when she continued. "I just can't bear to see Sarah so unhappy. That's why I'm desperate to find a more personal, one-on-one day-care situation. Someone who can give her the love and affection and attention that I would give her if I could be there. I guess your son thought you might be willing to pinch-hit, at least until I can find something more permanent. I'm hoping the same thing," she admitted frankly.

Anna carefully set her iced-tea glass on a coaster and looked at Kate, her face concerned. "I'd like to help you, my dear. But you do understand that I'm not experienced in day care, don't you?"

Kate smiled. "You're a mother. And you raised a fine son, from what I can see. You seem kind and caring. And Sarah seems to have taken to you. Those are good enough credentials for me." Kate had decided after five minutes in her presence that Anna was the answer to her prayer.

"Well, as Eric told me, this might be my one and only chance to play grandmother," the older woman reflected. "And I would enjoy that."

Kate looked at her curiously. "What do you mean?"

"Eric's divorced. Has been for almost five years. He and Cindy never had any children. Pity, too, when he loves children so much."

"But he might remarry."

Anna shook her head sadly. "Not Eric. So perhaps I'd best take my opportunity."

Kate was curious about Anna's enigmatic comment regarding Eric, but her attention was focused on the woman's second statement. She looked at her hopefully, her own heart banging painfully in her chest. "Does that mean you'll watch Sarah?"

Anna nodded. "At least for a while. Just tell me what kind of schedule you're thinking about."

Within ten minutes the details were settled, and Kate looked across at Anna. "I can't ever thank you enough for this, Mrs. Carlson. I feel like such a great burden has been lifted from my mind."

"First of all, it's Anna. And I'm glad I can help you with this. It seems like you've had far too many trials for someone so young."

"I don't feel very young these days," Kate admitted wearily. "I may only be thirty-six, but sometimes I feel ancient."

Suddenly Sarah burst into the room to proudly show off her drawings of George. As Anna exclaimed over them, Kate settled back with her iced tea. Once upon a time, Eric had saved her husband's life. In many ways, Kate felt he had just now saved hers. And in her heart she knew that she owed him a debt of gratitude she could never even begin to repay.

"So what happened?"

"I'm fine, thanks. How are you?" Anna's amused voice came over the wire.

"Sorry," Eric apologized sheepishly. "It's just that I've had your meeting with Mrs. Nolan on my mind all afternoon, and this is the first chance I've had to call."

"It's seven-thirty. It must have been a busy day."

"It was. I had an emergency at the hospital that delayed me."

He heard her exasperated sigh. "You work too hard, Eric. Especially since the divorce. I admire your dedication, but you need to have a life, too."

They'd been over this before—countless times. After Cindy had left and he'd decided that marriage and medicine didn't mix, he'd immersed himself in his work to the exclusion of just about everything else. He knew it wasn't healthy. He knew he needed to back off from some of his commitments, resign from a couple of the boards he was on, give some serious thought to his partner's suggestion that they bring another doctor into their practice. And he'd get around to all those things one of these days. In the meantime, he was more worried about the stress level of one beautiful-but-sad mother and her little girl.

"You're changing the subject, Mom."

"Well, I worry about you."

"Worry about Mrs. Nolan and Sarah instead. They need it more than I do."

She sighed again. "Yes, I think you're right. Oh, Eric, the minute I opened the door and looked at them, my heart just about broke. Sarah is such a precious, sensitive child. I can see where she'd feel lost in one of those big day-care centers. And Kate… Oh, dear, that poor woman. What a tragic story! And to have that accident happen on her wedding anniversary—I can't even imagine the horror. Anyway, she looked so lost and alone, standing there on the porch. And so tired and anxious. I just wanted to hug her.''

Eric could relate to that. He'd felt exactly the same way. "So you agreed to watch Sarah?''

"How could I refuse? As you said, it just seemed like the Christian thing to do. Besides, I liked them both. It won't be a hardship.''

"When do you start?''

"Tomorrow.''

Eric's eyebrows rose in surprise. "Pretty fast action.''

"Why wait? I don't have anything planned, and Kate can't get her daughter out of that place fast enough. Of course, I had to run to the store and pick up a few things. Peanut butter and jelly, ingredients for my sugar cookies, some coloring books and Play-Doh. You know, that kind of thing. I'm not used to entertaining a child.''

There was a new energy in his mother's voice, an enthusiasm that Eric hadn't heard in months. Apparently his instinct that this arrangement would be good for everyone had been right on target, he thought with satisfaction.

"Do you need me to do anything?''

"No. I have it all under control, thanks.''

"Well, I'll see you Sunday, then. And good luck.''

"Thanks. I think things will work out just fine.''

So did Eric. He was happy for his mother and Kate and Sarah— and strangely enough, for himself, as well. He wasn't quite sure why. Perhaps because now he could stop worrying so much about his mother. He could use some peace of mind on that score.

But there were other things about this arrangement that *weren't* conducive to peace of mind, he suddenly realized. Such as the link it provided with Kate Nolan. For reasons he preferred to leave unexplored, he didn't think that would necessarily lead to mental serenity.

"You know, one of these days I'm going to stop inviting you, since you never come, but Mary said I should try one more time. So…barbecue, Labor Day, five o'clock. What's your excuse this time?''

Eric slid the chart back into the folder and grinned at his partner. Frank Shapiro seemed the complete opposite of his colleague. Six inches shorter, with close-cropped, thinning brown hair and a wiry build, Frank exuded high energy in contrast to Eric's calm demeanor. While Frank was an outgoing extrovert, Eric stayed more to himself. But as they'd discovered during their residency together, in every other way—philosophical, ethical, political, religious—they were a good match. Their partnership had flourished, and Eric had only one complaint. Since his divorce, Frank had been unrelenting in his attempts to spice up Eric's practically nonexistent social life. Eric had always deflected his efforts, but he suddenly decided to throw his friend a curve.

"No excuse. I'll be there."

Frank stared at him. "What?"

"I said I'll come."

Frank tilted his head and looked at Eric suspiciously. "Are you serious?"

"Uh-huh."

"Well...gosh, that's great! Wait till I tell Mary our persistence finally paid off."

"Can I bring anything?"

"No, thanks. Except a date, that is." Frank grinned.

Eric grinned back. His friend was joking, of course. Frank knew he never dated. But suddenly Eric thought of Kate Nolan, and his expression grew thoughtful. He suspected she had even less of a social life than he did; that she rarely, if ever, allowed herself a night out, and that there was very little laughter and lightheartedness in her world. Not much of a life for a young, vital woman. Maybe he ought to ask her.

Eric frowned. Now where had that idea come from? What about his rule of keeping personal involvements at arm's length? Exceptions weren't a good idea, he told himself firmly. And yet, for some reason, ever since Kate had walked into his office he'd felt a sense of...*responsibility*—that was the word—for her. He couldn't explain it. Didn't even try. It was just there. And it nudged him to invite her. Just as a friend, of course. It would be an act of charity. Nothing more.

He laid the folder on the counter and purposely kept his tone casual. "I just might do that."

The look of surprise on Frank's face was almost comical. He stared at his partner for several seconds before he found his voice.

"Well...that's great!" He clearly wanted to ask more, but for once he seemed momentarily at a loss for words. And Eric didn't give him a chance to recover.

"On to the next patient," he declared, picking up a chart. As he walked away he could sense Frank staring after him, the dumbfounded look still on his face. And Eric couldn't help grinning. Everyone figured he was so predictable. Well, maybe it was time he started surprising a few people.

Then again, maybe it wasn't, Eric ruminated glumly as he stared at the phone in his office on Friday evening. The party was only three days away, and he still hadn't summoned up the courage to call Kate Nolan. What on earth had prompted him to make that impetuous remark to Frank? He should have been content with Frank's initial surprise when he'd accepted the invitation. There had been no need for overkill, he chastised himself.

And now he was stuck. Frank expected him to show up with a date in tow, and he'd never hear the end of it if he didn't. His partner would badger him about the "mystery" woman he'd "almost" brought. Even worse, thinking he was now willing to date, Frank would renew his efforts to set his friend up, much as he had—relentlessly—for a year or two after the divorce. Eric closed his eyes and groaned. He loved Frank. Like a brother. But not when he played matchmaker. No, he had to show up with someone. And Kate Nolan was the only option.

Besides, there were altruistic reasons for this invitation, he rationalized. Kate seemed to lead far too solitary a life. As far as he could see, she only had Sarah. The little girl was a charmer, he acknowledged, and she seemed to adequately fulfill her mother's nurturing needs. But what about Kate's other needs? Despite the tragedy that had taken the man she loved, she still needed adult companionship. And adult conversation. And someone who cared when she had a cold or a taxing day, who worried when she worked too hard or didn't eat right. He was certain those needs weren't being met. Inviting her to go with him to Frank's party wasn't a solution—but it might be a step toward a more normal, balanced life for her.

Feeling more confident, he picked up the phone and dialed her number, tapping his pen restlessly against the desk as he waited. When she answered, three rings later and out of breath, his hand stilled.

"Mrs. Nolan? It's Eric Carlson." That was odd. He sounded as breathless as she did.

There was a momentary pause, and he could sense her surprise, could imagine the look of astonishment on her face. His assessment of her reaction was confirmed by her tone of voice when she spoke.

"Hello, Doctor." He heard her draw a deep breath. "I was just opening the door when the phone rang. I had to run to answer it." *And why are you calling me?* The question, though unasked, hung in the air.

"I wanted to thank you for the note you sent me." She'd written him a warm, heartfelt letter after Anna had agreed to watch Sarah, and it suddenly seemed like a good way to open the conversation.

"Oh. You're welcome. I was very grateful for everything you did."

"I'm just glad it worked out. Mom seems much more like her old self, even though it's only been a week."

"Well, speaking for Sarah, this seems like a match made in heaven. She and your mom hit it off right from the beginning. Her morning tune has changed from 'Do I have to go?' to 'Hurry up, Mom. We'll be late for Aunt Anna's.' In fact, I'm not sure how she'll manage away from your mom for three whole days over the Labor Day holiday."

That gave him the opening he needed. "Maybe she doesn't have to."

He could hear the frown in Kate's voice. "What do you mean?"

Eric took a deep breath and willed his racing pulse to slow down. You'd think he'd never asked a woman out before, he thought with chagrin. And this wasn't even a real date, anyway.

"Well, I know this is a bit last-minute, but I was wondering if you were free Monday. My partner is having a barbecue, and I thought it might be a nice change of pace for you, after the stress of the last few weeks. And I could use a break myself."

Her stunned silence conveyed her reaction more eloquently than words. Well, what did he expect? he asked himself wryly. After all, they barely knew each other. In her position he'd probably react the same way. And he'd likely decline. So before she could do so, he spoke again, playing his trump card.

"I'm sure you're surprised by the invitation, but to be honest, you'd do me a real favor if you'd accept. Frank is a great guy, but he's always trying to fix me up and I'd like to avoid that. I'm just not interested in dating, and I can't seem to convince him of that. I usually turn down his invitations, but I figured if I came to one of his parties with a date, he might decide I could take care of my own social life after all and would lay off."

Kate stared at the phone, a frown marring her brow, her refusal dying on her lips. She wasn't in the dating mode and never would be again. What was the point, when she'd already had the best? That kind of love only came around once in a lifetime. Though Jack might be gone in body, she'd never let him go in her heart. He was her husband. He was Sarah's father. And no one could take his place. Ever. Period. She'd never even looked at another man since his death, let alone dated one. And she saw no reason to start now.

But then Eric had added that caveat: that she'd be doing him a favor by saving him from the well-meaning-but-unwanted match-making efforts of his friend. Then he'd gone on to say that he wasn't interested in dating, either. His mother had implied the same thing at their first meeting, Kate recalled. And she owed him—big time, after what he'd done to help her resolve her day-care dilemma. So what would be the harm in accepting his invitation? Nothing that she could articulate. Yet somehow it didn't feel quite right. The notion of spending an evening in Eric's company made her...uneasy.

As the silence lengthened, Kate realized she had to say something. And honesty seemed the best approach. "I don't know, Doctor," she replied frankly, toying with the phone cord as she spoke. "I try to spend all my free time with Sarah. And I'd have to find someone to watch her."

"That's where Mom comes in. She'd be happy to look after Sarah."

"You mean…you already asked your mother?" She was clearly taken aback.

"Uh-huh." He'd checked with her before he'd called Kate, wanting to remove any potential stumbling blocks in advance.

"Oh. Well, wasn't she…surprised?"

"Actually, no." Which had surprised *him.* He'd expected to be plied with questions when he'd made the request. Instead, his mother had simply said, "No problem." And frankly, that had made him a little nervous. It wasn't like her. But instead of pressing his luck, he'd simply said thanks and ended the conversation as soon as possible, before she slipped back into character and launched into the third degree.

"Oh." Kate was starting to sound like George, who had a tendency to repeat the same words over and over again, she realized. "Well, I do have school the next day."

"We can make it an early night."

It was getting harder and harder to think of excuses. Eric was being absolutely cooperative and understanding. How could she say no? With a sigh, Kate capitulated. "All right, Doctor. If it will help you out."

He closed his eyes and let out a long, slow breath. When he spoke again, she heard the teasing tone in his voice.

"There's just one thing."

"What?"

"I don't think this is going to work too well if you call me 'Doctor.' Frank might smell a rat, don't you think?"

Kate found herself smiling. "You could be right."

"So…how about if we switch to Eric and Kate?"

"I just hope I don't forget. I'm used to thinking of you as 'Doctor.'"

"I may have the same problem. Be sure to elbow me if I call you Mrs. Nolan."

But he wouldn't. Because oddly enough, since the moment she'd walked into his office she'd been "Kate" to him. In fact, he'd had to remind himself to call her "Mrs. Nolan." So this switch would be no problem at all.

"All right, Doct— Eric," she corrected herself.

They settled on a time, and as Eric replaced the receiver and leaned back in his chair, he experienced an odd combination of emotions. Relief. Satisfaction. Anticipation. Uncertainty. And last, but certainly not least, guilt.

He frowned over that last one. Why did he suddenly have this niggling sensation of guilt? He wasn't doing anything wrong. Professional ethics kept doctors from dating patients, but he knew of no such sanction against *mommies* of patients. And he hadn't exerted too much pressure on Kate. If she'd resisted too much, he would have backed off. The last thing she needed in her life was more stress. Finally, while it was true that he refrained from dating because he believed that in the eyes of the Lord he was still married, this wasn't a real date.

So why did he feel guilty? After all, he was doing this for her. Out of compassion. As a friend. He felt sorry for her. It was as simple as that.

Or was it? he asked himself. Because if his motives were so noble and unselfish, if he was only thinking of *her,* why was *he* looking forward to the barbecue so much?

# Chapter Three

Kate glanced in the mirror behind her bedroom door and absently adjusted the strap on her sundress. She'd been so taken aback by Dr. Carlson's—Eric's, she reminded herself—invitation that she hadn't thought to ask about attire. Was she too dressed up? What did people wear to a barbecue these days? It had been years since she'd been to one. To any purely social function, in fact. It actually felt odd to be dressing up for a night out. Odd—and a little uncomfortable.

Kate frowned. Even though Eric had made it clear that this wasn't a date, it had all the trappings of one. And that made her conscience twinge, as if she were somehow cheating on Jack. Which was ridiculous, of course. She loved Jack absolutely, with a devotion that was undimmed by the years. She was simply doing a favor for someone who had gone out of his way to be kind to her. There was no reason to feel guilty, she admonished herself sternly.

Resolutely she picked up her purse and stepped into the hall. Sarah glanced up from her perch on the couch and smiled as Kate approached.

"You look pretty, Mommy."

"Thanks, honey."

"I wish I could go to the party, too."

Kate's heart contracted and she sat down beside Sarah. She already felt incredibly guilty about leaving her daughter with a sitter—even if it *was* Anna—on a weekend, and Sarah's innocent comment was enough to send a pang through her heart. For just a moment she was tempted to back out on Eric. But she owed him this, she reminded herself. Just as she owed Sarah as much time as possible on her days off to make up for all the hours during the week when they had to be apart. It was a perennial dilemma, this conflict between her daughter's needs and other obligations. But she *had* promised Eric. And Sarah would be fine for one night with Anna, she assured herself.

"I wish you could, too, honey. But it's a grown-up party. And when Dr. Eric asked me to go with him I thought I should, since he was so nice to us. If it wasn't for Dr. Eric, we would never have met Aunt Anna," Kate reminded her, using the affectionate title for the older woman that she and Anna had decided upon.

"I like Aunt Anna," Sarah declared. "She said we would make cookies tonight and watch *Mary Poppins*. Have you seen that movie, Mommy?"

"Uh-huh. You'll like it. And I might even be back before it's over."

The doorbell rang, and Kate reached over to give Sarah a quick hug. "That's Dr. Eric now. Run and get your sweater and then we'll take you over to Aunt Anna's."

As Sarah scampered toward her bedroom, Kate rose and walked slowly to the door. She still felt ill at ease, but she tried to suppress her nervousness. After all, Eric seemed like a nice man. He wasn't looking for anything more than companionship. And she *had* been a pretty good conversationalist at one time, even if her skills were a bit rusty. Maybe she'd even have fun, she told herself encouragingly. But she knew that possibility was remote. Fun didn't play much of a role in her life these days. She reached for the knob and sighed. Wouldn't it be nice, though, if—

The sight of Eric's broad shoulders filling her doorway cut off her thought in mid-sentence and her polite smile of welcome froze on her face. He looked different today, she thought inanely, her lips parting slightly in surprise as she stared at him. More…human. And he exuded a virility that had been camouflaged beneath his clinical demeanor, white coat and stethoscope during their last encounter in his office. At work he looked professional and slightly remote, and his role was clear. In his present attire—khaki trousers and a cobalt-blue golf shirt that hugged his muscular chest and matched the color of his eyes—he seemed to be playing a much less precisely defined role. It was an unsettling and intimidating change. Yet his eyes—warm and genuine and straightforward, even while reflecting some other emotion she couldn't quite put her finger on—helped to calm her jitters.

Eric watched the play of emotions on Kate's face as he struggled to control his own expression. Her smile of welcome had faded to a look of surprise, and her slightly parted lips, along with the pulse that began to beat in the delicate hollow of her throat, clearly communicated her nervousness. She looked vulnerable and scared…and very, very appealing, he thought, as his heart stopped, then raced on. By anyone's definition, her simple sundress was modest, hinting at—rather than revealing—her curves. But the white piqué was a perfect foil for her dark hair and eyes. She wore a delicate gold chain at her neck, and his eyes lingered for a moment on the spot where it rested against the creamy skin at the edge of her collarbone.

Eric swallowed past the sudden lump in his throat, fighting a swift—and disconcerting—surge of panic. Until this moment he'd felt somehow insulated from Kate's beauty, gentle manner and earnest efforts to do the right thing for her daughter. He'd admired her, but he'd felt in control and able to keep a safe emotional distance. Suddenly he didn't feel at all in control. Or safe. Or distant.

But that wasn't *her* problem, he reminded himself. He'd just have to deal with his own surprising reaction later. Right now he needed to make her relax. And that would be no small chore, he realized. The pulsating shimmer of her gold chain clearly suggested accelerated respiration, indicating that she was as nervous about this setup as he suddenly was. Not a good sign.

Deliberately he tipped his lips up into a smile, and when he spoke his voice was warm and friendly—but purposely not *too* friendly. "Hello, Kate. I…"

"Hi, Dr. Eric." Sarah burst into the room, dragging her sweater by one sleeve.

He grinned at Kate as Sarah's exuberant entrance dissipated the tension in the room, then he squatted down beside his small patient and touched her nose. "Hello, Sarah. Are you still having those tummyaches?"

"No. They're all gone. You must be a very good doctor."

He chuckled. "I think maybe Dr. Anna can take the credit for your cure."

Sarah gave him a puzzled look. "Is Aunt Anna a doctor, too?"

He smiled. "In some ways. She always used to make me feel better after I fell off my bike and scraped my knees."

"I like her," Sarah declared.

"So do I."

"We're going to make cookies tonight and watch *Mary Poppins.*"

"Now that sounds like fun."

"You can come, too," Sarah offered.

"I'd like to. But I promised my friend I'd come to his party. Maybe we can watch a movie together sometime, though."

"Can Mommy watch, too?"

Eric glanced up at Kate apologetically, realizing he'd put her in an awkward position. "Sure. If she wants to."

"Oh, Mommy likes movies. Don't you, Mommy?"

Kate didn't answer. Instead, she picked up her purse. "Shouldn't we be leaving? I promised Sarah I wouldn't be gone too long, and it's getting late."

He rose slowly, aware that she was laying out the ground rules for tonight. Clearly, it was going to be a short evening. Still, it was better than nothing, he consoled himself. Even a couple of hours in the company of adults, where she could laugh and relax, might help chase the haunted look from her eyes.

"Yes, we should."

As he turned toward the door the phone rang, and Kate hesitated. Then she sighed. "I'd better get it. It will only take a minute."

"No rush."

Although Sarah's chatter kept him occupied during Kate's absence, Eric took the opportunity to glance around her modest apartment. There was a small living room, a tiny kitchenette with a counter that served as a dining table, and—judging by the three doors opening off the short hallway—apparently two bedrooms and a bath. The unit was barely large enough for two people, let alone three, he concluded with a frown. How had they managed in such a confined space when her mother was alive?

Apparently there'd been no choice. His mother had mentioned

Kate's comment about her finances being depleted, and this tiny, older apartment was eloquent testimony to a tight budget. Yet she'd made it a home, he realized, noting with appreciation the warm touches that gave the rooms a comfortable, inviting feel. One of Sarah's drawings had been framed and hung on the wall. A cross-stitched pillow rested on the couch. Green plants flourished in a wicker stand by the window. And several family photos were prominently displayed.

His eyes lingered on the photo on top of the television. Kate was holding a tiny baby and a man sat next to her, on the edge of a couch, his arm protectively around her shoulders. Jack. Eric recognized him from the night of the accident. And on the opposite wall hung a wedding picture in which Kate and Jack were slightly younger—and obviously very much in love.

"That's my daddy," Sarah declared, noting the direction of Eric's gaze.

He smiled down at her. "That's what I thought. He looks very nice."

Sarah turned to study the picture gravely. "Mommy says he was. She says he loved me very much." She transferred her gaze to the photo on the TV. "That's me in that picture, when I was a baby. That's my daddy, too. I don't remember him, though. He went to heaven right after I was born."

Eric felt his throat tighten, but before he could respond Kate spoke from the hallway.

"I'm sorry for the delay. We can go now."

He looked up, and the raw pain in her eyes tugged at his heart.

"Did you know my daddy?" Sarah asked Eric, oblivious to Kate's distress.

With an effort he withdrew his gaze from Kate's and glanced back down at Sarah. "No. I wish I had," he said gently.

"So do I. Then you could tell me what he was like. Mommy tells me stories about him, but sometimes she cries and it makes me sad."

"Sarah! That's enough about Daddy!" Kate admonished, her face flushed. When she saw Sarah's startled gaze, her eyes filled with dismay and she gentled her tone. "You don't want to keep

Aunt Anna waiting, do you? She's probably all ready to make those cookies.''

A slightly subdued Sarah walked to the door. "We were waiting for *you*, Mommy," she pointed out in a hurt voice that only made Kate feel worse.

Sarah talked nonstop to Eric during the short drive, and when they dropped her off, Anna wished them a pleasant evening and told them not to hurry. "We'll have lots of fun, won't we, Sarah?"

The little girl nodded vigorously, and Kate bent down beside her.

"You be a good girl, now. And Mommy will be back soon." Her voice sounded artificially bright, and the slight, almost-unnoticeable catch at the end tugged at Eric's heart.

"Okay."

It was Kate who seemed reluctant to part, he noted. Sarah seemed perfectly happy to spend the evening with his mother. Kate confirmed his impression as they drove away.

"You know, this is the first time I've ever left her with a sitter, except for day care," she admitted, her voice slightly unsteady.

"She'll be fine," he reassured her. "She and Mom get along famously."

"I know. And I'm grateful. But I feel guilty for leaving her with someone when I don't have to."

"You need a life, too, Kate," he gently pointed out. "Apart from Sarah. When was the last time you went out socially?" He caught her surprised glance out of the corner of his eye and turned to her apologetically. "Sorry. That's none of my business. But I have the impression you don't get out much, other than to your job. That's not healthy."

"Is that your professional opinion?"

"I'm not a psychiatrist. But balance is important to a healthy lifestyle."

"From what your mother has told me, it sounds like maybe you need to take your own advice."

He grimaced. "Touché. I do spend a lot of hours at work. But I also take time occasionally to socialize. Like tonight."

Kate turned to stare out the front windshield. "I *want* to be with Sarah, Eric. It's not a chore. Besides, I don't know that many people here. We lived in Cincinnati until a few months before Sarah was born. When we first moved to St. Louis we were too busy fixing up our house to socialize. And afterward… Well, I had no time to make friends. I was with Jack every minute I could spare. Since he died, I simply haven't had the interest or the energy to meet people. Besides, Sarah is all I need.''

''Have you ever thought that maybe *she* needs more?'' he suggested carefully.

Kate frowned. ''Like what?''

''Friends her own age. Is she involved in any activities with other children?''

Kate stiffened. ''There aren't many children in our apartment complex. And there's nowhere for her to play unless I take her to the park down the street. We get along, Eric. It's not ideal, but then, nothing is.''

Eric could sense Kate's tension in her defensive posture. Not a good way to start their evening, he realized. It was time to back off.

''I didn't mean to be critical, Kate. You're right. Nothing is ideal. And your social life is none of my business. But I appreciate your willingness to help me out tonight. You'll like Frank and Mary. And maybe we'll both have some fun.''

There was that word again. ''Fun.'' It seemed so foreign, so distant. She could hardly remember what it was like to indulge in pure, carefree fun with other adults. And she didn't expect her memory to be jogged tonight.

But much to her surprise, it was.

Kate wasn't sure at exactly what point she began to relax and enjoy herself. Maybe it was when Frank told the hilarious story about how he and his wife met after Mary ran into his car. Or maybe it was when Mary learned that she and Kate liked the same author, then loaned her the woman's latest book, even though Kate protested that she never had time to read anymore. ''Make time,'' Mary said, and extracted a promise that Kate would call her to talk about the book after she finished it. Or maybe it was when she got coaxed into a game of lawn darts, and much to everyone's surprise—including her own—proved that she had an incredibly accurate aim by trouncing one challenger after another.

All Kate knew was that suddenly she found herself laughing—

and relaxing. It took her by surprise, but it also felt good. So good, in fact, that for a moment it made her eyes sting as she recalled the fun and laughter that had once been part of her normal, everyday existence. Nothing had been ''normal'' in her life for years, but tonight reminded her of what she had once had—and so often had taken for granted. This brief reprieve from the deep-seated sadness that had shrouded her existence for so long was like a life vest thrown to one adrift, and she clung to it greedily. Even if it only lasted tonight, she thought, it gave her a precious moment in the sunlight after years of darkness.

As Kate won her fourth round of lawn darts, Frank held up his hands in defeat. ''That's it. I give up. I'm not a glutton for punishment. I duly declare Kate the Queen of Lawn Darts. And now I think it's time to move on to something more important. Let's eat.''

Mary poked him in the ribs good-naturedly. ''Is that all you ever think about? Food?''

He glanced down at her five-months-pregnant girth and grinned. ''Obviously not.''

She blushed and rolled her eyes. ''I'm not going to touch that one with a ten-foot pole,'' she declared. ''Let's eat.''

''Isn't that what I just said?'' he teased.

Kate watched their affectionate interplay with both amusement and envy. She and Jack had once shared that kind of closeness, where a look spoke volumes and a simple touch could unite two hearts. Even after all these years, whenever she saw a couple communicating in that special nonverbal way reserved for those deeply in love, her heart ached with the realization that for her those golden days were gone forever.

Eric saw the sudden melancholy sweep over Kate's face, and he frowned. He'd been keenly attuned to the nuances in her mood all evening, watching with pleasure as her initial uncertainty and subdued demeanor gave way to tentative smiles and then relaxed interaction. Eric was taken aback the first time he heard her musical laugh, then entranced by it. He was captivated when her eyes occasionally sparkled with delight. And he was charmed by her unaffected beauty and unconscious grace. It had been an incredible transformation—and he intended to do everything he could to sustain it.

"Did I hear someone say food?" he asked, coming up quickly behind her.

Mary gave him a rueful grin. "You men are all alike."

"Well, I certainly hope so," her husband countered with a wink. "Come on, we need to lead off or no one will eat." He took her arm and led her purposefully toward the buffet table.

Eric nodded toward the food line. "Shall we?"

Kate stepped forward, and he dropped his hand lightly to her waist, guiding her toward the serving table with a slight pressure in the small of her back. His touch startled her at first. She knew it was an impersonal gesture, born more of good manners than attraction, yet it sent an odd tingle racing along her spine. It had been a long time since she'd been touched like this. She'd almost forgotten the sense of protection it gave her—and how good it felt. She'd missed these simple little gestures, she realized with a pang. They went a long way toward making a person feel cared for. Yet she'd never recognized their importance until they were absent. And by then it was too late to experience again and savor those special, everyday moments that truly defined a relationship.

Eric heard her small sigh and looked at her with concern as he picked up two plates. "Is something wrong?"

She summoned a smile, but it was edged with sadness. "I was just remembering that old cliché, about how you never really appreciate something until it's gone." Her gaze strayed to Frank and Mary, who were holding hands as they carried their plates to a table. "They're a really nice couple."

Eric followed her gaze, then handed her a plate. "Yes, they are. It renews your faith in romance to see two people who are obviously in love."

They filled their plates in silence, and when they reached the end of the line he led the way toward a secluded table. Kate hesitated and glanced back toward the group.

"Shouldn't we mingle?"

"We've been doing that all night. Don't worry. Frank won't take offense." He deposited his plate on a table for two under a rose arbor and held out her chair. "This is a perfect spot for dinner, don't you think?"

Kate couldn't argue with that. It reminded her of an old-fashioned garden—the kind she'd once planned to have. Nowadays she had to content herself with a few ferns and African violets tucked into sunny corners of her apartment. She couldn't even give Sarah a proper yard to play in, she thought dispiritedly, her gaze drifting back to Frank and Mary. Their child would be blessed with two loving parents and plenty of room to stretch his or her legs—and wings, she thought wistfully.

As Eric sat down, one look at Kate's face made him realize that there was no way he could salvage her lighthearted mood. And maybe he shouldn't even try. Maybe she needed to talk about the things that had made the light in her eyes flicker and die.

"I have a feeling that watching Frank and Mary reminds you of your own marriage," he remarked quietly.

She looked at him in surprise, then gazed unseeingly at her plate as she toyed with her food. At first he wasn't sure she was going to respond. But a moment later she spoke.

"In some ways," she acknowledged softly, "Jack and I weren't as outgoing, but we had that same kind of special bond. I guess once you've experienced it, you just recognize it in others. Seeing Frank and Mary together makes me remember what I once had."

"I'm sorry about how things turned out, Kate. I guess the only consolation is that at least you had that special bond once."

She glanced at him. He was staring at his own plate now, apparently lost for a moment in his own memories. He seemed sad, and there was disillusion—and regret—in his eyes. Obviously she wasn't the only one with grief in her past, Kate realized with a sharp pang. Apparently Eric had not only gone through a painful divorce, but a painful marriage as well, devoid of the kind of love all young couples dream of. In some ways, perhaps the death of that dream was worse than living the dream and then losing it, she reflected. At least she had happy memories. His seemed depressing at best.

"Now it's my turn to say I'm sorry." She watched as, with an effort, he pulled himself back to the present.

He shrugged. "I survived—with the help of my family and my faith."

She looked down. "I had the family part, anyway."

Eric frowned. "No faith?"

"Not anymore."

"But Mom said that Sarah mentioned Sunday school."

"My mother used to take her. I feel badly that I haven't followed through, but my heart's not in it."

"What happened?"

She played with the edge of her napkin. "Jack and I went to church regularly. I used to think God really listened when we prayed," she said haltingly.

"And now?"

"Let's just say I haven't seen much evidence that He does. I prayed when Jack was injured. Pleaded, actually. And bargained. And begged. I put my trust in God's hands, always believing He'd come through for me. But He didn't. So I figured, what's the use? If God wasn't listening to me, why keep talking? That's when I stopped praying. And going to church. Mom picked up the slack with Sarah, but I've kind of dropped the ball since she…since she died. I feel guilty about it, but I just can't go back yet. Maybe I never will. I'm still too angry at God."

"You know, there's a simple fix for the guilt about Sarah, at least."

She gazed at him curiously. "There is?"

"Yes. Mom and I go to church every Sunday. We'd be more than happy to take her with us."

Kate looked at him in surprise, then frowned. "But you've both done so much for me already. It just doesn't seem right."

"Well, then, think of it this way. We'd actually be doing this for Sarah."

She conceded his point with a slight lift of her shoulders. "I can't argue with that. Are you really sure you wouldn't mind?"

"Absolutely. We'll start tomorrow. You'd be welcome to join us anytime."

"I'll keep that in mind."

"It really might help, you know," he pressed gently. "It was a lifesaver for me. We have a wonderful minister. He's helped me through some pretty rough times."

Kate didn't want to discuss the state of her soul with anyone. She had too many conflicting emotions about her faith, too many unanswered questions. But she *would* like to know more about what had happened to turn Eric so completely off marriage. So far, he'd asked most of the questions. It seemed only fair that she return the favor.

"I take it your marriage wasn't exactly…memorable," she ventured.

An expression of pain seared across his eyes, like the white-hot flash of fireworks—brief but intense. "Oh, it was memorable, all right." Though she saw he tried to mask it, the bitterness in his tone was unmistakable.

"Is it something you can talk about? Sometimes that helps. And I used to be a good listener. I'm a little out of practice, but I can give it a try."

Even as she spoke the words, Kate was startled by their truthfulness. For the last few years she had been so focused on her own pain that she'd been oblivious to the pain of others. In one blinding moment of revelation, she realized that she had slipped, without even being aware of it, into self-pity and self-absorption. It was a disturbing insight. One of the things Jack had loved about her was her openness to others and her ability to empathize. He would hardly have recognized her now, she conceded. Since his death she'd closed herself off to everyone and everything except Sarah, her mother and her sister. And it had been an effective coping mechanism, insulating her with a numbness that made the pain in her life bearable.

But living the rest of her life in darkness and grief wasn't going to bring Jack back, she acknowledged sadly. Somehow she had to find her way back to beauty and joy and hope, because suddenly she knew she couldn't go on marking the days instead of living them. It wasn't fair to her, or to Sarah—or to the memory of Jack, who had loved life intensely and lived each day with passion and appreciation, fully embracing all the blessings the Lord had bestowed on him.

But Kate had no idea how to begin the rebuilding process. It seemed like such a daunting task. Maybe listening to Eric, as he had listened to her, would be a way to start connecting with people again.

When her gaze linked with his, she found him watching her intently and she shifted uncomfortably. Was he angry that she'd turned the tables and asked about *his* private life? she wondered anxiously. She hadn't meant to offend him. "Listen, I didn't mean to pry, Eric. I'm sorry."

"It's not that," he assured her quickly. "It's just that you— I don't know, you had a funny look on your face for a minute."

"Did I?" His perceptiveness surprised—and slightly unnerved—her. "I guess I was wondering if maybe I'd overstepped my bounds, asking about your marriage," she hedged, reluctant to reveal the personal insight that had just flashed through her mind. "It's just that talking to you about Jack and my faith helped tonight. I thought maybe it might help you to talk, too. But I understand if you'd rather not."

He looked at her for a moment before he spoke, as if assessing whether her interest was real or just polite. "Actually, I haven't talked much about it to anyone. Except my minister. Maybe because there isn't a whole lot to say. And because it still hurts after all these years. And because it's hard to admit failure," he confessed candidly. "But I'll give you the highlights—or lowlights, depending on your perspective—if you're really interested."

"I am."

He gave a slight nod. "Cindy and I met when I was in medical school," he began. "She was blond and beautiful, carefree and fun, always ready for the next adventure. I was the serious, studious type and it was exciting just to be with her. I never knew what she'd do next. All I knew was that she added a whole new dimension to my life. As different as we were, something clicked between us and I proposed a year after we met. We got married a few months later."

"Sounds like a promising beginning," Kate ventured.

"Yeah. Except things just went downhill from there. She didn't like my choice of specialty, and she grew to resent the intrusion of my career on our personal lives. We both changed through the years—or maybe we just became more of what we'd always been. In any case, the differences we once found so appealing gradually became irritating and hurtful. In the end, we were barely speaking."

He paused and looked down at his iced tea. The drops of condensation on his glass reminded him of tears, and he suddenly felt sad. "To be honest, I don't think either of us was blameless in the breakup, but I feel most responsible," he said heavily. "Cindy was right about my career—it takes an inordinate amount of my time. And it was a self-perpetuating kind of thing. As our marriage disintegrated, I spent even more time in the office and at the hospital, which only made matters worse. I don't know.... Maybe she would have been more tolerant of my schedule if I'd been doing heart transplants or something.''

Kate frowned. ''What do you mean?''

''Cindy wanted me to be a surgeon. That's considered one of the more 'glamorous' specialties. And when we got married, I thought I wanted to do that, too. But eventually I realized that I didn't enjoy practicing medicine in that sterile environment. I wanted to interact with people. And I love kids. Pediatrics was a natural fit for me. But Cindy hated it. It didn't have enough prestige. She was bitterly disappointed in my choice—and in me. Over time, our relationship grew strained and distant, and in the end it just fell apart.'' Eric didn't tell Kate about the final hurt—the reason he'd finally agreed to the divorce. Even now, five years later, it made him feel physically ill to think about it.

Impulsively Kate reached out and touched his hand. ''I'm sorry, Eric.''

Startled, he dropped his gaze to her slender fingers lightly resting on his sun-browned hand. It was funny. He couldn't remember a single time during his entire relationship with Cindy when she'd touched him in quite this way, with such heartfelt empathy and simple human caring. His throat tightened, and he swallowed with difficulty.

''So am I,'' he admitted, his voice suddenly husky. ''I always believed marriage was forever, that if things got rough you worked them out. But by the time I brought up the idea of counseling, it was too late. Cindy had already given up. She finally asked for a divorce, and under the circumstances I agreed. But in my heart I still feel married. I spoke those vows in the sight of God, and I can't forget them as easily as she did.''

''What do you mean?''

''She remarried a few months after the divorce became final. She and her new husband live in Denver. It's not that I'm judging her, Kate. I leave that to God. But it wasn't the right thing for me.''

"So that's what your mother meant when she said she'd better take this opportunity to play grandmother," Kate mused aloud.

Eric looked surprised. "She told you that?"

"Yes. The day I met her."

"Well, maybe my message is finally sinking in. But I know she's disappointed. As the only child, I was her one hope for grandchildren," he said ruefully.

"Hey, hey, hey! This conversation looks way too heavy," Frank interrupted with a grin. "Time to liven things up a little. Okay, Kate, one more round of lawn darts. I feel renewed after that meal."

Kate smiled and glanced at her watch. "I really need to get home," she protested.

"Eric, convince her."

Eric shrugged. "He'll be a bear to work with if he doesn't get a chance to redeem himself."

Kate laughed. "Okay. One more round."

Fifteen minutes later, after she had once more soundly beaten her host, she and Eric said their goodbyes.

"He'll never live this down, you know," Eric told her with a chuckle as he escorted her to his car, his hand again placed possessively in the small of her back.

"Oh, people will forget," she replied with a smile.

"I won't," he declared smugly.

"Eric! You aren't going to use this against him, are you?"

"You'd better believe it," he asserted promptly, grinning as he opened her door. "What are friends for?"

Kate shook her head and slid in. A moment later he took his place behind the wheel. "You know, he's going to be sorry I came tonight," she predicted.

Eric smiled. "Maybe so. But do you know something, Kate?" At the odd note in his voice she turned to look at him. "I'm not. I had a really good time."

At his words, a feeling of warmth and happiness washed over her like a healing balm. "So did I," she admitted quietly. "Thanks for asking me."

"It was my pleasure." As he pulled away from the curb, he glanced over at her. "Maybe we can do it again sometime."

Again? Kate wasn't sure that was wise. It wasn't that she found

Eric's company lacking. He was a great conversationalist, an empathetic listener, intelligent, well-read—not to mention incredibly handsome. She liked him. A lot. And therein lay the problem. She liked him *too* much. While she might have reached a turning point in her life tonight, she wasn't ready to deal with relationships—at least, not the male/female variety. And that included Eric—despite the fact that he wasn't even in the market for romance.

Like Eric, Kate believed in that "till death us do part" vow. Even though she was no longer bound by it, in her heart she still felt married. Yet being with Eric tonight had awakened feelings long suppressed—and best left undisturbed, she decided firmly. Though her reactions had been subtle, they spelled danger. Intuitively she knew that Eric Carlson's very presence could disrupt her life by raising questions she wasn't yet ready to address and forcing her to examine issues she wasn't prepared to face.

She turned and gazed out into the night with a troubled frown, oblivious to the passing scenery. Even her mild reaction—or maybe *attraction* was a better word, she admitted honestly—to Eric tonight made her feel guilty; as if she were somehow betraying the love she and Jack had shared. It was *not* a good feeling. And the best way to keep it from happening again was to stay away from the disturbing man beside her.

It was as simple as that.

# Chapter Four

Okay, maybe it wasn't quite *that* simple, Kate conceded the next Sunday as she waited for Eric to pick Sarah up for church. Their paths were going to cross every Sunday at this rate unless she decided to take Sarah to services herself. And that wasn't likely to happen anytime in the near future. So she'd just have to get used to seeing him once a week and maintain a polite distance.

Except that would be easier said than done, she acknowledged with a sigh. There was just something about him that drew her. Maybe it was his eyes, she mused. They were wonderful eyes. Understanding. Warm. Caring. Compelling. She'd never seen eyes quite so intensely blue before—nor so insightful. When he gazed at her she felt he could almost see into her soul.

Strangely enough, that didn't bother her, even though she'd always been a very private person. Maybe because—stranger still—she felt as if they weren't just recent acquaintances, but old friends. Which made no sense. For all practical purposes, they'd met less than two weeks ago. Nevertheless, the feeling of familiarity persisted. It was disconcerting—yet somehow oddly comforting.

The doorbell rang, and Sarah dashed to answer it. Kate followed more slowly, grateful that Eric's attention was distracted by his young greeter long enough for her to take a quick inventory—and then struggle to regain control of a breathing pattern that suddenly went haywire as she stared at him.

Kate had always known that Eric was a handsome man. He had classic Nordic good looks, and in a different age might have stood at the helm of a questing ship. Yet his gentle manner and kind-heartedness were at odds with those Viking images of old. It seemed he had inherited the best of both worlds—ancient athletic virility and modern male sensibilities. It was a stunning—and extremely appealing—combination. And never had it come across more clearly than today. In a light-gray summer suit that emphasized his lean, muscular frame, and a crisp white shirt and dark blue, patterned tie, he was by far the most attractive man Kate had seen in a long time. Or maybe he was just the first one she'd *noticed* in a long time, she acknowledged with a frown.

He chose that moment to look up, and his smile of greeting faded when he saw her troubled expression. "Everything okay?"

She forced the corners of her mouth to lift and closed the distance between them. "Fine."

"Not having second thoughts?"

"No, of course not."

He studied her for a moment with those discerning eyes, as if debating whether to pursue the subject. Much to her relief, he let it rest. "We usually go to breakfast after services. Would you like us to swing by and pick you up? Make it a foursome?"

"Can we, Mommy?" Sarah asked eagerly. "I could get pancakes. I like pancakes," she told Eric.

He grinned. "So do I." He transferred his gaze back to Kate, and his expression softened. Or was it only her imagination? she wondered. "How about it, Kate?"

"I appreciate the offer, Eric, but your mom told me that's your special time together. We wouldn't want to intrude."

"Actually, it was her idea. But I had the same thought. She just brought it up first," he said with an engaging grin.

"Oh. Well, maybe another time. I really hadn't planned on going out at all today. I need to work on some lesson plans."

"Now what's that old saying? 'All work and no play makes Jack a—'" At the sudden pallor of Kate's face, Eric stopped short, his jaw tightening in self-reproach. Of all the stupid remarks! "Kate, I'm sorry. I just didn't think."

"It's...it's all right," she assured him shakily. "It's just that— Well, that saying was Jack's motto. He was a great believer in keeping things in proper perspective. He always made sure we took time for fun, and he never forgot to smell the flowers along the way.''

''I have a feeling I would have liked him,'' Eric said quietly.

She summoned up a sad smile. ''I think you might be right.''

''Are we going now?'' Sarah asked impatiently.

With an effort, Eric released Kate's gaze and smiled down at the little girl. ''I don't think I've ever seen anyone quite so anxious to go to church,'' he teased. ''God will be very happy.''

''I just want to show Aunt Anna my new dress. Mommy bought it for me this summer and we were saving it for a special occasion.''

Kate liked the deep, rich sound of the chuckle that rumbled out of Eric's chest. ''Well, we won't tell God that's the reason you want to hurry. We wouldn't want to hurt His feelings.''

''I want to go to church, too,'' Sarah assured him. ''I like the singing.''

''I'll walk out to the car with you,'' Kate said. ''I'd like to say hello to Anna.''

The two women exchanged a few words while Eric settled Sarah in the back seat, then he rejoined them.

''You're sure you won't come to breakfast, Kate?'' Anna asked.

''Maybe another time. But thank you.''

''I'll see you back to your door,'' Eric told her.

She looked at him in surprise. ''That's really not necessary.''

''Yes, it is. I have something I want to ask you.''

He fell into step beside her, and she looked up at him curiously. ''Is there a problem?''

He smiled ruefully. ''That depends on how you look at it, I guess. I have another favor to ask, and I'd like you to consider it while we're at church.'' He reached up and adjusted his tie, and Kate would have sworn he was nervous. ''In addition to my job, I'm on the board of several local health-related organizations. As Mom told you, I have a tendency to slightly overextend myself,'' he admitted wryly.

She smiled. ''I think her exact words were that it's harder for you to say no to a good cause than for a gopher to stop digging holes.''

He chuckled, and a pleasing crinkle of lines appeared at the corners of his eyes. ''That sounds like Mom. Anyway, next Saturday night there's a black-tie dinner dance that's the culmination of the annual fund-raising drive for one of the organizations. Usually I try to avoid these things, but I can't get out of this one. I could go alone, but to be honest, it always feels a little awkward." They reached her door, and he turned toward her. "So I wondered if you might go with me. Will you think about it while we're at church, Kate?"

She gazed up into his clear blue eyes, and for a moment she felt as if she were basking in the warmth of the summer sun under a cloudless sky. It was a good feeling—one that had been absent from her life for a long time. But it also made her nervous. She dropped her gaze, unsure how to answer. Something told her she should say no immediately. But she didn't want to hurt Eric's feelings. He had gone out of his way to be kind to her and Sarah. And besides, she had enjoyed their time together the evening before.

"Kate?"

She looked back up at him, took a deep breath and suddenly decided to follow her heart. "All right, Eric. I'll think about it," she agreed.

She was rewarded with a smile that lit up his face and made his eyes glow. A person could get lost in those eyes, she thought, mesmerized by their warmth. "Thanks, Kate. And don't work too hard while we're gone."

"N-no, I won't. See you later," she said breathlessly, then quickly slipped inside.

For a long time after he left, Kate stood with her back braced against the front door, trying to reconcile her conflicting emotions. She felt more alive than she had in years—but she was also troubled. And she knew why. Her gaze strayed to her wedding picture, and she tenderly traced the contours of Jack's dear, familiar face. Her love for him was as strong now as it had been on that day nearly eleven years before when they'd been joined as man and wife. It had not diminished one iota.

But other things had, she thought sadly, tears welling in her eyes. Certain images and sensory memories were slowly slipping away, despite her desperate efforts to hold on to them. The funny, dismayed face Jack always made whenever she served carrots. The deep timbre of his voice during their intimate moments. The feel of his freshly-shaved skin beneath her fingertips. The distinctive, woodsy scent of his after-shave. The way he always tilted his head as he cut the grass.

All of those things were fading, like an old photograph in which all that remained were vague outlines of images that had once been sharp and clear and vibrant. Soon she would only be able to remember the *fact* that those things had once been special, not the unique qualities that made them so. She was losing Jack, bit by bit, day by day, and there was nothing she could do to stop it. The sense of distance and the ebbing of memories had accelerated in the last few months, she realized, and it left her with a sick, hollow, helpless feeling that seemed destined to plague her well into the foreseeable future.

And then, out of the blue, Eric Carlson had stepped into her life. With him, she didn't feel as hopeless and depressed. In fact, he made her feel things she'd never expected to feel again—attractive, womanly, cared for. He'd awakened in her needs that she had suppressed for five long years; needs she'd thought were forever locked within the cold recesses of her heart. Slowly, under the warmth of his gaze, those needs were beginning to thaw. And that scared her. After all, she was a lonely widow. He was a handsome divorced man. Even if the widow was still in love with her husband and the divorced man still felt married, it just didn't seem like a safe combination.

Kate wasn't sure what to do. But she knew whom to call for advice. And she intended to place that call just as soon as she poured herself a cup of coffee.

"Kate? What's wrong? I thought it was my turn to call *you* this Sunday."

"Nothing's wrong, Amy. I didn't mean to scare you," she apologized quickly, dismayed by the alarm in her sister's voice. "I just had some free time and thought I'd call you first, that's all."

"Thank God! I didn't mean to overreact, but—"

"That's okay. You have good reason. My unexpected phone calls haven't always been exactly uplifting."

"Yeah, well, hopefully those days are over. So what's the occasion? It's not my birthday or anything. How come you're springing for this Sunday's call?''

"Can't I be generous once in a while?"

"Look, neither of us can afford to be generous. Why don't I call you back tonight, as usual? It *is* my turn. Every other week, remember?''

"I remember. But I just wanted to talk. Unless... Are you getting ready for church?''

"Nope. Cal pulled a midnight shift at the park last night and is sleeping in. We're going to the second service. So I've got the time. But you haven't got the money.''

"Will you quit with the money thing?''

"I'd like to. But neither of us can afford to treat money lightly— no pun intended. Just consider the facts. You're a single working mother with huge medical debts. I have three kids, my husband makes his living dressed like Smokey the Bear, we live in a log cabin and I make quilts to keep the wolf from the door. Case closed.''

That wasn't quite the whole story, but Kate let it pass with a smile. "You forgot one thing.''

"What?''

"You love every minute of your life.''

Kate heard her sister's contented sigh. "Yeah, I do. But we'll never have money to spare. I'm always sorry we couldn't do more to help you, Kate.''

"You did the most important thing, Amy. You were there. You and Mom. That was worth more than gold.''

"Still, gold comes in handy sometimes. Speaking of which—how are you doing with the bills?''

"Okay. I pay off a little every month. I figure at this rate I'll be free and clear about the time I'm ready to retire.'' She tried for a light tone, but didn't quite pull it off.

"You know, Kate, sometimes I think that... Well, I've never said this before, but...but since things turned out the way they did, it almost would have been better if—well—if Jack hadn't...'' Amy's voice trailed off.

"I've thought about that, too,'' Kate admitted slowly. "But at the time I was just grateful he survived the accident.'' She paused and took a deep breath, determined not to dwell on what might have been. She needed Amy's advice about the future, not about the past. "Actually, in a roundabout way, that's one of the reasons I called today. You'll never believe this coincidence, but the doctor who saved Eric's life at the accident scene is Sarah's new pediatrician."

"No kidding? That's weird! Did he recognize you?"

"Uh-huh. Even before I recognized him. As a matter of fact, his mother is watching Sarah for me while I teach."

"How in the world did you arrange that?"

"I didn't. He did." Kate explained, ending with Eric's offer to take Sarah to church each Sunday.

"Wow! I doubt whether my pediatrician, nice as she is, would ever take such a personal interest in *my* kids," Amy commented, clearly impressed.

"I've been really lucky," Kate acknowledged. "But I do have a sort of…dilemma."

"So tell me about it."

In halting phrases, Kate told Amy about Eric's marital situation, their evening together and his second invitation.

"So I honestly don't know what to do," she admitted at the end.

As usual, Amy honed right in on the key question. "Well, do you *want* to go?"

Kate frowned. "I—I think so. I like him, and we had a really good time. But when I'm with him I…I feel things I haven't felt in a long time. And then I feel guilty."

"You have nothing to feel guilty about," Amy declared firmly. "You're a healthy young woman who's been living in an emotional cave for way too long. Why shouldn't you go out and have a good time?"

"You know why."

"Because of Jack."

"I still love him, Amy. I still feel married. It just doesn't seem right, somehow, to go out with another man. Even one who's not interested in romance."

There was silence for a brief moment before Amy spoke. "Can I tell you something, Kate?"

"Why do I have the feeling you will anyway, even if I say no?"

"Because you know me too well," Amy replied pertly. Then her voice grew more serious. "Look, I'll just say this straight out, okay? I know you loved Jack. And I know why. He was a great guy. We *all* loved him. And we all still miss him. We always will. As his wife, I know you feel the loss more intensely than any of us can even imagine. When I think of life without Cal... Well, it makes me understand in a very small way the pain you've had to deal with. But Jack wouldn't want you to go through the rest of your life without ever really living again, Kate. And part of living is loving. I know you have Sarah. But I'm not talking about that kind of love. You're the kind of woman who blossoms when she's loved by the right man. That's not to say you're not strong or capable or independent. You're all of those things, and you've proved it over and over again these past five years. But don't close yourself off to life—and love—because of a misplaced sense of obligation or guilt. Jack wouldn't want that, and deep in your heart you know that. Nothing can ever take away the memory of the special love you two shared. That's yours forever. But maybe it's time to start making some new memories."

For a long moment there was silence. Sometimes Kate felt that Amy, though two years younger, was really the older of the two. She was so solid, so grounded, so blessed with common sense and the ability to quickly analyze a situation and offer valuable insight. People didn't always like what Amy said. But they could rarely deny the truth of her words.

"Kate?" Amy said worriedly. "Are you still there? Look, I'm sorry if I overstepped, but—"

"It's okay," Kate interrupted. "Actually, I think you're right in a lot of ways. It's just that... Well, it's not easy to let go."

"I know, hon," Amy murmured sympathetically. "But you're going to have to let go before you can really get on with your life."

Kate played with the phone cord. "Jack's kind of slipping away anyway, you know?" Her voice broke on the last word.

"Oh, Kate, I wish I was there right now to give you a hug!"

"Yeah, so do I."

"You know, maybe this slipping away is Jack's—and the Lord's—way of telling you it's time to move on."

"Maybe. But... I don't know. I guess I'm just scared, Amy."

"That's okay. That's normal. But don't let fear stop you. It's like that old saying about ships. They may be safe in the harbor, but that's not what they're built for. I think it's time for you to set sail, Kate.''

"How come you always know the right thing to say?'' Kate asked, smiling mistily as she swiped at her eyes.

Amy chuckled. "My kids wouldn't agree with that.''

"They will when they get older. Listen, thanks, okay? I feel a lot better.''

"So are you going with Eric?''

"I guess so. But don't start getting any romantic ideas. I told you, he's not in the market.''

"That's okay. At least he'll get you back into circulation, introduce you to some new people. That's a start. And I'll want a full report next Sunday. Except *I'll* call *you*. Agreed?''

"Agreed.''

"So, you've been holding out on your old pal all this time.''

Eric glanced up from the chart he was reading. Frank was lounging against the door of his office, arms folded, one ankle crossed over the other, his accusatory tone tempered by the twinkle in his eyes.

"What's that supposed to mean?'' As if he didn't know. He'd been waiting all afternoon for Frank to pounce and demand details about Eric's date.

"You know very well what I mean. Here I think you're a miserable, lonely, driven man desperately in need of female companionship and then you show up with a babe like Kate. Boy, you had me fooled! Where have you been hiding her all this time?''

"I haven't been 'hiding' her anywhere. And I'm not sure she'd appreciate the term 'babe,' even though I know you mean it in an entirely flattering way. How about if we just refer to her as the Queen of Lawn Darts?''

Frank grimaced. "Ouch! You would have to bring that up. I just had an off night. So…'' He ambled over and perched on the edge of Eric's desk, not about to be distracted. "Tell me everything. Where did you meet this goddess? And how serious are you two?''

"We're just friends, Frank. That's it.''

His partner gave a skeptical snort. "Yeah. Like Ma Barker was just a sweet old lady."

"I'm serious."

"You expect me to buy that after the way you were looking at her all night?"

Eric sent him a startled look. "What do you mean?"

"Oh, come on, man. You hung on her every word. You made it a point to keep tabs on her whenever you were apart—which wasn't often. And you have that look in your eye."

"What look?"

"Smitten. Enamored. Head over heels. Is that descriptive enough?"

Eric frowned. "You're crazy."

"Uh-uh. I know that look. Had it once myself. Still do sometimes, in fact."

"Well, with all due respect to your powers of perception, you're way off base this time, pal."

Frank tilted his head and considered his friend thoughtfully for a moment. Then he grinned and stood. "Good try. But no sale. However, I get the message—butt out. Okay, that's fine, don't bare your soul to me, even though I'm your best friend in the world. I can read a No Trespassing sign when I see one." He ambled to the door and disappeared into the hall, but a moment later he stuck his head back inside and grinned. "But I don't pay any attention to signs. I'll wear you down eventually, you know. In the meantime, don't worry, buddy. Your secret's safe with me."

Eric stared at the doorway, then frowned and leaned back in his chair, absently playing with his pen. Frank might be a bit outspoken and on the boisterous side, but his powers of perception were keen. Usually he nailed a person's personality within five minutes of meeting him or her. He was even more intuitive about friends and associates. Sometimes it was almost scary.

Like right now.

Eric's frown deepened. Was Frank overreacting? Or had he seen something Eric had overlooked? There was no question that he liked Kate. And he *had* carried a memory of her in his mind for more than five years—but only because he'd been struck by her beauty and obvious love for her husband. Her transparent devotion had made a tremendous impact on him in light of his own disintegrating marriage. But he hardly knew her. They'd only gone out once, had spent barely four hours in each other's company socially. And it hadn't even been a real date.

And yet... Eric couldn't deny that there was at least a kernel of truth in Frank's assessment. He *was* attracted to Kate. To her beauty, certainly, but even more to her person, to who she was, to her essence. Attracted enough to want to get to know her better. And that wasn't good. Because Eric truly believed that in the sight of God he was still married. Through the years he'd never had any trouble remembering that, though countless women had made it clear they were available if he was interested. But he hadn't been. Until now.

Eric reached up with one hand and wearily massaged his temples. He wasn't going to compromise his values by allowing himself to get involved with Kate romantically, even if the lady was willing. Which she wasn't. It was obvious that her late husband had never relinquished his claim on her heart. And even if *he* was free—which he wasn't—getting involved with someone whose heart belonged to another was a recipe for disaster.

Besides, medicine and marriage didn't mix. He'd learned that the hard way. And he'd better not forget it.

Asking Kate to the dinner had probably been a mistake, Eric conceded with a sigh as he pulled the next chart toward him and flipped it open. But he couldn't retract the invitation now. All he could do was make sure it was the last one. Keeping their contact to a minimum was clearly the right thing to do—for everyone's sake.

But if that was true, why did it feel so wrong?

Kate was nervous. She'd spent the entire week second-guessing her decision to go with Eric tonight, less sure with each day that passed about the wisdom of her decision. She'd almost called Amy for another pep talk. But she already knew what her sister would say: "You need to do this, Kate. It's time. It's a first step. Just think of it that way and you'll be fine."

And of course, Amy would be right. After all, it was just a dinner with a nice man who, for whatever reason, had found her engaging

enough to want to spend a second evening with her. A man who
had no interest in her beyond friendship. So why was she nervous?

"You look pretty, Mommy. Is that a new dress?"

Kate turned back to the mirror. A new dress? Hardly, she thought
wryly. The limited money available for new clothes was generally
spent on Sarah. Kate had foraged deep in the recesses of her closet
for this dress. She'd given away most of her dressier clothes when
she sold the house, having neither the room nor the need for them,
but she'd kept a couple of things that were classic in style and would
be serviceable for any number of functions. This sleeveless linen-
like black sheath with a square neckline could be paired with a
jacket for a "business" look or worn alone, accented with costume
jewelry, for a dressier effect. It had made the "keeper" cut because
it was practical. Tonight, a clunky hammered-gold necklace and
matching earrings added some glamour to its simple lines, and she'd
arranged her hair in a more sophisticated style. The outfit still might
not be dressy enough for a black-tie event, Kate acknowledged, but
it was the best she could do.

"No, honey. I've had this in my closet for a long time."

"From when Daddy was here?"

The innocent question made Kate's stomach clench, and she
gripped the edge of the vanity. She'd bought it shortly after Sarah
was born as an incentive to return to her pre-pregnancy measure-
ments, but she'd never worn it.

"Yes, honey. It's as old as you are," she replied, struggling to
maintain an even tone.

"Well, I like it. I bet Dr. Eric will, too."

The doorbell rang, and with an, "I'll get it," Sarah scampered
off.

Determinedly, Kate put thoughts of the past aside and forced
herself to focus on the conversation in the living room as she added
a final touch of lipstick.

"Hi, Dr. Eric. Hi, Aunt Anna."

"Hello there, Sarah." Eric's deep voice had a mellow, comforting quality, Kate reflected, her lips curving up slightly.

"Hello, Sarah," Anna greeted the youngster.

On hearing the older woman's voice, Kate felt a pang of guilt.
Anna had offered to keep Sarah overnight at her place so Kate and

Eric wouldn't have to worry about staying out too late. But Kate had balked. Sarah wasn't even five yet, she had rationalized. It was too soon for her to be gone all night, even though it would have been more convenient for everyone.

"Mommy is almost ready. She looks really pretty. Do you think Mommy is pretty, Dr. Eric?"

There was a momentary pause, and Kate felt hot color surge to her face. But it grew even redder at Eric's husky response. "I think your mommy is beautiful, Sarah."

She had to get out there now, before Sarah asked any other embarrassing questions, Kate thought desperately. Willing the flush on her cheeks to subside, she flipped off the light and hurried down the hall.

"Well, here's Kate now," Anna said brightly. "My dear, you look lovely."

"Thanks, Anna." Her gaze flickered to her escort. "Hello, Eric." She intended to say more, but her voice deserted her as their gazes met. He looked fabulous tonight, she thought in awe. The black tux was a perfect complement to his blond hair, and it sat well on his tall, muscular frame, emphasizing his broad shoulders and dignified bearing. Her heart stopped, then raced on. Good heavens, what was she getting herself into? she thought in panic.

Eric took in Kate's attire in one swift, comprehensive glance that missed nothing. Fashionably high heels that accentuated the pleasing line of her legs. A figure-hugging sheath that showed off her slender curves to perfection. A neckline that revealed an expanse of creamy, flawless skin. She looked different tonight, he thought, swallowing with difficulty. Gorgeous. Glamorous. And very desirable. His mouth went dry and his pulse lurched into overdrive.

As his stunned gaze locked with hers, he realized that she seemed equally dazed. Her eyes were slightly glazed and the hand she ran distractedly through her hair was trembling. But no less so than his, he realized, jamming it into his pocket. Electricity fairly sizzled in the air between them.

"Mommy, how come your face is red?" Sarah asked innocently.

Anna stepped in smoothly. "Because she put on extra blush to go with her fancy dress," the older woman replied matter-of-factly. "Now, you two better be on your way or you'll miss dinner."

With an effort Kate dragged her gaze from Eric's. "Yes, y-you're right. I'll just get my purse."

Eric watched her flee down the hall and then drew a shaky breath. He wasn't sure exactly what had happened just now. All he knew was that the smoldering look he'd just exchanged with Kate had left him reeling.

In the sanctuary of her bedroom, Kate forced herself to take several long, slow breaths. What on earth had gone on just now? She felt as if a lightning bolt had zapped her. Eric hadn't even spoken to her, yet they'd connected on some basic level that needed no words. Or had they? Maybe it was all one-sided. Could she have imagined the spark that had flashed between them? It didn't seem possible. And how could she walk back out there and pretend that nothing had happened? But she had no choice. She couldn't acknowledge a thing. The ramifications of doing so were way too scary.

She picked up her purse and walked slowly back down the hall, trying vainly to curb the uncomfortable hammering of her heart. When she stepped back into the living room, her gaze immediately sought Eric's. She searched his eyes, but it was impossible to tell if he'd been as deeply affected by the look that had passed between them as she had been. He seemed as calm and at ease as always. Good. At least one of them was in control.

"Now you two take off," Anna instructed. "And don't hurry. I'm deep into a mystery that will keep me entertained for hours after Sarah goes to bed."

"Ready, Kate?"

Did Eric's voice sound deeper than usual, Kate wondered? Was it slightly uneven? Or was it only her imagination?

"Yes." Her *own* voice was definitely unsteady, she noted with chagrin.

He stepped aside to let her pass, and when he dropped his hand lightly to the small of her back she knew that her last reply was a lie. She wasn't ready at all. Not for tonight. Nor for whatever lay ahead in her relationship with this man.

But then she remembered Amy's comment about the ship. And Amy was right, she told herself resolutely. It was time to chart a new course and set sail.

# Chapter Five

As they drove to the downtown hotel where the banquet was being held, Eric could sense Kate's tension. It mirrored his own. To pretend that nothing had happened just now in her apartment would be foolish. To acknowledge it would be dangerous. There was clearly only one way to deal with it: stay away from situations where it might happen again. Frankly, he didn't need the temptation. And she didn't need the stress. His earlier decision to make this their last social excursion was clearly the right one, he told himself resolutely.

However, they still had to get through tonight. He risked a sideways glance at her. She was staring straight ahead, her brow marred by a slight frown, the lines of her body taut with strain. Not good, he concluded. He had been hoping for a repeat of their first outing, when she had relaxed and laughed and had seemed, at least for a little while, less weary and burdened. But tonight they were definitely not off to a good start. This might be their last pseudo "date," but he wanted her to enjoy it. She deserved a pleasant evening. He needed to distract her, introduce a subject that would take her mind off the unexpected chemistry that had erupted between them a few minutes before.

"You know, Mom already seems more like her old self in just the two weeks she's been watching Sarah," he said conversationally.

Kate turned to him. "Does she? I'm glad. It's worked out well for us, too. Sarah looks forward to the time she spends with Anna.

What a difference from our brief day-care-center experience!'' She sounded a bit breathless, and her tone was a little too bright, but Eric persisted.

''I know there are cases like yours where mothers have to work, but I often think it's a shame that so many of today's kids are being raised by strangers just so the parents can bring in two incomes to support a more extravagant lifestyle. I really think kids would rather have time and attention from their parents than material things.''

Kate nodded eagerly, warming to the subject. ''You know, that's exactly how Jack and I felt! We waited a long time for Sarah, and we decided that if the Lord ever blessed us with a child, he or she would have at least one full-time parent. That's why I quit my job when she was born. Jack had a good job—he was an engineer—so he was able to provide for us comfortably. Nothing lavish. But then, we didn't need 'lavish.' We just needed each other.''

She sighed and turned to stare out the front window, but her eyes were clearly not focused on the road ahead of her. ''It was the way I was raised, I guess. We never had a lot when I was growing up,'' she said softly. ''But we never felt poor, either. Because our home was rich in love. That's what Jack and I wanted for our child. A home filled with love. You know, it's too bad more parents don't realize that kids would rather have your time on a daily basis than a week at some fancy tennis camp in the summer. Sometimes I think parents today spend so much on material things for their children out of guilt—as a way to appease their conscience for the *time* they should have spent instead.''

''I couldn't agree more.''

Kate looked at him curiously. ''I hope you don't think I'm prying, Eric, but… Well, you obviously like kids. And they just as obviously like you. Yet you never had your own.''

A flicker of pain crossed his face, but he hid it by turning briefly to glance in the rearview mirror as he debated how to answer Kate's implied question. Hedge or be frank? It was a painful subject, one he'd discussed with only a few trusted, longtime friends. Kate was new in his life. Yet he trusted her. And so he chose to be frank.

''You're right about my feelings with regard to children,'' he said quietly. ''I always assumed that if I ever got married, I'd have my own family. And I guess I also assumed that most people felt that way. Cindy and I somehow never discussed the issue directly. I tried a few times, but as I recall, her answers were always a little vague and noncommittal. I should have pursued it, but I suppose I was afraid of what I'd hear if I pressed the issue. And I didn't want to risk hurting our relationship by upsetting her. I'd figured that once we were married it would just be a natural next step, and any reservations she might have had would evaporate.

"As it turned out, I was wrong. About a lot of things, actually. Cindy didn't want kids, period. They would have 'cramped her style,' as she so succinctly put it. And as much as I wanted children, I didn't want them to have a mother whose heart wasn't in the job. Besides, as she often reminded me, if I was too busy with my career to spend time with her, how would I ever find time to spend with children? And I suppose she had a point," he conceded wearily. "But I still wanted children. Giving up that dream was very difficult."

Kate thought about all the joy Sarah added to her life; how even in her darkest hours, when her heart grieved most deeply for Jack, her daughter had always been the one bright ray of sunlight able to penetrate to the dark, cold corners of her soul and remind her that joy and beauty still lived. But on Eric's darkest days he had struggled alone, not only with disintegration of a marriage but also with the loss of a dream for a family. And now he would always be alone. It was such a waste, she thought, her heart aching for him.

"You would have made a good father, you know," she said gently.

He gave her a crooked grin. "You think so?" His tone was light, but there was a poignant, wistful quality to it that tugged at her heart and made her throat tighten with emotion.

"Yes. As my sister Amy would wisely say, you can tell a lot about a man by the way he treats children. And you can tell a lot about a man by the way children treat *him.* According to her, children have almost a sixth sense about people. Using Sarah—who's generally very shy around strangers—as a yardstick, you stand pretty tall. So, yes, I think you would have made a great dad."

Eric felt his neck redden at the compliment. Very few things made him uncomfortable, but praise was at the top of the list. So he quickly refocused the attention on Kate. "I can hear the affection in your voice when you mention your sister. I take it you and she are close?''

"Yes. It's too bad she lives in Tennessee. We have to be content with weekly phone calls," she told him with a sigh.

"Tennessee isn't too far. Don't you visit occasionally?"

"Not as often as we'd like. Her husband, Cal, is an attorney *and* a part-time ranger in Great Smoky Mountains National Park, so his busy season is summer. They can never get away then, and I'm teaching the rest of the year. Besides, it's tough traveling with three small children—four-year-old twins and a six-month-old.''

He gave a low whistle. "She *does* have her hands full.''

Kate smiled. "That's putting it mildly. She also hosts a bi-weekly program on a Christian cable station in Knoxville. Anyway, Sarah, Mom and I always went down in the spring, and then again at Thanksgiving. But that's about it.''

"Thanksgiving in the Smokies sounds nice," he remarked with a smile.

"It is. Especially at Amy's. She's become quite the earth mother. They live in a log cabin, and she makes quilts and bakes homemade bread and cans vegetables. It's an amazing transition, considering that in her twenties she was an absolutely gung-ho career woman who liked bright lights and traveling in the fast lane and thought life simply ceased to exist outside the city limits.''

"What happened?"

"Cal."

"Ah. True love."

"Uh-huh. It wasn't that she changed for him. She just discovered that all that time she'd been living a lie. Somewhere along the way she'd bought into the notion that success is only measured in dollars and prestige and power. But she was never happy, even though she had all those things. It took Cal to make her realize that.''

"That's quite a story, Kate. Sort of reaffirms your belief in happy endings.''

She smiled softly. "Yeah, it does. They're a great couple.'' As Eric turned into the curving drive of the hotel, Kate sent him a startled look. "You mean we're here already?''

"See how times flies when you're having fun?'' She smiled, and he was gratified to note that she now seemed much more relaxed. "Shall we go in and be wined and dined?"

"I think that's what we're here for," she replied.

Eric didn't have Kate to himself again until after dessert. As a board member, he knew many of the guests and it seemed that all of them wanted to spend a few minutes talking with him during the cocktail hour. Throughout the meal Kate was kept occupied by an elderly man seated to her right. Only when their dinner companions rose to mingle with other guests did Eric have a few minutes alone with her.

"You seem to have made a friend in Henri," he remarked, nodding toward the older man who was now greeting some guests at a nearby table.

Kate followed Eric's glance and smiled. "He's a fascinating person. You'd never guess by looking at him that he was an underground fighter with the French Resistance in World War II, would you?"

Eric stared at Kate. He'd known Henri Montand, a major contributor to this event, for ten years. But it seemed that Kate had learned more about his background over one dinner than he had in a decade.

"You're kidding!"

"No. You didn't know?"

He shook his head ruefully. "Speaking of having a way with people... I may be pretty good with kids, but you obviously have a knack with adults." Kate flushed at his compliment, and he found that quality in her endearing—and utterly appealing. "So, are you having fun?" he asked, trying unsuccessfully to minimize the sudden huskiness in his voice. Fortunately, Kate didn't seem to notice.

"Oh, yes! This is a lovely event." She glanced around appreciatively at the fresh flower arrangements on the tables, the crystal chandeliers and the orchestra just beginning to tune up.

"The fund-raising committee generally does a nice job. But most importantly, the organization does good work. Abused kids need all the help they can get."

"You really take your commitment to children seriously, don't you? On and off the job."

"It's pretty hard to leave it at the office," he admitted. "But I do too much sometimes, I guess. That's what Cindy always said, anyway. And since the divorce, I've gotten even more involved. Frank's always saying that I'm a driven man. Even Mom's been telling me to get a life. And they're right. My terms on two boards are up at the end of the year and I've already decided not to renew them. But I'll stay involved with this one. I've been on the board for almost ten years and—"

"Eric! Kate!"

They glanced up, and Kate recognized the man bustling toward them as an energetic, fortyish board member Eric had introduced her to earlier. "Listen, help us out, will you? We need some people to kick off the dancing. I think if I get five or six of the board members out on the floor, everyone will loosen up. Thanks, guys." Without giving them a chance to respond, he hurried off.

Kate stared after him, then glanced at Eric uncertainly. "I haven't danced in years."

"Neither have I."

She gave a nervous laugh. "Honestly, Eric, I don't even think I remember how. That was about the only thing Jack couldn't do. I haven't danced since my wedding."

"I haven't danced in six or seven years."

"So should we just pass? I mean, I'd like to help out, but..." She lifted her shoulders helplessly.

Eric looked at her thoughtfully. It would be easy to agree. And probably wise. But as he gazed at Kate, bathed in golden light from the centerpiece candle, the creamy skin of her neck and collarbone glowing warmly, the delicate curve of her neck illuminated by the flickering flame, he was suddenly overcome by a compelling need to hold her in his arms and sway to romantic music. It would be a memory of their brief time together that he could dust off when the nights got long and he was in a melancholy mood, or on those rare occasions when he let himself indulge in fantasy and wonder how differently his life might have turned out if he'd met someone like Kate a dozen years ago.

"I'm willing to give it a try if you are."

Her eyes grew wide. "Are you serious?"

"Absolutely."

"But I'm really not very good, Eric. I'll probably step all over your feet."

"I'm more worried about stepping on yours. Come on, we'll muddle through." He stood and held out his hand.

Kate hesitated. It was true that her dancing skills were extremely rusty. And it was also true that she was worried about looking awkward and embarrassing Eric. But she was even more worried about the close proximity that dancing entailed. It was one thing to sit next to this virile man in the car or at the table, and quite another to be held in his arms. She wasn't exactly sure how she would handle the closeness. But there seemed to be no way to gracefully decline. So she took a deep breath and placed her hand in his.

"You may be sorry," she warned, her voice not quite steady.

"I don't think so."

As he led her out to the dance floor, the orchestra began playing "Unforgettable." He glanced down at her and grinned. "You know, if we're both as bad as we claim, that's exactly what this dance might be."

Her insides were quaking, but she managed to smile. "You could be right."

As it turned out, the dance really was unforgettable. In every way.

From the moment he drew her into his arms, she felt as if she'd come home. They danced together perfectly, moving effortlessly to the beat of the music. And once she realized she didn't have to worry about her feet, she was able to focus on other things—the spicy scent of his after-shave, the way he tenderly folded her right hand in his left, tucking it protectively against his solid chest, and the strong, sure feel of his other hand splayed across her back, guiding her firmly but gently.

Kate closed her eyes and let his touch and the romantic music work their magic. It had been a long time, such a very long time, since she'd been held this way; since she'd felt so safe and protected and—the word *cherished* came to mind. Which was strange. After all, she barely knew Eric. But something about the way he held her made her feel all of those things. Of course, it might just be her imagination. But, real or not, she intended to enjoy the moment, because it might never come again. With a contented sigh, she relaxed against him.

Eric felt Kate's sudden relaxation, and instinctively he drew her closer, tilting his head slightly so that her lustrous hair brushed his cheek. Then he closed his eyes and inhaled, savoring the faint, pleasing floral fragrance that emanated from her skin. She felt good in his arms, he reflected; soft and feminine and very, very appealing. He swallowed with difficulty. *Dear Lord, why did you send someone like this my way?* he cried silently, overcome by a sudden sense of anguish and regret. *I made a vow in Your sight on my wedding day that I don't want to break. But I'm lonely, Lord. And Kate is getting harder and harder to resist. Her sweetness and values and kind heart are like a ray of sun in my life. I'm drawn to her, Lord. Powerfully. Please help me find the strength to do what is right.*

By the time the music ended, Kate was fairly quivering. And Eric didn't look much steadier, she reflected, as—with obvious reluctance—he released her. The hand that rested at the small of her back as he guided her toward their table felt about as unsteady as her legs.

"Eric! I knew you were here somewhere but I just couldn't seem to find you in this crowd."

They turned in unison as a man in his mid-fifties with salt-and-pepper hair approached them.

"Hello, Reverend Jacobs." Eric's voice sounded husky, she noted. But at least it was working. She wasn't sure about her own. "It's quite a turnout, isn't it?"

"It gets bigger every year, which is very gratifying."

"Reverend, I'd like you to meet Kate Nolan. Kate, Reverend Carl Jacobs, my minister."

"Nice to meet you, Mrs. Nolan." The man extended his hand, and Kate found her fingers engulfed in a firm, somehow reassuring clasp. She stared at the minister, struck by the kindness and serenity in his eyes. He radiated calm, like someone who was at peace with life, who understood the vagaries of this world and had not only accepted them, but had found a way to move beyond them. He seemed, somehow, like a man with answers. The kind of answers Kate had been searching for.

Their gazes held for a long moment, until at last Kate found her voice. "It's nice to meet you, too. Eric has spoken very highly of you."

"And also of you. I've met your daughter. She's charming."

"Thank you."

Suddenly Eric reached inside his jacket and retrieved his pager. He scanned the message, then frowned. "Would you two excuse me while I make a quick phone call?"

"Of course," Kate replied.

"I'll keep Mrs. Nolan company," the reverend promised.

They watched as Eric threaded his way through the crowd, then disappeared.

"He works too hard," Reverend Jacobs remarked. "But it's difficult to fault such dedication. And he's a fine doctor."

"I agree."

"Eric has mentioned you, Mrs. Nolan. Have you known each other long?"

"Please call me Kate. Actually, Eric and I have a somewhat unusual history. We met—if you could call it that—five years ago, when my husband was seriously injured in a car accident. Eric saved his life."

The minister's eyebrows rose. "Is that right? Eric never mentioned it. But then, I'm not surprised. To use an old cliché, he isn't one to blow his own horn. But I understood from Eric that you were a widow."

"Yes. My husband lived for several months after the accident, but he never regained consciousness."

"I'm so sorry, Kate. It must have been a very difficult time for you. Sarah would have been just a baby, I'm sure."

She swallowed and nodded. "She was six weeks old. She needed me, and so I managed to get through the days. But it was almost like my own life ended in some ways when Jack died," she said quietly.

"I know what you mean. I lost my wife of thirty years to cancer just five months ago. She left a void that can never be filled."

Kate's face softened in sympathy. "I'm so sorry, Reverend."

"Thank you. It's been a difficult time. But the Lord has sustained me."

A flash of pain and bitterness swept through her. "I wish I could say the same. I always felt He'd deserted me."

"Many people feel that way in the face of tragedy," Reverend

Jacobs returned in an understanding tone that held no censure. "But often the opposite actually happens. We think the Lord hasn't answered our prayers, so we turn away. But you know, He always does answer us. It's just that sometimes it's not the answer we want to hear."

Kate frowned. "I've never thought of it quite that way before. But why would He take someone like Jack, who was so young and had so much to offer? Why would He not only take my husband, but deprive Sarah of a father? What sense does that make?"

"The Lord's ways are often difficult to understand, Kate. And I certainly don't have all the answers," the minister said gently. "But maybe together we could find a few. I'd certainly be happy to talk things through with you. Why don't you stop by some day?"

Kate thought about Eric's comment at the barbecue—that Reverend Jacobs had helped him through some difficult times. Might he be able to do the same for her? Help her find the sense of peace that he so obviously had, even in the face of a recent, tragic loss? It seemed like an option that might bear exploring.

"I just might do that, Reverend."

"Please do." He extracted a card from his pocket and handed it to her, then glanced over her shoulder. "Well, here comes your host." He waved at Eric, who was weaving through the crowd, then turned to Kate and extended his hand. "I have several more people to see before I leave tonight. It was a pleasure to meet you. And do think about stopping by."

"I will."

Eric rejoined her a moment later, and the concern on his face made her breath catch in her throat. "What's wrong? Is Sarah...?"

"Sarah's fine," he reassured her quickly, noting her sudden pallor. "That was my exchange. I'm on call tonight. One of my patients has been in an accident, and her parents are on their way to the hospital with her now. I promised to meet them. Normally I'd just let the emergency room handle it, but she's got asthma as well and I thought a familiar face might help calm her down. She's only eight."

"Of course." She reached for her purse and tucked the minister's card inside.

"Kate, I'm sorry about this," Eric said regretfully. "I wanted us to have a nice evening."

"But we have! The dinner was lovely, and we even got to dance. That's more than I've done in a long time. Please don't worry about it."

He gazed down into Kate's sincere eyes and felt a lump form in his throat. He remembered Cindy's attitude on occasions when they'd had to cut a social evening short—resentful, put-upon, angry. It had put a strain on their relationship for days. Of course, Cindy had been through it many times. This was a first for Kate. Maybe, in time, she'd grow to feel the same way. But somehow he didn't think so. Not that the theory would ever be put to the test, he reminded himself firmly.

"Thanks for understanding," he said quietly.

She shrugged off his gratitude. "Don't be silly. If I was a parent with an injured child, I'd want *my* doctor there. It's the right thing to do."

"Nevertheless, I appreciate it. I'd take you home first, but the hospital is so close. How about if I call you a cab?"

"Why don't I just go with you?"

That was an offer he'd never heard before. "To the hospital?" he asked in surprise.

"Would that be okay?"

"Sure. I'd appreciate the company," he said honestly. "But it could be a while," he warned.

"If you're delayed I can just get a cab from there. I don't mind waiting, Eric." Which was true. She really didn't want their evening to end just yet.

"Okay, if you're sure."

As they turned to go, she expected him to place his hand at the small of her back and guide her toward the door, as had become his custom. But instead, he surprised her by taking her hand in his, linking their fingers and squeezing gently. The smile he gave her was warm and somehow intimate.

"Thanks for being a good sport."

As he led her out of the ballroom, Kate savored the feel of his strong fingers entwined with hers. And she wondered about Cindy's customary reaction to an interruption such as this. Not good, apparently, considering how grateful—and taken aback—Eric had been by her acceptance of it. She was beginning to form a picture of his married life. And it wasn't pretty.

A movement on the other side of the waiting room caught her eye, and Kate looked up from her magazine. The young couple whose daughter had been injured had risen anxiously, privy to something in the corridor hidden from Kate's view. A moment later Eric entered and walked toward them. Though they spoke in low tones, their voices carried clearly.

"How is she, Doctor?" The man's face was lined with anxiety, and Kate could tell even from across the room that his wife had a death grip on his hand. Her heart contracted in sympathy, and she blinked back sudden tears. She knew what it was like to wait in a cold, sterile anteroom for news about someone you loved.

"She'll be fine, Mr. Thomas. Let's sit down for a minute. Mrs. Thomas?" Eric nodded toward a cluster of chairs and gently guided the mother toward one, clearly attuned to the woman's emotional distress. Kate was impressed by his astuteness—and his thoughtfulness. In a medical world that was often clinical and impersonal, Eric appeared to be an admirable exception. Which somehow didn't surprise her.

When they were seated, he spoke again, his tone calm and reassuring. "Emily has lots of scrapes and bruises, but nothing requiring stitches. Her arm is broken—in two places, actually—but they're clean breaks and should heal just fine. Dr. West is a fine orthopedic surgeon and he took care of everything. She was having a little trouble with her breathing when I first arrived, but we got that under control very quickly. Once I started talking to her about your vacation to Walt Disney World, she calmed down and the asthma wasn't a problem. We'd like to keep her overnight just to make sure she's not in too much pain and monitor her breathing. There should be no problem with her going home in the morning."

The relief on the young couple's faces was visible from across the room, Kate noted discreetly.

"I can't thank you enough for coming in tonight, Doctor," the woman said gratefully, her voice thick with tears. "We told her all the way here in the car that you were coming, and that helped to keep her calm. We were so afraid she'd have an attack!''

''No thanks are necessary, Mrs. Thomas. I'm just doing my job.''

''You do a lot more than that,'' the girl's father corrected him. ''Most doctors just send you to the emergency room. They don't show up themselves. This means a lot to us. Especially when it's obvious we interrupted a special event.'' He nodded toward Eric's tux.

''I was glad to do it. I'll stop by in the morning and check on Emily, and by lunchtime she'll be ready to go home. Just tell her not to play soccer quite so aggressively in the future,'' he said with a grin.

''Do you think maybe we should take her off the team?'' the man asked anxiously.

''Not at all. We've got her asthma under control. And kids need to run and play and stretch their wings. Reasonable caution is prudent. Excessive caution is stifling. Sometimes accidents happen, but that's part of living.'' Eric rose. ''They're getting ready to move her to a room, so let me take you down to her and you can walk with her.''

Eric glanced at Kate and smiled as he ushered the couple out, mouthing, ''I'll be right back.'' She nodded.

When he reappeared a few minutes later, she was waiting at the doorway. He smiled at her ruefully. ''You look ready to leave.''

''Let's just say hospitals aren't my favorite places,'' she replied lightly, but he heard the pain in her voice. His gut clenched at the echo of sadness in her eyes and he frowned.

''I'm sorry, Kate. I didn't even think about that. I shouldn't have let you come. Instead of leaving you with pleasant memories of tonight, I've dredged up unhappy ones.''

''I wanted to come,'' she insisted. ''And I'm glad I did. It wasn't as hard as I thought it might be.''

He took her arm and guided her purposefully toward the door. ''But there's no reason to hang around now. It's my second trip today, anyway.'' He glanced at his watch and his frown deepened. ''It's probably too late to go back to the dance. Would you like to stop and get a cup of coffee on the way home?''

She looked up at him. He'd mentioned he was on call this weekend. And that he'd already made one trip to the hospital today. There were fine lines at the corners of his eyes, and slight shadows beneath them. Much as she'd like to extend the evening, she shook her head. "It's been a long week, Eric. And there's no reason to keep your mother up any later than necessary. Let's head back."

He studied her for a moment. "Are you sure?"

"Of course. But I had a good time tonight, despite the interruption."

He chuckled. "I guess we should look on the bright side," he said as they reached his car and he opened the door for her.

She glanced at him curiously. "What do you mean?"

"Well, we may have ended up at a hospital, but at least it wasn't because of any broken toes."

She smiled. He had a good sense of humor. And he wasn't afraid to laugh at himself. She liked that. "Good point. Actually, I think we did quite well for two very out-of-practice dancers."

Eric almost suggested that they polish up their skills another night, but he caught himself in time. There wouldn't be another time, he reminded himself soberly. It was too dangerous, because Kate was easy to be with, and he knew with absolute certainty that she could very easily become a part of his life—an important part. But given his situation, all he could offer her was friendship.

And his feelings were already running way too deep for that.

# Chapter Six

Kate drew a deep breath, then reached up and rang the bell on the parsonage. She wasn't sure exactly why she had followed through and made an appointment with Reverend Jacobs, except that she had been struck by the calm and peace he radiated even in the face of personal tragedy. She sensed that he had found the answers to some of life's harder questions, and that he might also have some of the answers *she* needed. It couldn't hurt to find out, especially since Anna had agreed to keep Sarah for an extra hour after school so Kate could take care of some "personal" business.

The door swung open, and Reverend Jacobs smiled at her kindly. "Kate. It's good to see you again. Come in."

She stepped into the foyer, and as the minister led her toward his office he paused beside an older woman seated at a word processor.

"Kate, this is Margaret Stephens. She's been with me for... how long, Margaret?"

The woman smiled indulgently. "Twenty-two years, Reverend."

"That's right, twenty-two years. She keeps my professional life in order. I'd be lost without her. Margaret, Kate Nolan."

They exchanged greetings, then the minister ushered his visitor into the office and closed the door. "I know you're on a tight schedule, Kate. Please make yourself comfortable." He indicated a small sitting area off to one side. "Can I offer you some coffee?"

"No, thanks. I've had my one cup for the day. My husband was the real coffee drinker in the family," she said, her lips curving up in affectionate remembrance.

Reverend Jacobs filled a mug and sat in a chair at right angles to hers. "Would you mind telling me a little bit about him, Kate? I can see that he's still a very important part of your life. I have a feeling that to know you, I also need to know him."

"I—I hardly know where to begin, Reverend," she faltered, her smile fading.

"How about telling me how you met?"

Under his gentle questioning, Kate found herself recounting their first meeting, courtship and eventual engagement. Halting phrases eventually gave way to a flood of words as she spoke about their wedding, their early years as a married couple, and their joy at Sarah's birth. Only when she came to the accident, the subsequent seven-month nightmare and her feelings of confusion and abandonment, did she once more struggle to find words.

"At first I refused to accept the prognosis," she said, her voice subdued and laced with pain. "I just couldn't believe the Lord would allow Jack to be paralyzed or to...to die. I prayed constantly, not only for my sake, but for Sarah's. I didn't want her to grow up without a father. I had faith, and every time I went to the hospital I believed there would be a breakthrough. But the months went by with no change, and eventually Jack was moved to a long-term-care facility. That's when I began to lose hope. Seven months after the accident, he died."

"Tell me about how you felt then, Kate," Reverend Jacobs said gently.

She lifted her shoulders wearily. "Numb. Devastated. Angry. Guilty. Confused. A whole tangle of emotions. I still feel a lot of them."

"Can you talk to me about the anger and guilt?"

She drew a deep breath. "I was angry at God," she said slowly. "I still am. And I was angry at Jack—which was totally illogical and only made me feel guilty. The accident wasn't his fault. But I still felt as if he'd deserted me. And then I kept thinking, if only he'd worn his seat belt. I should have reminded him to buckle up. I usually did. But it just didn't occur to me that night. So that added to the guilt."

"None of those feelings are abnormal, Kate. I experienced many of them myself when my wife died. I felt guilty, too, thinking that if only I'd insisted she go to the doctor sooner, she might have lived. And when she died, I was angry. She was taken from me just when we were reaching the stage in our lives when we'd planned to travel and spend more time together. All of the thoughts and emotions you mentioned are part of the natural grieving process. Knowing that others have gone through the same things often helps. Have you shared your feelings with anyone?''

''No. I just…couldn't find the words. And then I kept trying to figure out why God would take Jack from us. It just didn't make sense. I began to think that maybe…maybe I was being punished for something I did wrong,'' she said in a small voice.

The minister nodded sympathetically. ''People often feel as you did when they lose someone they love—that it's their own fault in some way. But that's not the case, Kate. Jack's death had nothing to do with you. It was simply his time to go to the Lord. We can spend our lives asking why about such things, but that's an exercise in futility. The better path is to simply let go and admit that even though we can't understand the Lord's ways, we accept them. That's the only way to find peace in this world. But it's not always easy.''

She nodded, and hot tears welled in her eyes. ''I know. I've been trying to find that peace for a long time.''

''You took a good first step today.''

Kate shook her head sadly. ''I'm not sure about that, Reverend. To be frank, I only came because I'm desperate. You found peace because your faith is strong. Mine isn't, or it would have sustained me through this trial. Instead, it died with Jack. So I guess on top of everything else, I've failed God.'' Her voice broke on the last word.

Reverend Jacobs leaned forward intently. ''Let me tell you something, Kate. Doubts and despair don't make you a bad person. They just mean you're human. That's how the Lord created us, with all the weaknesses and frailties that entails. He doesn't expect perfection. He knows we stumble and lose our way. In fact, the history of Christianity is filled with holy men and women who experienced a dark night of the soul at some point in their lives. The Lord didn't disown them because of that, even when they disowned Him. He just patiently waited for them to come home. That's the beauty of our faith, Kate. The Lord is always ready to welcome us back, no matter how far we wander, once we open our hearts to Him.''

Kate saw nothing but sincerity and compassion in the minister's eyes, and a little flicker of hope leaped to life in her soul. ''I'd like to believe that, Reverend. I'd like to try to find my way back. But I—I don't know how.''

''As I said, you've already taken the first step by coming here today. And I'll do all I can to help you. May I also suggest that you join your lovely little girl at Sunday services? Just hearing the words of Scripture may offer you some comfort and guidance. You probably won't find what you're seeking in one or two visits, but if you persist, in God's time you will.''

Kate wasn't convinced. But clearly Reverend Jacobs was. And her faith *had* been important to her at one time. Perhaps, with the minister's help, it could be again.

Kate nervously adjusted the belt on her navy blue knit dress, then ran a brush through her hair. She knew Eric would be surprised when he discovered he had two guests for services today. She probably should have called and warned him. But she hadn't decided for sure about going until this morning. And besides, he *had* told her she was welcome anytime. She hoped that was still true, considering she hadn't heard from him since the night of the dinner dance, a week before. But then, why should she? Their outings had been defined as ''favors,'' not dates. He probably didn't need any more of those. Neither of them was in the market for romance, but she had hoped that maybe they could be friends.

The doorbell interrupted her thoughts, and she headed toward the living room. ''I'll get it,'' she told Sarah as she passed the bathroom. ''You finish up those teeth.''

When she reached the door, she took a deep breath to steady her suddenly rapid pulse, then smiled before she pulled it open. ''Good morning, Eric.''

His own smile of welcome turned into a look of inquiry as his gaze swept over her. ''You're awfully dressed up for grading papers.''

She flushed. ''Actually, I thought I might— That is, if the invitation is still open I'd like to join you for church today.''

For a brief moment before he shuttered his emotions she thought she saw a flash of apprehension—and dismay—in his eyes, and her stomach clenched painfully. She stepped aside to let him enter, then turned to face him nervously.

"I stopped by to see Reverend Jacobs Friday after school, and we had a long talk. You were right. He's a good listener. I felt better about…about a lot of things after we spoke. He suggested I try coming back to church, so I decided to join you today, if that's okay."

"Mom will be delighted."

A telling response, she reflected, suddenly acutely embarrassed. His *mother* would be delighted. Not him. She hadn't imagined his reluctance. For some reason he was pulling back, retreating from the relationship he'd initiated with her, she realized as a flush rose to her cheeks.

"Listen, Eric, maybe this isn't such a good idea. After all, I have my own car. It isn't as if we have to go together. I don't want to impose and take you out of your way when there's no need. I should have called you earlier and just said we'd see you there. I'm sorry to—"

The words died in her throat as he reached over and touched her arm.

"Kate."

She stared at him with wide, uncertain eyes. He looked down at her, frowning. She'd obviously picked up on his sudden discomfort, he realized. His resolve to stay away from her was shaky at best, but he'd figured it would hold if he just stopped by once a week to pick up Sarah and only saw Kate long enough to say hello. Her unexpected decision to go to church complicated things tremendously. But that was *his* problem. He *had* invited her to join them. She didn't strike him as the kind of woman who reached out easily, and his response had been far from enthusiastic. He needed to reassure her without telling her the real reason for his hesitation.

"You surprised me, that's all. I think it's great you've decided to go back to church."

She looked into his eyes, searching for the consternation she'd seen earlier, but it was gone. Had she imagined it? she wondered in confusion.

"We can go on our own in the future," she offered, her voice still uncertain. "I just thought it might be easier this first time to be with people we know."

His hand still rested on her arm, and its warmth seeped through the thin fabric of her dress as he gave her a gentle squeeze. "We'll talk about the future later, okay? Let's just worry about today for now."

It was a vague answer, but his voice was kind and his smile genuine. Besides, the future might not even be an issue. She might never go back to church again. She wasn't convinced that it would make that much difference, despite Reverend Jacobs's confidence.

But half an hour later, sitting in a pew beside Eric, she had the oddest sense of homecoming. As she listened to the words of Scripture, joined in the old familiar hymns and reflected on the sermon appropriately titled "All You Must Do Is Knock," she was surprised at just how much the experience touched her heart. And Reverend Jacobs's warm greeting afterward made her feel good—and welcome.

"I'm so glad you came, Kate," he said, taking her hand in a firm grip.

"So am I."

"Eric, Anna, good to see you both. Hello, Sarah."

"Hello," the little girl said shyly, staying close beside Kate.

"You know, I bet you'd enjoy our Sunday school," he told the youngster before turning back to Kate. "The fall session is just starting. Sarah would be most welcome."

"Thank you. I'll think about it."

"Just give us a call if you'd like to enroll her."

They moved on then, so others could speak with the minister, and she reached for Sarah's hand as Eric cupped her elbow.

"You'll join us for breakfast, won't you?"

"Can we, Mommy?" Sarah asked eagerly.

Kate glanced quickly at Eric, but his face was unreadable.

"Of course you can," Anna chimed in. "We won't take no for an answer, will we, Eric?"

"Absolutely not," he replied firmly.

"I really don't want to intrude on your time together," Kate protested.

"It's three-to-one, Kate," Eric said with a smile that made her feel warm all over. "Give it up."

She swallowed. "Okay, you win. For today, anyway."

"Oh, goody!" Sarah exclaimed, hopping from one foot to the other. "Can I have pancakes?" she asked Eric.

"Of course."

"This is the best Sunday I can ever remember," she declared happily.

Kate didn't respond. It was one of her best Sundays in a long time, too. But she had an uncomfortable feeling that it wasn't one of Eric's. And for some reason that made her spirits, which had been buoyed by the church service, take a sudden nosedive.

"Did you and Kate have some sort of misunderstanding?"

Eric frowned and positioned the phone more comfortably against his ear as he closed the chart in front of him. "Hello, Mom," he replied wryly.

"Oh. Hello. Well, did you?"

"Did I what?"

"Have a misunderstanding with Kate," she repeated impatiently.

"No."

"Then why won't she go to church with us this Sunday?"

Eric's frown deepened. "You mean she isn't?"

"No. She stayed for a cup of tea today when she picked up Sarah and told me that they would be going by themselves from now on, and to please let you know and thank you for all your help."

Kate had obviously picked up on his momentary panic last Sunday when she'd announced that she was going to accompany them. But maybe that was for the best, he reasoned. He didn't want to hurt her, but he couldn't afford to get too close, because if he did, they could *both* be hurt. Badly. Given his marital status and the demands of his profession—which had ruined one marriage already—she was a temptation he didn't need.

"Eric? Are you still there?" his mother prompted.

"Yes."

"So did something happen between you two to upset her?"

"I haven't even talked to her all week, Mom."

"Why not?"

"I hardly know her."

"Well, I'd hoped you'd be trying to remedy that. Women like Kate don't come along very often, you know. She's a wonderful person."

"She's also still in love with her husband."

"Of course she is. I'm sure she always will be. Love like that doesn't die, Eric." His mother's voice suddenly grew subdued and sad, and his heart contracted in sympathy—and in shared loss. His father's death had been extremely hard on both of them, leaving a gap that could never be filled. "But that doesn't mean you can't ever love anyone else. And I just thought..." Her voice trailed off.

Eric sighed. He knew what she thought—that he needed to find someone new. But aside from the fact that he still considered himself married, there were other pitfalls to a relationship: namely, the demands of his profession.

"That's not an option, Mom," he said gently but firmly.

"But Eric, you've been divorced for almost five years," she argued. "Cindy is remarried. It doesn't seem right for you to be alone. You should have a wife and family."

"I tried that once. It didn't work."

There was a brief hesitation before she quietly declared, "Maybe it was just the wrong woman."

Eric's eyebrows rose in surprise. Though his mother was usually outspoken in her opinion, she'd never before come this close to saying what he'd always suspected she felt about his marriage: that he and Cindy had not been a good match.

"Maybe," he admitted. "But it's too late now for second-guessing."

Her sigh came clearly over the wire. "Sometimes I think you're too hard on yourself, Eric. I'm sure the Lord doesn't expect you to spend the rest of your life alone when the divorce wasn't even your fault. As I recall, Cindy was the one who wanted out. You were willing to work at it."

"I'm not blameless, Mom. I have a demanding career, and it got in the way of our relationship. Marriage and medicine just don't seem to mix."

"That's nonsense," she declared briskly. "Most doctors are married and they manage just fine. Look at Frank."

"Well, maybe he knows some secret I don't."

"There's no secret, Eric. It just takes love and understanding on both sides."

"I can't debate that with you, Mom. All I know is that it didn't work for me. And even if I was free, I'm not willing to take that risk again. Besides, Kate obviously isn't interested. So let it rest. It's probably for the best."

Eric knew his mother wasn't happy with his response. She wanted him to have another chance at love. And as he hung up the receiver, he had to admit that he wanted that, too. Especially now. The hours he'd spent in Kate's company had given him a glimpse of the life he might have had with the right woman. But his error in judgment had cost him dearly, he thought with a disheartened sigh. And he was still paying the price.

Kate read the thermometer gauge worriedly. One hundred and two.

"I don't feel good, Mommy," Sarah whimpered.

Kate smoothed the hair from her daughter's damp forehead with a slightly unsteady hand. "I know, honey. I'm going to call Dr. Eric right now. You just lie here and be very quiet, okay?"

Kate tucked the blankets around Sarah, then headed for the phone to call Eric's exchange. She also spoke with Anna to let her know she was keeping Sarah home tomorrow.

"It's probably just a flu bug, Kate," the older woman reassured her. "Don't worry too much. Children get these things, you know. They bounce back quickly. When did she get sick?"

"A couple of hours ago, right before dinner. It just came on suddenly. She was fine this morning and had a great time at Sunday school."

"Oh, you must have gone to the later service, then. Eric was concerned when we didn't see you at church."

Was he? Kate wondered with a wistfulness that surprised—and disconcerted—her as she rang off. Deep inside she'd like to think his concern was prompted by more than polite consideration. After all, they'd spent two very enjoyable social evenings together. And she liked him. A lot. Too much, maybe, because the feelings he awakened in her made her feel disloyal to Jack. And she wasn't sure how to deal with that. But since he seemed to be putting a distance between them, it apparently wasn't something she needed to worry about, she reminded herself firmly.

But he wasn't putting distance between them today, Kate realized when she opened the door forty-five minutes later and found Eric. Her eyes widened as she noted the well-worn jeans that clung to his long, lean legs and the blue cotton shirt with rolled-up sleeves, open at the neck. Kate had never seen him dressed so informally before, and the effect was…well, stunning. In this rugged clothing, he literally took her breath away. She clung to the edge of the door and stared at him.

"Kate? Are you okay?"

Okay? No, she wasn't okay. In fact, her hand on the edge of the door was trembling. Which was ridiculous! She tried to get a grip. She barely knew this man, she reminded herself. They were practically strangers. Yes, he was handsome. Yes, he was nice. Yes, she found herself attracted to him at some basic level that she didn't understand. But he wasn't in the market for romance, and neither was she. She needed to remember that. She drew a shaky breath and somehow found her voice.

"Yes. I'm fine. But Sarah's not."

"That's why I'm here."

He held up his black bag, which had somehow escaped Kate's notice. Her gaze had gotten stuck on his broad shoulders and muscular chest. "A house call?" she said in surprise, her voice slightly breathless.

He smiled and shrugged. "Mom said you sounded really worried."

Kate stepped aside and motioned him in. "I am. But I didn't expect you to come over. It's your day off, isn't it? The answering service said Frank was taking the calls this weekend."

"He is. But I told him I'd handle this one."

"Why? I mean, you don't do this for all your patients, do you?"

He gazed down at her, and the blue of his eyes seemed to intensify. "No, Kate, I don't."

She stared at him, and her mouth suddenly went dry. He'd answered her second question, but not her first. Which was probably just as well, because she wasn't ready to deal with the answer she might get. At least, not yet. Nervously she tucked her hair behind her ear and looked away. "Well, I—I appreciate it, Eric. Sarah's back here."

Eric followed as she led the way down the short hallway. He was glad she hadn't pressed for an answer to her first question, because he wasn't sure himself why he had come. There had been no need to make a house call. Frank could easily have dealt with the situation by phone. But he'd experienced such a letdown when he didn't see Kate in church this morning that he'd grasped at the first excuse to see her. It wasn't wise, of course. But when it came to her, his heart seemed more in control of his actions than his mind was. Which was a problem he needed to address—and soon.

"Dr. Eric came to see you, honey."

Eric smiled at Sarah as he followed Kate into the charmingly decorated little girl's room and sat down on the bed beside his patient. "Hello, Sarah. I heard you were sick."

"Uh-huh. I threw up."

He glanced at Kate.

She nodded. "Twice in the last hour. And her temperature is still a hundred and two."

"Well, that doesn't sound like much fun." He snapped his bag open as he spoke. "I'd better take a look. Is that all right with you, Sarah?"

"I guess so. You aren't going to give me a shot, are you?"

He chuckled. "Not today. I'm just going to listen to your heart and look in your ears and check out those tonsils."

He conversed easily with Sarah while he did a quick exam. When he finished he removed the stethoscope from around his neck and placed it back in his bag.

"Well, little lady, I think you have the flu. But you know what? You should feel a whole lot better by tomorrow. In the meantime, I want you to drink a lot of soda and water and juice and take aspirin whenever your mom gives them to you. Okay?"

"Okay."

He turned to Kate. "Do you have any white soda?"

She nodded. "I'll get some—and the aspirin."

As Kate disappeared down the hall, he turned back to find Sarah studying him quite seriously. "Dr. Eric, do you have a little girl of your own?" she asked suddenly.

A pang of regret ricocheted through him, almost painful in its intensity, but he managed to smile. "No."

"Do you wish you had a little girl?"

"Sometimes."

"Sometimes I wish I had a daddy, too." She pointed to a picture of Jack on her bedside table. "He was my daddy. Mommy says he watches out for me from heaven now, but I wish I had a daddy who could hold me in his lap and tell me stories."

"I wish you did, too, Sarah." Eric reached over and smoothed the hair back from her flushed face as his throat constricted. If everything had gone the way he'd planned, he would have his own children right now, and a wife who loved him. But he'd never have the former. Nor had he ever had the latter, he thought sadly. Through the years he had gradually come to realize that Cindy had never really loved him—not in the fullest sense of that word. It had been a hard thing to accept. It still was.

"Maybe you could be my daddy," Sarah said brightly. "Then you could read me stories at night and—"

"Sarah!"

Eric turned to find Kate in the doorway, her face flushed.

"What's wrong, Mommy?" Sarah asked innocently, her eyes wide.

Eric watched silently as Kate drew a deep breath. "Nothing's wrong, honey. But you need to drink your soda so you can go to sleep. Then you'll be all better tomorrow, just like Dr. Eric said."

Eric stood as Kate moved into the room. She avoided his eyes, and bright spots of pink still burned on each cheek.

"I'll let myself out," he said quietly.

"No." She looked up at him, obviously still embarrassed by Sarah's remark, though good manners took precedence. "I put the kettle on. Please stay and have a cup of tea or coffee. And some cake. It's the least I can do after you came over here on your day off."

He hesitated, then nodded. "All right. I'll wait for you in the living room."

Kate watched him leave, then turned back to Sarah and helped her sit up enough to drink the soda.

"Are you mad, Mommy?" Sarah asked in a small voice.

"No, honey. Of course not."

"You seemed mad when you came back in the room."

Kate shook her head. "I wasn't mad, Sarah. I heard what you and Dr. Eric were talking about, and I just got sad for a minute because your daddy isn't here with us. He loved you very much, honey. Before you were born we used to plan all the things the three of us would do together. I'm just very sorry he can't be here to do them with us." Kate picked up the photo from the bedside table and gently traced Jack's face with her finger. "Don't ever forget how much he loved you, Sarah. He's part of you. See? You have his eyes. And you have that little dimple in your cheek, just like he had. So part of Daddy will always be with us in you."

Sarah studied the photo for a moment. "He was pretty, wasn't he, Mommy?"

Kate blinked to clear the sudden film of moisture in her eyes. "Yes, Sarah. He was very pretty."

"Do you think he misses us up in heaven?"

"I'm sure he does."

"But he can't come back, can he, Mommy?"

"No, honey."

"Do you think he would be mad if I got a new daddy sometime? Just for while I'm down here?"

Would he? Kate wondered, as she replaced the photo. She'd never thought of it quite that way. And in that context, she knew the answer. Jack wouldn't want Sarah to grow up without the influence of a kind, caring father in her life. They had always talked about how they wanted her to experience all the joys of a real family—two loving parents and at least a sibling or two. Jack would still want that, even if he couldn't be the one to provide it.

"No, Sarah," Kate replied slowly. "I don't think he'd mind. Your daddy would want you to have a father."

"But how would I get one?" Sarah asked, clearly puzzled.

"Well, I would have to get married again."

"Would you do that, Mommy?"

"I don't know, honey. Your daddy was a very special man. It would be hard to find someone like him again."

"Is Dr. Eric like him?"

Kate glanced toward the bedroom door and dropped her voice. "I just met Dr. Eric, honey. I don't know him well enough to answer that question."

Sarah scooted down in the bed and pulled the covers up to her chin. Already her eyes were drifting closed. "Well, then I think you should get to know him better," she declared sleepily.

Kate adjusted the covers, then reached over and touched the photo of Jack, her gaze troubled. For several long moments she just sat there. She didn't want to do anything that would diminish the love they had shared. It was a beautiful thing, and she would always treasure it in her heart. But it was only a memory now. And memories could only sustain one for so long.

Kate sighed as she reached over and turned off the light. Even if she was ready to move on—and she wasn't convinced that she was—Eric wasn't available. He'd made that eminently clear. In his mind, he still had a wife. And after his first disastrous marriage, he truly believed that medicine and marriage didn't mix. So, if and when she decided to consider romance again, she'd have to look elsewhere.

Except, for some strange reason that plan held no appeal.

# Chapter Seven

Eric listened to the murmur of voices as he restlessly roamed around Kate's living room. He couldn't distinguish the words, but he could guess what they were talking about. Sarah's last remark had clearly embarrassed Kate. And probably upset her, as well. He suspected that she'd done everything she could to make Jack as real as possible for Sarah. But it was a hard thing to do when the little girl had no memory of him. To her he was only an image, like the characters in her storybooks, with no basis in reality. What she wanted was a real daddy—someone who could hold her hand and share her life. Kate was fighting a losing battle, Eric thought with a sigh. Sarah was too young to be comforted by stories of a father she had never known.

Eric wandered into the kitchen, shoving his hands into the pockets of his jeans as he glanced around. The room was small but homey, with several of Sarah's drawings displayed on the refrigerator. The remains of a hardly touched dinner lay strewn next to the sink—macaroni and cheese, green beans, salad. Sarah must have started to feel badly before they ate more than a few bites.

His gaze swept over the eat-in counter that separated the living room and kitchen, taking in the pile of half-graded school papers, a copy of the church bulletin—and a loan statement at his elbow reflecting a balance of nearly six figures. Eric frowned and quickly glanced away. The latter was obviously private business. But he knew what the debt most likely represented: Jack's medical bills—probably for the extended-care facility where he'd spent his last months. Eric had seen too many instances where insurance covered only certain expenses in situations like that, leaving the survivors deep in debt. He could make a reasonable guess at Kate's salary, and he knew it would take her years to repay the loan. It just didn't seem fair, he reflected, his frown deepening as his eyes strayed back to the statement. He could write a check for the entire amount and not even miss it. To Kate, it was obviously a fortune.

"She's sleeping now."

Eric's gaze flew guiltily to hers and hot color stole up his neck. Kate glanced down at the counter, and a flush reddened her cheeks as she moved to gather up the papers, putting the statement at the bottom of the stack.

"Sorry. The place isn't usually so cluttered."

"I wasn't looking, Kate. It was just lying there," Eric said quietly. To pretend he hadn't seen the piece of paper would be foolish.

She sighed and her hands stilled, but she kept her eyes averted. "I know."

"For Jack's care, I assume?"

She hesitated briefly, then nodded. "The health insurance covered a lot, and the life insurance helped—later. But the expenses piled up so quickly. The debt was absolutely staggering. It still is. And with nothing to show for it," she added wearily, her voice catching in a way that tugged at his heart.

There was silence for a moment, and then she straightened her shoulders and looked up at him. "But you didn't come here tonight to hear about my problems. Let me get you that cup of coffee and cake I promised."

Actually, he wished she *would* share her problems with him. But he understood her reluctance. Their acquaintance was still too new. So he let it drop, nodding instead toward the sink. "It looks like you haven't even had dinner yet."

She glanced disinterestedly at the remains of the meal. "I had enough. I haven't been that hungry lately, anyway."

Eric frowned as she moved to the stove to fill the kettle, his gaze sweeping over her too-thin figure. "You can't afford to skip too many meals, Kate."

She shrugged as she set out two plates. "I eat when I'm hungry."

"Do you rest when you're tired?"

She paused in surprise, holding the knife motionless above the cinnamon coffee cake, and sent him a startled look. Then she turned back to her task. "I rest when there's time."

"Why do I think that's never?"

She turned to face him again, the smile on her face tinged with sadness. "You sound like my mother."

Eric didn't *feel* like her mother. Far from it. As his gaze took in her ebony hair tumbling around her face, her dark eyes shadowed with fatigue, her slender, deceptively fragile-looking form, he felt a fierce surge of protectiveness sweep over him—as well as something else he tried to ignore. He cleared his throat.

"You're the only mother in this room, Kate. And father, too, for that matter. It can't be easy, raising a child alone, trying to play both roles."

Her eyes grew troubled, and she turned away to reach for the kettle as it began to whistle. "Listen, Eric, I'm sorry about what Sarah said. She has a way of coming out with things that aren't always...well, discreet."

He waved her apology aside. "Don't worry about it, Kate. I hear all kinds of things from kids. Most of it I don't take seriously."

She placed their cake on the counter, then reached for her tea and his coffee, pushing aside the school papers as she sat on a stool next to him.

"Looks like you have some work ahead of you," he commented, nodding toward the pile.

"That's the lot of a teacher, I suppose. A never-ending stream of papers to grade. I usually work on them after Sarah goes to bed so I don't have to give up any of my time with her."

He looked at her. She was seated only inches away from him—so close he could clearly discern the faint lines of strain around her mouth. "Does sleep enter into the equation anywhere?" he asked gently. "You look tired, Kate."

The concern in his voice touched her, and her throat tightened as an unaccustomed warmth swept over her. "I catch up on my sleep in the summer," she replied, striving for a light tone. The truth was, she needed to take a summer job as well, at least something part-time.

"I have a feeling you're the kind of woman who never gives herself a break."

She propped her chin in her hand and played with her tea bag, swirling it in the amber liquid. "Jack always said I was too intense," she admitted quietly. "That I took everything too seriously. But that's just the way I am. If I commit to something, I can't do it halfway. Like teaching. I didn't want to go back to it. I wanted to stay home with Sarah. But that wasn't to be. So as long as I have to work, I intend to give one hundred percent. The same with raising Sarah. I want to be the very best mother possible under the circumstances. That's why I spend every spare minute with her. It's why I grade papers and do lesson plans at night." She paused and looked over at him speculatively. "You strike me as being equally committed to your profession, Eric. I can't imagine you ever doing anything halfway."

He conceded the point with a nod. "You're right. But maybe that's not the best way to be. Sometimes I wonder if..." His voice trailed off and he stared down pensively into his coffee.

Kate knew he was thinking about his failed marriage, and impulsively she reached over and lightly touched his hand. The simple contact jolted him. "I have a feeling you're being too hard on yourself about...the past," she said quietly.

He stared down at her delicate hand as its warmth seeped into his very pores. It took only this simple innocent touch, filled with tender compassion, to remind him how lonely and empty his life had become. That reminder left a feeling of bleakness in its wake. Carefully he removed his hand on the pretext of reaching for his fork.

"How did we get into such a heavy discussion?" he asked, forcing his lips up into the semblance of a smile as he speared a bite of cake.

"I don't know. I think we started off talking about food."

"Well, then, let's get back to that topic," he declared, "because this cake is wonderful. Did you make it?"

"Uh-huh."

He devoured another large bite, clearly savoring the dessert. "You know, the only time I ever have home baking anymore is at Mom's. I could live on this cake. What it is?"

"Sour-cream cinnamon streusel coffee cake," she recited with a smile. "It was one of my mom's favorite recipes. Kind of a family standard."

"Well, you can bake this for me anytime. I'd make more house calls if I always got treats like this in return."

"Do you actually make house calls?"

"Once in a great while."

"Well, I'm glad you did tonight. Although my checkbook might not be," she teased with a smile.

Eric stopped eating for a moment and looked at her. "There's no charge for this, Kate."

Her smile faded. "Wait a minute. This was a professional call, Eric. I expect to be billed. You don't owe me any favors. And I always pay my debts."

He finished off the last of the cake, then stood. "Okay, then bake me one of these sometime and we'll be even."

"That's not…"

"Kate." He picked up his bag and turned to her. "I know you pay your debts. I saw evidence of that tonight. If you want to repay me, then do me a favor. Bake me one of these—" he tapped on the cake plate, then turned to look at her "—and get more rest. You're doing a great job taking care of Sarah. Now you need to take care of yourself."

She followed him to the door, prepared to continue the argument, but when he turned there was something in his cobalt-blue eyes that made her protest die in her throat. Their expression was unreadable, but the warmth in their depths was unmistakable. And when he spoke, his voice was slightly husky.

"Good night, Kate. Call me if Sarah isn't a lot better by tomorrow."

She swallowed, with difficulty. "I will. And thank you, Eric."

"It was my pleasure."

He looked at her for a moment, his gaze intense, and her breath got stuck somewhere in her chest. Slowly he reached up and touched her face, and she felt every muscle in her body begin to quiver. His fingers were gentle, the contact brief and unplanned, but as their gazes locked for an instant, Kate saw a flame leap to life in his eyes. Her stomach fluttered strangely, and she remembered

Sarah's words to her earlier—*"I think you should get to know him better."*

Her mouth went dry and she seemed unable to move. Eric's gaze seared into her soul—assessing, discerning, seeking. She stopped breathing, not at all sure what was happening. Or if she could stop it. Or—most disturbing of all—if she even *wanted* to.

And then, abruptly, he turned away, striding quickly down the stairs. Kate stared after him, her heart hammering painfully in her chest as she thought about what had just happened. Had Eric been thinking about kissing her? Or had she only imagined it? But she hadn't imagined his touch. Her cheek was still tingling where his hand had rested.

And what did that touch mean? she wondered with a troubled frown as she slowly closed the door. And why had he done it?

Why did you do that? Eric berated himself as he strode angrily toward his car. He tossed his bag onto the passenger side and slid behind the wheel, his fingers gripping its curved edge as he stared into the darkness, struggling to understand what had just happened.

The self-control he'd carefully honed through the years had slipped badly tonight, he admitted. He wasn't normally an impulsive man. But as he'd looked at Kate's willowy form silhouetted in the doorway, he had been overwhelmed by a powerful urge to touch her, to reassure her in a tactile way that she wasn't as alone as she seemed to feel. He had wanted to tell her that she could always call on him, for anything. Had wanted to pull her into his arms and hold her. Had wanted to kiss her, to taste her sweet lips beneath his.

Eric let out a ragged breath and closed his eyes. Thank heaven he hadn't given in to that impulse; that he'd resisted his instincts and confined himself to a simple touch. But it hadn't been easy. And he had a sinking feeling in the pit of his stomach that the next time, it would be even more difficult.

Eric knew that he should strengthen his resolve to keep their contact to a minimum. He knew that just being around Kate was a dangerous temptation he didn't need. But he also knew it was a risk he was going to take—as soon as he regained his equilibrium and self-control. He figured that would take a week, maybe two. It wouldn't be easy to wait that long to see her again, he acknowledged. But he would manage it.

Three days later, Eric was already trying to think of an excuse to call Kate. So much for resolve, he thought grimly as he pulled into the attached garage of his modest bungalow, then headed down the driveway to retrieve the mail. She hadn't contacted him, so he'd assumed Sarah was feeling much better. Which had meant no more house calls. That was good, of course. For Sarah, anyway.

Eric reached into the mailbox and withdrew the usual assortment of bills and ads, flipping through the stack disinterestedly until a letter with his former sister-in-law's return address caught his eye. He frowned. Odd. He hadn't heard from Elaine since the divorce, more than four years ago. He closed the garage door and entered the kitchen, tossing the bulk of the mail on the counter and loosening his tie before slitting open the envelope and scanning the letter.

I know you will be surprised to hear from me, Eric, but I was reasonably certain that unless I wrote, you might never hear about Cindy. I know there was no love lost between the two of you by the time your marriage ended, but I think it's only right to let you know that she died a month ago. She was diagnosed with lung cancer a year ago—so far along that it was hopeless from the start. I guess her chain-smoking finally caught up with her.

Cindy never talked much about the divorce, although she did say that it was her idea. She was my sister and I loved her, but I want you to know that I always felt she had thrown away something pretty wonderful when she left you. I'm sure there was fault on both sides—there always is—but I suspect, much as I loved Cindy, that the bulk of it lay with her. I can only imagine what a devastating experience the breakup was for you, knowing what I do of you from our contact during your marriage.

I hope life has treated you more kindly since the breakup, Eric, and wish you only the best in the future.

Elaine

Eric stared numbly at the paper, then slowly sat down at the table. Cancer was a devastating disease that ravaged its victims physically. He couldn't even imagine how Cindy, who had always taken such care with her appearance, had coped with that—not to mention all the pain and suffering that cancer inflicted.

For a moment he allowed himself to recall how she had looked at their wedding, her blond beauty absolutely radiant and perfect; and how his heart had been so filled with love on that dream-come-true day. But over the next few years he'd watched that dream slowly disintegrate, until the night of the accident, when it had become a nightmare.

Eric raised a shaky hand and raked his fingers through his hair. He hadn't thought about that night in a long time, had purposely kept the memory of their confrontation at bay. But now the scene came back with startling clarity, the sequence of events unfolding in his mind as if on a movie screen.

At Eric's insistence, they'd cut their evening short. He hadn't been able to get the accident out of his mind, and the smoke at the party had actually begun to make him feel nauseous. Usually he'd deferred to Cindy at such events, enduring them until she was ready to call it a night. But that evening he'd simply told her they were leaving. She'd fumed all the way home in the car, then had confronted him the moment they walked in the door, turning on him in cold fury.

"Okay, do you want to tell me what that caveman act was all about?"

Eric wasn't up to a fight. But her tight-lipped, pinched features and belligerent tone told him there was no avoiding a confrontation.

"I just couldn't handle it tonight, Cindy. Not after the accident. It all seemed so…shallow. And the smoke was making me sick."

She uttered an expletive that made him cringe. "Why do you have to take everything so personally, anyway?" she demanded harshly. "You did your best. More than you needed to, probably. Why can't you just walk away? It's only a job."

He thought of the accident scene, of the woman's devastated face, the man's mangled body. And of his wife's inability to understand, even after all this time, that walking away simply wasn't in his nature. "It's not that easy, Cindy," he replied wearily.

She reached for her purse and extracted a cigarette, staring down his look of disapproval defiantly as she lit it and inhaled deeply.

"You and I need to talk, Eric."

She was right. But he was too tired tonight for the kind of discussion she had in mind. "Tomorrow, Cindy."

"No. Now."

There was an odd note in her voice, and he looked at her with a frown. Her gaze flickered away from his, as if she was suddenly nervous, and his frown deepened. He suddenly felt sick again—not from the smoke, but from a premonition that whatever Cindy had on her mind was going to change their relationship forever. And he didn't want to hear it. Not tonight.

"Look, can't this wait?"

"No. It's waited too long already." She moved restlessly to the other side of the room, paused as if gathering her courage, then turned to face him.

"Eric, this isn't working anymore, if it ever did. You know that. Let's face it. This marriage was a mistake from the start. We're not a good match. You can't have enjoyed these last six years any more than I have."

Eric wanted to pretend that this wasn't happening. But the tenseness in his shoulders, the sudden feeling of panic, the hollowness in the pit of his stomach, made it all too real.

"We took vows before God, Cindy. We can't just toss them aside. Remember the 'For better, for worse'?"

She gave a brief, bitter laugh. "Oh, I know all about the 'for worse' part. When do we come to the 'for better'?"

That hurt. There had been some moments of happiness, at least at the beginning. "We had some good times."

"A few," she conceded with an indifferent shrug. "But not enough to sustain this relationship. And I want more, Eric. In this marriage I'll always be competing for your attention with a bunch of sick kids. And I'm tired of losing."

"You knew I was a doctor when you married me."

She dismissed the comment with an impatient gesture. "I thought you were going to be a *surgeon,* Eric. With decent hours most of the time. Doing really important work. I didn't know you were going to turn into the pediatric version of Marcus Welby, always on call, always ready to jump every time some kid has a runny nose.''

Eric's mouth tightened. Cindy had always made her opinion clear on the subject, but she'd never before used such hateful language.

Something in his expression must have registered, because when she spoke again she softened her tone. ''Look, Eric, let's not make this any harder than necessary, okay? Let's just agree to call it quits and go our separate ways.''

''You're asking for a divorce.''

''Yes.''

''Why now?''

She shot him an assessing look. ''You want the truth?''

Suddenly he wasn't sure he did, but he nodded nonetheless.

She took a deep breath and reached down to tap the ash off her cigarette. ''Okay. I've met someone I…like…a lot. There's potential there. And I want to be free to explore it.'' She paused, and as she watched the color ebb from his face, she spoke again. ''I'm not having an affair, if that's what you're thinking. I wouldn't go that far, not while we're married. You know that.''

He didn't know much of anything at the moment. He just felt shocked—and numb. He sat down heavily and dropped his head into his hands.

''Look, Eric, it's not that bad. Lots of marriages fail. This way we can both be free to try to find someone who is more compatible.''

Slowly he raised his head, his face stricken, and looked at her. ''I married for life, Cindy.'' His voice was flat, devoid of all emotion.

''I thought I did, too. But it didn't work out. I don't think God expects people to stay in miserable marriages.''

''I think He expects people to try as hard as they can to make it work.''

''I did try,'' she replied defiantly. ''And it still didn't work. I'm sorry, Eric.''

But she didn't sound sorry, he thought dully. She sounded almost…relieved. As if she'd made up her mind about this a long time ago and had been waiting for the right moment to tell him.

When he didn't reply, she glared at him impatiently. "So are you going to make this easy, or am I going to have to fight you on it?"

He raked the fingers of his hand through his hair and his shoulders drooped. "I'm tired of fighting, Cindy. I can't hold you if you don't want to stay."

"Good." The relief in her voice was obvious. "I'm glad you're being sensible. It's for the best, Eric. Maybe you'll find someone in the future who'll make you a better wife."

He looked at her sadly. "I already have a wife, Cindy. We may be able to break the bonds of our marriage in the eyes of the law, but in the sight of God we'll always be married. 'Till death us do part.'"

Eric returned to the present with a start and stared at the letter from Elaine. "Till death us do part." The words echoed hollowly in his heart. He'd remained faithful to that vow, but the cost had been deep-seated loneliness and episodes of dark despair. Now he was free. He wasn't sure what that meant exactly. But there would be time to think about it later. Right now he needed to talk with the Lord. He closed his eyes and bowed his head. *Dear Lord, be with Cindy,* he prayed. *Show her Your infinite mercy and understanding. And forgive me for all the times I failed her. May she find with You the peace and happiness I couldn't provide her with in this life. Amen.*

Kate peered at the mailbox, verified the address, then pulled up to the curb and parked. She surveyed the small bungalow, surprised at its modest proportions and its location in this quiet, family-oriented neighborhood. She'd assumed that a successful doctor like Eric would live in more ostentatious surroundings.

She reached for the coffee cake, then paused as her nerves kicked in. She knew Eric hadn't really expected her to follow through on his "payment" suggestion for the house call. But it had given her an excuse to see him again. Just being in his presence made her feel good. In fact, since he'd come into her life she felt better than she had in a long time. Thanks to him, she was taking steps to renew her relationship with the Lord. Thanks to him, she'd found a wonderful caregiver for Sarah. And thanks to him, the spot in her heart that had lain cold and empty and dead for five long years was beginning to reawaken.

Actually, she wasn't sure whether to thank him for the latter. In fact she wasn't sure how to handle it—especially considering that Eric was off-limits. He'd made that very clear. Plus, she didn't know if she was ready to say goodbye to her past yet, despite Amy's advice. But something had compelled her to come here today. It might not be wise, but she had listened to her heart. She only hoped that it would guide her through the encounter to come. After their parting on Sunday night, Kate wasn't at all sure what to expect when Eric opened the door.

What she hadn't expected was his shell-shocked appearance. There were deep furrows between his brows, his hands were trembling and his face was colorless. She looked at him in alarm, her own trepidation forgotten as panic set in.

"Eric? What is it? What's wrong?"

He stared at her for a moment, as if trying to refocus. "Kate? What are you doing here? Is Sarah all right?"

"She's fine. I dropped her off at church for Christmas-pageant practice, and I wanted to stop by and repay you for the house call." She held up the coffee cake. "But…well, you look awful! Are you sick? What happened?"

He sighed and wearily passed a shaky hand over his eyes. "I had some…unexpected news. Come in, Kate." He stepped aside to let her enter, but she hesitated.

"Look, I don't want to intrude, Eric. Maybe I should come back another time."

"You're not intruding. And I'd like you to stay, actually. I could use the company."

Kate searched his eyes, but his invitation seemed sincere rather than just polite, so she stepped past him into the hallway.

"I was just going to make some coffee. Can I offer you some tea?"

"Thanks. But why don't you let me make it? You look like you should sit down."

He smiled wryly at her concerned expression as he led the way to the kitchen. "Don't worry, Kate. I'm not sick. Just shocked. But you look tired. Go ahead and sit down and I'll put the kettle on."

He indicated a sturdy antique wooden table and chairs in a large bay off to one side of the kitchen.

She complied silently, watching as he stepped between the stove and the oak cabinets. He moved with an easy grace, a quiet competence that was restful and reassuring. She glanced around her. The kitchen was a lovely spot, cheerful and bright, with big windows that offered views of what appeared to be a large tree-shaded backyard. But the room itself was somewhat sterile, with few personal items other than a letter addressed to Eric on the table. Though Cindy had been gone a long time, Kate was surprised that there was so little evidence of the decorating touches usually initiated by the woman of the house. But the room was comfortable and clearly had great potential.

"I like your house, Eric," Kate remarked as he set plates and forks on the table.

"Do the honors on the cake, would you, Kate? And thanks. The house *is* nice. It's the kind of place I always wanted."

"Me, too. Jack and I had a house something like this when we first moved to St. Louis."

Eric heard the wistful tone in her voice, and it tugged at his heart. He knew from his mother that Kate had sold the house after Jack died. She'd needed the money for other things—like paying medical bills. But he didn't want her dwelling on the past.

"The only problem with this place is the decorating—or lack thereof. It needs to be warmed up, but I'm not even sure where to begin."

"I'm surprised Cindy didn't do more," Kate admitted.

"Cindy never lived here, Kate. I bought this place after the divorce."

"Oh. I'm sorry."

"No need to be. Believe me, this wasn't her style. We lived in a condo in West County when we were married. It was what she wanted, and it suited her."

*But what about you?* Kate wanted to ask. *Didn't your wants count? What about whether it suited you?* But she remained silent, for he suddenly grew pensive as his gaze came to rest on the letter. Kate suddenly realized that whatever it contained accounted for his recent shock. And that it had something to do with Cindy.

She looked over at him, and their gazes met. She didn't want to pry, but she wanted him to know that she cared. "I'm a good listener, Eric," she said quietly.

He studied her for a moment, then sighed and turned away to retrieve their mugs. Kate tried not to be hurt by his silence. After all, they were recent acquaintances. She couldn't blame him for wanting to keep his problem private. But when he sat down he surprised her.

"That letter is from Cindy's sister."

Kate looked at him curiously but remained quiet.

"Cindy died a couple of weeks ago."

Kate stared at him in shock. Now she understood why he had looked so shaken when he answered the door. "What happened?"

"Lung cancer. I was always afraid her smoking would kill her."

"I'm so sorry."

He sighed. "I am, too. For her. For what might have been. For all the mistakes we both made. My strongest feeling at the moment is regret. It's odd, Kate. I have no sense of personal loss. No grief in that way. Cindy and I parted long ago, even before the divorce. By the end of our marriage we were really no more than strangers."

Kate couldn't imagine the living hell of that kind of relationship. She and Jack had had arguments on occasion, but deep down they'd always known that their marriage was rock solid, that it would endure, no matter what obstacles life put in their path. Eric had clearly never enjoyed that kind of relationship.

Impulsively she reached over and laid her hand on his, just as she had three nights before. "I'm so sorry, Eric," she repeated. "Not only for Cindy's death, but for the death of your marriage. In some ways, I think that would be even harder to bear than the physical death of a loved one. I was devastated when Jack died, but I had wonderful memories to cling to and sustain me. I'm sorry you never had that."

Eric looked into Kate's tear-filled eyes and something deep within him stirred. It was such a foreign emotion that it took him a moment to identify it as hope. Here, with this special woman, he suddenly felt that his future no longer needed to be solitary and devoid of love. Which was strange. Because though he might now be free to marry in the eyes of the Lord, there were still major obstacles to overcome before he could even begin to consider a future with Kate. First of all, she was still in love with Jack. That was no small hurdle. And second, he was still a doctor, committed to a profession that didn't seem to mix with marriage—or at least, not for him. There seemed no way around that barrier.

And yet...Eric couldn't suppress the optimism that surged through him. It was as if a heavy burden had been lifted from his shoulders, as if the floodgates had opened on a parched field. Yes, the problems were significant. But all things were possible with the Lord. And maybe, with His help, out of the darkness of these past years a new day was about to dawn.

# Chapter Eight

"So…I hear I have some competition in the baking department." Kate took a sip of her tea and smiled at Anna. "Hardly."

"I don't know." The older woman's tone was skeptical, but there was a twinkle in her eye. "The way Eric raved about that coffee cake—it must be something special. It was nice of you to make one just for him."

"It was the least I could do after he stopped by to see Sarah— and on a Sunday night." Kate poured herself another cup of tea and sighed contentedly. "Mmm. This is the perfect antidote to a long, drawn-out teachers' meeting. Thanks for watching Sarah later than usual, Anna."

"My pleasure. She's a delightful little girl and no trouble at all." They simultaneously glanced out the window toward the patio, where the youngster was engrossed in some make-believe game, wringing every moment out of the rapidly diminishing daylight. "She's so excited about the Christmas pageant at church. It's all she's talked about for the last two days. If you need any help with the angel costume, I'd be more than happy to lend a hand."

Kate smiled and shook her head. "Speaking of angels—how did I get lucky enough to find you?"

"Well, you can thank my son for that. And it wasn't luck at all. It was just part of God's plan."

"What plan is that?" Kate inquired with a smile.

The doorbell rang before the older woman could reply. "Goodness! I don't usually have visitors at this hour," she remarked, a flush rising to her cheeks. "Will you excuse me for a moment, my dear?"

"Of course. We need to be leaving anyway." Kate started to get up, but Anna put a hand on her shoulder.

"Not yet!" There was an anxious note in her voice, and Kate looked at her curiously. Anna's flush deepened and she quickly backtracked. "At least finish your tea first," she said, before quickly leaving the room.

Kate stared after her, a sudden niggling suspicion sending an uneasy tingle down her spine. The older woman was up to something, she concluded. But what?

She had her answer a few moments later when Anna reentered the kitchen followed by Eric, who was toting two large white sacks.

"Well, look who stopped by," Anna declared, feigning surprise.

Kate sent her a chiding look, which the older woman ignored. Kate was beginning to realize that Anna was a matchmaker at heart and now seemed to be directing her efforts at her son and the mother of her young charge. Of course, she wouldn't get very far without the cooperation of said son, Kate reflected, directing her glance his way. And he wasn't in the market for romance. But as their gazes connected she somehow got lost in his blue eyes and warm smile and forgot all about conspiracy theories.

"Hi."

How did he manage to impart such a warm, personal tone to a single word? Kate wondered as she distractedly returned the greeting.

He held up the sacks. "I heard you were working late tonight and thought maybe we could all share some Chinese. I brought chicken fingers and fries for Sarah."

Kate smiled, touched by his thoughtfulness. "She'll love that. It's not a treat she gets too often."

"How about you, Kate? Is Chinese all right?"

"Perfect. A treat for me, too."

Anna looked from one to the other with a satisfied expression. "I'll just call Sarah," she offered, heading toward the back door.

Kate rose to get some plates and eating utensils while Eric unpacked the bags. "You're going to spoil us, you know," she told him over her shoulder.

"You could use some spoiling."

She turned to him in surprise, and as their gazes met, a faint flush rose in her cheeks. There was something…different about Eric tonight, she decided. She couldn't quite put her finger on it. He seemed less tense. Less worried. And definitely less distant. Which shouldn't surprise her, considering how much he'd shared with her Wednesday night about the deep-seated hurts and disappointments of his marriage. In fact, she'd been surprised by his openness. Most men she'd met kept their feelings to themselves—especially the darker ones—as well as their doubts. Even Jack. Despite his outgoing nature, he'd had a hard time talking about feelings, preferring instead to express them.

But Eric had told her things that many men's egos would never have let them admit—his sense of failure when the marriage had faltered, his doubts about the compatibility of a family and his career, his sense of betrayal and deep hurt when Cindy had asked him for a divorce and told him she'd met someone new. It touched her deeply that he'd chosen to share his feelings with her. And as she'd left he'd looked at her as he had the prior Sunday, and had touched her cheek in just the same way.

Kate had thought about that evening a great deal over the last two days. She'd wondered what it meant, where it would lead. Now she was beginning to get a clue. Eric's visit tonight had clearly been planned. He was making an effort to see her, to get to know her better, to spend time with her. In other words, he was letting her know he was interested in her. At the same time, she sensed that he would wait for her to give him a sign that she wanted their relationship to move to a deeper level.

But Kate wasn't prepared to do that yet. She needed more time to sort through her conflicting emotions—and loyalties. With a self-conscious smile, she turned back to the cabinet and busied herself with the plates and glasses.

Eric got the message. Kate wasn't ready to cross the line from friendship to anything else yet. And frankly, he wasn't sure he was, either. So he would wait. And in time the Lord would show them both the way.

Somehow the Friday-night dinners became a regular event. So did Sunday church, with breakfast afterward. And Eric began calling her during the week to share amusing stories about his young patients and to ask about her day. Sometimes he would drop in unexpectedly for coffee, or sweep everyone off to an impromptu dinner out, much to Sarah's delight—not to mention her mother's.

Occasionally their evenings would be interrupted by Eric's pager, and though he always apologized, Kate assured him that she didn't mind. His deep compassion and fervent commitment to his work were part of who he was. To change that would be to change his very essence. And she liked him just the way he was.

By late October, he had become so much a part of their lives that the loneliness of the last five years began to recede in her mind until it was only a dim, unpleasant memory. In fact, not only did she begin to forget what life had been like before Eric, it was becoming harder and harder to imagine a future without him.

"Okay, partner, we need to have a talk."

Eric glanced up from his paperwork as Frank strode in with a determined look on his face, then dropped into the chair across from Eric's desk.

"What's up?" Eric asked mildly.

"We need to add a third physician to this practice," he declared without preamble.

Eric's eyebrows rose. "We've talked about this before."

"I know. And you were always reluctant. But that was when we were just getting established and *needed* to work twelve hours a day. We're past that now. We have a thriving practice. There's plenty of work for a third doctor. Plus, we'll only have to cover calls every third weekend instead of every two. With the baby coming, Mary thinks I need to lighten up my work schedule so I have more time to spend with the family. And I agree."

"So do I."

Frank opened his mouth to argue, stared at Eric, and shut it. "What did you say?"

"I said I agree."

"Just like that? No protest? No litany of reasons why this isn't a good time?"

"Nope."

Frank stared at him, his expression slowly changing from aston-ishment to smugness as the light dawned. "Oh, I get it. It's Kate."

"Kate?"

"Don't give me that innocent act. Of course it's Kate. Things are heating up, huh?"

Eric thought about their basically platonic relationship and smiled ruefully. "I wouldn't say that exactly."

"Oh, come on, buddy. You can tell me. Just because I haven't pestered you with questions about her lately doesn't mean I forgot the way you looked at her at the barbecue. I knew then something was in the wind. You're seeing her a lot, aren't you?"

"As a matter of fact, yes."

Frank grinned. "I thought so. Listen, I think that's great. It's about time you had something more in your life than a job and charity work. I'm glad for you, pal. This third partner will help us *both* out."

"Do you have someone in mind?"

"Absolutely. Carolyn Clark."

Eric knew her. She was one of the hardest-working pediatric res-idents he'd ever met, and her educational credentials were impres-sive. She'd be a good fit. "Is she interested?"

"Yep."

"Let's talk to her, then."

Frank shook his head incredulously. "You know, I thought I was going to have to do a real sell job on you about this."

Eric chuckled. "Not this time."

"So...I take it things are going well with Kate." Frank leaned back and crossed an ankle over a knee, clearly settling in for a long interrogation.

Eric looked at his friend speculatively as he recalled something his mother had said to him weeks ago about his partner's ability to balance marriage and medicine. He hesitated for a moment, then spoke carefully. "Can I ask you something, Frank?"

At the serious tone in Eric's voice, Frank straightened. "Sure. Shoot."

Eric steepled his fingers and sighed. "I guess it's no secret that Cindy and I made a mess of our marriage. And one of the biggest problems was my career. She hated how it intruded on our relationship and interrupted our private life. It was a major problem, and I just couldn't seem to solve it. If I had been able to, our marriage might not have fallen apart.''

Frank's eyes narrowed. "It wasn't just *your* problem, Eric."

"What do you mean?"

Frank spoke slowly, obviously choosing his words carefully. "Doctors' lives—whatever their specialty—don't belong completely to them. That's just the nature of the job. And good doctors—the ones who really care, who take the Hippocratic oath seriously—always serve two masters. Yes, we care for our families and the people we love. But we also have an obligation to do our best for the people we serve. Our patients' lives are literally in our hands. You don't have to marry a doctor to realize that. Cindy knew what she was getting into, Eric. Don't beat yourself up about that. She just wasn't willing to play second fiddle—ever. I think that reflects more on her than on you."

Eric wanted to believe Frank. But the doubts went too deep and were of too long a duration to be dispelled so quickly by his partner's reassurance. "What about you and Mary, Frank? How do the two of you deal with the demands? Doesn't Mary ever resent them?"

"Honestly? No. Which doesn't mean she isn't disappointed on occasion when my professional obligations interfere with our plans. But she accepts it as part of what makes me tick. And she knows I do everything I can to put her first the rest of the time and make time for us as a couple—like pushing for a third partner," he said, flashing a grin. "So we've never had any problems."

Eric looked at Frank silently for a moment, then sighed. "I wish I could be sure it worked like that for everyone."

Frank stood, his expression serious. "Don't let one bad experience stop you from having a good one, Eric. I don't know Kate very well. But I liked what I saw. Cindy's gone now. There's nothing except fear to keep you from moving forward. And let me say one more thing. You're just about the most conscientious, caring person I know. If you couldn't make a marriage work, nobody could. And if you ever tell anybody I got this mushy, I'll deny it," he finished with a smile as he exited.

Eric stared after him thoughtfully. He and Frank had been friends for a long time. Usually his colleague hid his deeper feelings under an umbrella of humor. But just now he'd spoken from the heart. Eric appreciated his flattering words, as well as his honesty. And Frank was right. He *was* afraid. Now the question was, could he get over those fears enough to take another chance on love?

Anna handed Kate another pin, then backed up and critically surveyed the hem of Sarah's angel costume. "I think that will do it. I'll run it up for you on the machine tomorrow, Kate."

Kate stood and lifted Sarah down from the sturdy kitchen chair, giving her a hug as she lowered her to the floor. "You're a beautiful angel, honey."

"Are we going to make the wings next week?" the little girl asked excitedly.

"Absolutely. Dr. Eric said he'd get some wire for us at the hardware store for the frame."

"Mommy's been working on the wreath for my hair at night after I go to bed," Sarah told Anna. "It's really pretty!"

"I think you'll be the loveliest angel there ever was," Anna declared with a smile. "Now let's get that gown off so it stays clean. Angels always look nice and neat, you know."

"I can't thank you enough for all your help, Anna," Kate said warmly when Sarah scampered off to play. "In a way, I feel that Sarah has a brand-new grandmother."

"Well, it's a role I always wanted to play," Anna reminded her as she laid the gown over the sewing machine. "I love taking care of her. It's given me a new sense of purpose. I still miss Walter every day, of course, but it's easier to bear, somehow, knowing that you and Sarah are counting on me." She paused and turned to the younger woman. "And speaking of watching Sarah—I know this is rather short notice, Kate, but my cousin called last night. She and a friend were planning to go on a cruise the week of Thanksgiving, and her friend had to back out at the last minute. She asked me to go instead. I've always wanted to take a cruise, and this seemed like a providential opportunity. So I told her yes. But I'm afraid that means I can't watch Sarah on Monday and Tuesday of Thanksgiving week."

"Oh, Anna, don't give it another thought!" Kate assured her.

"I'm thrilled for you! And Thanksgiving is still three weeks away. I have plenty of time to make other arrangements."

"Actually, I spoke with my neighbor—a lovely young woman, very responsible, with two small children of her own. Sarah's played with them on occasion. She said she'd be happy to watch her. I know you're leaving for your sister's Wednesday, and I'll be back Sunday night. So it's only for two days."

Kate was touched by the older woman's consideration. "Thank you, Anna. That sounds perfect," she said warmly. "And I hope you have a wonderful time on your cruise."

"Oh, I expect we will. Except…"

"Except what?" Kate prompted when Anna's voice trailed off.

"Well, I'm a little concerned about Eric. He'll be by himself on Thanksgiving, and I'm afraid it will be hard for him. It's always been the three of us on holidays. But when I spoke to him last night about the trip, he encouraged me to go and assured me he'd be fine. So I suppose I shouldn't worry. He'll probably go to Frank's."

Kate frowned. Eric wouldn't be spending the holiday with Frank because they were going to Mary's parents' house. He'd probably end up working the whole four-day weekend. Unless…

"Is something wrong, dear?" Anna asked, eyeing the younger woman with concern.

Kate forced herself to smile. "Not a thing." There was no sense mentioning the idea that had just popped into her head. Especially when she wasn't sure she would follow through on it, anyway.

"Hi, Amy."

"Kate? It's my Sunday, isn't it?"

"Yes. But Eric is stopping by in a little while, so I thought I'd just go ahead and call. Are you in the middle of something?"

"You mean other than the usual mayhem around this place?"

Kate chuckled. "What's going on now?"

"A friend of Cal's had to go out of the country on business for a few weeks and somehow conned my good-natured husband into baby-sitting his iguana. The twins are fascinated. Personally, when it comes to pets I prefer the warm, cuddly variety. However, as long as I don't have to touch it, I suppose I can put up with a reptile in

my house for a limited time. But speaking of 'warm and cuddly'—
how are things with Eric?"

Kate flushed. She'd tried to downplay their relationship, but Amy
wasn't inclined to buy the "just friends" routine. Which, in a way,
might make it easier to broach the subject that was on her mind.
"Things are fine."

"'Fine,' hmm. Would you define that?"

"I see him a lot. We go to church together and all of us eat
dinner at his mother's every Friday night. Sometimes he drops over.
Like tonight."

There was silence for a moment. "Look, Kate, I don't want to
pry—or push. So if you want to tell me to mind my own business,
it won't hurt my feelings in the least. But is it really just a friendship
thing with you two?"

Kate played with the phone cord. "Yes. Although sometimes I…
Well, I think maybe he'd like for it to be more. I mean, I know he
still has concerns about mixing medicine and marriage. He got
burned pretty badly the first time he tried that. So he's gun-shy. But
I have a feeling if I gave him some encouragement he might be
willing to at least…consider it."

"And I take it you haven't?"

"No. I'm still trying to put my own past behind me," Kate admitted, her gaze coming to rest on the wedding picture that hung
over the couch. "It's really hard to let go, you know? Even after
all this time."

"Yeah, I know." Amy sighed. "I guess you just need to listen
to your heart and do things at your own pace, Kate. You'll know
when it's the right time to move forward."

Kate took a deep breath. "Actually, that's one of the reasons I
called. I think maybe it *is* the right time. At least to take a few
small steps." Kate explained Anna's Thanksgiving plans and her
concern about Eric being alone. "So I wondered if maybe… Well,
I thought that—"

"Invite him," Amy interrupted promptly.

"Honestly?"

"Of course. One more mouth to feed in this household won't
even be noticed. And there's plenty of room. We'll kick out the
iguana if we have to."

Kate laughed. Amy had always had a knack for making her feel better. "You're a pretty terrific sister, you know that?"

"Just paying back an old debt. Seems to me you were a pretty good sounding board once when I really needed guidance. If it wasn't for you I might never have married Cal and ended up living in the heart of Tennessee. You know, come to think of it..."

Kate smiled at her teasing tone. "You wouldn't trade your life for anything and you know it."

"You're right about that. Listen, you bring that overworked doctor down here and we'll show him a Thanksgiving he won't forget."

"Thanks, Amy."

"My pleasure. Just do me a favor, okay? Warn him about the iguana."

Kate didn't mention the holiday that night when Eric stopped by for cake and coffee. In fact, it took her a whole week to work up the courage to broach the subject. And when she did, it was at the last minute, as he walked Sarah and her to the door after Sunday services.

Kate fitted her key in the lock and ushered Sarah inside, then turned to Eric, struggling to get her suddenly-too-rapid pulse under control. "Thanks again for the ride. And for breakfast," she said a bit breathlessly.

"You're welcome."

Though there was a chill in the early-November air, his smile warmed her all the way to her toes. "Uh, Eric..."

He looked at her curiously, alerted by something in her tone. "Yes?"

"I'm glad your mother is going on that cruise."

"So am I. It will be a nice change of pace for her. She sounds like a kid when she talks about it—which is most of the time. I didn't think we'd get a word in edgewise at breakfast today."

"I know. She's so excited! But... Well, what about you? It won't be much fun to spend the holiday alone."

He shrugged dismissively. "I'll be fine."

"Your mom is kind of concerned about you being by yourself."

He tilted his head and eyed her quizzically. "Did she tell you that?"

"Uh-huh."

He frowned. "I told her not to worry."

"That's how mothers are. It's in the job description." She paused and took a deep breath. "To be honest, I'm not too happy about the situation, either. So I thought you might like to... Well, I talked to Amy and...you know we always go there for Thanksgiving, and there's plenty of room—Amy said so. Except she did tell me to warn you about the iguana. Cal's watching it for a friend of his. Amy's not too happy about that, but the kids love it and—'' Her nervous babbling ceased abruptly when Eric laid his hand on her arm and gazed down at her.

"Kate, are you asking me to spend Thanksgiving with you and your family?" he asked quietly.

She swallowed with difficulty and nodded. "Listen, I know it's kind of a long trip and they're all strangers to you, so it's okay if..."

"I accept."

She looked at him in surprise. "Really?"

"Really. Because between you and me, I *wasn't* looking forward to spending this holiday alone. And I can't think of anywhere I'd rather be on this Thanksgiving than with you. And Sarah. And Amy and her family...and the iguana," he teased, a twinkle springing to life in his eyes.

Kate's gaze was locked on his, and she watched, mesmerized, as the twinkle suddenly changed to an ember that quickly ignited, deepening the color of his eyes. Her breath caught in her throat as he slowly reached over and touched her face, letting his hand linger before gently raking his fingers through her hair.

Though the touch was simple, its effect on Kate's metabolism was anything but. She longed to lean against his solid chest, to feel his arms protectively and tenderly enfold her. She closed her eyes and sighed softly, instinctively swaying toward him.

Eric read her body language, recognized the invitation she was unconsciously issuing, and fought down the sudden urge to pull her close. *Dear Lord, give me strength,* he prayed, his heart hammering in his chest. He wanted to hold her tightly, to touch her, to caress the soft waves of her ebony hair and the silky smoothness of her cheek. He wanted to press his lips to hers and taste their sweetness.

Bottom line, he wanted a whole lot more than he *should* want at this point, he reminded himself as he struggled to control his desires. Get a grip, admonished himself sharply. This is not the time. Or the place.

With a triumph of willpower that surprised him, he dropped his hand and stepped back, drawing a long, shaky breath as he did so.

Kate opened her eyes and blinked, as if trying to clear her vision, then reached out to grip the doorframe as she stared at him.

"I'll call you," he promised, his gaze locked on hers.

She nodded jerkily. "Okay." It was barely a whisper.

He held her gaze for a moment longer, then with obvious effort turned and strode quickly away. Not until he was out of her sight did he pause for a moment to take a deep, steadying breath. He knew that Kate was close to reaching out to him. The real question now was whether they were both ready. During the last couple of weeks he'd thought a lot about his conversation with Frank, and he was gradually beginning to believe that maybe…just maybe… marriage and medicine could mix—with the right woman. Namely, Kate. But even if he resolved his own issues, there was still Jack. Could she let him go? And could she ever find it in her heart to love someone else as intensely as she'd loved her husband?

Eric wasn't sure. And that uncertainty left him discouraged. For if he truly set out to win the heart of this special woman, he realized he could face a daunting task. The simple fact was, his experience in dealing with *living* rivals was extremely limited. And he was at a total loss about how to deal with a dead one.

# Chapter Nine

Kate glanced over her shoulder at Sarah, whose excited chatter had finally been silenced by sleep, and smiled. Her gaze connected with Eric's as she turned back, and he glanced briefly in the rearview mirror, his own mouth lifting at the corners.

"Looks like the sandman finally won."

"Thanks for being so patient, Eric. I'm sure you would have preferred a quieter drive."

"Honestly? No. Most of my drives are far *too* quiet. This was a nice change."

"Well, Sarah isn't usually this wound up. It's just that she's been so excited about the trip. She was up at dawn, ready and waiting."

"Which means her mother was up at dawn, as well."

She shrugged. "I had things to do anyway."

"You must be tired, Kate. Why don't you grab a nap, too?"

The sudden tenderness in his voice made her stomach flutter, but she tried to ignore the sensation. "I'm okay. The fact is, I'm excited, too. I've been looking forward to seeing Amy and her family as much as Sarah has. The kids are cute, Cal is great and Amy... Well, Amy's special. I hope you like her, Eric."

"I'm sure I will. Especially if she's anything like you."

She felt a warm flush rise to her face. "Actually, we're pretty different," she replied, striving to maintain a conversational tone. "Amy has always been more outgoing and self-confident, sort of a take-charge kind of person—in the best sense of the term. She's a doer and an organizer and always has things under control. Unlike me.''

Eric frowned and glanced over at her. ''I think you're selling yourself short.''

Kate gazed unseeingly into the deepening dusk. '' 'Control' isn't a word I would apply to my life in recent years,'' she said quietly.

''The things that happened were *beyond* your control, Kate,'' Eric reminded her gently but firmly. ''You coped admirably under extremely difficult circumstances and through it all you've been an exceptional mother. That ranks you pretty highly in my book.''

Kate turned to study his strong profile, trying unsuccessfully to read his expression in the dim light. ''I have a feeling you're just being kind, Eric, but in any case, thank you.''

His gaze flickered momentarily to hers. ''I'm not just being kind, Kate. Trust me.''

That tender, intimate quality was back in his voice, and her heart stopped, then raced on. ''You know, Dr. Carlson, you're going to turn my head with all these compliments. Pretty soon I'll have to add conceitedness to my list of faults,'' she quipped, unwilling yet to deal with the implications of his flattery—and his tone. She was relieved when he picked up on her cue and responded with a chuckle.

''Why do I doubt that?'' he countered.

They lapsed into companionable silence then, and by the time they pulled into the drive that led to Amy's log house it was after ten. The crunch of the tires on the gravel announced their arrival, and as they pulled to a stop, the front door was flung open to reveal a silhouetted, jeans-clad figure.

Kate smiled softly. ''Amy's been watching for us.''

Before Eric could respond, the woman in the doorway called something over her shoulder, then raced down the steps, bypassing the last one with a leap. Kate pushed open her door, and the two women met in front of the car, clinging to each other in a fierce hug.

''Oh, Kate, it's so good to see you!'' Amy said fervently.

When Kate replied there was a trace of tears in her voice. ''I've missed you so much!''

Eric leaned against the car and folded his arms across his chest as he silently watched the reunion. Though it was difficult to see much in the dim light, there were definitely some physical differences between the two women. Amy was taller than Kate, and her hair wasn't nearly as dark. While Kate was softly rounded in all the right places, Amy's build seemed more angular and athletic. And her movements suggested a more boisterous, impulsive nature than Kate's. But whatever their physical or personality differences, it was clear that the sisters shared a strong emotional bond. He felt touched—and honored—that Kate had included him in this family gathering.

When Amy at last extricated herself from the hug, she strode toward him and extended her hand. ''You're obviously Eric. Welcome.''

He straightened quickly and took her fingers in a firm grip. ''And you're obviously Amy. Thank you for inviting me. I'm looking forward to being part of your holiday.''

Amy tilted her head and planted her hands on her hips. ''I hope you still feel that way when you leave on Sunday. Kate did tell you about the iguana, right?''

He smiled. ''I've been duly warned about your temporary guest.''

''Well, I'm glad you used the term 'temporary,''' she confessed with relief. ''We're eccentric enough without having strangers think we regularly keep weird animals in our house. You'll be happy to know that Wally isn't sleeping in your room.''

'''Wally'?''

''The iguana.'' She rolled her eyes. ''An iguana named Wally, can you believe it? The next time Cal agrees to—''

''Did I hear my name mentioned?''

A tall, dark-haired man slipped his arm around Amy's shoulders and she turned to look up at him. Her expression softened, though her tone was teasing. ''You did. We were discussing Wally.''

Cal grimaced good-naturedly. ''Why do I think I'll never hear the end of this?''

''Because you won't,'' she replied pertly. ''But enough about Wally for the moment. Eric, this is my husband, Cal. Cal, Eric Carlson.''

While the two men shook hands and exchanged greetings, Amy

slipped from under Cal's arm, peered inside the car and grinned. "Looks like someone nodded off."

"About a hundred and fifty miles ago," Kate informed her.

"Well, I'm sure you're all exhausted after that long drive. Are you hungry?" She glanced from Kate to Eric, and they shook their heads.

"We stopped for dinner along the way," Kate told her.

"Okay. Then let's get you all to bed. We can visit tomorrow."

By the time everyone was settled, it was nearly eleven. Sarah and the twins were happily rolled into sleeping bags in the living room, while Kate took the twins' room. Eric was assigned the sleeper sofa in the den.

"Now, is there anything else you need tonight?" Amy asked.

"We're fine," Kate assured her. "Get some rest yourself."

Amy chuckled and glanced at her watch ruefully. "Fat chance. Believe it or not, Caitlin still likes a midnight bottle. My six-month-old," she explained to Eric.

He smiled. "A healthy appetite is a good sign."

"I'll remind myself of that while I'm feeding her in the wee hours," she replied with a wry grin. "Good night, you two."

They watched her disappear up the rough-hewn split-log stairway, and then Eric turned to Kate. The warmth in his eyes banished the evening chill. "Sleep well," he said huskily.

She opened her mouth to reply, discovered she'd somehow misplaced her voice, and forced herself to take a deep breath before trying again. "I usually do when I'm here. I like being in the country."

"I do, too. This seems like a perfect spot to celebrate an all-American holiday. Thanks again for inviting me, Kate."

She smiled. "Like Amy said, save your thanks until we leave. It can get pretty crazy around here with all the kids."

"It's a good kind of crazy, though."

Her smile softened. "Yeah, it is."

Kate expected him to turn away then, but instead he propped a shoulder against the doorframe and shoved his hands into the pockets of his jeans. He drew a deep breath, and in the dim light of the hall Kate could see twin furrows etched between his eyes.

"Is something wrong?" she asked in concern.

He glanced down at her, and his frown eased. "No. I'm just thinking how nice it is to be in a home so obviously filled with love. Amy and Cal seem to have created something really special in this house. I can feel it, even in the short time I've been here. It's heartwarming to see such a successful marriage."

"They do happen, Eric. I know."

He looked down into her eyes and nodded slowly. "I know you do. I guess the question is…"

His voice trailed off, and Kate felt her breath catch in her throat. She could guess what he was thinking, and she knew she ought to leave his comment alone. But she spoke anyway. "The question is what?" she ventured hesitantly.

Eric gazed at her for a long moment. Then, instead of replying, he withdrew one of his hands from his pocket and reached over to cup her chin, his thumb stroking her cheek. It was a casual, uncomplicated gesture. But the warmth of his gentle touch, the compelling look in his eyes, turned it into so much more. A deep yearning surged through Kate, and she felt her heart pause, then race on. She wanted more, she realized. She wanted him to hold her in his strong arms, to tenderly claim her long-neglected lips. Instinctively Kate knew Eric's briefest kiss would transport her to a land of emotion from which she had long been estranged.

Eric saw the longing in Kate's eyes and could no longer ignore—or suppress—the attraction that sparked between them. It was time to test the waters. Slowly he leaned toward her, his gaze locked on hers. His own pulse was none too steady, and he closed his eyes as their lips came whisper close, eager to taste the sweetness of—

"Oh, I'm glad you're both still up. I forgot—"

Kate heard Eric's sharply indrawn breath and pulled back, startled. She felt hot color suffuse her face as she turned to her sister.

Amy paused on the bottom step and quickly assessed the situation. "Uh, listen, leave it to me to barge right in at the wrong time. I just wanted to let you know that we planned to go to services tomorrow morning at ten, if that's okay with you two."

"Th-that's fine. Thanks." Kate tried unsuccessfully to control the tremor in her voice.

"So…good night again. This time for good," Amy promised as

she made her way up the stairs. A few seconds later a door very deliberately clicked shut.

There was a long moment of awkward silence. Then Kate wrapped her arms around her body and tried to smile. "Amy always did have impeccable timing," she said shakily.

Eric let out a long breath and raked the fingers of one hand through his hair. "That's for sure."

"Listen, it's getting late anyway. We're both tired. Maybe... maybe we should just call it a night."

He looked down at her for a moment, the haze of desire still evident in his eyes. Finally he sighed and nodded. "I guess you're right. But remember one thing." His voice was husky as he reached over and touched her cheek.

"Wh-what?" she stammered, her gaze locked on his.

"To borrow a line from *Gone With the Wind,* 'Tomorrow is another day.'"

And with that enigmatic comment, he turned and disappeared down the hall.

Tomorrow was, indeed, another day. But it was a family affair—from the pancake breakfast to the church service to the dinner preparations, when everyone was recruited to help. Eric found himself peeling potatoes after Amy slapped a paring knife into his hand and said she figured if he could handle a scalpel, he could handle that.

The meal itself was a joyous, boisterous affair, and afterward everyone pitched in on the cleanup. They paid their respects to Wally, admired the gazebo Cal was building in a grove of rhododendrons at the back of the property, and stayed up late, reminiscing and playing board games. The next day was equally busy, and the evening not conducive to privacy—Amy was up till all hours with a fussy Caitlin. On Saturday Cal took them into Great Smoky Mountains National Park for a "VIP tour," as he laughingly called it.

"This isn't the best time of year for the park, but it has its beauty in all seasons," he told them as they wandered down a particularly lovely path by a crystal-clear stream. As the children ran ahead, and Cal and Amy strolled arm in arm, Caitlin sleeping—finally!—in the carrier on Cal's back, Eric slowed his pace and turned to Kate.

"Alone at last," he declared with a grin.

She gave him a wry glance. "Hardly."

"Why do I think this is as good as it's going to get while we're here?"

Kate looked up at him apologetically. "It's been a bit overwhelming, hasn't it? I'm sorry, Eric. I guess I didn't realize that—well, that you were hoping for some time alone."

He reached over and deliberately laced his fingers with hers. A tingle ran down her spine at his touch, and she felt warm color rise in her cheeks when he spoke. "I guess I didn't, either—until the night we arrived. As you've probably realized by now, I tend to be the slow-moving, cautious type when it comes to relationships. Maybe too much so. At least that's what Frank says."

Kate smiled understandingly. "I'm the same way. Just ask Amy. I like to be sure about things, and sometimes...sometimes that holds me back."

"I know. Unfortunately, life doesn't seem to offer many certainties."

"Maybe...maybe there are times when you just have to trust your heart."

He looked down at her, his eyes serious. "I haven't been willing to do that for a long time," he admitted honestly.

She gazed up at him, searching his eyes, wanting to ask the question that hovered on her lips but feeling afraid to do so. Yet he seemed to read her mind, and answered it.

"I've felt...differently about a lot of things since I met you, Kate," he told her quietly.

"So...so have I," she confessed haltingly. "But I'm still not sure about what to do. Reverend Jacobs has been really great, though, in helping me sort out my feelings. And I've been following his advice to pray for guidance."

He smiled and squeezed her hand. "Since I've been doing the same thing, why don't we leave it in the Lord's hands for the moment? He'll show us the way in His own time."

She nodded. "I think that's a good plan. But can I tell you something?" she added impulsively. "I hope He doesn't wait too long."

Eric chuckled. "You and me both."

\* \* \*

"Okay, I put Cal in charge of Caitlin's midnight feeding and very firmly told him that it was now or never for our sister-to-sister tête-à-tête. Here's your hot chocolate. Let me throw another log on the fire and then we're all set," Amy said briskly.

Kate tucked her feet under her and smiled as Amy joined her on the couch a moment later. "This is nice."

Amy sighed contentedly and nodded. "Yeah, it is, isn't it?" She settled herself comfortably into the cushions and took a leisurely sip of her hot chocolate, then turned to find Kate grinning at her. "What's wrong?"

Kate chuckled and reached over to wipe the sticky marshmallow mustache from her sister's upper lip. "It's nice to see that some things never change," she teased.

Amy grinned impudently, but a moment later her face grew melancholy. "Too bad other things do, though," she reflected wistfully.

Kate's expression sobered. "You're thinking about Mom, aren't you?"

"Yeah. It seemed so strange not to have her here for Thanksgiving. It's like a puzzle with a missing piece. She was always such a rock. No matter what scrapes I got into, I could always count on her to get me back on the straight and narrow, or to point me in the right direction when I was lost. Now I feel kind of like a ship adrift without an anchor. And on top of everything else, I missed her gravy at dinner. No one made it like Mom."

Kate nodded. "I thought about that, too."

"It must be doubly hard for you, Kate," Amy reflected with a frown. "She was part of your everyday existence. I can't even imagine the gap her death left in your life."

Kate blinked back her tears and turned to gaze into the fire. "It was pretty awful. Sometimes, in those first few weeks, I'd get so lonely... You'll think I'm crazy when I tell you this, Amy, but there were times I actually talked out loud to Mom. Like she was still there. Meeting Anna has helped a lot, though. It's not the same as having Mom, of course, but in many ways she reminds me of her. And she's taken Sarah and me under her wing. It was a godsend that she came into our lives when she did. I was grieving so much for Mom and at my wit's end about the day-care situation. Then she just appeared, out of the blue. I'll never get over it.''

"The timing was pretty incredible,'' Amy concurred. "I'm glad you met her. And Eric, too.'' She took a sip of her hot chocolate and then spoke carefully. "I know you insist that your relationship is pretty platonic, but I have to say things didn't look like 'just friends' the other night when I interrupted you two.''

Kate blushed and gazed down into her mug. "I think maybe it won't be platonic for much longer,'' she admitted quietly.

"Can I say I'm glad?''

Kate looked at her curiously. "Why?''

"Because I like what I've seen of Eric these few days. Because Sarah obviously adores him. And most of all because I think it would be good for you to let love back into your life. The question is, are you willing to open that door?''

Kate nodded slowly. "I think so, Amy. In fact, I think I'm... Well, I think I'm falling in love with Eric. But I still love Jack. Sometimes I feel so confused. I mean, how can I love them both?'' she asked helplessly.

"How does a mother love more than one child? The heart has an infinite capacity for love, Kate. We can love many people in our lives, all in different ways. The love you have for Jack will always be there. Part of your heart will be his and his alone until the day you die. But that doesn't mean there isn't room for someone else. Love Eric for himself—for all the special qualities that are uniquely his. That won't diminish in any way the love you have for Jack. It's just different. A new dimension of love, if you will.''

Kate reached over and took Amy's hand. In the firelight her eyes shimmered with tears. "Thank you, Amy.''

"For what?''

"For understanding. For trying to help me find a way to let go.''

Amy squeezed her hand, and when she spoke her voice was slightly unsteady. "It's time, Kate. In your heart I think you know that. And I have a feeling that one very special doctor is waiting for you to close the door on the past and open the one that says Future. Because until you do, things will go nowhere. There's no place for him in your past. But unless I'm way off the mark, I think he'd very much like to be part of your future.''

\* \* \*

Kate glanced toward the passenger seat and her lips curved up into a tender smile as she gazed for just a moment at that very special doctor, who was now sleeping quite soundly. In repose his face looked younger, more relaxed, more endearingly vulnerable. Reluctantly she turned her attention back to the road. Though she'd insisted they take her car for the trip, he'd been equally insistent about driving them down. But for the trip back she'd convinced him that they'd both arrive more rested if they took turns. She'd even encouraged him to sleep on this final lap, and he'd taken her up on it. In fact, both of her passengers had drifted off.

Absently Kate switched on her wipers as a soft drizzle began to fall. She was actually glad to have some quiet time to think. Since her conversation with Amy the night before, she'd felt a new sense of peace and resolution. Everything suddenly seemed more clear. Months before, when her pediatrician had retired, she could have chosen any number of doctors as a replacement. But she'd selected Eric, a man who had once saved her husband's life. Though some would dismiss it as an odd twist of fate, Kate believed there was more to it than that. Things happened for a reason. The Lord had guided her toward Eric, and through him, to Anna. Both had enriched her life tremendously. And now it seemed that she was being given the chance to find love once again. The choice about whether to pursue it was hers; but the opportunity had come from the Lord. And, with His help, she resolved to start building the future Amy had referred to.

The rain intensified, and Kate's full attention snapped back to the road. Ever since the accident five years before, she'd hated driving in bad weather, especially at night, and avoided it whenever possible. But she could handle a little rain, she told herself encouragingly.

Twenty minutes later, however, when the rain turned to sleet, her confidence faltered. As the small ice particles zinged against the windshield, she frowned worriedly and tightened her grip on the wheel. She detested sleet. It brought back the nightmare of the accident with harrowing intensity. Her heart began to thump painfully, and she risked a quick glance at Eric, who was still sleeping soundly. She knew he'd take over in a minute if she asked him to, but she hated to wake him. He worked too hard and slept too little as it was. And she wasn't at all sure he'd gotten much rest on this trip, between the sleeper sofa and Caitlin's nighttime fussiness. She glanced at her watch. They were less than an hour away from home. She could do this if she took it a mile at a time, she told herself firmly. Her fears were irrational, after all. She had to get over them sooner or later. She might as well take the first step tonight.

Eric wasn't sure exactly what awakened him. But as he slowly came back to reality an odd noise registered in his consciousness. He frowned, struggling to identify the sound. Once he opened his eyes, the icy buildup on the windshield quickly gave him his answer. Sleet. His gaze flickered to the road. Judging by the glaze, the freezing rain had been coming down for some time.

Eric quickly straightened and turned to Kate. Though the car interior was dim, the tension in her body was evident in her rigid posture and white-knuckled grip on the wheel. She was driving slowly and cautiously, with absolute concentration, and seemed completely oblivious to everything but the task at hand. These conditions must be a stark reminder of a similar night five years before, he realized, suddenly filled with compassion.

"Kate." He spoke softly, trying not to startle her, but she jumped nonetheless as her gaze jerked toward his.

"Oh! You're awake." Her voice sounded tight and was edged with panic.

"How long has the weather been this bad?" he asked with more calm than he felt. It was obvious that he needed to get her out from behind the wheel as quickly as possible. She was terrified. The hazardous conditions had clearly brought back the traumatic memories of the accident.

With a hand that shook badly, she reached up and tucked a strand of hair behind her ear. "About…about half an hour."

"Why don't you pull onto the shoulder and let me take over?" he suggested quietly.

"It's too icy to stop here. And there's…there's a drop-off at the edge." There was a note of hysteria in her voice now.

"There's plenty of room, Kate," he reassured her soothingly. "Just take it slow and easy. There's no one behind us. I'll help you." He placed his hand protectively over hers on the wheel, alarmed by her frigid fingers. "Come on, sweetheart, just guide it over real gently. That's right."

With his help she edged the car halfway onto the shoulder. Eric glanced into the rearview mirror as they rolled to a stop, and was relieved that there were no other vehicles in sight. "Can you just slide over here, Kate? I'll go around to the driver's side."

Jerkily she nodded. By the time he'd slipped and slid around the front of the car and settled himself behind the wheel, she was huddled into the passenger seat. Her face was totally devoid of color, a thin film of perspiration beaded her upper lip and her breathing was shallow. He frowned as he reached over to take her cold hands in his.

"Kate?" She turned to him, her eyes slightly dazed. "Everything's going to be fine. We're almost home. You'll be back in your apartment in less than an hour. Okay?"

She nodded mutely.

He released her hands reluctantly. What he wanted to do was take her in his arms until her trembling ceased. But he suspected the best way to calm her was to get her out of the car and into her apartment.

The remaining drive was made in silence, though he glanced her way frequently. She stared straight ahead, her hands clenched in her lap, her posture still rigid. And, in truth, her concern—if not its intensity—was valid, Eric admitted. The roads were slick and hazardous, and continued to worsen as the minutes passed. He didn't realize how tense *he* had become until they pulled into a vacant spot in front of her apartment and he shut off the engine. Only then did the knotted muscles in his shoulders and the tension in his neck register. He took a deep breath and turned to Kate.

"Home at last," he said quietly.

Shakily Kate reached up and brushed her hair back from her face. "Th-thank you for driving, Eric. I'm sorry you had to take over."

"I didn't mind, Kate. I just wish you'd woken me up sooner."

"Are we home?" A sleepy voice from the back seat interrupted them.

Eric turned, lightening his tone. "Indeed we are, Miss Sarah."

She rubbed her eyes and stared out the window. "Oh! It's snowing!"

"Not yet. But it wouldn't surprise me if we didn't wake up to a winter wonderland tomorrow. Right now it's just ice. And very slippery. So I'm going to carry you up to the apartment, okay?"

"Okay. Can I build a snowman tomorrow if it snows, Mommy?"

Eric glanced at Kate. "Your mommy's awfully tired right now, honey. She drove for a long time. We'll decide about the snowman tomorrow." He turned to Kate and reached over to rest his hand on her knee. "Sit tight, okay? I'll take Sarah in and come back for you."

"I can manage, Eric."

"Humor me, okay? I don't think we want any trips to the emergency room for broken bones on a night like this."

He had a point. "Okay." She reached for her purse and fumbled around for her keys.

He squeezed her shoulder as she handed them over, then opened his door and carefully stepped out. The pavement was like a newly cleaned skating rink, he concluded, moving with extreme caution as he reached in for Sarah. "Hold on tight, sweetie."

He was back more quickly than Kate expected, his collar turned up against the pelting sleet. "Take it slow and easy, Kate," he cautioned as he opened her door and held out his hand. "Walking is pretty treacherous."

She took his hand and stepped out, steadying herself on the car door. "What about the luggage?"

"I'll come back for it. First I want to get you inside where it's safe and warm."

She didn't argue. At the moment, anywhere safe and warm sounded like heaven.

Eric kept a firm grip on her arm as they made their way slowly up the steps from the parking lot and along the walk. He was right— the night was too dangerous for either walking *or* driving, she reflected. Not until she'd stepped inside did she finally relax, her shoulders drooping as she drew a weary sigh.

"I've never been all that thrilled with this apartment, but right now I could get down and kiss the floor," she admitted, summoning up a shaky smile.

"I have a better idea." He took her hand and led her to the couch, then gently urged her down. "Sit for a minute and take a few deep breaths. You'll feel a lot better. I'll get the luggage and then head back to my place before it gets any worse."

"But Eric, it's too dangerous to drive!" she protested in alarm.

"Why can't Dr. Eric stay here tonight, Mommy?" Sarah piped up. "He can sleep on the sofa bed, just like you used to do before Grandma went to heaven."

Kate looked up at Eric. His eyes were unreadable. "Would you consider it?" she asked uncertainly. "I'll be so worried if you try to drive home. It's not safe out there."

Eric studied her. She seemed so vulnerable, her eyes huge in her white face, her body still trembling, her dark hair loose and mussed around her face. She was right about the danger outside. But suddenly he was a whole lot more worried about the danger inside.

# Chapter Ten

The sudden whistling of the kettle bought him a moment's reprieve. "I put the water on to boil when I brought Sarah in," he said over his shoulder as he headed for the kitchen. "I figured you could use a cup of tea. Let me make it and then we can discuss the situation."

Except what was there to discuss, really? he thought as he mechanically pulled a mug from the cabinet and added water and a tea bag. The weather was terrible. It didn't make sense to take risks. But what about the risks right here? he countered silently. Kate was an extremely desirable woman. He'd been attracted to her for weeks. So far, past experience and a conviction that marriage and medicine didn't mix had allowed him to exercise some discipline in their relationship. But this weekend he'd almost kissed her. And though Amy's untimely interruption had effectively derailed his passion, the desire was still there. It might not be wise to stay. But common sense told him that venturing out again tonight would foolish.

With sudden decision he picked up the mug and stepped out of the kitchen, frowning as he glanced around the deserted living room. A moment later, Sarah's girlish giggle, followed by the low murmur of voices, echoed down the hall and he headed in that direction.

Kate looked up guiltily when he entered Sarah's bedroom. "I know you asked me to wait, but I wanted to get Sarah into bed as quickly as possible. It was a long trip for her."

He handed her the mug, noting the lingering quaver in her hand.

"It was also a long trip for her mother," he replied quietly. "Go on back into the living room and relax. I'll put Sarah to bed."

"Oh, goody!" the little girl exclaimed, clapping her hands. "Will you read me a story, too?"

"A short one, if you get your pajamas on really quick."

As she scampered down the hall to the bathroom, Kate looked up at Eric. "Are you sure you don't mind doing this?"

"Not in the least. Go back out there and put your feet up. Doctor's orders," he added, flashing her a grin.

She rose slowly. "Listen, Eric, I'm sorry Sarah put you on the spot about staying tonight. And I understand if you don't want to. But the weather is so bad and..."

He reached over and gently grasped her upper arms, effectively stilling her voice. "I'm staying, Kate," he said deliberately. "I was just taking a minute to...think about it."

His gaze was locked on hers, and Kate stared up at him silently, certain he wasn't referring to the weather. A swarm of butterflies suddenly took flight in her stomach.

"Oh. Well, okay. I'll...I'll be in the living room."

And then she fled.

At first, as Kate waited for him to join her, she sat perched on the edge of the couch, her shoulders hunched nervously, her hands tensely gripping the mug. But as she slowly sipped the soothing liquid and listened to the voices in the back bedroom—Sarah's high and excited, Eric's deep and mellow—she gradually began to relax. It was an odd feeling, to let someone take care of *her* for a change and help her with her daily chores, she mused. And it suddenly occurred to her that she could get used to this.

But she had better not, she warned herself. After all, the man had never even kissed her. Not that he hadn't tried, she conceded, her lips curving up into a smile. It was ironic that Amy, who had been the one urging her to put some romance back in her life, had also been the one to derail Kate's first romantic encounter in years.

Eric had thrown her the classic line from *Gone With the Wind* as they'd parted that night. Was tonight the "tomorrow" he'd referred to then? she wondered, as a warm surge of adrenaline shot through her. It had been such a long time... She wasn't even sure she remembered *how* to be amorous. Her only consolation was that

Eric was equally rusty. She shook her head ruefully. They were quite a pair.

"Want to share the joke?"

Startled, Kate looked up to find Eric smiling at her from the doorway. She tried vainly to stifle the flush that rose to her cheeks, desperately searching for a truthful but evasive response.

"I was just thinking about...about Amy."

"Hmm." She wasn't sure he believed her, but fortunately he let it pass. "Let me get a cup of tea and I'll join you."

She scooted over to make room for him, noting as she placed her mug on the end table that her hands were once again trembling. She clasped them together tightly in her lap and took several long, deep breaths. This was ridiculous, she scolded herself. After all, she was a grown woman. She could handle this situation. Okay, so maybe she was a little out of practice. But if she just remained calm, she'd be fine. Eric was probably just as nervous as she was, she told herself consolingly.

Except he didn't look in the least nervous as he settled down comfortably beside her, she noted enviously. In fact, the man looked totally relaxed.

"Feeling better?" he asked.

She nodded stiffly. "Uh-huh. The tea helped a lot. Thank you."

"My pleasure." His gaze swept over her face appraisingly. She did look better now, he decided. There was more color in her cheeks and the dazed look had left her eyes. "I'm just sorry you had to go through that."

She sighed, and her eyes grew troubled. "You'd think after all these years I'd have gotten over my fear of being in a car in bad weather. But I can't seem to shake it. Even here in town I try to avoid driving when the roads are slick. Especially at night. Sometimes I have to, of course, but it always shakes me up."

"I noticed."

She flushed. "It's so embarrassing. I feel like I should be able to put that night behind me and move on. But I can't seem to get past it."

Eric draped an arm loosely over her shoulders and gently massaged her stiff muscles. "Don't apologize, Kate. You weren't just involved in a fender bender. It was a nightmare situation. That kind of trauma can linger for years. In fact, you may never get over it completely. You'll probably always be extra careful in winter-weather driving—which isn't necessarily a bad thing, by the way. But eventually the fear should subside to a more manageable level. There's no need to rush it. Things usually happen in their own time.''

His reassuring comments and the soothing touch of his hand went a long way toward easing Kate's tension. She sighed and relaxed against his arm.

''That feels good,'' she murmured. ''I guess I was more tense than I realized.''

He set his cup on the coffee table. ''Turn around and I'll do both shoulders.''

She did as he instructed, angling herself on the couch so that her back was to him. With a gentle but firm touch he massaged her shoulders, her upper arms, her neck, until the tension at last evaporated.

''Has anyone ever told you that you have great hands, Doctor?'' she asked languidly, dropping her head forward.

Eric stared at her slender shoulders, at the dark hair spilling over his fingers, and drew a deep breath. ''Not lately,'' he replied, his voice suddenly husky.

Kate heard the different nuance in his tone and felt her pulse quicken as his touch changed subtly from therapeutic to sensual.

''You have beautiful hair, Kate. Has anyone ever told *you* that?''

''Not lately,'' she echoed breathlessly.

Slowly she drew in her breath and held it as he combed his fingers through her hair. A moment later a jolt of electricity shot through her when she felt his lips on the back of her neck.

''You taste good, too,'' he murmured.

Kate closed her eyes and uttered a small, contented sound deep in her throat as he moved her hair aside and let his lips travel across the full width of her neck. ''Oh, Eric,'' she breathed. ''I'd forgotten how good this could feel!''

''Me, too.'' He turned her then, urging her to face him with gentle hands on her shoulders. Their gazes connected, and she could see the fire smoldering in the depths of his eyes. ''But I'd like to remember,'' he continued. "And I'd like to make some new memories. With you.''

She stared at him, mesmerized by the profound emotion and honesty she saw reflected in his eyes. Her throat contracted with tenderness. "I'd like that, too,'' she whispered, and was rewarded with a smile that warmed her through and through. Slowly he reached over to touch her face, but stopped when she backed off slightly.

"What's wrong?'' he queried in concern.

She blushed self-consciously. "It's just that I'm...I'm really out of practice. And I guess I'm a little bit afraid that I won't be...that you won't like... I haven't kissed a man in years, and I feel so awkward and schoolgirlish and— Boy, I'm really blowing this, aren't I?'' she finished artlessly.

Eric's expression eased and he chuckled. "Can I tell you something? I have exactly the same fears. So what do you say we both just relax? I have a feeling everything will turn out fine.''

Kate forced her trembling lips into a smile. "If you say so.''

He reached out to her again, and this time she remained still, letting her eyelids drift closed as his fingers made contact with her skin.

Eric moved slowly, taking time to savor the feel of her skin beneath fingertips that were suddenly hypersensitive as he traced the sweet contours of her face, memorizing every nuance. She felt so soft—so good. He knew that they were breaking new ground in their relationship tonight; knew that there was no turning back once they started down this path. And part of him was still afraid. The wounds from his first marriage had left scars that ran deep. But somehow he sensed that with Kate, things would be different. He'd prayed for guidance, had asked the Lord to give him the courage to trust his heart, and so now he stood poised at a crossroads: he could either stay on the safe, predictable, lonely path he'd been following, or move in a new, uncharted direction that could bring love. The choice was his.

He gazed tenderly down at Kate's upturned face, at the soft fanning of her dark lashes against her cheeks. There was a fineness to her; a goodness that radiated from deep within. It wasn't in her nature ever to be hurtful or selfish or inconsiderate. He knew that as surely as he knew the sun rose in the east. She was a kind, caring woman who had shown great courage and endurance in the face of tragedy. She was also a loving and conscientious mother. And though she had strayed from her faith for a time, she had eventually found her way home again.

And then there was her beauty. With her flawless complexion, lovely features and slender, toned body, she looked closer to twenty-five than thirty-five. And her hair—it was soft and full and made for a man's hands to tangle in, he thought, combing his fingers through the wavy tresses.

In short, she was an incredibly desirable woman.

And yet…she'd remained alone for five long years, true to the memory of her dead husband. That, too, he admired in her. Loyalty and enduring love were qualities to be respected and honored. He knew she was still struggling to reconcile the possibility of a new relationship with her devotion to Jack, and was reluctant to do anything that diminished the memory of their love and commitment. So he felt deeply honored that she was willing to open her heart to him. Not to mention deeply attracted. Until Kate, he hadn't so much as *considered* the option of falling in love again. Now it wasn't just an option; it was a very real possibility.

Eric let his other hand drop to her waist and closed the distance between them. He felt her begin to tremble again, and he knew she was afraid, just as he was. Where would this lead? Were they making a mistake? Would they both end up hurt? Eric didn't know. But there was only one way to find the answer to those questions. Taking a slow, deep breath, he leaned toward her and tenderly claimed her lips.

Though his touch was gentle, Kate was momentarily stunned by the electric sizzle that shot through her. At the same time, she felt as if she'd been waiting for this moment for years. And maybe, in a way, she had. There had always been physical affection in her life—as a daughter, a mother, a sister. But this kind of affection had long been absent. And she'd missed it. A sweet shiver of delight swept over her and her heart soared with an almost-forgotten thrill as Eric's lips moved tenderly over hers, igniting long-dormant desires deep within her. Without consciously realizing what she was doing, she put her arms around his neck and pulled him even closer.

Eric was momentarily taken aback by her complete surrender to his embrace and by her ardent, uninhibited response. He'd expected her to be tentative and uncertain. Instead, she was giving herself fully and willingly to the kiss. And he was delighted. Because it meant that she not only cared for him, but also trusted him. And he had no intention of betraying that trust.

Kate felt his firm, sure hand on her back, through the thin fabric of her turtleneck. She could feel the hard, uneven thudding of his heart. She could feel his ragged breath. But most of all she could feel his lips, hungry yet tender. And she responded willingly, reveling in the embrace of this wonderful, caring man.

At last, with obvious reluctance, he drew back enough to gaze down at her.

She stared up at him, able to utter only one, breathy word. ''Wow!''

His lips tilted up into an unsteady, crooked grin. ''Yeah. Wow!''

She touched his face wonderingly, hesitantly reaching out to trace his lips with her fingertip. His sudden, sharp intake of breath made her pause, and she started to withdraw her hand. But he grasped it and held it firmly in place.

''Don't stop,'' he said hoarsely, closing his eyes.

Slowly she continued her exploration, her fingertips memorizing the planes of his face. Only when she'd finished did he open his eyes. He held her gaze compellingly as he lifted her hand to his lips and kissed the palm.

This time it was her turn to gasp. He paused and raised his eyebrows questioningly.

''Don't stop,'' she murmured, echoing his words.

He kissed each fingertip before enfolding her hand protectively in his, his fingers warm and strong around hers. Then he drew a long, ragged breath. ''You know what you said earlier, about being out of practice?'' he reminded her with a crooked grin. ''If this is what you're like when you're rusty, I have serious concerns for my blood pressure when you're up to speed.''

She blushed and smiled shyly. ''I guess I got a little carried away.''

''Hey, I'm not complaining! I just didn't expect things to get so…intense…so quickly.''

''Me, neither.''

"Are you sorry?" His tone was serious now, his face concerned.

She considered the question for a moment, finding it hard to concentrate when one of his hands was stroking her nape and the other was entwined with hers. "No. I think in my heart I realized at some point that this was inevitable. And we're not exactly strangers on a first date. We've known each other for over three months, Eric. This evolution of friendship into romance—well, it feels right to me. And natural. And comfortable. Not to mention…exciting." Her face grew warm, and he gave a relieved chuckle.

"I'm glad you added that last adjective. For a minute, there, I was beginning to feel like a pair of old slippers," he teased.

She smiled. "'Old slippers' is hardly the way I would describe you. More like a pair of fancy shoes I once bought—classy and sophisticated and guaranteed to make a woman feel drop-dead gorgeous and desirable."

"Well, you're definitely all of the above. And I plan to do everything I can to make you feel that way every day from now on."

Kate looked up at him, and the tenderness in his eyes made her throat constrict with happiness as her heart soared with hope. For the first time in years she began to think that maybe, just maybe, she wouldn't spend the rest of her life alone.

The smell of freshly brewing coffee wafted into the bedroom, slowly coaxing Kate awake the next morning. But even though the aroma was appealing, she fought the return to full consciousness. She wanted to hold on to this lingering, inexplicable feeling of contentment—most likely a remnant of some already forgotten dream—for just a little longer.

But she couldn't ignore the knock on her door a few minutes later. And she especially couldn't ignore the husky male voice that accompanied it.

"Are you decent?"

Her eyelids flew open and she stared at the ceiling in shock. The feeling of contentment *wasn't* an illusion, after all. It was as real as the man standing on the other side of her door. She struggled to a half-sitting position and frantically pulled the blanket up to her neck, clutching it against her chest with both hands as her pulse skyrocketed.

"Y-yes. Come in."

Eric opened the door, a coffee mug in one hand, and paused for a moment to smile at her. His gaze, intimate and tender, lingered on her face, then did a leisurely inventory of the dark mass of hair tumbling around her shoulders, the demure neckline of her gown, the cheeks still flushed from sleep. With her wide eyes, slightly parted lips and endearingly modest posture, she looked vulnerable...and beautiful...and very, very appealing.

With a jolt that rocked him to his core, Eric suddenly realized that he wanted to wake up beside this special woman every morning for the rest of his life. But how could things have progressed so quickly? he wondered in confusion. When he'd claimed Kate's lips last night, he'd considered it a first step down a new path in their relationship. Yet he now realized that it hadn't been a first step at all. It had simply verified what his heart had known for weeks. He was in love with her. But was he ready for that kind of commitment?

And then she smiled—a tentative, endearing smile that tugged at his heart and chased away his doubts. Yes, he *was* ready, he realized. Maybe past ready. But he wasn't so sure about her. Though she'd responded fully to his overtures last night, she might be having second thoughts in the light of day. He knew she still had issues to deal with, and he couldn't push her. But he also knew with absolute certainty that one day in the not-too-distant future he would ask her to be his wife. It was just a matter of waiting for the right time.

"Hi, Mommy." Impatient about the delay in seeing her mother, Sarah squeezed past Eric and plopped on the bed beside Kate.

Lost in the intensity of Eric's gaze, Kate needed a moment to refocus and respond. "Hi, sweetie. Do I get a good-morning hug?" She leaned over to kiss her daughter, holding her close for a long moment as she willed her breathing to calm. She glanced at the clock as she released Sarah, and her eyes grew anxious. "Oh, no! I forgot to set the alarm last night. I'll be late! I've got to get up!"

Eric moved beside her and placed a hand on her shoulder. "Your school declared a snow day. You're a lady of leisure today."

Her posture relaxed and she drew a deep breath. "It must be pretty bad out there. They never call snow days."

"It is."

He handed her the coffee, and she gave him a warm smile. "Thank you. I'm not used to such service. Do you do windows?" she teased.

He chuckled and gave her a wink. "Depends what the job pays."

She flushed but was saved from having to reply when Sarah spoke up.

"Are you staying here all day, Dr. Eric?"

"I wish I could," he declared regretfully. "But kids still get sick when it snows. So I need to go and take care of them."

Kate looked at him worriedly. "What are the roads like?"

He shrugged. "Manageable in daylight. The radio said the main routes are clear and I'll be careful, Kate," he promised gently, reaching out to touch her cheek.

She swallowed. "Okay."

"I'll call you when I get to the hospital."

She gave him a grateful look. "Thank you."

"Take it easy today, okay? Get some rest."

She nodded mutely.

He hesitated, then turned to Sarah. "Do you think you could find a piece of paper and a pencil for me in the kitchen, honey?"

"Uh-huh." She scooted off the bed and skipped down the hall.

As soon as she was out the door, Eric looked back at Kate. "I enjoyed last night," he said huskily.

"So did I."

"And I couldn't leave without doing this." He leaned over, and her lips stirred sweetly beneath his promise-filled kiss. "I wish we had more time," he admitted. His breath was warm on her cheek as he reluctantly broke contact.

"There's always tonight."

He gazed down at her with a warm, amused smile. "Is that an invitation?"

"Yes."

"I accept."

At the sound of running feet, he quickly turned to the doorway.

"Is this okay, Dr. Eric?" Sarah asked, holding out a tablet and pencil as she reentered the room.

"That's perfect, honey." Eric took it and scribbled something, then handed it to Kate. "That's my pager number, just in case you need me."

Her spoken reply was a simple, "Thank you," but in the silence of her heart another voice responded differently. "I'll always need you," it said.

For a moment, Kate was taken aback by those words. Though they were simple, too, their implication was not. And suddenly she knew that the time had come to put her past to rest. Only then could she give herself a chance at a future that included this very special man.

Kate climbed onto the kitchen chair she'd dragged into her bedroom and carefully withdrew a box from the top shelf of her closet. As she deposited it in the living room, she glanced at the clock. Sarah had gone to the park down the street with the little boy next door and his mother, which meant Kate had about an hour to herself. That should be plenty of time, she decided, as she made herself a cup of hot chocolate and put on the CD of classical music that Amy had given her last Christmas.

Kate settled herself comfortably on the couch, took a deep breath and lifted the lid of the box. The familiar cream-colored envelope on top produced the usual melancholy pang, though it wasn't quite as intense this year. She fingered the envelope gently, then withdrew the formal invitation. As her eyes scanned the conventional wording, she found it hard to believe that eleven years ago today she had walked down the aisle as a radiant bride. So much had happened since then. So much had changed. In many ways, she felt like a different person. The youthful girl in white, so optimistic, so filled with dreams for the future, so deeply in love with her husband-to-be, seemed almost like a stranger, or a character in a story she had read—not actually lived.

She set the invitation aside and reached for the album, pausing to take a sip of her hot chocolate as she flipped open the first page. It was an annual ritual that she and Jack had begun on their first anniversary. They would usually open a bottle of champagne and slowly work their way through the photos, sometimes laughing, sometimes stopping to kiss, sometimes pausing to offer toasts. She'd continued the tradition after his death, substituting hot chocolate for the champagne.

When Kate reached the last page—a close-up portrait of the two of them—her eyes misted as her gaze lovingly traced Jack's handsome, dear face. He had been a wonderful husband. There had been no one else like him—no one who touched her heart in quite the way he had, no one who had his knack for making her find that special place inside herself where the child still lived. And there never would be again. She knew that with absolute certainty. And she accepted it.

With Reverend Jacobs' help, she had also accepted Jack's death, had made her peace with the Lord's decision to call him home sooner than either of them had expected. She felt ready, at last, to move forward with her life—and her relationship with Eric. Much of the credit for that went to Amy, who had put into words what Kate had begun to feel in her heart: that her love for Eric in no way diminished what she and Jack had shared. That time in her life—those memories—stood apart and belonged always to them. She and Eric would create something new that was theirs alone, touch places within each other that no one else had ever touched. They would move forward together, leaving doubts and guilt behind, and face tomorrow with hope.

Suddenly Kate remembered the counted-cross-stitch sampler she'd worked on at Jack's bedside during the months he'd been in the long-term nursing facility. With a frown, she tried to recall where she'd put it. Somewhere in her closet, she was sure. A few minutes later, after rummaging around on the floor, she emerged triumphantly with a dusty bag. She waited until she was seated again on the couch before she carefully withdrew her handiwork and gazed at the partially stitched words from Jeremiah. She read them once, twice, a third time. They had given her hope as she'd sat by Jack's side, she recalled, but she'd bitterly put the sampler away unfinished—just like her life—after he died.

Kate looked again at their wedding portrait on the last page of the album, and her throat tightened with emotion. For she knew that this ritual, which had helped sustain her during the last few years, was now coming to an end.

"I love you," she whispered, her voice catching. "I always will.

You were my sunshine, Jack. You filled my life with joy and beauty and laughter. I'll never forget that. And I'll never let Sarah forget what a wonderful father she had in you. But it's time now for me to let you go. I know you're with the Lord, and that you've found the contentment and wholeness that only comes when we are one with Him in heaven. But I still have a road to travel here. And I don't want to make the journey alone. I think Eric is going to ask me to marry him soon, and I'm going to accept. He's a wonderful man. You would have liked him, I think. And it's my most fervent prayer that you'll always know I love you no less because I also love him.'' She paused as her eyes misted with tears. ''Goodbye, my love. Until we meet again.''

And then, very gently, she closed the album.

# Chapter Eleven

"I'll get it!" Sarah called as she raced from the living room to the front door.

Kate smiled and wiped her hands on a dish towel. It might have taken *her* a long time to figure out where Eric fit in the scheme of things, but for Sarah, who had no memories holding her back, he had immediately meshed seamlessly and naturally into their lives.

"Hi, sweetie. Did you build a snowman today?" she heard Eric ask.

"Yes. Mark and me and his mommy went to the park and made a gigan—gigan—really big snowman with a carrot for a nose and charcoal for eyes."

Kate liked the sound of his chuckle—deep, rich and heartwarming. "Now that sounds like a first-class snowman. Did your mommy go, too?"

"No. She said she had stuff to do."

Kate stepped into the living room then and smiled at Eric. The snow had started up again, and delicate white flakes clung to the shoulders of his dark wool coat. He looked rugged and masculine, she thought, as her heart skipped a beat.

"Hi."

He glanced up to return her greeting, but the words died in his throat. She looked absolutely radiant tonight, he thought in awe. On a peripheral level he noticed her deep blue angora sweater and black stirrup pants, and her hair, brushed loose and full, lying softly on her shoulders. But it was the glow on her face that stunned him.

For the first time in their acquaintance she seemed truly relaxed and at ease, he realized. There was a profound calmness, a serenity about her that reached out and touched his very soul. Something about her had changed—and changed dramatically—in the hours since he'd reluctantly left her to enjoy her snow day. It was as if an event of great significance had occurred. But what?

Kate saw the sudden look of speculation on his face and flushed. Was her newfound inner peace so obvious? But Eric was a perceptive man. She should have realized he'd immediately sense the change in her, just as she should have realized that he'd quickly notice the changes in the room, as well. In one quick, discerning sweep his gaze passed over, then returned to the spots where photos of her and Jack had once been displayed.

Sarah's powers of perception were none too shabby, either, Kate acknowledged wryly. The little girl was watching the proceedings with interest, and quickly noted the direction of Eric's glances.

"Do you like our new picture?" she piped up.

His brain was so busy trying to process the significance of Kate's redecorating efforts that it took a moment for the question to register. When it did, he transferred his attention from the Monet print behind the couch to Sarah. "It's very pretty."

"I like it, too," she declared. "It was in the hall closet. Mommy said it was too pretty to keep hidden away. So she took the wedding picture down. She said sometimes you have to put things away to make room for new things."

Eric turned to Kate, whose cheeks were tinged with warm color.

"Mommy let me put the picture from the TV in my room, too," Sarah continued, oblivious to the intense atmosphere. "She said we're going to get some tulip bulbs in pots to put there instead, and that we can watch them grow all winter. She said they'll help us keep spring in our hearts even when it's cold and snowing outside. Isn't that right, Mommy?"

Eric's gaze remained locked on hers. "That's right, honey," Kate replied unsteadily, reaching up distractedly to push her hair back from her face. And that was when Eric noticed the most significant thing of all.

The ring finger of her left hand was bare.

"Aren't you going to say hi to Mommy?" Sarah demanded when the silence between the two adults lengthened.

Once again, it took him a moment to collect his chaotic thoughts. "Of course I am. In fact, I'm going to do better than that." His gaze never leaving Kate's, he closed the distance between them, hesitated long enough to give her time to protest, then leaned over and kissed her.

"Hi," he greeted her huskily, one hand resting lightly at her waist. "I missed you."

"We missed you, too," Sarah added. "But Mommy said you'd be back."

"Mommy was right."

"We're having chicken and dressing and biscuits tonight," she announced. "And chocolate cake!"

"And broccoli," Kate reminded her daughter.

"Sounds like a celebration. Broccoli and all," Eric remarked.

Kate's flush deepened and she turned toward the kitchen, trying to steady her staccato pulse. "Sarah, you have just enough time to finish watching your video before dinner."

"Okay." The little girl happily returned to the TV set and sat down, cross-legged.

As Kate walked toward the counter, she was aware of Eric close behind her. And she wasn't at all surprised when he placed his hands on her shoulders and leaned close, his breath warm on her neck.

"I like the redecorating."

She took a deep breath as she turned to face him, and he looped his arms loosely around her waist. They were only inches apart, and she felt lost for a moment in the depths of his deep blue eyes. "It was time," she replied quietly.

"You're sure about this?"

She nodded. "I don't want to live in the past anymore, Eric. I'll never forget my life with Jack. And I'll always love him," she added honestly. "But memories can only sustain you for so long. I've tried to hold on to them, but as a result I've ended up putting my *life* on hold. I've felt like a hollow, empty shell for too long. There was a time when my life was rich and full and filled with promise. I want to feel that way again. I want to move forward and make new memories.''

She didn't say, ''With you,'' but somehow she had a feeling he knew what was in her heart. And his next words not only confirmed that, but sent her hopes soaring.

He reached over and tenderly cupped her face with his strong, capable hands. ''I feel the same way, Kate,'' he told her huskily. ''What do you say we start making those memories together?''

Kate couldn't remember a Christmas season so filled with joy and breathless anticipation. For once she didn't mind the cold weather, and moved with renewed energy and a lightness of step. Her daily chores, formerly dreary, no longer seemed burdensome and endless. Because always, at the end of her day, there was Eric. Whether it was a simple dinner at her apartment or an impromptu meal out, whether it was a ''family outing'' with Sarah and Anna, or quietly sipping hot chocolate with Eric by the tree after Sarah went to bed, each moment was golden. And Kate treasured every single one, storing them in a special place in her heart reserved just for Eric. Their relationship, so long purely friendship, blossomed rapidly into a genuine romance.

Once, Kate paused in surprise as she passed a mirror, hardly recognizing for a moment the woman with the sparkling eyes, flushed cheeks and animated face who stared back her. She shook her head and smiled ruefully. There was no hiding it, she admitted. It was there for all the world to see. She was in love.

Even Sarah noticed. As Kate tucked her daughter into bed one night after Eric had been summoned to the hospital for an emergency, the little girl suddenly looked up at her, her expression quite serious.

''Are you going to marry Dr. Eric?'' she asked solemnly, without preamble.

Kate's heart stopped, then tripped on. She'd been expecting this question, but she still wasn't sure how to answer it—or the others that would inevitably follow. Slowly she sat down on the bed and took Sarah's hand, silently asking the Lord for guidance.

''He hasn't asked me yet, honey.''

''But what if he does?'' she persisted.

"Well, what do you think I should do?"

She considered for a moment. "Would he live with us if you got married?"

"We'd all live together. Probably at Dr. Eric's house."

"Would he be my daddy?"

This was the tough one. Kate struggled to find the right words—words that would keep Jack's memory alive but leave room for Eric, as well. "Actually, Sarah, you'd have *two* daddies." She reached over and picked up the photo of Jack. "When you were born, this was your daddy. He's in heaven now, so you can't see him, but he still loves you very much. And so does Dr. Eric. He'd be your daddy here. So you see how lucky you would be? You'd have a daddy in heaven and one here on earth."

"Do you still love my first daddy?"

Tears pricked her eyes, and Kate swallowed. "Of course, honey. I always will. He was very special to me. But he wouldn't want us to be lonesome. And I know he'd like Dr. Eric. I think he would probably be very happy if Dr. Eric took care of us, since he can't be with us himself."

Sarah thought about that for a minute. "You know something, Mommy?" she said at last.

"What, sweetheart?"

"I would really like to have a daddy I could see. If Dr. Eric asks you to marry him, I think you should. Then we could be a real family. And that would be my best Christmas present ever!"

As Kate bent over to kiss Sarah, her heart gave a silent, fervent reply.

*And mine as well.*

"Kate? Eric. Listen, I've got a problem at the hospital."

Kate frowned and glanced at her watch. Sarah had to be at church in forty-five minutes for the Christmas pageant, and Eric had planned to take them.

"Kate?" Eric prompted when she didn't reply.

"I'm here. Will you be tied up long?"

She heard his weary sigh over the line. "Possibly. I've got a little boy who was just diagnosed with meningitis."

Kate's throat tightened and she closed her eyes. She'd read stories about the dangerous, fast-moving illness. "Oh, Eric! I'm sorry. How old is he?"

"Seven. Even worse, he's an only child. The parents are panic-stricken."

"How bad is he?"

"Bad."

She swallowed. The tone of his voice said everything. "Listen, don't worry about tonight, okay? I'll take Sarah. Maybe you can meet us later if things improve."

"Kate, I'm sorry. Sarah will be so disappointed."

He was right. Her daughter had been looking forward to having all three of them—Kate, Eric and Anna—in the audience. "Like a family," she'd told Kate happily. But it couldn't be helped.

"I'll explain it to her, Eric. Don't worry."

"I wish Mom hadn't agreed to go early to help set up refreshments." She heard the frustration in his voice. "At least you could have ridden together, then."

"Please, Eric. It's okay. We're fine. Just do what you can for that poor child and his parents."

"Thanks, Kate."

"For what?"

"For understanding. For not making me feel guilty. For not hating my work and resenting the demands and the disruption."

Once again Kate had a glimpse of the hell he must have lived through with Cindy.

"Eric, your profession is part of who you are," she said quietly. "Your conscientiousness and caring are two of the things I lo—" She paused and cleared her throat. "Things I respect in you and find appealing. So stop worrying and go do your job, okay?"

"Okay. And I'll get there as soon as I can. You'll explain to Sarah? Tell her I'm sorry?"

"Yes. Everything will be fine. We'll see you later."

"Count on it."

As Kate slowly replaced the receiver, Sarah trailed excitedly into the kitchen, holding her halo. "When do we have to leave, Mommy?"

Kate took her hand and drew her into the living room, tucking her under her arm as they sat down. "In about fifteen minutes. Honey, you know how Dr. Eric was supposed to take us?"

Sarah looked up at her with wide eyes that were suddenly troubled. "Yes."

"Well, he's at the hospital. There's a very sick little boy there who needs him very much. And his mommy and daddy are very worried and they need Dr. Eric, too. So he has to stay with them for a while and try to help that little boy get well so he can go home for Christmas."

Sarah's lower lip began to quiver. "Isn't Dr. Eric coming to see me in the Christmas pageant?"

"He's going to try his very best, honey. But he isn't sure he'll be able to get there in time. This little boy needs him. Just think if you were sick and had to go to the hospital. Wouldn't you want Dr. Eric to stay with you?"

"Yes. But he said he'd come to my show. And I need him, too."

"I know, honey. And Dr. Eric knows, too. It's just that sometimes, when you're a doctor, other people need you more. This little boy is so sick that he might die if Dr. Eric doesn't stay with him."

"You mean like Daddy?"

"Yes. Just like Daddy. And then his mommy and daddy would be all alone, just like we were after Daddy went to heaven."

"And they would be very sad, wouldn't they? Like you used to be?"

"Yes, they would."

Sarah bit her lip and struggled with that idea. "I guess maybe they do need Dr. Eric more," she said at last in a small voice.

Kate's heart swelled, and she pulled Sarah close. "Oh, sweetie, I'm so proud of you. You're such a big girl! Why don't we say a prayer for the little boy so that God will watch over him?"

"Okay."

As they held hands on the couch and sent a heartfelt plea to the Lord, Kate also took a moment to silently give thanks—for the wonderful, caring man who had come into her life, and for a precious daughter who had shown a compassion and unselfishness beyond her years.

\* \* \*

"Oh, my, will you look at that!"

Anna stood at the window of the church hall and gazed outside. A mixture of sleet and snow had begun to fall during the program, and the roads were already covered. Kate, who stood at her elbow, felt the color drain from her face. Eric hadn't made it to the pageant, and there was still no sign of him. The road would only get worse the longer she waited, and even though the social was just beginning, she decided to call it a night.

"I think I'm going to head home, Anna," she said, trying to control the tremor in her voice. "I'm not much for driving in bad weather."

Anna turned back to her. "Well, I can't say I blame you. But you'll have to pry Sarah away from the dessert table."

Kate glanced at her daughter, whose obvious delight in the wonderland of sweets brought a fleeting smile to Kate's face. "We'll just have to get a plate to go. How about you? Will you be okay getting home?" she asked worriedly.

"Oh, absolutely. Fred and Jenny have a four-wheel drive. In fact, if you want to wait, you could ride with us and just leave your car here."

Kate considered the offer for a moment, then regretfully shook her head. "Thanks, Anna. I'd love to take you up on that, but I need the car for school tomorrow."

"Well, you be careful then, okay?"

"I will."

By the time Kate and Sarah were strapped into their older-model compact car, the icy mixture had intensified. Kate glanced nervously at Sarah, but fortunately she was so busy sampling her smorgasbord of desserts that she seemed oblivious to her mother's tension. Which was just as well, Kate concluded. With any luck, they'd be home before Sarah even made a dent in her plate of goodies.

Eric swung into the church parking lot, skidding slightly as he made the turn. For the first time he realized that it was sleeting. He'd been so distraught since he'd left the hospital that he hadn't even noticed the weather. He'd simply turned on the windshield defroster and made the drive to the church on automatic pilot, his mind in a turmoil.

Was there anything else he could have done? he asked himself for the dozenth time in the last hour. Had he reacted quickly enough? Had he pushed the tests through as rapidly as possible? Would it have made any difference if they'd made the diagnosis even half an hour sooner? And dear God, how did you explain to two grief-stricken parents that you'd let their only child die? They'd stared at him numbly, in shock and disbelief, and all he'd been able to say was, "I'm sorry." "Inadequate" didn't even come close to describing those words.

Eric parked the car and took a long, shaky breath. Even after years of dealing with scenarios like this, he'd never gotten used to it. Some doctors learned to insulate themselves from the pain. He never had. On nights like this it ripped through him like a knife, leaving his heart in shreds, his spirits crushed.

Wearily he climbed out of the car and made his way toward the church hall. He wasn't in the mood to see anyone, not even Kate, but he'd promised to come if he could. And he wasn't a man who gave his word lightly. So when he'd left the hospital he'd just automatically headed in this direction.

"Heavens, Eric, are you all right?"

Anna met him inside the door, her face a mask of concern.

He jammed his hands into the deep pockets of his jacket. "Not especially."

"Kate told me about your patient. Did he…"

"He didn't make it." His voice was flat and lifeless.

Anna's eyes filled with tears and she reached out to touch his arm. "Oh, Eric, I'm sorry. I know how losses like this tear you up."

"I'm in great shape compared to the parents."

"I know you did all you could," Anna said quietly.

He sighed and wearily raked the fingers of one hand through his hair. "I hope so." He glanced around the room and frowned. "Is the pageant over?"

"It's been over for twenty minutes. Would you like some coffee?"

Distractedly he shook his head, his gaze once more scanning the room. "Where's Kate? And Sarah?"

"They left about five minutes ago. Kate said she didn't want to wait in case the weather got any worse."

For the first time since leaving the hospital his mind switched gears. Kate hated to drive in this kind of weather. And now she was out there on roads that were rapidly becoming treacherous, probably as terrified as she'd been on the drive home from Tennessee. His frown deepened and he turned toward the door.

"I'll call you tomorrow, Mom," he called over his shoulder, not waiting for a reply.

As Eric set off on the familiar route from the church to Kate's apartment, his heart began to hammer against his rib cage. He drove as quickly as the deteriorating conditions would allow, peering ahead, his hands gripping the wheel. *Please, Lord, watch over her,* he prayed. *Let her feel Your presence and Your guiding hand.*

By the time he caught sight of her, she was only about a mile from her apartment. She was driving slowly and cautiously, but she was safe, he reassured himself, his shoulders sagging in relief. In a couple of minutes he'd be right behind her, and a few minutes after that, she'd be home.

Eric watched as Kate stopped at an intersection. She took plenty of time to look in both directions, then continued across. But for some reason she stopped right in the middle. Or perhaps her car stalled or got stuck on the ice. He wasn't sure. All he knew was that he suddenly saw headlights approaching too quickly, heard the squeal of brakes, and then watched in horror as the other car slammed into the passenger side of Kate's vehicle.

For the second time in a handful of hours, Eric felt as if someone had kicked him in the gut. He stepped on the accelerator, oblivious to the road conditions, and skidded to a stop with only inches to spare. The other driver was already out of his car and clearly unhurt.

"Do you have a cell phone?" Eric shouted as he slipped and slid across the icy surface. The man nodded. "Call 911," Eric barked harshly.

He didn't want to look inside Kate's car. But he had no choice. Hiding from what was inside the car was as impossible as hiding from what was in his heart.

He tried Sarah's door first, but it was too smashed to budge and he couldn't tell how seriously hurt she was by peering in the window. All he knew was that she was crying.

Eric moved around to the driver's side as quickly as the icy conditions would allow, and when he pulled open the door the wrenching sound of Sarah's sobbing spilled out. Kate was leaning across the seat, frantically trying to unbuckle her daughter's seat belt, but she was too constrained by her own. Eric reached in and unsnapped it, freeing her.

"Kate, are you all right?"

If she heard him, she didn't respond. Her attention was focused solely on her daughter.

He tried again, this time more forcefully, his hands firmly on her shoulders, a touch of desperation in his voice. "Kate, look at me. I need to know if you're all right."

She turned then, her eyes frantic. For a moment she didn't even seem to recognize him, and when she did, her face crumpled. "Eric? Oh, God, where were you? We needed you! Please...help us! Help Sarah!"

Eric felt as if a knife had just been thrust into his heart and ruthlessly twisted. Those few words, and the look of hurt and betrayal on her face, sent his world crashing so rapidly that it left him reeling. But he couldn't think about that now. There were other, more pressing things that demanded his attention.

"Kate, are you hurt?" he repeated, his voice broken and raspy.

Jerkily she shook her head, then clutched at his arm. "No. I'm okay. Please...just help Sarah!"

"I'm going to. Can you get out? I can't get in from her side."

Kate nodded and scrambled out, swaying unsteadily as she stood. He reached for her, but she shook him off impatiently, clinging to the frigid metal of the car as the sleet stung her face. "Go to Sarah."

Eric climbed into the front seat and reached over to touch Sarah, speaking softly. "Sarah, it's Dr. Eric. I'm going to help you, okay? Sarah? Can you look at me?"

Her sobbing abated slightly and she turned to him, her eyes wide with fear. At first he thought the dark splotches on her face were blood and his stomach lurched. But then he noticed the plate of cake and cookies on the floor and realized it was chocolate. He drew a steadying breath.

"Sarah, can you tell me what hurts?"

"M-my ar-arm," she said tearfully.

"I'll tell you what. I'm going to unbuckle your seat belt and take a look, okay?'' He tried to keep his voice calm and matter-of-fact, but it took every ounce of discipline he had.

"I want my mommy," Sarah declared, her lower lip beginning to tremble.

"I'm here, Sarah." Kate leaned into the car. "Do what Dr. Eric says, okay?"

She sniffled. "Okay."

"Sarah, honey, can you turn toward me? I just want to take a look at your arm. I promise I'll try not to hurt you." Eric reached over and unsnapped her seat belt as he spoke, holding it away from her body as it slid into its holder.

She angled toward him slightly, her sobs subsiding. Fortunately she was wearing a down-filled parka, he noted. It had probably padded her somewhat from the impact. But it also hampered his exam. He reached over and took her small hand in his, forcing himself to smile.

"It looks like you had chocolate cake tonight. Was it good?'' he asked, gently manipulating her arm.

"Yes. But I didn't get to finish it.''

"Well, we'll just have to get you some more. Maybe your very own cake.''

Her eyes grew wide. "Really?''

"Really.'' He unzipped her parka and eased it off her shoulders. "Do you want chocolate or yellow?''

"Chocolate.''

"Ah. A woman after my own heart.'' He carefully pressed her arm in critical places through the thin knit of her sweater, slowly working his way up. "I think that's a good choice. Chocolate or white icing?''

"Chocolate. And maybe it could have— Ouch!'' She gave a startled yelp when he reached her elbow.

"I'm sorry, honey. Does it hurt up here, too?'' Carefully he pressed along her upper arm to her shoulder. Silently she shook her head.

"How is everything in here, Doctor?''

Eric turned, suddenly aware of the flashing red lights reflecting off the icy pavement. A police officer was looking into the car.

"Nothing too serious, as far as I can tell.''

"Should I call an ambulance?"

That would only upset Kate and Sarah even more, he decided. "I'll take them to the hospital."

"Okay. I'll send one of my men over to take a statement."

Eric nodded, then turned back to Sarah and draped the parka over her shoulders. "I don't want to hurt your arm, honey. Can you scoot over and put your other arm around my neck?"

Sarah nodded, and a moment later he eased himself out of the car, with Sarah in his arms. Kate reached out to her daughter and touched her face, then turned anxious eyes to Eric.

"I don't think there's any real damage," he said reassuringly. "But I'd like to get you both checked out at the hospital, just to be sure."

Kate shook her head. "I'm fine. I'm just worried about Sarah."

Kate didn't look fine. She looked terrible. Her face was colorless and she was visibly shaking. But he wasn't about to stand around in the sleet and argue.

"Hold on to my arm. We'll take my car."

She frowned. "What about my car? Is it drivable?"

"Yes, ma'm," the police officer replied, coming up next to them. "The keys are still in the ignition, so if you'll give us your address, we'll drop it off when we're finished here."

Kate complied, and a few moments later they were on their way to the hospital. Though Eric tried to convince Kate to be examined, she refused.

"I told you, Eric. I'm not hurt. Just shaken up. I'll feel much better when I know for sure that Sarah is all right."

Which she was, except for a badly bruised elbow, Eric concluded after a complete exam at the hospital. Kate's shoulders sagged with relief when he told her, and she lifted a weary, trembling hand to her forehead as tears spilled out of her eyes.

"Thank God!" she whispered fervently.

Eric wanted to reach out to Kate, wanted to take her in his arms and comfort her. Wanted to feel the comfort of *her* arms. But he held himself back. Her words at the accident scene, though spoken in a moment of panic and fear, had seared themselves into his soul, "Where were you? We needed you!" In circumstances like that, people often said what was truly in their heart. Cindy had just been more direct about it. "You're never there when I need you," had been her frequent refrain. And she had been right. Just as Kate had been right a couple of hours before. If he'd attended the pageant, as he'd promised, the accident would never have happened. They would have stayed for the social, and their paths would never have crossed with the other driver. Once again, his profession had gotten in the way of his private life—and with consequences that could have been so much worse. And it could very likely happen again. Which led Eric to the disheartening conclusion he'd reached long ago.

Marriage and medicine didn't mix.

# Chapter Twelve

Something was very wrong.

Kate frowned and slowly replaced the receiver, then turned to stare out the window at the leaden skies and the barren trees cloaked in a dull, gray fog. *Everything* suddenly looked gray to her, she realized, her eyes misting with tears—including the future that so recently had seemed golden.

Ever since the accident four days ago, Eric had been like a different person. He'd brought Sarah her own miniature chocolate cake, just as he'd promised in the car on the night of the accident. He'd offered to drive Kate anywhere she needed to go, even though she had a rental car while her own was being repaired. He checked daily to see how she and Sarah were doing. In fact, she'd just hung up from his call. But in many ways she felt as if she'd been talking to a polite stranger. There was a distance between them, an almost palpable separation that made her feel cold and afraid.

At first Kate thought it was because of the little boy he'd lost. And that probably *was* part of it, she reflected. He wasn't the kind of man who would ever be able to insulate his heart from such a tragedy. But the distance she felt was due to more than that, she was sure. For some reason the accident that had damaged her car had also damaged something far more valuable—their relationship. And she wasn't sure why. She'd tried to bring it up a couple of times, but Eric had simply said that he was busy at work, and they could talk about it after the holidays. Which did nothing to ease her mind.

Restlessly Kate rose and began to pace, her worry deepening. Eric was slipping away. She could feel it as surely as she'd felt the sting of sleet against her cheeks on the night of the accident. And she couldn't let that happen. Not without a fight, anyway. Not when she'd begun to build her whole future around this special man. But how did you fight an unknown enemy? How did you tackle a phantom, a shadow?

Kate didn't know. But suddenly she thought of someone who might.

"Kate! This is a surprise!" Amy exclaimed. "Did you change your mind and decide to come down for Christmas? You know you and Eric and Sarah are more than welcome. And you won't even have to put up with Wally this time. I'm pleased to report that our guest has thankfully been returned to his owner in good health and with good riddance, just in time for the holidays. Hallelujah!"

Kate found herself smiling despite her anxiety. "Since you did such a good job, maybe Cal's friend will ask you to iguana-sit again next year."

"Bite your tongue!" Amy declared in horror.

"Just a thought."

"And not a good one. But speaking of good thoughts, I'm serious about the invitation. Do you think you can drag that hardworking doctor down here for a quick visit?"

Kate played with the phone cord. "Frankly, I doubt I could convince him to visit anyone. Even me."

There was a moment of silence while Amy processed this information. When she spoke, her voice was laced with concern. "Do you want to tell me what happened?"

"I honestly don't know," Kate admitted, struggling to control the tears that suddenly welled in her eyes. "It's just that ever since the accident, he…"

"Whoa! Back up! What accident?" Amy demanded in alarm.

A pang of guilt ricocheted through Kate. She should have told Amy sooner, but she'd had other things on her mind—namely her relationship with Eric. "It wasn't bad, Amy. Don't worry. Some guy ran into our car the other night on the way back from the Christmas pageant. It was sleeting, and he lost control."

"Are you and Sarah all right?"

"Sarah's elbow is bruised, but it's nothing serious. I'm fine."

"How about Eric?"

Kate frowned. "What do you mean?"

"Was he hurt?"

"Oh. He wasn't in the car. He was delayed at the hospital. By the time he got to church we'd left, so he followed us. He was right behind us when the accident happened."

"You mean he saw the whole thing?"

"Yes."

"Wow! That must have played havoc with his nerves. It gives me chills just to think about it. And that's when things changed between the two of you?"

"Yes."

"Maybe he's just upset, Kate," Amy speculated. "Watching something like that unfold in front of your eyes, seeing people you care about in danger and not being able to do anything about it... It probably shook him up pretty badly."

"I know. And to make matters worse, he'd just lost a patient." Kate briefly explained about the little boy with meningitis.

"Oh, Kate!" Amy exclaimed in horror. "Having met Eric, I imagine he was devastated."

"Yes, he was."

"Okay, so let's try to piece this together," she reasoned. "He'd already had a terrible day at the hospital. Then, not only did he disappoint Sarah, who was looking forward to having him at the pageant, but he wasn't able to drive you. You told me once that his first marriage was more or less a disaster, largely because of conflicts between his career and personal life. And that for a long time he was afraid marriage and medicine didn't mix. Maybe those old fears have resurfaced. He probably figures that if he had taken you, the accident might never have happened. But his job got in the way." She paused, and when she spoke again her voice was thoughtful. "You know, I'd lay odds that right now he's waging a pretty intense battle with guilt. And fear."

As usual, Amy's analytical mind had distilled the essence of the situation. "You might be right," Kate conceded.

"Maybe he thinks you're upset because he didn't make the pageant. Maybe he thinks you blame him for what happened."

"But that's ridiculous! It wasn't his fault!"

"Did you tell him that?"

Kate frowned. No, she hadn't. In fact, what *had* she said to him the night of the accident? The whole incident was still so fuzzy. She remembered him pulling open her door, and she recalled the immense relief she'd felt, and her silent "Thank God!" But she hadn't said that. Nor had she said, "I'm so glad you're here," though she'd thought that, as well. She struggled to remember her first words to him, and was almost sorry when she did, for her heart sank.

"Oh, no! I couldn't have..." she whispered bleakly, closing her eyes, wishing with every ounce of her being that she could take back those accusatory words, spoken without thinking, in a moment of panic.

"Kate? What is it?"

"I just remembered what I said when Eric arrived on the accident scene," she said in dismay.

"What?"

Kate drew a deep breath. "Basically, I implied that he wasn't there for us when we needed him. Which of course only played right into the guilt he was already feeling. Big time. Oh, Amy, what am I going to do? I didn't mean it the way it came out! I was just so frightened and worried about Sarah. I don't even know where those words came from. He must have felt like he was reliving a nightmare. Just when he was starting to believe that marriage and medicine *could* mix, I say something stupid like that and blow the whole thing. He had enough guilt laid on him in his first marriage to last a lifetime. He's sure not going to put himself in that position again. No wonder he backed off!"

"You do have a problem," Amy conceded soberly. "Up until that point, do you think things were getting pretty...serious?"

"Very. In fact, I think he was..." She swallowed past the lump in her throat. "I think he was going to ask me to marry him, Amy."

"Were you going to accept?"

"Yes."

"Then you can't let this setback stand in the way," she declared resolutely.

"But I can't take back those words. And he isn't likely to forget them."

"I agree. What you need now are some more words."

"Do you want to explain that?"

"Let me ask you something first, Kate. How much do you love Eric?"

"So much that I can't even imagine a future without him anymore," she replied softly, without hesitation.

"Then you love him enough to do something totally out of character?"

"What exactly do you have in mind?" Kate asked, suddenly cautious.

"Just answer the question."

Kate drew a deep breath. She wasn't sure she was going to be comfortable with whatever Amy was going to suggest. But she also knew that her sister's advice would be sound. It always was. "Yes."

"Good," Amy declared with satisfaction. "Because I have a plan."

Eric frowned as he pulled up in front of his mother's house. Why was Kate's car here? He and Anna were supposed to pick up Kate and Sarah later, in time for Christmas Eve services, and they were all going to spend the day together tomorrow. Kate had canceled her usual holiday trip to Amy's when they'd made those arrangements. If she hadn't, he would have begged off from the whole thing. It was bound to be awkward.

Eric knew that Kate was confused and troubled by the change in their relationship. The intimacy they'd begun to create had been replaced by polite formality, the closeness by distance. In fact, if Christmas hadn't been only days away, he'd have cut the ties entirely by now, as painful as that would be. God knew, it wasn't what he wanted to do. But he felt he had no choice. During the last few weeks he'd gradually begun to believe that with Kate, things could be different; that she wouldn't come to resent the demands of his profession—and ultimately him—as Cindy had. And yet, in a moment of crisis, at a time when the heart often spoke truths even *it* hadn't recognized, she'd voiced a resentment, a blame, that had pierced him to his very core. He doubted whether she even recalled what she'd said. But though *she* might not remember her words, they were ones *he* could never forget.

Eric closed his eyes and gripped the steering wheel as his gut twisted painfully. With all his heart he wished there was a way out of this dilemma, an answer to the same question that had plagued him during his marriage to Cindy: where did his first loyalty lie? It was a conflict he'd never been able to reconcile. Cindy had made her opinion clear. And—intentionally or not—so had Kate. He desperately wished he could promise her it would never happen again, but that would be a lie. It *would* happen again. And again. And again. Until finally she, too, grew disillusioned and bitter. He couldn't do that to her. Or to himself.

Wearily Eric climbed out of the car. For everyone's sake he needed to be upbeat for the holiday. There would be time for sadness, for dealing with the loss of a dream, later. But getting through the next thirty-six hours with even a semblance of holiday cheer wasn't going to be easy.

The fragrant smell of pine mingling with the aroma of freshly baked cookies greeted him as he stepped inside the door, and he paused for a moment to let the warm, comforting holiday smells work their soothing magic. They took him back many years, to the happy days of his boyhood, and his lips curved up at the pleasant memories. If only life could be as simple as it had been in those idyllic days of youth, when the most pressing question he faced was whether there would be a shiny red bike under the tree, come Christmas morning.

"Eric! I thought I heard you," Anna greeted him with a smile as she stepped into the small foyer.

"Hello, Mom." He bent and kissed her cheek. "Merry Christmas."

"Merry Christmas to you. I'm glad you came early."

"You asked me to."

"So I did. It's nice to see you still listen to your mother once in a while," she teased.

"You know I'm always at your beck and call. But I'm surprised to see that Kate and Sarah are here," he remarked, striving for a casual tone. "I thought we were picking them up for services later."

"Well, when Kate called earlier, she sounded awfully lonesome. She and Sarah were all by themselves, so I invited them to come over early. I figured, why not spend the time together? I baked a ham, and there's plenty for two more. I didn't think you'd mind," she teased.

Eric hadn't said anything to his mother about his plans to stop seeing Kate, and tonight wasn't the time to break the news—not when he knew she had hopes for a wedding in the not-too-distant future. It would ruin her Christmas. And one ruined Christmas was enough. "Of course not."

"Hi, Dr. Eric!" Sarah dashed into the hallway and launched herself at him.

He reached down and swept her up. "Hi, yourself, sweetie. How's that elbow?"

She cocked it for him to see. "It's still kind of blue." Then she put her small arms around his neck and smiled. "You know what?"

His throat tightened. This was something else he was going to miss—the trusting touch of a child who loved him. "What?"

"This is the best Christmas ever!"

Eric's gut clenched again. How he hated to hurt this child! He was sure Kate would find a way to explain their breakup without making him sound like a villain. That was her way. But he sure *felt* like one. And as he looked into Sarah's happy, guileless face, so filled with the optimism of youth, he suddenly felt old.

"Sarah, honey, are you ready to decorate that next batch of cookies?" Anna asked.

"Yes. Do you want a cookie, Dr. Eric? Aunt Anna made them, and I decorated them," she told him proudly.

"I'll have one a little later," he promised as he set her down. He glanced at his mother as Sarah scampered back to the kitchen. "Where's Kate?"

"Right here," she replied breathlessly, coming up behind Anna.

As always, Eric was moved by the translucent beauty of her face. These last few weeks it had seemed almost luminous, filled with a soft light and a peace that reflected a soul at rest. But today she seemed a bit...different. He couldn't quite put his finger on it. Her eyes were a little too bright, for one thing. And her face was flushed. There was also an unusual energy radiating from her, making her movements seem agitated. He frowned, both curious and concerned.

"Are you all right?" he asked.

Her flush deepened. "Yes, of course. A little warm from all that cookie baking, though. Anna, I think I'll take a walk. I love this crisp weather, and I feel a touch of snow in the air. I won't be gone long," she promised, opening the hall closet to retrieve her coat.

"Kate, dear, do you think you should?" Anna asked worriedly. "It's getting dark."

"I'll be fine. A little fresh air will do me good."

Anna turned to Eric with a frown. "I'm not crazy about her walking alone, even if it is Christmas Eve."

"Please don't worry, Anna. I won't be gone long. Just down to the park and back," Kate reassured her as she pulled on her gloves.

Eric wasn't crazy about the idea, either. But Kate seemed determined to go. He frowned, waging an internal debate. Spending time alone with her was the last thing he wanted to do. The temptation to touch her, to feel her melt into his arms, was hard enough to resist when there were other people present. He wasn't sure his self-control would hold when it was just the two of them. Despite recent events and his subsequent resolve to end their relationship, he still loved her. He still wanted her to be his wife. And deep in his heart, he still wanted to believe they could work out the conflict between their personal life as a couple and his career. But his confidence had been badly shaken. He just couldn't find the courage to trust his heart—or his judgment. They had betrayed him once. How could he be sure they wouldn't again?

"Eric, I really don't like this," Anna prompted more forcefully.

His gaze swung from Kate to Anna's concerned face, then back to Kate. He didn't, either. It wasn't safe for Kate to be wandering around in the dark by herself. There was really no choice.

"Why don't I go with you?" he suggested. "If you don't mind the company."

Did her smile seem relieved? Or was it just his imagination?

"I don't mind in the least. Thank you." She picked up a tote bag, slung it over her shoulder and gazed expectantly at Eric.

He hesitated for a moment, then pulled open the door and stepped aside. "We won't be long, Mom," he said as Kate moved past him, leaving a faint, pleasing fragrance in her wake.

"Don't hurry. We won't eat for at least an hour," she assured them.

Kate waited while he shut the door, then fell into step beside him as they headed down the sidewalk. Dusk was just beginning to fall, and the lights from Christmas trees twinkled merrily in the windows. Few cars passed, leaving the peace and stillness of the evening largely undisturbed.

"I've always liked Christmas Eve," Kate said softly. "I remember as a child it was filled with such a sense of wonder and hope and anticipation. As if great, exciting things were about to happen. Was it like that for you?"

Eric shoved his hands into the pockets of his overcoat. His breath made frosty clouds in the cold air, but his heart was warm as he thought of Christmases past. "Yes, it was. Thanks to Mom and Dad. They made me feel that somehow anything was possible during this magical season. It's a shame we have to grow up and lose that belief in endless possibilities."

They strolled for a few minutes in silence, and just as they reached the park a few large, feathery flakes began to drift down. The distant strains of "Silent Night" floated through the quiet air as carolers raised their voices in the familiar, beloved melody.

"My favorite Christmas song," Kate murmured, her lips curving up sweetly. "Could we sit for a minute?" She nodded toward a park bench tucked between two fir trees bedecked with twinkling white lights.

Eric hesitated. He was already pushing his luck, going on this walk. He'd had to fight the impulse to reach over and take her hand every step of the way. Sitting on a park bench, where the shimmering lights were sure to add a luster to her ebony hair and bring out the sparkle in her eyes, was downright dangerous. "It's getting awfully dark, Kate," he objected.

"Please, Eric? We don't have to stay long. But the song is so beautiful."

There was no way he could refuse her when she looked at him like that, her eyes soft and hopeful, her face glowing. He drew a deep breath and slowly let it out. "Okay."

Kate led the way to the bench and sat down, carefully setting the tote bag beside her. He joined her more slowly, keeping a modest distance between them. As they sat there quietly, listening to the distant, melodic voices, Eric stole a glance at Kate. She seemed oblivious to the snowflakes that clung to her hair like gossamer stars, giving her an ethereal beauty. Her gaze was fixed on something in the distance, and he wondered what she was thinking.

*Please, Lord, give me the courage to go through with this,* Kate prayed silently. *I've never been the bold type, but I think Amy's right. This may be the only way to convince Eric how much I care. Please, let me feel Your presence and help me to find the right words.*

As the last strains of "Silent Night" faded away, her heart began to hammer painfully against her rib cage. So before her courage could waver, she clasped her hands tightly in her lap, took a deep breath and turned to him.

"Eric, I've been thinking a lot about what happened the night of the accident. And I think we need to talk about it," she said as firmly as she could manage, considering her insides were quivering like the proverbial bowlful of jelly.

Startled, he jerked his gaze to hers. Confrontation wasn't her style, yet there was a touch of that in both her voice and the determined tilt of her chin. And she was right, of course. They did need to talk. But he didn't want to do it on Christmas Eve. "Kate, can't we put this on hold until after…"

"No." Her tone was quiet but resolved. "My life has been on hold too long, Eric." She reached into the tote bag at her feet, withdrew a flat, rectangular package and held it out to him. "Let's start with this."

He stared at the gift wrapped in silver paper. "Kate, I…"

"Please, Eric. Unlike Amy, I'm not really good at this assertiveness thing, so just humor me, okay?"

The pleading tone in her voice, the strain around its edges, tugged at his heart, and without another word he took the package and tore off the wrapping. He angled the counted-cross-stitch sampler toward the light from the bushes as he slowly read the words from Jeremiah that had been so carefully and elaborately stitched around a motif of the rising sun. "For I know well the plans I have in mind for you, says the Lord, plans for your welfare not for woe! Plans to give you a future full of hope.''

''I started working on this when Jack was in the hospital,'' Kate told him quietly, her gaze resting on the sampler. ''I came across the passage one night when I was idly leafing through the Bible, and it seemed to speak directly to my soul. Because after the accident I felt that there must have been something I did—something wrong—to deserve such a tragedy and loss. Taking Jack away was the Lord's way of punishing me, I thought. So whenever I started to feel overwhelmed, I'd pull this out and work on it to remind me that the Lord was *for* me, not *against* me. And it also encouraged me to look to the future with faith and hope. It made me believe that things would get better, that tomorrow my life would again be filled with joy.''

Kate paused and transferred her gaze from the gift to his deep blue eyes. ''When Jack died, I put the sampler away. I felt empty and hollow inside, and the words seemed to mock me rather than offer comfort. For a long time I lived in an emotional and spiritual vacuum. The guilt became all-consuming again, and I lost hope that the kind of love I shared with Jack, which had made my world so bright, would ever touch my life again. All I could see in my future was an endless string of dark days. And then you came along.''

She drew a steadying breath, willing her courage to hold fast. ''Eric, the simple fact is that until I met you, my life was like this sampler—on hold and unfinished. But you made me realize that it was time to tie up the loose threads and move on. So I did exactly that—literally and figuratively. Because when I took this out of storage, I took out my heart, as well. For the first time in five years, I let myself not only believe again in the endless possibilities of life, but I opened myself to them. I want you to have this because I think you've been held captive by the same demons that plagued me for years—guilt and hopelessness. And I think it's time for you to do what I did—put your past to rest so you can create a new future.''

She paused and reached into her bag again, this time withdrawing a smaller, square box, which she handed to him. She noticed that her hands were trembling, and clasped them tightly in her lap as Eric silently unwrapped the second package, then lifted the lid. Nestled on a bed of tissue lay a delicate, heart-shaped blown-glass Christmas-tree ornament with a loop of green satin ribbon at the top, anchored with sprigs of holly.

"Just as today we celebrate the birth of a baby who brought new life to the world two thousand years ago, I'd like us to celebrate our own rebirth of hope and faith that this day symbolizes," Kate said softly. "When Jack died, I never thought I'd love again. But the Lord seemed to have other ideas when he sent you my way. Because how could I help but fall in love with your tenderness and caring and sense of humor and those deep blue eyes and all of the thousands of things that make you so very special and unique? I love you, Eric Carlson, and I can't imagine my future without you in it. So I give you this ornament as a sign of what you've already claimed—my heart. And I would be very honored if...if you would marry me."

Eric stared at her, speechless, then looked down at the shiny red ornament cradled in his hands. It was so fragile and so easily broken—just like her heart. Dear God, had she really offered to entrust it to his care? Or was he caught up in some sort of Christmas Eve fantasy? His confused gaze moved to her hands, clasped tightly in her lap, and he could sense the tension vibrating in every nerve of her body as she waited for his reaction. So it was real, after all.

A rush of tenderness and love and elation swept over him, so swift and powerful that it took his breath away—and scared him out of his wits. There was no question that he returned her love, with every ounce of his being. Yet doubts about making a success of marriage, given the pressures of his career, remained. He struggled against the urge to throw caution to the wind and pull her into his arms and shout "Yes!" for all the world to hear. It was what his heart told him to do. But he had to make sure she understood the dangers.

"Kate, I—" His voice broke and he cleared his throat.

Kate felt the bottom drop out of her stomach. She'd obviously shocked him into speechlessness, and her courage suddenly deserted her. How could she possibly have asked this man to marry her? Amy's bold plan had seemed reasonable when they'd discussed it, but given his reaction, it was way off base. Now she needed to find a way to smooth over the awkwardness she'd created.

"Listen, Eric, I'm sorry," she said jerkily. "Y-you don't have to answer that question. I understand if…"

He reached out and took her hand, his look so tender and warm that her voice deserted her. "I *want* to answer the question. I was just…overwhelmed for a minute. No one's ever proposed to me before." His lips quirked into a crooked grin.

Although the ardent light in his eyes set her heart hammering, she sensed a hesitation in his manner. She had hoped her bold question would assuage any doubts he might have about her willingness to accept the demands his job would make on their life, but apparently it hadn't, she realized with dismay.

"I—I understand if you need to think about it," she stammered, stalling for time, suddenly afraid to hear his answer. If he was going to refuse, she didn't want to know tonight. Not on Christmas Eve. She averted her gaze and reached for the tote bag. "Like you said, we can talk about this after Christmas."

She started to stand, but he restrained her and pulled her trembling body close beside him, into the shelter of his arm. "You can't just drop something like that on a man and then walk away, you know. Let's talk."

She lowered her head and stared at the snowflakes falling gently to the ground, willing the peace of that sight to calm the turbulence in her heart. "I don't know what else to say," she responded softly, her voice choked with emotion.

Eric reached over and with gentle pressure urged her chin back up until their gazes met. "Then I'll start. First of all, I love you, too," he said huskily.

Kate's throat constricted, and joy flooded her heart. Those were the words she'd been praying to hear for weeks! And yet…he hadn't accepted her proposal. She searched his eyes, afraid to ask but knowing she had to. "I sense a 'but' there," she ventured, her voice quavering.

He laced his fingers with hers and absently stroked his thumb across the back of her hand.

"There is," he conceded. "I'm just not sure marriage would be good for either of us."

"How can you say that, when we love each other?"

"Because love implies certain obligations. Like being there for a child's Christmas play. And making sure the woman you love doesn't have to deal with her private terrors alone. And protecting the people you love from danger. And honoring promises. And a million other things that my profession won't always allow me to do. What happened four days ago could happen again, Kate. I can't promise you it won't.''

"I'm not asking you to. I admire your dedication to your work, Eric. It's part of what makes you who you are. Don't you think I know that you're torn between what you see as conflicting loyalties, that you anguish over balancing the two responsibilities? I wish you wouldn't let it tear you up inside. Yet one of the reasons I love you is that you care enough to *feel* anguish. And my feelings about *that* will never change.''

He wanted to believe her. Desperately. But experience had been a harsh teacher. "I'd like to think that's true, Kate," he said wearily. "And I know you believe it is—right now. But I'm afraid that in time you'll come to resent my work. Whether you realize it or not, you were upset the night of the accident because I wasn't there for you.''

"You're thinking about that stupid comment I made when you opened my door, aren't you?'' she said quietly.

He looked surprised. "You remember what you said?''

"Yes. And obviously you do, too. Eric, I don't know where those words came from. I was distraught. And shaken up. And afraid Sarah was hurt. I wasn't even thinking straight. Do you know what my *thoughts* were when you appeared? 'Thank God.' I can't even find the words to describe the relief I felt when I saw you. I know my words didn't reflect that. But that was what was in my heart.'' She paused and took a deep breath. "Believe it or not, Eric, I can handle the fact that you have a demanding career that sometimes requires you to make difficult choices. I may be disappointed sometimes if your duties take you away from us, but I'll never stop loving you. Because I know you'll always do your best to *give* your best. To us *and* your job. I would never ask for any more than that. And I truly believe that if we trust in the Lord, He'll show us the way to make this work.''

Eric gazed into the face that had become so precious and dear to him during these last few months. The sincerity in her eyes, and the love, were unquestionable. What had he ever done to deserve a woman with such an understanding heart, and an inner beauty that surpassed even her physical loveliness? he wondered, his throat tightening with emotion. She seemed so sure, so confident about their future. Why couldn't he put his own doubts and fears to rest, as well?

"You seem to have such faith," he said quietly.

She looked at him steadily. "Enough to move mountains. I'm not Cindy, Eric. I love you for who you are—not in *spite* of who you are. And on this Christmas Eve, for the first time in years, I believe great, exciting things are about to happen. I believe that anything is possible. And I believe in you. And us."

Eric looked at her, his heart so full of love that for a moment he couldn't speak. She was everything he'd always wanted, and he suddenly knew with absolute certainty that he'd be a fool to pass up this chance for happiness. As if to confirm his sudden lightness of heart, the distant voices of the carolers came once more through the air, jubilantly proclaiming, "Joy to the World." As he reached over and touched her face with infinite tenderness, his doubt was replaced by a gladness and peace that truly reflected this most joyous, holy season.

"When I got to Mom's tonight, Sarah said that this was the best Christmas ever," Eric told Kate huskily. "And you know something? She's absolutely right."

Kate studied him cautiously, trying not to infer too much from his tender tone of voice and the promise in his eyes. Yet she was unable to stop her hopes from soaring. "Is that a yes?" she ventured.

He chuckled as his own spirits suddenly took wing. "That is most definitely a yes. And even though this proposal wasn't exactly traditional, I think we should seal it in the traditional way. Don't you agree?"

The sudden flame of passion in his eyes made her tingle. "Most definitely, " she concurred.

He reached for her, and she went willingly, savoring the haven of his strong arms and the wondrous feeling of homecoming. And in the moment before his lips claimed hers, the words of the distant carol echoed in her ears, making her heart rejoice.

"Let heaven and nature sing. Let heaven and nature sing. Let heaven, and heaven, and nature sing."

*Amen,* she said silently. *And thank you.*

# Epilogue

*Five months later*

It was a perfect day for a wedding.

Kate gazed out the window of Amy's log cabin at the blue-hazed mountains, fresh with spring. New green shoots decorated the tips of the spruce trees, and the masses of rhododendrons and mountain laurel on the hillsides were heavy with pink-hued blossoms. A cloud of yellow swallowtail butterflies drifted by, undulating playfully in the warm morning sun, while classical flute music played a duet with the splashing water from a nearby stream.

Kate smiled and slowly drew in a deep breath. The peaceful setting, reflecting the beauty of God's creation and the rebirth of nature after a long, cold winter, seemed symbolic; within a few moments, she and Eric would start a new life together after their own long, cold winter of the heart.

"You look happy."

Kate turned at the sound of Amy's voice. Her sister stood in the doorway with Sarah, holding two bouquets of mountain laurel still beaded with silver drops of dew.

"I am."

"And beautiful."

Kate flushed and turned to look in the full-length mirror beside her. The simple but elegant style of her A-line, tea-length gown enhanced her slender figure, and the overlay of delicate chiffon that flared out near the hem softly swirled as she moved. Long sleeves—sheer and full, cuffed at the wrist—emphasized her delicate bone structure, and the deep blue color was a perfect foil for her dark hair and flawless complexion.

"I *feel* beautiful," she admitted. And young. And breathless. And hopeful. And all the things every bride should feel on her special day, she thought with wonder.

"Do I look pretty, too, Mommy?" Sarah asked.

Kate turned to her daughter and smiled. In her white eyelet dress, with a basket of flowers in her hands, she would fit right in at a Victorian garden party.

"You look lovely," Kate replied, kneeling down to hold her close. Without Sarah, she knew she would never have survived the months following Jack's death. Only her daughter's sunny disposition and innocent laughter had kept her sane and grounded in the present, prevented her from slipping into the abyss of total despair. She hugged Sarah fiercely, thanking God for His gift of the precious child who had filled her life with a special love during the difficult years when she'd felt so deserted and spiritually alone.

When Kate finally released her, Sarah lifted her basket and pointed to a bluebell. "I picked that flower for Dr. Eric. Aunt Amy says I can give it to him later."

Kate smiled, deeply grateful that Sarah adored Eric. And equally grateful that the feeling was returned.

"I'm sure he'll like that. It's just the color of his eyes."

"Well, if you two ladies are ready, I don't think we should keep the groom waiting any longer," Amy announced.

Kate gave Sarah one more quick hug. "I love you, honey," she whispered.

"I love you, too, Mommy."

Kate rose and Amy handed her one of the bouquets. For a long moment their gazes met and held.

"You know how happy I am for you, don't you?" Amy said softly.

Kate nodded, and when she spoke her voice was choked with tears. "I know. And thank you, Amy. For everything. For your love and support and for always being there. You and Mom were my lifeline for so many years."

Amy's own voice was none too steady when she replied, "I always will be, Kate. But I'm more than happy to share the job with someone else. Especially Eric."

The flute music suddenly changed, and Kate recognized the melody of the hymn they'd chosen for the opening of the ceremony.

"It's time," Amy said.

Kate nodded. Amy took Sarah's hand and they preceded Kate down the steps and out the door. She waited for a few moments, then stepped out into the sunshine and walked slowly toward the gazebo banked by blossoming rhododendrons and surrounded by the people she loved most in the world.

Anna was there, of course, beaming with joy. Cal smiled at her and winked, juggling Caitlin in one arm while the twins clung to his leg and stared wide-eyed at the proceedings. Frank grinned and gave a subtle thumbs-up signal.

And Eric—her breath caught in her throat as she gazed at him. He looked incredibly handsome in a dove-gray suit that hugged his broad shoulders. The morning sun had turned his blond hair to gold, and as she gazed into his face—so fine and strong and compassionate and caring—tears of happiness pricked her eyes. His own eyes, so blue and tender, caught and held hers compellingly as she drew closer. They spoke more eloquently than words of the passion and love and commitment in his heart, and she trembled with wonder that God had blessed her with a second chance at love.

As the pure notes of "Amazing Grace" drifted through the mountain air, she was glad once again that they'd chosen this hymn to begin their wedding ceremony. For she had, indeed, once been lost. But now she was found. And today, as she prepared to start a new life with the man she loved, she felt filled with God's amazing grace.

Eric watched Kate approach, and his own heart overflowed with joy. The significance of the song wasn't lost on him, either. He knew that without the Lord's help, he wouldn't be standing here today. On his own, he would never have had the courage to take another chance on love. But God had sent him Kate, whose sweetness and understanding had broken through the barriers he'd erected around his heart and made him believe once again in endless possibilities. And as Kate stepped up into the gazebo and took his hand, her eyes shining with love and faith and trust, he knew beyond the shadow of a doubt that they would have a rich, full marriage. For the Lord would always help them, just as His grace had led their hearts home.

\*    \*    \*    \*    \*

Dear Reader,

Christmas has always been the most magical day of the year for me. When I was a little girl, my parents would labor long into the night on Christmas Eve after my brother and I went to bed, putting up the tree, draping it with tinsel and lights, and arranging the presents from "Santa" under the graceful boughs.

I will never forget that first, wondrous glimpse of the twinkling tree in the predawn darkness of Christmas morning. (Yes, my parents always gave in to our excited pleas and dragged themselves out of bed at the crack of dawn!) What had been a bare area in the living room the night before was now filled with the glowing tree and piles of gaily wrapped packages. And beneath the tree, in a place of honor, rested our manger.

I must admit that as a child I noticed the presents more than the manger. But as I grew up, I began to understand the greater significance of the holiday—or, more accurately, holy day. I also came to realize that the best gifts—the ones that truly add magic and wonder to our lives—don't come in gaily wrapped packages. Hope that sustains. Good health. Enduring faith. The comfort of a warm and close-knit family. And most of all, abiding love.

At this joyous season, may Kate and Eric's story fill your heart with hope and inspire you to trust in that special child born one starry night two thousand years ago. And may you, too, have one special Christmas this year.

*Irene Hannon*

**Books by Lenora Worth**

Love Inspired

*The Wedding Quilt* #12
*Logan's Child* #26
*Wedding at Wildwood* #53
*His Brother's Wife* #82
*Ben's Bundle of Joy* #99
*The Reluctant Hero* #108
*One Golden Christmas* #122
\* *When Love Came to Town* #142
\* *Something Beautiful* #169
\* *Lacey's Retreat* #184

*In the Garden

## LENORA WORTH

grew up in a small Georgia town and decided in the fourth grade that she wanted to be a writer. But first, she married her high school sweetheart, then moved to Atlanta, Georgia. Taking care of their baby daughter at home while her husband worked at night, Lenora discovered the world of romance novels and knew that's what she wanted to write. And so she began.

A few years later, the family settled in Shreveport, Louisiana, where Lenora continued to write while working as a marketing assistant. After the birth of her second child, a boy, she decided to pursue her dream full-time. In 1993, Lenora's hard work and determination finally paid off with that first sale.

"I never gave up, and I believe my faith in God helped get me through the rough times when I doubted myself," Lenora says. "Each time I start a new book, I say a prayer, asking God to give me the strength and direction to put the words to paper. That's why I'm so thrilled to be a part of Steeple Hill, where I can combine my faith in God with my love of romance. It's the best combination."

# I'LL BE HOME
# FOR CHRISTMAS
## Lenora Worth

To Jean Price and Dee Pace,
for taking a chance on me,
and
to my mother, Myla Brinson Humphries,
who's in heaven with the angels.

# Chapter One

He was tired.

He was hungry.

He wanted a big roast beef sandwich from that roast Henny had baked early in the week, and then he wanted to go to bed and sleep for at least fourteen hours.

Nick Rudolph shifted against the supple leather seat of his Jaguar sedan, his impatient foot pressing the accelerator further toward Shreveport, Louisiana, the interstate's slippery surface spewing icy rain out around the sleek black car.

He was also late. Very late. Carolyn would be fuming; he'd have to smooth things over with her. Right about now, he was supposed to be escorting her to the mayor's Christmas party. Instead, he was making his way along a treacherous stretch of icy road, on the coldest night of the year.

His mind went back to the meetings in Dallas he'd had to endure to cut another deal for Rudolph Oil. After all the hours of endless negotiations, he still wasn't sure if he'd closed the deal. They wanted to think about it some more.

That he wasn't coming home victorious grated against his ego like the ice grating against his windshield wipers. Over the last few years, work had always come first with Nick Rudolph. It was an unspoken promise to his late father, a man Nick hadn't understood until after his death. Now, because he'd seen a side of his father that still left him unsettled, Nick preferred to concentrate on tangible endeavors, like making money.

Nick Rudolph wasn't used to losing. He'd been blessed with a good life, with all the comforts of old money, and he didn't take kindly to being shut out. He'd win them over; he always did. He might have given up every ounce of his self-worth, but he wasn't about to let go of his net worth.

As the car neared the exit for Kelly's Truck Stop, he allowed himself a moment to relax. Almost home. Soon, he'd be sitting by his fire, the cold December rain held at bay outside the sturdy walls of his Georgian-style mansion. Soon.

Nick looked up just in time to see the dark shapes moving in front of his car, his headlights flashing across the darting figures rushing out onto the road in front of him.

Automatically slamming on his brakes, he held the leather-covered steering wheel with tight fingers. His mind screamed an alert warning as the car barely missed hitting a small figure standing in the rain before it skidded to a groaning halt.

"What in the world!" Nick cut the engine to a fast stop, then hopped out of the car, his mind still reeling with the sure knowledge that he'd almost hit a child. Coming around the car, his expensive loafers crunching against patches of ice, he looked down at the three people huddled together on the side of the interstate. Tired and shaken, he squinted against the beam of his car's headlights.

The sight he saw made him sag with relief. He hadn't hit anyone. Immediately following the relief came a strong curiosity. Why would anyone be standing in the middle of the interstate on a night like this?

The woman stood tall, her chin lifted in proud defiance, her long hair flowing out in the icy wind, her hands pulled tight against the shoulders of the two freezing children cloistered against the protection of her worn wool jacket.

The two children, a small boy and a taller, skinny girl, looked up at Nick with wide, frightened eyes, their lips trembling, whether from fear or cold, he couldn't be sure.

He inched closer to the haphazard trio. "Are you people all right?"

The woman pushed thick dark hair away from her face, shifting slightly to see Nick better. "We're all okay. I'm sorry. We were trying to cross over to the truck stop. We...you...I didn't realize how fast you were going."

Nick let out a long, shuddering sigh, small aftershocks rippling through his body. "I almost hit you!"

The woman stiffened. "I said we're all okay." Then as if realizing the harshness of her words, she repeated, "I'm sorry."

Something in her tone caught at Nick, holding him. It was as if she'd had a lot of experience saying those words.

"Me, too," he said by way of his own apology. He'd never been good with "I'm sorry", because he'd never felt the need to apologize for his actions. But he had been driving way too fast for these icy roads. What if he'd hit that little boy?

He ran his hand through his damp dark hair, then shoved both hands into the deep pockets of his wool trench coat. "Where... where's your car? Do you need a ride?"

The woman moved her head slightly, motioning toward the west. "We broke down back there. We were headed to the truck stop for help."

"I'll drop you off," Nick offered, eager to get on his way. Turning, he headed back to his car. When the woman didn't immediately follow, he whirled, his eyes centering on her. "I said I'd give you a lift."

"We don't know you," she reasoned. "It's not that far. We can walk."

"And risk getting hit again?" Regretting his brusque tone, Nick stepped closer to her, the cold rain chilling him to his bones. "Look, I'm perfectly safe. I'll take you to the truck stop. Maybe they can call a wrecker for your car."

"I can't afford a wrecker," the woman said, almost to herself.

"We're broke," the little boy supplied, his eyes big and solemn, their depths aged beyond his five or so years.

"Patrick, please hush," the woman said gently, holding him tight against her jeans-clad leg. Gazing up at Nick, she shot him that proud look again. "I'd appreciate a ride, mister."

"It's Nick," he supplied. "Nick Rudolph. I live in Shreveport." As he talked, he guided them toward his car, wondering where they were from and where they were headed, and why they'd broken down on such an awful night. "I'm on my way back from Dallas," he explained, opening doors and moving his briefcase and clothes bag out of the way.

"We used to live near Dallas," the little boy said as he scooted onto the beige-colored leather seat. "Wow! This is a really cool car, ain't it, Mom?"

"It's *isn't,*" his sister corrected, her voice sounding hoarse and weak.

The boy gave her an exaggerated shrug.

Nick stepped aside as the woman slid into the front seat. Her eyes lifted to Nick's, and from the overhead light, he got his first really good glimpse of her.

And lost his sense of control in the process.

Green eyes, forest green, evergreen, shined underneath arched brows that dared him to question her. An angular face, almost gaunt in its slenderness, a long nose over a wide, full mouth. Her lips were chapped; she nibbled at the corner of her bottom lip. But she tossed back her long auburn hair like a queen, looking regal in spite of her threadbare, scrappy clothes.

Nick lost track of time as he stared down at her, then catching himself, he shut the door firmly, his body cold from the December wind blowing across the roadway. Running around the car, he hurried inside, closing the nasty night out with a slam.

"Mom?" the little boy said again, "don't you like Nick's car?"

"It's very nice," the woman replied, her eyes sliding over the car's interior. "And it's Mr. Rudolph, Patrick. Remember your manners."

The expensive sedan cranked on cue, and Nick pulled it back onto the highway, careful of the slippery road. "What's your name?" he asked the woman beside him.

"Myla." She let one slender hand rest on the dashboard for support as the car moved along. "Myla Howell." Nodding toward the back of the car, she added, "And these are my children, Patrick and Jessica."

The little girl started coughing, the hacking sounds ragged and raspy. "Mama, I'm thirsty," she croaked.

"They'll have drinks at the truck stop," Nick said, concern filtering through his need to get on home.

"We don't got no money for drinks," Patrick piped up, leaning forward toward Nick.

"Patrick!" Myla whirled around, her green eyes flashing. "Honey, sit back and be quiet." Her tone going from stern to gentle, she added, "Jesse, we'll get a drink of water in the bathroom, okay?"

Nick pulled the car into the busy truck stop, deciding he couldn't leave them stranded here, cold and hungry. He'd at least feed them before he figured out what to do about their car. Turning to Myla, he asked, "Is everything all right? Can I call somebody for you? A relative maybe?"

She looked straight ahead, watching as a fancy eighteen-wheeler groaned its way toward the highway. "We don't have any relatives here." A telling silence filled the car. Outside, the icy rain picked up, turning into full-fledged sleet.

"Where were you headed?" Nick knew he was past late, and that he probably wasn't going anywhere soon.

"To Shreveport." Myla sat still, looking straight ahead.

"Mom's found a job," Patrick explained, eager to fill Nick in on the details. "And she said we'll probably find a place to live soon— it'd sure beat the car—"

"Patrick!" Myla turned then, her gaze slamming into Nick's, a full load of pain mixed with the pride he saw so clearly through the fluorescent glow of the truck stop's blinding lights.

His mouth dropping open, Nick gave her an incredulous look. "What's going on here?"

"Nothing." Her chin lifted a notch. "Thank you for the ride, Mr. Rudolph. We'll be fine now."

The car door clicked open, but Nick's hand shot out, grabbing her arm. "Hey, wait!"

Her gaze lifted from his hand on her arm to the urgent expression on his face. "Let me go."

"I can't do that." Nick surprised himself more than he surprised her. "If you don't have any place to go—"

"It's not your problem," she interrupted. "If I can just make it into town, I've got a good chance of still getting the job I called about yesterday. Once I find steady work, we'll be fine."

"I can help," he said, almost afraid of the worn wisdom he read in her eyes. "I can call a wrecker, at least. And find a place for you to stay."

From the back seat, Jessica went into another fit of coughing, the hacking sound reminding Nick of memories he'd tried to suppress for too long.

"That does it." He reached across Myla to slam her door shut. The action brought them face-to-face for a split second, but it was long enough for Nick to get lost in those beautiful eyes again, long enough for him to forget his regrets and his promises and wish for things he knew he'd never have. And it was long enough for him to make a decision that he somehow knew was about to change his life. "You're coming with me," he said, his tone firm. "I won't leave a sick child out in this mess!"

The woman looked over at him, her eyes pooling into two misty depths. "I...I don't know how to thank you."

Nick heard the catch in her throat, knew she was on the verge of tears. The thought of those beautiful eyes crying tore through him, but he told himself he'd only help the family find a safe place to spend the night. He wasn't ready to get any further involved in whatever problems they were having.

"You need help," he said. "If you're worried about going off with a stranger, I'll call someone to verify my identity." A new thought calculating in his taxed brain, he added, "In fact, my sister is a volunteer counselor for Magnolia House. I'll call her. She's always helping people." Having found a way to get out of this sticky predicament, Nick breathed a sigh of relief.

Myla turned back, her eyes wary. "What's Magnolia House?"

He waved a hand. "It's this place downtown, a homeless shelter, but a bit nicer. According to my sister it has private rooms where families can stay until...until they get back on their feet." He really didn't know that much about his sister's latest mission project, except that he'd written a huge check to help fund it.

Giving him a hopeful look, she asked, "And we don't have to pay to live there?"

"No, not with money. You do assigned tasks at the home, and attend classes to help you find work, things like that. My sister helped set the place up and she's on the board of directors. She'll explain how it works."

"Can you get us in tonight?"

Putting all thoughts of a roast beef sandwich or a quiet evening with Carolyn out of his mind, Nick nodded hesitantly. "I'll do my best. And I'll send a wrecker for your car, too."

She relaxed, letting out a long breath. Then she gave him a direct, studying stare, as if she were trying to decide whether to trust him or not. Clearing her throat, she said, "Thank you."

Admiration surfaced in the murky depths of Nick's impassive soul. He knew how much pride those two words had cost this woman. He admired pride. It had certainly sustained him all these years. Debating his next question, he decided there was no way to dance around this situation. Starting the car again, he carefully maneuvered through the truck stop traffic.

"How'd you wind up...?"

"Homeless, living in my car?"

Her directness surprised him, but then this whole night has been full of surprises.

"If you don't mind talking about it."

"My husband died about a year ago." She hesitated, then added, "Afterward, I found out we didn't have any money left. No insurance, no savings, nothing. I lost everything."

Nick glanced over at her as the car cruised farther up the interstate, leaving downtown Shreveport at Line Avenue to head for the secluded privacy of the historic Highland District. Taking her quiet reluctance as a sign of mourning, he cleared his throat slightly, unable to sympathize with her need to mourn; he'd never quite learned how himself. So instead, he concentrated on the fact that she was a single mother. All his protective instincts, something he usually reserved for his sister, surfaced, surprising him. *Must be the Christmas spirit. Could I possibly have some redeemable qualities left after all?*

"What did you do?" he asked, mystified.

Lifting her head, Myla sighed. "I left Dallas and looked for work. I got a job in Marshall, but the company I worked for closed down. I ran out of money, so we got evicted from our apartment."

Nick could hear the shame in her voice.

"After that, we just drove around. I looked for work. We stayed in hotels until the little bit of cash I had ran out. That was two weeks ago. We've been sleeping in the car, stopping at rest areas to bathe and eat. The kids played or slept while I called about jobs."

She slumped down in her seat, the defeat covering her body like the cold, hard sleet covering the road.

Then she lifted her head and her shoulders. "I don't want to resort to going on welfare, but I'll do it for my children. We might be destitute right now, but this is only temporary. I intend to find work as soon as I can."

It was Nick's turn to feel ashamed. He was more than willing to write her a fat check, but he had the funny feeling she'd throw it back in his face. She had enough pride to choke a horse, but how long could she survive on pride? And why should he be so worried that she'd try?

Nick didn't have time to ponder that question. Minutes later, he pulled the car up a winding drive to a redbrick Georgian-style mansion that shimmered and sparkled with all the connotations of a Norman Rockwell Christmas. Suddenly, the wreaths and candles in the massive windows seemed garish and mocking. He'd told Henny not to put out any Christmas decorations, anyway. Obviously, the elderly housekeeper hadn't listened to him, not that she ever did.

Now, seeing his opulent home through the eyes of a person who didn't have a home scared him silly, and caused him to take a good, long hard look at his life-style.

"Man!" Patrick jumped up to lean forward. Straining at his seat belt, he tugged his sleeping sister up. "Look, Jesse. Can you believe this? Santa's sure to find us here. Mr. Nick, you must be the richest man in the world."

The woman sitting next to him lowered her head, but she didn't reprimand her son. Nick saw the pain shattering her face like fragments of ice.

Nick Rudolph, the man some called ruthless and relentless, sat silently looking up at the house he'd lived in all his life. He'd always taken it for granted, his way of life. His parents had provided him and Lydia with the best. And even in death, they'd bequeathed an affluent life-style to their children.

Nick had accepted the life-style, but he hadn't accepted the obligations and expectations his stern father had pressed on him. When he could no longer live up to those expectations, he'd acted like a rebel without a cause—until he'd seen the truth in his dying father's eyes.

Everything his father had drilled into him had become a sham. And Joseph, overcome with emotion because he loved his Ruthie too much, had tried to tell Nick it was okay to be vulnerable when it involved someone you loved.

But it had been too late for Nick. He'd learned his lessons well. Now, he guarded his heart much in the same way he watched over Rudolph Oil—with a steely determination that allowed no room for weakness.

Maybe that was why he'd felt so restless lately. Maybe his guilt was starting to wear thin. Though he had it all, something was missing still. Nick had never wanted for anything, until now. All his money couldn't buy back this woman's pride or settle her losses. All his wealth seemed a dishonest display compared to her honest humility.

"No, Patrick," he began, his voice strangely husky, "I'm not the richest man in the world, not by a long shot."

"Well, you ain't hurtin' any," Patrick noted.

"No, I suppose I'm not," Nick replied, his eyes seeking those of the woman beside him. "Let's go inside where it's warm."

Opening the car door, he vented his frustration on the expensive machine. He *was* hurting. And he didn't understand why. How had the night become a study in contradiction and longing? How had he fallen into such a blue mood? Well, he'd just had an incredibly bad day, that was all. Or was it?

No. It was her—Myla. Myla Howell and her two needy children. He couldn't solve all the problems of the world, could he? He'd make sure they had a decent place to stay, maybe help her find a job, then go on with his merry life. Things would go back to the way they'd been up until about an hour ago.

*And how were things before, Nick?* an inner voice questioned.

Normal. Settled. Content.

And lonely.

And that was the gist of the matter.

These three ragamuffins had brought out the loneliness he'd tried to hide for so long. Denying it had been pretty easy up until tonight. But they'd sprung a trap for him, an innocent but clever trap. They'd nabbed him with their earnest needs and unfortunate situation. He'd help them, sure. He certainly wasn't a coldhearted man.

But he wouldn't get involved. At all. His formidable father had drilled the rules of business into Nick—no distractions, show no emotions. In the end, however, Joseph Rudolph had forgotten all his own rules. In the end, his own emotions had taken control of his life. Nick had learned from Joseph's mistake. So now, he let Lydia do the good deeds while he took care of business. It was a nice setup. One he didn't intend to change.

"I'll call Lydia. She'll know what to do," Nick said minutes later as he flipped on lights and guided them through the house from the three-car garage. A large, well-lit kitchen greeted them as the buzz of the automatic garage door opener shut them snugly in for the night. Nick headed to the cordless phone, intent on finding his sister fast. Then he'd have to call Carolyn and make his excuses. When he only connected with Lydia's perky answering machine, he left a brief, panicked message. "Lydia, it's your brother. Call me—soon. I'm at home and I could really use your help."

*We make him uncomfortable,* Myla Howell reasoned as she watched the handsome, well-dressed man talking on the phone. She knew she and her children were an inconvenience. When you didn't have money, or a place to sleep, you became that way.

She'd learned that lesson over the last few months. People who'd called themselves her friends had suddenly turned away. She wasn't good enough for them now. They didn't have time for her now. They couldn't be seen associating with a homeless person.

This man was the same. He couldn't wait to be rid of them. But, he had saved them tonight. She'd give him credit for that. She watched him moving about the kitchen, taking in his dark, chocolate-colored hair, remembering his gold-tinged tiger eyes. Golden brown, but missing that spark of warmth. Calculating eyes? She'd seen that kind of eyes before; still bore the scars from trusting someone who could be so ruthless. Would this man be any different?

She hoped so, she prayed so, for the sake of getting her children to a safe place. Refusing to give in to her fears or her humiliation, she focused on her surroundings instead. What a joy it would be to cook in a kitchen like this! She missed having a kitchen. Cooking was one of her pleasures and with hard work and lots of prayer, it could soon be her livelihood, too.

The gleaming industrial-size aluminum stove shouted at her while the matching refrigerator-freezer told her there was lots of bounty here to explore. The long butcher block island centered in the middle of the wide room spoke of fresh vegetables and homemade breads and pastries. Myla closed her eyes briefly, almost smelling the aroma of a lovely, home-cooked holiday meal. She'd miss that this Christmas. But next year...

Nick watched her in amazement. Under the surreal lights of the truck stop, she'd looked pale and drawn. But here in the bright track lights, Myla seemed to glow. She was tall, almost gaunt in her thinness. Her hair was long and thick, a mass of red, endearing curls that clung to her neck and shoulders. Even in her plain clothes, this woman exuded a grace and charm that few women would possess dressed in furs and diamonds. Obviously, she hadn't always been homeless. Her clothes and the children's looked to be of good quality and in fair shape. Not too threadbare; wrinkled, but clean.

Mentally shaking himself out of his curious stupor, Nick watched her closely, noticing the dreamy expression falling across her freckled face. Then it hit him. "You're probably hungry."

His statement changed Myla's dreamy expression to a blushing halt. "I'm sorry...this is such a beautiful kitchen...I got carried away looking at it." Nodding at the expectant faces of her children, she pushed them forward. "The children need something to eat. We had breakfast at a rest stop—donuts and milk."

The implication that they hadn't eaten since this morning caused Nick to lift his head, but he turned away before she could see the sympathy in his eyes. "Well, don't worry. Our housekeeper, Henrietta Clark, has been with the family for most of my life. She always stays with a friend down the street when I'm away, so she's not here tonight. But she cooks a lot, way too much for my sister and me. We usually wind up giving half of it away—"

"It's all right, Mr. Rudolph," Myla said to ease his discomfort. "We'll be glad to take some of your leftovers off your hands, right, kids?"

She was being cheerful for the children's sake, Nick realized. Relaxing a little, he dashed over to the gleaming refrigerator. "Let's just see what we've got. We'll have ourselves a feast."

Patrick hopped up on a wooden stool, yanking his fleece jacket off with a flourish. "My mom's the best cook, Mr. Nick. She can make just about anything, but her bestest is bread—and cookies."

"Oh, really?" Nick glanced over at Myla. "Well, come on over here, Mom. I could use an expert hand. I'm not very good in the kitchen."

Eyeing Jesse and unsure what to do with her, he lifted the quiet little girl up on the stool next to Patrick. With an unsteady smile, he registered that she felt warm, almost too warm, but then he wasn't a doctor or a daddy. What did he know about little girls?

Myla stepped forward, then took off her threadbare wool coat. "Anything I can do to help?"

Nick watched as she hovered beside him, as if waiting for him to issue an order. Tired and unsure what to do himself, he unceremoniously loosened the red-patterned tie at his neck, then yanked off the tailored wool suit jacket he'd worn all day. Tossing the jacket across a chair, he watched as Myla straightened it and hung it over the back of the chair, her hands automatically smoothing the wrinkles out.

"Thank you," he said.

He watched as a flush bathed her cheeks. "I'm sorry," she said. "Force of habit. My husband liked everything in its place."

Nick nodded, then wondered about her marriage. Had it been a happy one? Not that it was any of his business, but the sad, almost evasive look in her eyes made him curious. Did she miss her husband? Of course, she probably did, especially now when she was struggling so much.

"How about a roast beef sandwich?" he asked as he lifted the heavy pan of meat out of the refrigerator. "Henny cooked this for Sunday supper, but I didn't get back into town to enjoy it."

"That's a shame."

"No, that's the life of an oilman. Lots of trips, lots of leftovers." Searching through a drawer, he found a large carving knife. "I say, let's cut into this thing."

"Yeah, let's cut into that thing," Patrick echoed, clapping his hands. "My mouth's watering."

Jesse smiled, then coughed.

"Are you hungry, Jesse?" Worry darkened Myla's eyes. "She has allergies and she's fighting a nasty cold."

A spark of warmth curled in Nick's heart. "Maybe some good food will perk her up." He offered Jesse a glass of orange juice.

Nick found the bread, then poured huge glasses of milk for the children. Myla located the coffeemaker and started a fresh brew. She sliced tomato and lettuce, then made some thick roast beef sandwiches. Soon all four of them were sitting around the butcher block counter. Nick picked up his sandwich for a hefty bite, but held it in midair as Myla and her children clasped hands and bowed their heads.

Seeing his openmouthed pose, Myla said quietly, "We always say grace before our meals. I hope you don't mind."

Nick dropped his sandwich as if it were on fire. "No, of course not."

When Myla extended her hand to his, something went all soft and quiet in his ninety-mile-an-hour mind. When was the last time he'd said a prayer of any kind? He listened now to Myla's soft, caressing voice.

"Thank you, Lord, for this day and this food. Thank you for our safety and for the warmth you have provided. Thank you for sending us help when we needed it most. We ask that you bless each of us, and this house. Amen."

Stunned, Nick wasn't so sure he wanted his house blessed. He felt awkward as he lifted his hand away from the warmth of Myla's. To hide his discomfort, he said, "Let's eat."

Patrick didn't have to be told twice. He attacked one half of his sandwich with gusto. Nick flipped on a nearby television to entertain the children, but mostly to stifle the awkward tension permeating the room.

He watched them eat, hoping Lydia would call soon. Patrick wolfed his food down in record time, while Jesse nibbled at hers between fits of dry coughing. Their mother broke off little bits of her sandwich, as if forcing herself to eat, her eyes darting here and there in worry.

Finally, out of frustration more than anything else, Nick said, "That hit the spot. I was starved."

"Me, too," Jesse said, speaking up at last.

Nick's eyes met her mother's over her head. It didn't help to know that Jesse probably had been really hungry, when to Nick the words were just a figure of speech. Myla only gave him a blank stare, though, so to hide his confusion he munched on a chocolate chip cookie while he watched the children, and their mother when she wasn't looking.

The baggy teal sweater brought out the green in her expressive eyes. Worn jeans tugged over scuffed red Roper boots encased her slim hips and long legs. Couldn't be more than thirty, just a few years younger than him, yet she carried a lot of responsibility on her slim shoulders.

"You've got a pretty name," he said to stop the flow of his own erratic thoughts.

"I was named after my grandmother," she said. "She hated her name because people would always call her Mi-lee. My mother named me after her to make her feel better about it."

"Where's your family?" he asked, hoping to learn more about her situation.

She shot him that luminous stare before answering. "My parents passed away several years ago—a year and a half apart. First my mother, from a stroke. Then Daddy. The doctors said his heart gave out, and I think that's true. He died of loneliness. They'd been married forty years."

Nick felt a coldness in the center of his heart, a coldness that reminded him of his firm commitment to keep that part of himself closed away. "Same with my parents. My mother died of cancer, and my father was never really the same after her death." He looked down at his half-eaten sandwich. "He...he depended on his Ruthie, and her death destroyed him. It was as if he changed right before my eyes." Not wanting to reveal more, he asked her, "Do you have any brothers or sisters?"

She nodded. "A brother in Texas—he's got five kids. And a sister in Georgia. She just got married a few months ago." She sat silent for a minute, then finished. "They don't need me and my problems right now."

"Do they know...about what's happened to you?"

Her flushed face gave him his answer. She jumped up to clean away their dishes. "No, they don't. Not yet." Turning toward the sink, she added, "I really appreciate your help, but I don't intend to live on handouts. If my job hunt pays off—"

"What sort of work are you looking for?"

"A waitress, maybe, for now. I love to cook. One day, I'd like to run my own restaurant."

Nick wanted to touch her face for some strange reason. She had that dreamy look about her again, and it endeared her to him. He felt an overwhelming need to buy a building and turn it into a restaurant.

But he didn't touch her, and he didn't offer to fund her venture. Instead, he looked down, as embarrassed by being wealthy as she obviously was by being destitute.

Myla's touch on his arm brought his head up. "I want to thank you, Mr. Rudolph, for helping us. All day, I prayed for help, and then you came along. You offered us shelter, and that's something I'll never forget. So thank you, for your kindness and your understanding."

Nick looked in her eyes and felt himself falling, falling, as if in slow motion. Moving away abruptly, he said, "Call me Nick, please. And you don't have to thank me."

The confused look she gave him only added to his woes. He couldn't tell her that he rarely let people get close enough to touch him, either physically or emotionally. He couldn't erase the hurt look in her eyes.

When a special news bulletin interrupted the noisy cartoon on the nearby television, Nick was thankful for the distraction until he heard the report.

The familiar face of the local weatherman filled the screen, and after going over the progress of the ice storm covering the city, the newscaster suggested everyone stay put for the night. "The roads are becoming treacherous and travel may be hazardous until this storm passes. We should be able to resume normal activities by midmorning when higher temperatures and sunshine clear this system out."

Nick eyed the television, willing the man to say it wasn't so. When that didn't happen, he looked toward the silent phone, all hopes of Lydia's much-needed help freezing up like his winding driveway outside. With three pairs of questioning eyes centered on him, he could only give a gracious but shaky smile.

Thoroughly at odds, he wanted to ask Myla Howell why him? Why'd she have to pick him? And what was he supposed to do with her now? Instead, he took her hand. "Well, that settles it. You heard the man. You can stay here tonight."

"What?" Myla gave him a stunned look. "But what about your sister? What about Magnolia House?"

"It can wait," Nick stated firmly, silently wishing Lydia would call and rescue him before he drowned in those questioning green eyes. Or was he silently hoping she wouldn't call? To counter his treacherous thoughts, he added, "It's late and Magnolia House is downtown. It's too dangerous a trip in these icy roads. You'll have to stay here tonight."

"Are you sure?"

"Very sure." His tone was firmer than his confidence. Right now, he wasn't very sure of anything—except that he couldn't send this family back out into that cold, dark night.

# Chapter Two

"Henrietta, please don't cry."

Nick ran a hand through his tousled hair, then gratefully accepted the cup of coffee the whimpering housekeeper handed him before she burst into tears again.

"Ah, Henny, don't do that. It's too early in the morning for theatrics. I didn't know my Christmas present would move you to tears."

"But, Nicky," the older woman began, her shimmering gray curls not moving a centimeter even though she bobbed her head with each word, "it's the sweetest thing anyone's ever done for me. God bless you. You're a good man...a good one..." Her words trailed off as her watery eyes centered on something beyond Nick's head.

Nick turned to find Myla Howell standing in the doorway, wearing the same clothes she'd had on the night before.

"I'm sorry," Myla said, sensing she'd interrupted something important. "I heard voices...."

"Nicky?"

Myla looked from the old woman who stood with her hands on her hips to the man sitting like a king at the head of the long Queen Anne dining table. He was trying to read the newspaper, and judging from the frown marring his handsome face, he was losing patience with the woman standing before him.

"Who's this?" the woman asked, smiling kindly over at Myla.

Nick looked up. Myla didn't miss the surprise or the grimace on his face. "Oh, hello. Henny, this is Myla Howell. Due to the bad weather, Myla and her children were forced to spend the night in one of the guest rooms." He extended a hand toward the woman. "Myla, this is Henrietta Clark, my housekeeper and best friend."

Myla was thankful when the woman didn't ask any questions. "Nice to meet you."

Henny smiled and waved a hand. "Did I wake you up with my wailing, honey? I'm sorry, but I'm so excited. Nicky gave me the best Christmas present before he left for Dallas the other day—a trip to see my daughter and her children in Arkansas."

"And she's wailing because she's so touched," Nick added on a droll note. "She's leaving today."

"That's wonderful," Myla said. "I know you'll have a great time."

"I plan to," Henrietta said, "if I don't spend the whole time worrying about Nicky and Lydia."

"We'll be fine," Nick said, his attention already back on his paper. Then he asked Myla, "Would you like some breakfast, a cup of coffee, maybe?"

Myla took the cup of coffee Henny pressed into her hand, but she didn't sit down. "Actually, I came down to ask for some medicine. Jesse's had a bad night. She's running a fever."

Nick scowled. "Is she all right?"

Afraid that he wasn't pleased at this added problem, Myla nodded. "I think she'll be okay. I just need to bring her fever down."

"Your child?" Henny asked.

"Yes. My oldest. I'm not sure about her temperature, but she feels awfully hot."

Henny whirled around. "There's a thermometer around here somewhere. Nicky won't let me use it on him anymore."

A smile slipped across Myla's face. In spite of her concern for Jesse, she couldn't resist the mental image of the stout Henrietta chasing a snarling Nick around with a thermometer.

Nick's scowl went a few grooves deeper. "She still thinks of Lydia and me as her babies." He gestured for Myla to sit down. "Does Jesse need anything else?"

Myla appreciated the warmth in his words, even if it didn't quite reach his eyes. "I don't think so. Just rest and good food. If you don't mind, I'll feed them breakfast before we leave."

He looked down at the table. "I put in another call to my sister. You can't take chances with this weather."

"No, I wouldn't do that to Jesse. I appreciate your letting us stay here, Mr. Rudolph."

"Call me Nick."

"Okay." Myla sensed, knew, he couldn't wait to be rid of them. "I'm sorry we've disrupted your life."

"It's no problem," he said. "Did you sleep all right?"

"Yes, we all did until Jesse started coughing."

Myla wouldn't tell him that she'd tossed and turned in spite of the warm, cozy room and the enormous bed. She felt so alone, so out of place in this grand old house. But she was certainly thankful that they hadn't had to spend the night in the car.

When she looked up, Nick's gaze softened. "Don't worry about your daughter. If she's sick, we'll get her to a doctor."

"Thank you."

Henrietta burst through the swinging door from the kitchen, a bottle of pills in one hand and a thermometer in the other. "How old's the child?"

"Eight."

"Half a tablet, then. And I'll fix her up some of my special hot lemonade with honey to help get that down. The lemons—good for a cold." She turned to strut back to the kitchen, then whirled to face Nick. "Oh, Nicky, I almost forgot. Are you sure you and Lydia can handle things tonight?"

Nick looked confused, his gaze moving from Myla to his housekeeper. "Tonight? What's going on tonight?"

"Your dinner party," Henny said with arms akimbo. "Don't tell me you forgot to call the temp service. You told me not to worry about a thing, that you and Lydia would take care of calling someone to fill in for me."

Nick sat up, realization hitting him. "You mean my sister and I are in charge of...kitchen duty?"

Henrietta shook her head. "I knew you weren't listening to me the other day." She shot Myla a knowing look. "A one-track mind, that one. If it don't have to do with oil, he don't want to deal with it."

"I guess I *wasn't* listening," Nick agreed. "And I think we'd better round up someone to take care of that. We both know Lydia's as useless in the kitchen as I am."

The housekeeper mumbled something about preoccupied executives, then explained, "It's too late to call the temp service. They're booked through Christmas, I imagine." Looking disappointed, she asked, "You want me to stay?"

Myla listened, then squeaked, "I can do it." When both Nick and Henrietta looked at her as if she'd gone daft, she wanted to drop through the tapestry rug underneath her feet. But this would be a good way to pay Nick back for his help, and it would make her feel a whole lot better about things. "I can cook. I can do whatever needs to be done." When Nick kept staring at her, she rushed on. "Well, if I'm going to stay here all day anyway, I can't just sit around twiddling my thumbs. I'd like to help, to pay you back for your kindness."

Henny smiled from ear to ear. "Well, now, isn't that a nice gesture on your part, honey."

"I'll pay her, of course." Nick gave Henny a sharp look, then turned a questioning glance at Myla. "Do you have experience with this sort of thing?"

Myla didn't tell him that she'd once been considered the best hostess in her neighborhood. That had been one of her husband's demands, along with all his other demands. Instead she said, "I've been in charge of dinner parties before, yes. Henrietta can show me where everything is." Lifting her chin, she added, "And I could use the money."

She watched as Nick weighed his options, hoping for this reprieve, this time out of the cold. Finally, he spoke.

"Well, I certainly don't have time to find anybody else. Okay, you've got the job. But I expect everything to run smoothly—and that means making sure your children—"

"They'll stay out of your way," Myla said. "I promise."

"Good." He turned to Henny. "After breakfast, you can get things settled up between you."

"You're the boss," Henrietta said, smiling to herself as she ambled into the kitchen.

Nick watched her, and Myla saw the doubt clouding his features. Wanting to reassure him, she said, "Don't worry. I can do whatever needs to be done. I want to help and I won't let you down."

"That's good," he contended, "since I'm trusting you alone in my house."

Not liking his tone, she retorted, "I'm a Christian, Mr. Rudolph. I won't steal anything if that's what you're implying."

"I wasn't implying anything. And I certainly didn't mean to insult you."

Seizing the opportunity, Myla rushed on. "Then you might consider letting me fill in for Henrietta. I could work for you until she gets back from her trip."

That got his attention. "I hadn't planned on a long-term replacement. I don't go all out for the holidays."

"That's a shame," she countered. "Christmas is such a beautiful, blessed time of year."

"I don't like Christmas," he insisted. "In fact, this dinner party tonight is more of an obligation to my clients than a celebration."

"Why wouldn't you want to celebrate?" she had to wonder out loud. "The birth of the Savior is a joyous time."

He didn't give her the answer she wanted. Instead, he said, "Henny's planning to be gone until the first of the year. Are you willing to work through Christmas?"

Myla was glad, but surprised that he wanted her to stay that long. She needed a job, but hadn't counted on this becoming a long-term arrangement. This would give her some time, though, and a safe place for her children. "A month? That would help us get a good start on the new year."

Nick's next words were dusted with doubt. "And, it would solve both of our predicaments—you need a job, I need a good worker."

"What about my children? You obviously don't want them underfoot."

"We'll get them enrolled in school. You were planning on doing that, weren't you?"

Resenting his superior attitude, she retorted, "I hadn't thought past getting them to a warm bed."

Nick countered. "Hey, it was your idea. After Christmas you can take the money you've earned here and do whatever you like. This is a sensible solution for everyone concerned.''

Myla had to agree. "So you're asking me to stay here and work for you for the next few weeks?''

He almost grinned. "I don't remember doing any asking, but yes, I guess I am.''

She held out her hand. "Deal, unless that other job I came here for is still open. Then, I'll help you only until I can start there.''

"Deal," he said, shaking her hand. "I'm glad you understand that this is only temporary.''

"Oh, I understand. And I'll need to get my car. We've got a few belongings left in the trunk.''

"I'll take care of that. You take care of your daughter, then get together with Henny so she can explain how everything's run around here." He started toward the long, central hallway, then turned. "We'll put you in Henny's apartment off the kitchen. It's more private.''

"That's fine," Myla said. At least it would be a roof over her head for a while, and it would be much more suitable than the spare guest room, since this was a strictly business arrangement. "I'd better get back up to the children. Jesse needs this medicine.''

"Don't forget Henny's hot lemonade with honey," he reminded her. "Works wonders. I've got to get to work. Oh, and one other thing. I always do a background check on my employees. Any problem with that?''

Hesitating, Myla stammered, embarrassed. "No, but I think you should know a few things. I haven't held a job since high school. I was…I chose to stay at home after my children were born. And my credit is shot because…I had to file bankruptcy.''

He gave her a sympathetic look that hid his own doubts as to the wisdom of this arrangement. "Anything else?''

"Isn't that enough?" she replied with a small smile. "I'll do a good job, I promise," she added sincerely.

Nick stared down at her a moment, nodded briefly, then turned to go.

She watched Nick walk away, then she sent up a silent prayer. *Don't let me mess this up, the way I've messed up my life.*

She'd be so ashamed if he knew the whole truth.

*        *        *

"This is so exciting!"

Lydia Rudolph stood at the window of her brother's downtown Shreveport office, gazing out at the Red River some twenty floors below. "I mean, I'm twenty-five years old, big brother, and this is one of the few times I've actually seen you do something almost human." She fluffed her shining blond bob and beamed brighter than the lighted Christmas stars twinkling insistently on the building across from them. "This only goes to show what I've tried to tell you all along—doing something good for someone brings out the best in people, even an old Scrooge like you."

"I am not a Scrooge," Nick said in protest. "I can't help it if I don't feel the same strong sense of religion that you do, Lydia. I'm quite happy with my life the way it is, thank you. In fact, I'm just a happy-go-lucky kind of guy."

Lydia snorted, causing her bright red hoop earrings to jingle. "Right. You're a great faker, Nick, and we both know it. But this is a start. I'm glad to see you involved with something besides this oil company."

"Yes," Nick responded dryly from his perch on the massive teakwood desk. "Having two rambunctious children and their pretty mother in my house for the holidays is about the most exciting thing I can imagine. And here I was hoping you'd help me out of this mess."

"They're people, Nick, not a mess." Lydia swung around, the fringe on her red suede jacket almost hitting her brother on the head. "I think you needed this. You couldn't wait to tell me all about it when you got here this morning."

"I told you all about it because what I need is your help, little sister. *They* need your help. This is a very temporary situation."

Nick wished he'd just kept his mouth shut. This whole business was starting to get to him. Still amazed that he'd hired Myla to run his house, he had to wonder at his own sanity. He was reeling from the strange turn of events in his life. In the span of less than twelve hours, he'd committed himself to saving a homeless mother and her two waifs. Not involved? Hah! He was involved up to his eyeballs.

Resolving to get this situation cleared up—another of his father's rules: no loose ends—Nick gave his sister a pleading look. "This dinner party is important, Lydia. I need to reassure some of our local stockholders. We've pulled through our slump, but I've still got people jumping ship. Are you going to help me?"

"I'm thinking," Lydia said, settling herself down in the comfortable black leather swivel chair behind Nick's desk. "If I help you with this woman and her children and your precious party, will you go to church with me on Christmas Eve?"

Nick gulped his coffee too fast and burned his tongue. "That's blackmail," he said, spurting out hot coffee in the process. "You know how I feel about that."

Lydia's knowing smile didn't help his bad mood. "What happened to that almost-human I was just talking to?"

He scowled, rubbing his burned tongue against his top teeth. "I'm the same as ever. And I refuse to be pushed into a situation about which I feel uncomfortable. If you can't agree to help me, please leave. I've got work to do."

Lydia jumped up to come around the desk. "Oh, Nick, remember when we were little? Remember Mother taking us to the Christmas Eve service? You in your Christmas suit, me in my velvet dress? You cared then, Nick. You loved Christmas."

"Well, I don't love it now," he said, his mood getting darker by the minute. "And I have work to do."

Lydia stood staring at him. "And I thought helping someone out of a jam would make you less grumpy. When are you going to stop being mad at God, Nick?"

"Probably never," he said, tired of this argument. Thinking back about last night, he remembered Myla's prayer. She'd thanked God for simple things. Basic things. Things most people took for granted every day. Arrh, there he went again, daydreaming about a woman he'd just met last night. "Look, Lydia," he said, "I won't kick them out. You know that. But we do need to help them. And since this sort of thing is your department…"

Lydia nodded. "Of course I'll help. But you made the right decision, Nick. Giving her a job was the best thing you could do."

"I didn't have much choice. She was available on the spot and I needed someone immediately. Now I hope I don't live to regret it."

"You won't," Lydia assured him as she headed toward the door, her long black wool skirt swishing around her matching boots. "You did need someone immediately, and I don't think you'll regret it at all."

"Hey, you're the bleeding heart, remember?" he replied. "While you've been out trying to save the world, I've been breaking my back to save this company."

"And you've done a good job," his sister acknowledged. "The latest stock report shows we're up forty cents per share. We haven't had to dip into that old pile of money Daddy left us, so why don't you relax?"

Nick's eyes grew dark. "I promised him—"

"No, you swore on his grave," she reminded him. "Nick, when are you going to forgive and forget? Yes, he was harsh, but he was only human. It's just that we didn't see his human side until it was too late. I don't want it to be too late for you, Nick. But you're already headed down the same road he took—giving orders and doling out cash, never getting your hands dirty, never facing reality. It's not too late for you yet, not if you realize that money isn't everything."

Nick eyed his little sister curiously, still amazed that she'd escaped their father's ironhanded approach to life. Lydia was so like their mother, good, kindhearted, openly loving. And, Nick reminded himself bitterly, he was his father's son. "Look, Lydia, doling out cash is what I do best. Money, I've got."

"Uh-huh. And that's about all you've got."

Defending himself, he said, "Well, I haven't heard any complaints. We've both got everything we need."

She shook her head. "Except faith, Nick. That's the one thing I've got that you lack." With that, she shut the door and left.

She was wrong, of course. He didn't need the added assurance of some higher power watching over him, which she insisted on believing. He had everything he needed. Didn't he? Head of a successful company, owner of one of the finest homes in Shreveport, possessor of a social book that rivaled anybody's in Louisiana. His list of attributes spoke volumes about his life.

*But that's about all you've got.* Lydia's words taunted him again. Oh, all this Christmas sentiment was affecting his better judgement.

It was normal to feel at odds with so much Christmas hype being shoved down his throat.

Remembering other, happier Christmases, Nick stared out the window, mindless of the crawling traffic below. His father had taught him to keep his emotions at bay, and had set a firm example by never showing any sort of affection or compassion himself. Until Ruth died. Watching his proud, self-sufficient father crumble had only reinforced Nick's own need to stay in control.

Now, he was trapped, so trapped, in a firmly encased persona that gave him a ruthless outlook on life. He'd get through Christmas the same way he had each year since his parents' deaths, by celebrating with a detached kind of fascination, like the cynical kid who didn't believe in Santa anymore.

Except this year, he reminded himself, he'd be doing it with a lovely widow and her two noisy kids. "Why do I have a bad feeling about this whole thing?" he asked himself.

"The whole thing is going to be a disaster," Myla mumbled to herself as she once again checked preparations for the dinner party that loomed less than two hours away. Henrietta had gone over all the details with her. The food was ready; it only needed to be heated when the guests arrived. But Myla wasn't so sure about herself.

She wore a white long-sleeved blouse and black trousers, courtesy of Lydia's closet. Henrietta had insisted Lydia wouldn't mind or even miss the functional outfit.

"All you have to do is keep the food coming," the older woman had explained. "Nicky likes everything to run smoothly—these people are clients and stockholders, but this is a casual dinner. Just put it out on the buffet, real nice and hot, and keep your eyes open for seconds. The bar's fully stocked, and Nicky'll mix what drinks are needed."

Since she didn't condone drinking, Myla was glad she didn't have to play bartender. The rest sounded simple enough. After all, she'd done this hundreds of times before. Smoothing the knot of hair coiled at the nape of her neck, she took a deep, calming breath. The children were tucked away in Henny's small sitting room, armed with books to look over, coloring pads and crayons, and various other things Henny stockpiled for her grandchildren. They could watch a little television before they were to go on to bed. Surely, nothing could go wrong.

The kitchen door swung open. Nick marched in, whistling to himself. He'd saved the Dallas deal, another coup for Rudolph Oil, and a nice nibble to share with his fidgety stockholders. Stopping in midwhistle, he looked around the kitchen, and then into the set of exotic eyes watching him.

"Who did all of this?" he asked in a deadly calm voice as his gaze trailed over the fresh ivy and holly berry greenery adorning every available corner. The scent of bayberry candles lifted through the air, giving the room a cozy holiday effect.

Seeing the scowl on his face, Myla said, "I...I did. I found the decorations in the garage. I thought it would look nice for the party."

"I don't care for a lot of frivolous decorations," he said, noting that she looked right at home. "I just wanted a simple, quiet evening with no fuss. Did the cake I ordered come?"

She nodded, swallowing back her embarrassment. "Yes, your coconut cake is right here on the counter."

So it was. To avoid lashing out at her for her innocent assumptions, he concentrated instead on the rich cake he'd had a local restaurant prepare for tonight.

Before he could speak, she spoke to him. "I'm sorry about the decorations. I didn't realize—"

"Never mind," he said on a tired sigh. "It is Christmas, after all, and I do need to appear all jolly-holly for these people."

Myla leaned against the counter to steady her nerves. "Everything's in order. The table's set. The food's ready. I really didn't have that much to take care of."

"Plenty to drink?" he asked as he scanned the mail lying on the countertop.

She lifted her shoulders. "Yes, but I must tell you, I don't drink and I'd prefer not to have to mix drinks for your guests."

He shrugged. To each his own. "I'll take care of that, then. But don't worry. I don't expect this stoic crowd to get too wild."

Relieved to hear that, Myla relaxed a little. "Henny told me how important this is to you."

He moved into the room, throwing his briefcase on a desk in the corner before heading to the refrigerator. "Henny's very efficient. She knows how these functions work. The old-boy networking system never slows down."

Myla noticed the lines of fatigue around his eyes. He seemed so cool and in charge that she found it hard to believe he could be worried. "Can I get you anything?" she asked.

"Nah, I'll just have some juice." Spying a tray of appetizers in the refrigerator, he picked up a cracker covered with a shrimp mixture and popped it into his mouth. "That's good," he said between chews.

"I found the shrimp in the freezer," she explained. "I know the recipe by heart."

"You're in charge of the kitchen," he said by way of appreciation. "Do you need anything?"

*I need to have my head examined,* she thought. She was terrified of being here, but she needed this job. She wouldn't allow her children to be homeless again.

"No, Henny went over the schedule with me."

"Good." Nick placed the empty juice glass in the sink. "Guess I'll head up to get a shower." Turning back on his tasseled loafers, he asked, "How's Jesse?"

"Much better." Touched that he'd bothered to ask, Myla guessed he was just being polite. "Her fever is down." At his questioning look, she added, "They're in Henny's room, all settled in."

He nodded, wondering why he'd become so tongue-tied all of a sudden. "By the way, your car's in the auto shop. It should be fixed in a couple of days. Your belongings will be delivered tomorrow."

"But..." Myla began, not knowing how to ever thank him. He'd taken care of everything in such a businesslike manner. She supposed he was used to taking matters into his own hands, while she was just beginning to learn how to deal with everyday problems on her own. "Thank you," she said, her voice tapping down the tad of resentment she couldn't deny.

He raised a hand to ward off her gratitude. "It was no trouble and besides, I'm depending on you to run my house. You can't do that if you're out trying to get your car fixed."

"Good point," she reluctantly agreed. He didn't take compliments or praise very well. "I'm sorry for all this trouble."

Nick shrugged. "Don't worry. If it'll make you feel better, I'll send you the bill."

"I insist," she said as she watched him plow through the swinging door to the hallway. Somehow, she'd pay him back for his kindness, but she couldn't say if it would make her feel better or not.

Nick's bellowing call from the den brought her head up. Rushing through the swinging door, she flew down the hall to the other room to find him standing in front of the tree she and the children had put up that afternoon.

"What's this?" he asked, his hands on his hips, his chin jutting out as he stared at the eight-foot-tall evergreen.

"It's a Christmas tree, of course," she said, wondering why the fresh-cut tree seemed to be bothering him so much. "Henny called a nursery and had it delivered."

Nick ran a hand through his hair and gave another long sigh. "I told her in no uncertain terms, that I did not want a tree in this house."

"She never mentioned that to me."

"No, I don't suppose she would have. Well, too late to take it down now."

Finding her courage, Myla stepped closer to the tree to touch one of the brilliant ornaments she'd found in a huge box in the garage. "The children had such a great time decorating it, I'd appreciate it if you would try to enjoy it."

Nick's gaze moved from the tree to the woman at his side. Her eyes were almost the same shade as the lush branches reaching out toward him. And they sparkled every bit as brightly. He couldn't deny her this one concession to his rigid holiday rules.

"Okay. The tree can stay up, but no more decorating without consulting me first, no matter what Henny tells you."

"All right."

He didn't like her tone or the hurt look in her eyes. "What are you thinking?"

She smiled then, but her eyes still held a certain sadness. "That you have a beautiful house. Six bedrooms, is it? And four baths?

And those sunrooms. I've always loved having lots of live plants in a sunny room.''

Nick hadn't really noticed the plants. He shrugged, his gaze sweeping casually over his surroundings. "It's almost too big for a bachelor and his baby sister, but it's home.''

"Is it?" she couldn't help but ask.

"Is it what?"

"Home?"

"I live here, don't I?"

"Yes, but...oh, never mind. This place is like something out of a dream, but it just seems as if something is missing in this great, old house.''

She'd sensed it, when she'd gone through the rooms earlier, dusting and gawking at the same time. The house was as reserved and cool as the man who lived in it, and just like him, it cast out a false sense of contentment.

Nick sighed, then turned to go. "Don't try to analyze me, Myla. There's nothing missing here. Everything is as it should be.''

"If you say so.''

She watched as he left the room and stalked up the curving staircase. How sad that he couldn't enjoy the holidays. Myla wondered what had made him this way. She turned back to the tree, her gaze fixed on the gold and white angel watching her from the top of the sturdy blue spruce. "I think Nick Rudolph needs your help,'' she whispered.

An hour later, the house was filled with the sound of laughter tinkling on the air as crystal glasses tinkled with ice. The aroma of mulling cider wafted through the night while the fire in the massive marble fireplace located across one wall of the den crackled and popped. Myla viewed the cluster of people scattered around the tree, making sure each guest had plenty to eat and drink, while she listened to the carefully selected group's conversation.

"Nick, I love the house this year,'' a stout woman covered in diamonds said between bites of puffed pastry stuffed with artichoke filling. "I haven't seen it this festive and bright in a long time.''

Nick's smile was all calculated charm. "Glad you approve, Dottie. I'm not much on the holidays, but my new housekeeper insisted

I put up a tree, at least.'' He guided Dottie away from the tree, then said, ''Remind me to show you Rudolph Oil's fourth-quarter report. I'd love to have you serve on the board again. We could use your input.''

Clearly enthralled, the woman practically preened. ''You know, I've been telling Jacob we need to reconsider that decision.''

Jacob, a tall gray-haired man, listened diligently. ''Whatever you say, dear.''

Nick grinned, then caught Myla's eye. He saw the disapproving look she cast his way and wondered what he'd done to offend her. Excusing himself from Dottie, he cornered Myla by the buffet.

''Is everything all right?''

''Fine,'' she replied, her gaze scanning the crowd. ''Would you like another glass of soda?''

He finished off the cool liquid left in the bottom of his glass, then shook his head. ''No, but I'd like to know why you were glaring at me earlier.''

''No reason,'' she said, busying herself by putting out more cans of soda for his guests. ''I was just watching you work the crowd.''

''And you disapprove?''

Myla gave him a direct stare. ''No, I'm just surprised. One minute you're acting like a regular grizzly bear and the next you're turning on the charm.''

Recalling their earlier encounter right here in this room, Nick replied, ''Look, I'm sorry I got angry about the decorations and the tree. You were smart to spruce this place up...and it looks wonderful. Perfect.''

''Glad you approve,'' she said, not at all convinced of his sincerity.

Sensing that she didn't exactly trust his motives, Nick smiled over at her. ''I do approve. So far, everything's going according to schedule. And I owe that to you.''

Before she could respond, he turned away to greet some more guests, leaving her with the memory of his aftershave. She'd smelled it earlier when he'd entered the kitchen. He was a handsome man. A self-reliant man, who liked to rule over his domain.

This was his world, not hers. She'd had a similar life with her husband, but now...now, she intended to make her own way, with her faith to shield and guide her. She wouldn't put her trust in another ruthless man. And Nick Rudolph was exactly that.

She watched him play host to the hilt as he mixed business with pleasure and made her feel like an out-of-place Cinderella watching the prince dance with all the other girls at the ball.

"Bill, you rascal," Nick said, laughing as he playfully slapped the tall, blond-headed man on the back. "How are things looking for your re-election to the Senate? Can I depend on you down in Baton Rouge?"

"Can I depend on your donation to my next campaign?" Bill countered with a hearty laugh, thus beginning a rather long and detailed account of his political aspirations. His wife, a slender brunette in a pricey red pantsuit gave a bored smile as her eyes fell across Myla, then moved on.

The look of dismissal galled Myla, but she knew her place. She'd been poor before she married Sonny Howell. And now, she'd come full circle. She could afford to be gracious to the woman; she'd once been so like her.

Once again, Nick excused himself from his guest to head toward Myla with a purposeful stride. Afraid that she'd done something wrong again, she moved to meet him.

"Everyone's here except—" Nick stopped in midsentence when a loud screeching noise, followed by a bellowing bark and the crash of dishes, rose from the back of the huge house. "What was that?"

The doors of the kitchen burst open as a tall woman with flowing blond hair ran into the room, her black dress clinging to her slender curves.

"Carolyn?" Nick looked surprised, then laughed in relief. "Leave it to you to make a grand entrance."

The lovely Carolyn fumed with indignation. "Nick Rudolph, how dare you laugh at me? It's bad enough that you stood me up last night, but now this. You've got to do something!"

"Do what?" Nick looked confused. "What's the matter?"

The other guests had gathered around now, each waiting and watching as Carolyn pulled at a torn spot in her black hose. "It's Pooky," she said on a low moan. "He's in the kitchen—"

Another wailing scream rose from the kitchen, followed by a

growl and another scream, this one human. Several loud crashes joined in with the screams.

Nick plopped his glass down on a walnut table. "What's going on in there?"

Carolyn moaned again and tugged at her hair. "That's what I'm trying to tell you, Nick. I brought Pooky along with me to ward off muggers and when I went to put him in Henny's room, a...a cat ran out and now Pooky's chasing the crazed creature around the kitchen and when I tried to stop him, well...that cat lurched into my leg and well, look, a fifteen-dollar pair of nylons ruined." Tossing her evening bag and black velvet cape into Nick's face, she added, "And I'm bleeding. You know I'm allergic to cats!"

The uproar in the kitchen increased now, the crowd moving in closer, each guest hovering near the swinging doors, afraid to go in and see what Pooky and the mysterious cat were doing to each other.

"Cat?" Nick shook his head. "I don't have a cat."

Another scream brought Myla into action. Pushing through the dazed spectators, she called to Nick, "The children!"

"Children?" Carolyn eyed Nick suspiciously. "I thought I saw something unusual hiding behind Henny's couch. Nick, what's going on here?"

Nick looked over at Carolyn, prepared to explain everything until he heard Myla's low agony-filled moan. That moan did not bode well, not at all. Giving Carolyn's things to the skinny brunette in red, he dashed toward the kitchen. The sight that greeted him caused him to echo the same low-pitched moan.

A tabby cat, scrawny and hissing, sat on a blade of the still ceiling fan, one paw extended in the attack position while a howling, barking Saint Bernard sat underneath, his tongue fairly hanging out of his big, toothy mouth as he waited for the next chase to begin.

Patrick sat in the middle of the counter, surrounded by what had once been the carefully arranged entrees for the dinner party. Now those entrees were not only arranged all over the counter, but also all over Patrick and all over the once white tile floor. Jesse hovered in the doorway leading to Henny's apartment, her wails matching pitch with the cat's. The Saint Bernard, tired of playing chase with the pitiful cat, turned and started lapping up what remained of the platter of roast that Myla had carved so lovingly and garnished with parsley and star-burst carved cherry tomatoes.

Myla's eyes met Nick's. Of their own accord, her hands came up to cover her face. He's going to send all of us packing, she thought.

Nick's face burned with a rage born of shock. ''What happened here?'' His voice grew deeper and more deadly with each word. ''Would someone like to tell me what in blazes happened in here?''

The room, filled with twelve warm, curious bodies, remained silent, except for the occasional hissing from the ceiling fan and the melodious lapping on the tile floor.

''I'm waiting.'' Nick circled the carnage, his eyes brown with a fire of rage. ''I want some answers, now!''

Finally, a feeble voice rallied from the direction of Henny's room. Jesse stepped forward, shivering with fear, her eyes bright with freshly shed tears. ''Mamma, we forgot to tell you about the cat,'' she said before she burst into another round of high-pitched sobs

# Chapter Three

The door leading from the garage burst open. Lydia bounced into the room, wearing a black crepe dressy pantsuit, her blond bob shining as brightly as her diamond earrings.

Myla recognized her from the many pictures of Nick and Lydia hanging around the house. But Carolyn…was she Nick's girlfriend? Nick had been busy doing a good deed last night and now look what it had caused him. Even Lydia's upbeat mood didn't help the situation.

"Sorry I'm late," she began, her earrings twinkling like twin stars, "but I had to stop by—" Her eyes registered shock for a split second before she burst out in a fit of uncontrollable laughter. "Food fight? Nick, why didn't you tell me? You know how I love to throw my food at you!"

"Not now, Lydia," Nick said, his growl more pronounced than the drooling Pooky's. "We've had a bit of an accident and I was just trying to get to the bottom of it."

"Looks like Pooky here beat you to it," Lydia countered, rushing forward to pet the massive Saint Bernard. "Hey, boy, what did you get into this time?"

"It's not Pooky's fault," Carolyn said as she sidestepped a pile of shrimp dip to comfort the hyper dog. "I walked over for the party, so I brought Pooky with me. I had no idea that a cat and two strange children would attack us when we entered the back door."

"Next time, try using the front door like the other guests," Lydia replied sweetly, though her eyes indicated she felt anything but sweet.

"Ladies, please," Nick said, raking a hand through his crisp dark curls. Turning to Myla, he watched as she knelt to comfort her sobbing daughter. Instantly, he regretted his anger from before. "Jesse, how'd we manage to acquire a cat?" he asked, his tone deceptively soft, his eyes centered on Myla as if to say *this is your fault.*

Jesse looked up to her mother for reassurance. Myla, stung by Nick's anger and by Carolyn's high-handed attitude toward her children, shot him a defiant look. Thinking she could kiss this new job goodbye, she patted Jesse on the shoulder. "Just tell the truth, honey."

Jesse took a deep breath to clear away another round of sobs. "Mr. Nick, I'm sorry. But today when Momma was getting stuff ready for your party, me and Patrick went for a walk out in the backyard. We weren't supposed to, 'cause I'm sick and Patrick gets into stuff, but we snuck out.... Anyway, we heard a cat meowing behind that big building by the pool. Patrick came back in the house when Momma wasn't looking and got some food for the cat. It was real hungry." Sniffing, she looked up at Nick. "We wanted to help it so it wouldn't freeze to death, like you helped us, Mr. Nick." She wiped her nose again with her hand, her big blue-green eyes wide with the importance of her confession.

Nick looked uncomfortable, but Myla saw the touch of warmth Jesse's innocent words had provoked in his eyes.

"Why didn't you tell me about the cat, sweetie?" she asked her daughter, her heart breaking. Jesse loved animals. She'd never let one starve or stay out in the cold, in spite of her allergies around certain animals. Hunger wasn't pretty—in animals or humans.

"We were afraid you'd make us let it go," Jesse said, dropping her eyes to the floor.

"Yeah, and we didn't want Mr. Nick to kick us out," Patrick piped up as he held out his dip-covered fingers. "I tried to catch it, Mamma, but it was too fast. And besides, I'm scared of that big dog."

"Pooky wouldn't hurt a flea," Carolyn protested, looking from one child to the other accusingly. Then she turned to glare up at

Nick. "You told me you helped some people out last night; you didn't tell me they were staying in your home."

Bristling, Myla shot Carolyn a proud look. "I'm *working* for Mr. Rudolph while his housekeeper is on vacation."

"Working for Nick?" Carolyn whirled around. "Is that true—even after what you told me last night?"

Nick's look warned her to drop it. "Things have changed since then. I'll explain later."

Myla's eyes met his. He was embarrassed, but she saw the hint of an apology. He was too much of a gentleman to make a scene. Obviously though, he'd avoided telling Carolyn everything. Wondering if he was ashamed of her being here, Myla felt like a circus sideshow.

Deciding she'd really give them all something to talk about and try to save Nick's reputation and her much needed job in the process, she pinned Carolyn with a level look. "Yes, it's true. Mr. Rudolph was kind enough to help us out last night. You see, we've had a rough time lately. We've been living in our car." That statement caused an audible rumbling through the room, but it didn't stop Myla. "He found us stranded on the interstate during the ice storm, and he brought us here. Knowing I needed a job, he asked me to work for him while his regular housekeeper, Henrietta, is on vacation. And as long as he doesn't have a problem with that, I don't, either. I'm just very thankful that he was kind enough to care about my children and me.

"The Bible says, 'Blessed are ye that hunger now: for ye shall be filled. Blessed are ye that weep now: for ye shall laugh.' Yesterday, I was hungry and weeping. Today, thanks to Mr. Rudolph's kindness, I'm warm and full and laughing, in spite of all of this mess." Dismissing Carolyn's surprised, cynical look, she turned to Nick. "Isn't this the true spirit of Christmas? You took us in, when there was no room at the inn. You did something entirely unselfish. It's the best Christmas present I could ask for, and I thank you. And I take full responsibility for my children's actions."

Nick stood still, in shock. He should be angry that she'd turned his party into a sermon on the mount. Instead, he felt a great rush of warmth moving through his body. Ashamed, he blinked to hold back the blur of tears forming in his eyes. He'd never seen a woman as brave as Myla Howell. She had more courage among this crowd of cutthroats than he'd ever possessed, ruthless as he was supposed to be.

Of course, her courage was one thing. Being called a pushover was quite another. Glancing around, he waited for the looks and whispers that were sure to come. But to his surprise, his guests didn't condemn him or laugh at him. They came, one by one, to pat him on the back.

The senator was the first in line. "Perfect, my friend. Helping the homeless is one of my campaign pledges. I'll hold you up as an example."

That comment was followed by Dottie's tear-filled pledge. "How could I ever doubt your sincerity again, Nick? Jacob and I will be happy to serve on the board of Rudolph Oil, and I intend to call our broker first thing tomorrow and instruct her to buy a substantial amount of Rudolph Oil shares." Then, glancing at Myla, she whispered, "And I'll leave a check for your housekeeper, too. A little Christmas gift. Such a tragedy."

"But..." Nick didn't know what to say. Myla had single-handedly turned a disaster into a public relations dream. Now, after giving her eloquent speech, she went on to introduce herself to the group and assure them that they would have a decent meal, after all.

Sending Nick a daring look, she called, "Pizza, anyone?" Then, turning to him with a gracious smile, she whispered, "You can't fire me now."

"I wouldn't dream of it," he whispered back, his eyes full of a grudging admiration, and his heart full of something warm and unfamiliar.

All the guests started talking and laughing, except Carolyn. Myla saw the blonde throw Nick a scrutinizing look.

Carolyn stood, then smiled sweetly at Nick. "Since when did you find religion, Nicky?"

Nick didn't answer. Instead, he said, "Carolyn, why don't you wait for me in the den?"

"I'll order the pizza," Lydia said, jumping over broken dishes to find the phone. "How about three vegetarians and three with pepperoni and sausage, all large with extra cheese?"

Everyone clapped their approval. Lydia herded the humans and Pooky toward the den. "Just make yourselves at home while I dial the emergency pizza number."

Carolyn gave Myla a cold look, then pranced into the den with the rest of the crowd. As she walked past Nick, she said, "We really need to talk."

Nick watched her go, then turned to stare at his wrecked kitchen, before settling his gaze on Myla and her daughter. Lifting Patrick down, he sent the little boy scooting toward his mother. A long sigh escaped from deep within Nick's lungs as he watched Patrick hug Myla's neck and smear her with shrimp dip. How could he be mad at them when they stood huddled together as if he were about to issue an order for their execution?

"I'll clean it up immediately," Myla said, her voice firm while her hands shook. "I'm so sorry, Nick."

He held up a hand to ward off her apology. She'd put up a good front for his guests, but he could see she was visibly upset. She'd said she'd handled a few dinner parties, but never one such as this, he'd wager.

"It's okay," he said, pushing away his questions for now. Swallowing the lump of pride caught in his throat, he added, "Thanks. You sure handled that better than I did. You made me sound like a saint."

"Saint Nick," Patrick said, giggling as he wiped a glob of dip on his pajamas.

"Not a saint, Patrick," his mother corrected, "just a very kind and understanding man."

"Flattery will get you everywhere," Nick retorted, smiling in spite of himself. "You obviously have me confused with someone else."

She wouldn't let him get away so easily. "Oh, no. I know what I'm talking about. You're uncomfortable in this role, being heroic, I mean. What happened to make you so afraid of reaching out to others, Nick?"

Lydia hung up the phone, interrupting before he could answer. "I can't believe Carolyn. She knows that dog doesn't belong at a dinner party. She should have left the big brute at home to run around on that two-acre lot she calls a backyard."

"She brought him along for protection," Nick said, glad to change the subject.

Lydia snorted. "I've never know Carolyn to need protection."

"Careful, sis."

Lydia turned to Myla and the children. "He's right. I have to remember not to judge too harshly. It's so nice to meet you. Nick's told me all about you."

Myla looked at Nick. Yes, she was sure he'd called Lydia first thing this morning, telling her how much he regretted being a Good Samaritan. "Well, he apparently didn't tell *Carolyn* all about us."

Getting back to the immediate problem, Nick said, "I'm not worried about Carolyn or her dog right now." Motioning toward the fan, he said, "What about that?"

The cat still sat on guard, its bright yellow eyes narrowing suspiciously each time anyone made a move.

"We'll get it down and clean it up, don't worry," Lydia said. "How about we call it Shredder, kids?"

"Yeah, Shredder," Patrick agreed, clapping his sticky hands together.

"Who said we were going to keep it?" Nick asked, his hands on his hips.

"The worst is over." Myla turned to Lydia. "Would you mind getting Shredder out of the way so I can clean this up?"

"Sure." Lydia called softly to the frightened animal. "We'll take him to Henny's sitting room and teach him some manners while you two straighten things out." The meaningful gaze she shot her brother told him she was referring to much more than the mess on the floor.

"Gee, thanks." Nick pulled off his navy-and-burgundy patterned wool sweater, then rolled up his blue shirtsleeves so he could get down to work. "Lydia, you just want to see me get my hands dirty, right?"

Lydia bobbed her head and grinned.

Myla stepped forward as Lydia bribed the cat down with a piece of roast beef. "Nick, you don't have to help."

The animal refused to come into Lydia's arms, but did jump down and run into the safety of Henny's apartment. Lydia and the giggling children followed, discussing the now famous battle with animation.

Left alone, Nick and Myla could only stand and stare around them. Everything was ruined. Nick moaned softly when his eyes lit on the mashed remains of his prized coconut cake.

"You have guests," Myla stated, picking up the cake plate to remove the source of Nick's woes. "Go ahead. I'm sure Carolyn needs comforting after her horrid ordeal."

Nick heard the sarcasm in her words and saw the twitch of a smile pulling at her lips. He relaxed and smiled back, his eyes meeting hers. "Carolyn Parker and I grew up together," he explained. "She's divorced and rich, and expects me to jump when she calls. We escort each other around town on various occasions. And about last night—"

"You don't have to explain anything to me." Myla sidestepped a pile of spinach salad. "Your social life is your business. But why didn't you tell her everything...about me?"

"Because I didn't think I owed her an explanation. I didn't feel the need to go into detail about your situation."

"That was considerate," she said, thinking he was one of the most gentlemanly men she'd ever met. Then again, maybe he used his impeccable manners as a shield.

Nick tried to take the flattened cake from her. He wanted a little taste of that wonderful cake before she threw it out. "I'm glad you understand."

"Oh, I understand." She turned, looking for the trash can. "And I'm really sorry the children ruined your party." He tried to pry the cake out of her hand, but she pulled it away. "Nick, I've got it. Why don't you get a mop from the—"

Nick made one last-ditch effort to reach for the cake, leaning forward from the waist so he wouldn't have to step in the pile of spinach salad. But just as he lunged forward, Myla turned to dump the cake in the trash.

Nick came crashing against her, knocking Myla completely off balance. The cake sailed up as she whirled around. He got a taste of his cake, all right, in the face, as he slipped in salad dressing, with cake and Myla sliding right into his arms. By the time the impact was complete, Myla had cake all over her face and shoulders, too. Unable to move or breath, she watched as Nick licked creamy almond-colored icing off his lips.

His arms holding her, and the remains of the mushed cake, against him, he asked, "Are you all right?" When she nodded, he licked his lips again, causing something like kindling wood to spark and curl in Myla's jittery stomach. "Ah, that's so good," he said, lifting his hands to dump the ruined cake into the trash. "I could have handled anything but losing my coconut cake. I think I'm going to cry."

Myla huffed a breath, then turned to find a towel. "Please, if you do, don't mess up the floor."

"Very funny."

Nick raised a hand to take the towel from her, his fingers gripping her wrist. Lifting her head, she saw a set of bronze-colored eyes lazily assessing her. Gone was the cold indifference, the quiet reserve, and in its place, a heated brilliance that took her breath away.

"Let me go, Nick," she said on a soft whisper.

"Wait, you have a big glob of cake on your right cheek."

Reaching up, she touched her face. "I'll get it off. Now, let me go so we can clean up this mess."

"Let's start right now."

Before she could move or protest, he began wiping her face, his fingers gently lifting icing and cake filling off her cheek, his amused gaze causing sparks to ignite again in her stomach. She tried to pull away, but he held her steady.

"Right there." He took the towel and wiped it across her jaw. "Yep, that's it." He held her away to inspect his handiwork. "All clean now."

Myla could only stare at him. What on earth was the man trying to do to her? Here she was, covered with cake and shrimp dip, in the middle of his kitchen, with her children and his sister in one room and a pack of hungry guests as well as a jealous girlfriend in the other. Everything was ruined, and Nick should be angry with her. Instead, he was treating her with such intense concern that she thought she might cry from the sheer sweetness of his gesture. She could have handled his anger; his kindness was much harder to bear.

"Are you finished?" she managed to ask as she gritted her teeth to keep the lump in her throat from choking her.

Nick, seeing the torment in her eyes, stood back, then carefully wiped bacon-and-mustard salad dressing from his khaki trousers. Thinking he'd made her uncomfortable, he said, "I'm sorry. I didn't mean to offend you, Myla."

To calm her own wayward feelings, Myla turned to the sink. "It's all right. I…I'm just surprised that you didn't…that you aren't—"

"What?" Confused, Nick tugged her around again.

Myla sighed, then took the towel from his hands. "You should be mad—I promised you everything would work out fine tonight, and now I've ruined your party. Why didn't you just get mad at me?"

A bit amused, Nick lifted a brow. "So, you're upset because I'm not upset?"

She bobbed her head. "Yes. No! I mean, I could have handled you shouting and ranting. Why did you have to be so nice to me?"

Nick watched as she frantically tried to wipe the counter, not knowing how to comfort her. "I am so sorry," he repeated, a mock glare coloring his face. "What was I thinking?"

"Exactly," Myla agreed, unaware that he was smiling behind her back. "You don't have to be nice!"

Nick understood that she wasn't used to any tenderness and that realization bothered him. What had she suffered, to make her so wary of a kind gesture? He wanted to ask her, but decided she'd just clam up if he tried. So instead, he teased her. "I promise, if this happens again, I'll try to be justifiably angry."

She whirled around just in time to see the sparkle in his eyes. Hiding a smile, Myla relaxed a little. "Guess you miss Henny, huh?"

He laughed. "Yeah, but her dinner parties were never this exciting, I have to admit." Pivoting, he said, "I'll go get the mop."

Her hand shot out to stop him. "Wash your face first."

Lydia stuck her head around the corner from Henny's apartment. "By the way, Nick, I thought you both should know—I stopped by Magnolia House on my way over here. They're full, probably will be until well after the first of the year. But Myla, I did put your name on the waiting list."

Myla looked up at the man who'd saved her, praying he'd let her stay until she could find somewhere else to go.

Nick didn't say anything, but she could tell by his blank expression that he wasn't too pleased with the news. Together, they silently cleaned the kitchen while Lydia got the children and Shredder off to sleep.

Finally, when they'd finished and the whole room had been restored to order, Nick turned to Myla. "Well, at least you can stay here until the first of the year."

"Yes, and I'm thankful that the good Lord led me to you."

He gave her a puzzled look, then said, "Maybe it's the other way around, Myla."

Myla's heart soared. Maybe he was beginning to feel differently about Christmas and helping others. She followed him into the den where Pooky lay fast asleep in front of the roaring fire. The guests were playing a game that involved telling the truth regarding scruples.

Carolyn turned to Nick. "Your turn, darling. Are you willing to test your scruples?"

"Scruples?" Nick laughed, his shrug indifferent. "Why, you all know I don't have any. None at all."

Myla sat watching him. He had deliberately downplayed his good side, the side she'd seen firsthand. *You're wrong, Mr. Rudolph. You have scruples—you just haven't used them in a while.*

Again, she had to wonder what had caused Nick to turn into himself. As she watched him, his eyes touched on her and she saw the warmth shining there. She said a silent prayer. *Dear Father, help Nick to find his way back to you. And thank you for leading me to him.*

The next night when Nick came home from work, he found a freshly baked pound cake sitting on the counter, its buttery aroma filling the house. The kitchen sparkled and gleamed. Holly branches from the garden decorated the counters, giving the room a homey effect.

The back door opened and Myla, Patrick and Jesse all rushed into the room, giggling and chattering. All three held arms full of firewood. Myla looked up, a hesitant smile cresting her lips.

Patrick said, "Hey, Mr. Nick. We're gonna start a fire."

"So I see."

He nodded toward the boy's mother, noticing the way the December wind had brightened her cheeks and pinkened her lips, giving her fair skin a perfect contrast to her fiery wind-tossed copper-colored hair. As was his nature, Nick watched and waited as she ordered the children to place the wood in the den.

"And don't try to light a fire. I wouldn't want you two to burn down the Christmas tree." Turning back to Nick, she said, "Dinner will be ready in an hour."

"That's fine." He gazed at the fat cake sitting on the counter. "That smells wonderful."

"Want a slice?" She headed toward the refrigerator to pull out the milk. "Milk or coffee?"

"Milk." Nick slid out of his khaki trench coat. "This looks good."

"Well, it's not coconut cake, but I wanted to make up for last night. I hate seeing grown men cry."

He chuckled, then took the glass of milk and a generous slice of the still-warm cake, his eyes following her as he bit into the flaky lemon-flavored mound. Myla waited as he chewed it with glee, a little moan of appreciation escaping as he swallowed.

"I think I'm in love," he murmured as he closed his eyes. After another hefty bite, he said, "Oh, you wouldn't believe the phone calls I've been getting all day."

Concerned, she asked, "About what?"

"About you. About the pizza party. We really impressed the stockholders. They're throwing their support toward Rudolph Oil, and you."

"Me?"

"They want to help you out."

Myla had to turn away to keep him from seeing the tears welling in her eyes. Maybe there was hope, after all. Of course, these people didn't know her background. She wondered how they'd feel about her if they knew the whole story. "I can't take any charity, Nick," she said to hide her fears.

"Of course you can," he reasoned. "They admire your strength, Myla. Last night, you showed them something they've taken for granted."

She shrugged, her back still turned away. "I only told the truth according to my beliefs. It's what I live by."

Thinking she was about to launch into another sermon, Nick cleared his throat. "I have some checks here. Will you take them? You can use the money after...after you leave here."

"Charity," she said, dreading the thought of not being self-reliant.

Nick came to stand beside her. "Yes, charity, but given with the best of intentions. And besides, they can write it off on their income tax, so take the money, Myla."

She stopped stirring the steaming pot of vegetables. "The Lord loves a cheerful giver."

"That's the spirit. You can always pay them back."

She smiled then. "Did they write checks?"

"Yes, why?"

"I'll record their names and addresses and offer them my services. I want to start my own catering business."

He stared over at her. "Catering...you'd be good at that." Shaking his head, he added, "I admire your ingenuity. You'll do just fine in life, Myla." With that declaration, he finished the last bite of his cake.

Myla turned back to her cooking. She had to stop watching this man eat. She wanted to cook him hearty meals and take care of him. He needed more than a housekeeper; he needed a spiritual partner. And after ten years of marriage to Sonny Howell, she wasn't sure she was ready for that yet.

Answering him finally, she said, "I have to do this, Nick. I have to provide for my children."

Nick put his empty plate and glass in the sink. "I believe you will. Patrick was right. You are a good cook."

"Thank you. Cooking's about all I have to offer." She faced him at last. "I need to tell you—the other job I came here to see about—it was a cook in a restaurant. I called today...and they've already hired someone."

Nick put a hand on her shoulder. "You found this job, Myla. Maybe...maybe you'll be better off here, for now." Not sure how to comfort her, he added, "And hey, if you keep this up, I'll be as fat as Santa by Christmas."

She laughed then. "You can work it off by starting that fire Patrick and Jesse want."

"Good idea. I rarely build a fire for just myself." He headed toward the swinging doors, then whirled. "By the way, how's Shredder doing?"

"He won't come out of Henny's apartment."

She waited, but when he just stood staring over at her, she asked, "Is there anything else, Nick?"

"Yes," he said, lowering his head a bit. "You're wrong, you know."

"About what?"

"Cooking isn't the only thing you have to offer, Myla."

He turned to go, leaving her to wonder what he'd meant by that statement. *Careful, Myla,* an inner voice warned. Nick was just being polite, trying to boost her ego. He didn't know anything about her, and right now, she didn't have the nerve to tell him the truth.

An hour later, Nick looked at the place set for one in the formal dining room. In spite of the Christmas centerpiece sitting in the middle of the long, shining Queen Anne table, the room still seemed empty and vast. In spite of the plate of steaming vegetables and hot-buttered noodles, the baked chicken and delicate dinner rolls, he couldn't seem to get excited about eating.

Too much cake, he reasoned, plopping down on an antique chair to try to enjoy Myla's marvelous efforts. "At last, peace and quiet."

With his first bite, he heard Myla's soft voice lifted in prayer. She was blessing their food in the other room. Sheepishly, Nick closed his eyes and listened. Glad when she'd finished, he whispered his own animated "Amen," then straightened his linen dinner napkin to get on with his meal.

Before he got a bite of succulent chicken between his teeth, he heard giggles from the kitchen, followed by voices all talking at once. They were a close trio, his little pack of strays. Myla seemed very protective of her children. Nick had to wonder what kind of man would leave her and her two children with nothing.

It's not your problem, Nick, he reminded himself. Sit up straight and eat your dinner.

With his first bite of the flaky roll, he remembered holding Myla the night before. Somehow, he'd managed to lose all decorum right there in his own kitchen. Carolyn would just love to have the details of that.

Of course, he didn't owe Carolyn or anyone else any explanations. He liked having no strings attached, and no obligations to anyone. Memories of his loving parents moved through the room like ghosts, haunting Nick with a poignancy he refused to acknowledge. He couldn't deal with the responsibilities of that kind of devoted love. He had other obligations—to Lydia and Rudolph Oil. Wishing Lydia didn't always work so late, he tried once again to eat his dinner.

By his third bite, Nick could stand it no longer. Used to his house being quiet, he hopped up on the pretense of telling them to keep it down so he could eat. Making a beeline for the swinging door, he opened it to find three sets of surprised eyes looking at him as if he were the abominable snowman.

"Are we bothering you?" Myla asked, jumping up to take the glass he had in his hand. "Can I get you anything?"

Nick threw up his hands. "Yeah, a chair. You all are having entirely too much fun in here. I decided I'd better eat in here with you, just so we could avoid anymore surprises like last night's."

"Sure!" Patrick patted the stool nearest him. "Come on in, Mr. Nick. We don't mind him eating with us, do we, Mom?"

"Of course not," Myla replied softly. "After all, this is his house. He can eat in any room he chooses."

Nick's smile spread across his face like cream over strawberries. "I'll go get my food."

In a few minutes, he was settled in, packing away Myla's dinner like a man starved. Between bites, he regaled the children with tales of the adventures of Lydia and Nick as they were growing up.

"See this scar?" He showed Jesse a faint white dent right in the middle of his forehead. "Lydia gave me that with a roller skate. Had to have seven stitches. Mother made both of us go to bed early for a month."

"Why'd she hit you with a roller skate?" Jesse asked, her hoarseness making her voice soft-pitched.

"I chased her with a granddaddy long-legs," he explained, a grin encasing his face. "She hates spiders."

"I'm not scared of bugs," Jesse stated. "We lived in the country. I played with bugs all the time."

"Yeah, but we don't have that house no more, Jesse," Patrick reminded his sister. "It was repo—repur—"

"Repossessed," Myla finished, the flush on her cheeks indicating her discomfort. "Hush up now, and finish your dinner. We have to get up early tomorrow to get you both enrolled in school."

Nick steered the conversation away from the house they'd lost. "School? You two are too smart for that, aren't you?"

"Lydia's helping me get them straightened out," Myla said over the children's giggles. "She's been such a help—she's even looking into low-cost housing in this district, in case I don't get into Magnolia House."

"Trust good ol' Lydia," Nick replied.

Wondering why he sounded so sarcastic, Myla said, "You don't share the same strong faith as your sister, do you?"

Shocked by her directness, Nick became defensive. "I've learned to rely on myself. I don't need to turn to a higher being to help me through life."

Myla leaned forward on her stool, her voice quiet. "Being self-reliant is good. After all, the Lord gave us brains. But sometimes, Nick, we can't do it all by ourselves. We need His help. And it's all right to ask for it."

She could see the anger sparking through his eyes.

"I don't need His help." Waving his arms, he spanned the room. "As you can see, I'm doing okay on my own."

She nodded. "Oh, yes, you're doing great material-wise. But what about spiritually? You don't like Christmas. Why is that, Nick?"

"That's none of your business," he said, getting up to stomp to the sink. "Your job is to run this house efficiently, not delve into my personal life."

She followed him. "Of course. You make perfect sense." She started stacking the dishes he absently handed her. "But then, you're in charge, right?"

"And what does that mean?" They stood shoulder to shoulder, heads up, eyes flashing.

"I know what's expected of me here, Nick. I work for you and

I intend to do a thorough job. But I can't help but notice you don't have a strong sense of faith. That bothers me.''

Wanting to turn the tables on her, he said, ''Yeah, well, you need to be more concerned with your own problems. After all, you're the one without a home!''

Hurt, she said, ''I'll find one. And I'll find a good job, too.''

He groaned as she almost sliced his palm with a knife in her haste to load the dishwasher. ''You'll barely make ends meet, Myla. It's going to be a struggle.''

''I'll manage,'' she retorted. ''I have a higher help than you'll ever know.''

''Oh, that's right. Your faith. Well, faith won't get you through a cold winter night, now will it?''

''It did,'' she replied calmly. ''I prayed for help and the Lord sent it.'' She gave him a meaningful look.

''Fine,'' he said, sighing in defeat. ''So, why can't you just do the job you were hired to do, instead of wasting your time trying to save me?''

''I just thought you could use a friend.''

''I don't need a friend, and you need to concentrate on getting your own life back in order.''

''I will, but in the meantime, if you need to talk…''

''I don't need anything, Myla.'' Trying to change the focus back to her, he added, ''I'm willing to help you in any way I can, though. And I'm worried about you moving into that homeless shelter too soon. Having faith is one thing, but surviving is quite another.''

''I would think you'd want me to move out,'' she replied. ''You spout all this encouragement, then hand me a few checks to cover your own embarrassment. I'm trying to start over—on my own, and while I appreciate everything you and Lydia and your friends are doing, I have to do this for myself. If that means giving myself over to blind faith, if that means putting my trust in the Lord, then I can do it. I won't let anyone ever make me question my faith again.'' She stopped loading dishes to stare across the room at her two suddenly quiet children.

''What do you mean?'' Nick asked, his hand on her arm. ''What happened between you and your husband, Myla?''

"I...we'll talk later, maybe." Pulling away, she called to the children. "Jesse, Patrick, time for bed."

Patrick immediately followed Myla to Henny's room, but Jesse held back. Running up to Nick, she tugged on his jeans. "Daddy wasn't a bad man, Mr. Nick. Momma told us to always remember that. My Daddy wasn't a bad man. He just had some problems, is all."

"Jesse!" Myla's voice echoed through the house.

The little girl ran away before Nick could question her further. What did all this mean? Up until now, he'd believed Myla to be a grieving widow, but there was obviously more to this.

"Who are you really protecting, Myla?" he whispered. "Yourself and your children? Or your dead husband?"

# Chapter Four

The next week passed in a busy rush for Myla. After getting the children back in school, and finding a church nearby to attend while she was working for Nick, she fell into the daily routine of cleaning and cooking, and learning more about Nick's life. Each detail drew her closer to the man who'd reluctantly saved her from the streets, and each detail showed her that Nick needed to find his own faith again. He'd refused her invitation to attend church.

"I send them a hefty check each month," he informed her. "I catch up on paperwork on Sundays."

"You should rest, and spend the day in worship," she replied. And have some fun, she wanted to add.

He'd shot her one of his famous scowls, but his words hadn't been as harsh as he'd have her believe. "You should mind your own business."

"Yes, sir." She certainly knew her place, and she needed the money. She'd have to be more cautious in her resolve to help him spiritually. And more cautious about her growing feelings for her employer.

But how could she resist being drawn to this intriguing man? She watched him leaving the house in a hurry each morning at the crack of dawn. He hardly bothered to stop and sip the coffee and orange juice she had waiting. She watched him come dragging in at night to wolf down the dinners she prepared before he went straight into his spacious office and clicked on the computer. Nick often worked long into the night. She knew, because she couldn't sleep very well in her new surroundings and she'd seen the light on in his office many times.

Myla had had an instinctive urge to go and check on Nick in the middle of the night, the way she used to do with her late husband. But that wasn't part of her official duties. And neither was being so attracted to him.

Her duties this morning involved cleaning the master bedroom. As she stood in the wide upper hallway, she prayed for guidance.

*Dear Lord, give me the strength to get my work done, and not think about the man who's helped me so much.*

But the minute she entered the big masculine room decorated with tasteful plaids and subtle stripes, Nick's presence shouted out at her. His suit from yesterday was draped across the standing valet. Out of habit, she brushed it out and hung it up, so he could wear it once more before she took it to the cleaners.

His shoes were shelved in the long, well-lit closet off the dressing room. He had several pairs, some black and brown leather, some gleaming white athletics, all expensive and classic in design, just like their owner. His shirt, impeccably white, was tossed on a chair, waiting to be laundered and pressed at the cleaners, along with all his other tailored shirts.

So much about Nick's habits reminded her of Sonny. Sonny had been a perfectionist, almost fanatical in his demands. Nick wasn't quite that bad, as far as she could tell. He demanded loyalty, hard work, and the best in everything—but he demanded those things in himself first and foremost.

Myla picked up the shirt, catching the scent of his spicy, crisp aftershave. The shirt spoke of the man. Solid, honest, clean. And lost. He was a good man, but he was a lonely, sad man. His quiet, aloof nature drew her to him, then his rare burst through smiles and dry humor held her.

She couldn't fight her feelings, but she reminded herself she'd been on the bottom for so long, coming up for air was scary. She couldn't read anything into Nick's smiles and concerned gestures. He was just being kind. And he was used to having someone wait on him hand and foot. He was selfish and stubborn at times, and other times, he was caring and compassionate. Just his nature. She didn't think she was ready to deal with another domineering male just yet, though.

"Come on, Myla," she told herself as she hastily cleaned the large, elegant room. "You work for him. He gave you a job and a place to stay and food for your children. Nothing more. He owes you nothing."

Since she was alone in a twenty-room mansion, she could talk out loud. "And I owe him everything."

Silently, she thanked the Lord for giving her this reprieve and remembered that she'd promised to do things differently this time.

Moving into the bathroom, she cleaned the large garden tub with a new vigor, putting images of Nick Rudolph's handsome face out of her mind. Then she hurried out of the room, determined to stick to business.

And ran right smack into the arms of the very man she was trying to escape.

Myla's dust rag and cleaning supplies went in one direction and her armful of laundry went in the other as she plowed into Nick, sending him back against the sturdy oak railing on the second floor landing.

Catching her just as his back hit the banister, Nick gripped her shoulders to keep both of them from toppling down the stairs. "Goodness, is there a fire in there?"

She leaned against him in relief. "Nick, you scared me!"

"I'll say. Are you all right?"

Myla glanced up at him, embarrassed and acutely aware of his arms holding her. She had to learn not to be so clumsy! "I'm fine. What are you doing home so early?"

Nick hesitated, his smile as wry as ever. Then she noticed with a mother's keen eye, he looked flushed and his dark eyes were glazed over with a red-rimmed heat.

Concerned, she automatically put a palm to his forehead. "Why, you're burning up with fever!"

He pushed her away with a gentle shove. "Tell me something I don't know. Don't get too close. According to my friend and racquetball partner, Dr. Loeffler, I've got the flu. That's the only way he'd ever beat me and he knows it."

Myla kicked her scattered cleaning supplies out of the way and steered him toward his room. "You went to work like this, and played racquetball! Honestly, don't you ever know when to quit?"

He drew his brows together, amused at her righteous indignation and her bossy nature. "I felt kind of tired this morning, but things got progressively worse as the day wore on. Dr. Loeffler checked me over after our game and told me to get home. Guess he couldn't believe he'd actually beaten me."

Myla clucked over him with all the vigor of a mother hen. "Will you stop making jokes and get into bed? I'll make you some chicken soup and get you some medicine for that fever. What did the doctor tell you to do?"

Nick gave her a lopsided grin. "He told me to let a beautiful woman serve me chicken soup and give me something for my fever."

Laughter bubbled in her throat, but she managed to keep her tone stern. "You're impossible. You'd better be all tucked in when I come back."

"Yes, ma'am, Nurse Myla."

She put both hands on her hips. "And don't expect me to baby you. I'm busy and you need to rest. I know you must really feel horrible. You never come home early."

He sent her a mock scowl. "No, I don't, but I still intend to get some work done. So, hand me my briefcase before you head down to concoct your flu survival kit."

Hissing her disapproval, she picked up the heavy leather satchel he'd left on a chair. Shoving it at his midsection, she said, "You do love your work, that's for sure."

Nick watched as she pranced out of the room, then he dropped like a lead weight onto the big bed. Holding his hands around the stuffed briefcase, he nodded to himself. He did love his work, but right now it was the last thing on his mind.

He fell back in a heap against the fluffy plaid pillows. Well, if a man's gotta be sick, he reflected with a grin, at least it helps to have a spunky redheaded nurse waiting on him hand and foot. This might turn out to be a good thing. He could actually enjoy being here, that is, if his body would just stop hurting all over.

\* \* \*

A few minutes later, Myla was back with the promised soup and medicine, glad to see he was dressed in a blue sweat suit. He sat propped against pillows with paperwork scattered all around him, and a laptop computer centered in front of him on the bed.

"Are you going to eat and then rest?" she questioned as she set the bed tray down in front of him, then pulled the laptop away.

Giving her a mock angry glare, he brought the laptop back beside him. "Can you spoon-feed me?" he teased, enjoying the way her denim skirt whirled around her boots as she fussed with his discarded clothes.

"I don't think so," she retorted, a smile creasing her lips in spite of her reprimanding look. "You don't seem that weak to me."

"Gee, such a caring nurse."

"I'm sorry," she finally said, taking his droll humor seriously. "I'm just not used to you being home during the day. You've thrown me completely off schedule."

Nick knew his smile was awfully smug. He'd also brought a becoming blush to her apple cheeks. He liked knowing that his presence distracted her. That meant she was interested. Although, he reassured himself as he watched the winter sun dancing off her radiant auburn hair, he really didn't have time to indulge in a relationship. And he had no earthly idea where this one was going.

He put the laptop aside, then sampled the soup before sitting back to stare up at her. "I think you're just not used to me, period. But I'd say, all in all, this arrangement is working out okay. Other than that one unfortunate incident with Shredder and that overgrown puppy of Carolyn's, you and the children haven't been any trouble, if that's what you're worried about."

"I'm not," she said, backing away, memories of being in his arms in the middle of the kitchen floor reminding her that she needed to concentrate on her job. "I'd better get back to work."

"Myla, wait." He gave her a questioning look. "Tell me how you do it?"

A look of confusion colored her green eyes. "Do what?"

"Keep that serene expression on your face. After everything you've been through, including putting up with my demands, you seem so at peace."

She looked up then, her not-so-serene gaze meeting his. "I found my strength again," she said simply. "I found my faith again, after I thought I'd lost it forever."

Uncomfortable with this turn in the conversation, he said, "How'd you manage a thing like that?"

She lifted her chin. "Prayer. You know, Nick, when you have nothing left, you always have prayer."

No, he didn't know that. It had been a very long time since he'd relied on prayer. "Why...how did you lose your strength?"

She backed farther away, like a frightened bird about to take flight. "I don't want to discuss that."

"I'd really like to know...and to understand."

When she didn't answer immediately, he said, "Look, I'll take my medicine, and I promise I'll eat my soup. Sit down in that chair over there and talk to me."

Myla hesitated only a minute. Wanting him to see that he, too, could find his strength in faith, she sat down and watched as he diligently took two pills with a glass of juice; then, his eyes on her, he dutifully ate his soup.

Satisfied that he'd finish the soup, she leaned back for a minute. "You see, at one time, I thought God had abandoned me."

Surprised, he stopped eating. Funny, he'd thought that very thing himself, right after burying his father. "Why would you think that? You seem so sure about all this religious stuff."

She lowered her head, her hands wringing together, her eyes misty with memories. "I wasn't so sure for a while. Because of something I did, or rather, something I didn't do—and I'd rather not talk about it. It took me a long time to see that God hadn't abandoned me. It was the other way around."

"You mean, you abandoned Him?"

She nodded. "I gave up on Him. I didn't think I was worthy of His love."

"Why would you think a thing like that?"

"I had it drummed into me enough," she said, then gasped. "Oh, never mind. I shouldn't have said that."

"Well, you did. What do you mean?"

When she didn't speak, Nick sat up to stare across at her. "Does this have something to do with your husband?"

Her silence told him everything he needed to know. And brought out all the protective instincts he'd tried so hard to ignore. "Myla, did your husband do something to hurt you?"

Myla didn't want to cry. She'd learned not to cry. But now, after she'd heard Nick voice the truth, her worst secrets floated up to the surface of her consciousness, causing the tears to roll down her cheeks like a torrent of rain coming from a black cloud. Holding her eyes tightly shut, she tried to block out the painful memories. She couldn't let him see her like this. Lifting out of the chair, she said, "I need to get back to work."

Nick moved his tray away with a clatter and stood up. "Myla, did you and he...was it a good marriage?"

She bit her bottom lip, then gave him a soul-weary look. "In the beginning, yes. But, it turned ugly after a few years."

Nick closed his eyes, then opened them to look at her with dread. "Did he...did he abuse you?"

She brought her hands up to her face and cried softly.

Nick pulled her hands away, his eyes searching her face. "Did he?"

"No, not physically," she said, her hands automatically gripping his. "Nick, please don't make me talk about this now." She didn't want the bond they had developed to be destroyed, not yet.

"I want...I need to know," he said, his voice husky, his words gentle. "I won't judge you, Myla."

But she was afraid he would, just as so many others had. "I'm...not ready to tell you everything."

The pain in her green eyes stopped Nick from pushing her any further. Instead, he said, "What can I do, to help you?"

She looked up at him, unable to ask for his help, unable to ask for his understanding.

But Nick knew instinctively that she needed both. So before she could bolt, he tugged her into his arms and rocked her gently, as if she were a child who needed reassuring. "No more questions," he promised. "But if you want to cry, you go right ahead."

Myla did cry. Shutting her eyes tightly closed, she let him hold her for a while, thankful that he didn't press her any further about her marriage. Just to be held, unconditionally, that was comfort enough for now.

"All right," he said after a while, letting go to pat her shoulder.

"Feel better now?" At her silent nod, he added, "You can't keep this inside. Lydia knows people, therapists and counselors, who can help you. And...I want to help, too."

She lifted her head, then wiped her eyes with the back of her hand, resolve settling back over her like a protective winter cloak. With a shaky smile, she said, "You're a fine one to be giving me advice. I am a lot better now, though, really."

He looked doubtful. "How can you say that?"

"I told you, I found my faith again—alone, on a dark cold night. I was huddled in the car with the children, with nothing left... nothing. In the moonlight, I saw my worn Bible lying on the dashboard. I hadn't read it in months. I did that night, though, with a flashlight. While my children slept in the cold, I found my faith again in that single beam of light, and I cried long and hard, and I prayed, really prayed, for the first time in a very long time."

Nick swallowed back the lump forming in his throat. "What did you find there in that light, that helped you?"

She sniffed, then lifted her head. "He said He would not leave me comfortless, but I had forgotten that promise. In First Corinthians, chapter thirteen, verse thirteen, the Bible says, 'And now abideth faith, hope, love, these three: but the greatest of these is love'."

Nick stood there, his heart trembling. Love. The one thing he'd been so afraid of since his father's breakdown and death. "How did that verse sustain you?"

She smiled then. "I knew that no matter what, I had my children with me and I loved them above all else, except the Lord. They were my gift, and no matter what kind of life I'd had with their father, they were my responsibility. Love, Nick. Love is the greatest gift of all. It gives us our strength. It gives us a reason to go on living, even when we'd rather curl up and sleep. I realized that God gave us unconditional love when He sent His son to save us from our sins. I realized that God hadn't abandoned me. He was reaching out to me on that dark night."

Nick sighed, his own fears cresting in the midst of her eloquent story. "But...unconditional love is so hard to give and so very hard to expect. To love so completely, you have to give up so much control. How can you trust something that abstract, something that can make you seem so weak?"

"That's the whole point," she said, her expression changing from sorrowful to hopeful. "Love doesn't make us weak, Nick. Love gives us the strength to go on. That night, alone and afraid, I remembered God's unconditional love for me. I'd lost that, as well as my trust. I'd been emotionally stripped of that love and that trust, by a man who didn't know how to give either."

"Your husband."

She nodded, then stepped back. "I'm all right now. I won't be afraid of the dark, ever again. I made a promise to take care of my children. They don't deserve to have to live like this—they didn't do anything wrong."

"Neither did you. You seem so brave. Is that for your children's sake?"

"I have to be strong, for them."

Nick felt his heart melting in half. He'd never seen such a fierce defense of love, or heard such a strong testimony. She had come to him with nothing, yet she had more to give than any woman he'd ever known. "Is there anything I can do?"

Unable to look at him, Myla couldn't speak about her pain. Leaning close, she whispered, "Just hold me again."

He did, for a long while, his arms wrapping her in what little protection he could offer. Finally, he brought a hand up to her chin so he could wipe her tears away. Gazing down at her, Nick wanted badly to kiss her.

But Myla stood back, her voice clear once again. "You'd better rest. And I'd better get away from you. I don't have time to get the flu."

He laughed at that. "Always the practical one." Leaning back down on the bed, he added, "I am feeling a little wobbly. Are you sure you're all right?"

"I'm fine now," she said as she lifted his tray away, her eyes downcast. "Do you need anything else?"

He looked up at her, thinking how right it seemed to have her here with him, thinking he needed her strength. "No, thanks. You've spoiled me quite enough, I believe."

His words soothed Myla like a balm. "Nick?" she called from the door.

"Hmmm?"

"Thank you, for understanding."

He wanted to tell her he didn't understand, really. But the weight of sleep blocked out his reply. He didn't understand how one minute he could be so sure, so secure in his firm, smug convictions, then the next, begin to doubt everything he stood for.

He wasn't as fearful as he should be. He wasn't so much afraid of reaching out for love now. Myla had done that for him. She'd opened up her heart and told him a story of faith that left him humbled and ashamed. For so long now, he'd been afraid of the power of love. He'd believed loving someone could make a person weak, just as his grieving, dying father had become. But he'd been so very wrong. Nick needed to hold Myla again, just to be held himself.

Instead, he reached for his pillow and buried his dreams and his doubts in a deep, troubled sleep.

Nick woke hours later to find his room dark, except for the flickering light from the fire someone had lit in the sitting area fireplace. The room was cozy, but a flash of thunder and lightning told of the wintry chill settling over the city. He shuddered to think Myla and her children could have been out there, alone, in that cold night. And he wondered how many people were cold and shivering and afraid this night.

Groaning, Nick rolled over, acutely aware of his own discomfort. This was a mean flu bug, that was for sure.

His throat felt like he'd swallowed a jalapeño pepper and his head throbbed with each beat of his pulse. Craving a long, hot shower, he rose to calculate the distance to the bathroom. A bold knock hit the bedroom door before he could attempt the trip, causing a ricocheting rumble in his head.

"Come in," he called in a raspy voice.

Lydia popped her head in the door. "Well, big brother, sleeping the day away won't get your Christmas shopping done."

He moaned, rolling over to face the fire. "Go away."

"Glad you're feeling better," she replied as she tossed him a bag of prescription medicines. "Dr. Loeffler sent you these—antibiotics and a decongestant. He said to take all of it."

"He's just trying to poison me so I won't beat him at racquetball again.'' Giving her a false smile, he added, ''I don't like being sick.''

Lydia handed him two drawings. ''Maybe these will cheer you up.''

Nick grinned. Jesse had reproduced the kitchen disaster, complete with Shredder sitting on the ceiling fan and Pooky lapping away amidst a pile of food. Patrick had drawn a Christmas tree loaded with colorful gifts.

''Your two biggest fans send their regards. Aren't those two adorable?''

Nick laid the pictures on the nightstand. ''Yeah, and very well-behaved, as far as children go. Lydia, has Myla told you anything about their past?''

''A little. Why?''

''We had a long talk today. She's had a rough time, but she won't tell me exactly what happened in her marriage.''

Lydia sat down to stare at her brother. ''Well, don't press her. I introduced her to Reverend Hillard. I'm sure he can give her some spiritual guidance.''

''Maybe,'' Nick said, remembering the story Myla had told him. ''But I think her faith's intact. It's her self-esteem I'm worried about.''

Lydia sat up, her eyes squinting toward him. ''You're worse off than I thought. Did I hear you say something good about someone's faith? And that you're actually aware of another person's mental stability?''

He nodded, then shot her a wry smile. ''Yes, you did. I want to help her, Lydia. She's a good woman.''

''Well, praise the Lord.'' Lydia hopped up to give her brother a breath-stopping hug. ''Oh, Nicky, I knew you'd come around. You really want to help, really, really?''

''Yes, really, really,'' he said, laughing. ''I'd be a real Scrooge if I didn't see how much Myla and her children have been through. But don't make more out of this than it is. I think this flu's gone to my head.''

''Or maybe Myla's gone to your heart,'' Lydia said softly. ''After all, it is Christmas. A time for miracles.''

He patted her on the back. ''I'd forgotten what a joyous time it can be. And I'm sorry, really sorry, for being so hard to live with since Father's death.''

She kissed him on the temple. ''No need to apologize. Welcome back, Nick.''

When Nick came out of the bathroom, his food was sitting on a tray in front of the leather armchair by the fireplace. Glancing around, he was disappointed that Myla wasn't there to make sure he ate everything on his plate. He still had a lot of questions to ask her.

Lydia was right. He did have a soft spot in his heart for Myla and her two children. And the spot was opening to include other possibilities such as attending church and opening the Bible he'd tossed aside years ago.

He should be scared, yet when he searched for the old fear, he only found a new, growing strength. Now, he was beginning to dread the time when Myla would have to leave.

Two weeks until Christmas. Usually, this old house was hushed and quiet around this time of year, haunted by the memory of his parents. Not this year. This year, things were going to be different.

A soft knock at the door caused him to put down the spoonful of beef stew he'd been about to eat. Two reddish blond heads bobbed just above the ornate door handle. Patrick and Jesse eyed him curiously.

''You two going to stand out in the hall all night, or are you going to get in here before your mother catches you?''

''We ain't supposed to be here,'' Patrick said in a small whisper. ''But we wanted to say hi.''

''It's *aren't*—we *aren't* supposed to be here,'' Jesse corrected as she pushed Patrick into the room.

Patrick made a face at his sister's redundancy. ''I know that. That's what I just said.''

''Where's your mother?'' Nick asked, smiling at them.

Jesse tossed her ponytail. ''Talking to Miss Lydia. Mama's gonna go to school at night and she's looking for another job, for when Miss Henny comes home. We'll just have to live in the shelter for a while, that's all.''

Nick didn't want to think about that, so he changed the subject to more pleasant things. "Well, Santa'll be coming soon," he said, hoping to find two worthy allies in the children. "What do you want him to bring you?"

Both children rushed to his side, talking at once. Nick heard it all, registered each request and vowed to travel to the North Pole if he had to, just to get them all the loot they wanted.

"And what about your mom?"

"Oh, that's kinda hard," Jesse said, giggling. "Mama wants stuff you can't find in the mall."

"Yeah, like what?"

Jesse settled down on the floor, wiping her nose with her hand. "She wants a house, of course. She talks about having a home of her own again. And she wants a job. She doesn't like not having any money. Oh, and once, she told us she'd like a long soak in a tub of hot water, then get dressed up in a pretty green dress for a special Christmas dinner. She loves to cook, you know."

Nick once again marveled at the simple things he'd taken for granted. Clearing his suddenly clogged throat, he said, "Are you sure that's all she wants?"

Thinking for a minute, her nose scrunched, Jesse held her hands wide. "Oh, and roses. She loves yellow roses."

Patrick nodded. "Yeah, and one day, Daddy got real mad and mowed all of hers down."

Nick went still inside. Trying to keep his tone light and casual, he asked, "Why would he do a thing like that?"

"'Cause she didn't have dinner ready on time," Jesse said in a matter-of-fact voice. "She cried when he wasn't looking."

Dinner. No wonder she'd tried so hard to make his dinner party a success. No wonder she'd been so shaken when it had gone bad. She was used to fixing things up, hiding her fear behind a false bravado.

Patrick pulled on Nick's sleeve, bringing him out of his numbed state. "I don't want much, Mr. Nick. I just wish we didn't have to leave here, ever."

Nick was beginning to wish that very same thing.

Before Nick could reply, however, the door swung open and Myla stomped into the room, a mother's wrath apparent in her expression. "What in the world! You two are supposed to be in bed! How'd you get up here?"

"We snuck by you," Patrick blurted out in spite of his sister's glaring look.

"That's obvious enough." Myla pointed a finger toward the door. "Get back downstairs with Miss Lydia. Do you both want to catch the flu?"

"I didn't breathe on them," Nick said, glad to find a light moment in the children's misdeeds. "And I'm glad they came by for a visit. I was getting downright lonely."

"Want us to stay awhile?" Patrick offered hopefully.

"No, he doesn't," his mother interjected. "Go on down. I'll come and read to you and help you with your prayers in a little while."

Nick managed a chuckle as he watched the children scoot out of the room. "Well, you certainly got rid of those two varmints."

She looked at his half-eaten food. "Why didn't you eat your supper?"

"I wasn't very hungry."

"Are you feeling better?"

"A little. I heard you and Lydia were plotting down there."

"Planning," she corrected. "There's a difference."

"I've never looked at it that way."

She started to take the tray, but his hand shot out to stop her. "Myla, could we talk some more?"

"No," she said, not daring to look at him. "I'd rather not."

"I won't press you about your life before," he said. "I just have some questions, about…this unconditional love about which you speak so highly."

She glanced up then, her eyes wide. "You want to discuss… religion?"

"Yes," he said, smiling slightly. "I think I'd like that."

And so they talked. She told him the stories of the Bible that he'd forgotten. As she talked, memories washed over him; memories of his mother, telling him these very same stories, her faith as strong and as shining as Myla's. How could he have forgotten the beauty in that? How could he have let it slip so far away?

After Myla said a gentle prayer for him to feel better, both physically and spiritually, he sat in the darkness alone, watching the fire. And realized he was tired of being alone in the dark.

Then it hit him—Myla had said something earlier about being afraid of the darkness. They were so alike, he and his Myla. They'd both been out in the cold for too long. Together, maybe they could find the warmth of that unconditional love she'd told him about. Together, with the help of a higher being watching over them.

Outside, the rain fell in cold, indiscriminate sheets and Nick shuddered, thinking again that she might have been out there tonight, all alone and frightened.

But she wasn't out there. For some strange reason, God had sent her to him instead. He wouldn't take that obligation lightly.

"Not again, Myla," he whispered to the fire. "Not ever again, if I can help it."

Then he did something he hadn't done in a very long time. He folded his hands and he prayed.

# *Chapter Five*

❧

It was well past midnight. Myla tiptoed into the kitchen, careful not to wake the children sleeping in the bedroom just down the narrow back hallway. With Nick being home sick the last couple of days, her mind was in turmoil. Sleep was impossible.

She didn't want to admit that she'd enjoyed playing nurse to him. The first morning, they'd talked and laughed together, sitting on the sunporch off the second-story hallway. Nick had insisted she sit with him while he had breakfast. It had been a comfortable, cozy distraction, complete with frolicking squirrels putting on a show in the great oaks lining the sloping backyard. Then, later in the day when he'd woken up feeling better, he'd come downstairs to eat a sandwich in the kitchen, reading the paper in silence while she went about her work. So domestic, so homey. So *wrong,* Myla reminded herself.

Setting the bags she carried on the counter, she pulled out the small treasures her first paycheck from Nick had allowed her to buy for her children. This would take her mind off of dreaming about a man she shouldn't be thinking about.

A sweater set for Jesse—pink-and-blue striped with little white bows on the Peter Pan collar. An inexpensive fashion doll with two sets of clothes. Some new jeans and an action toy for Patrick, along with a set of army men with tanks and jeeps. It wasn't much, but they'd have something under the tree. This year especially, it was important to her that her children understand the real Christmas celebration, so she didn't want to make a big deal out of gift giving. Yet she couldn't help but breathe a sigh of relief tonight.

She'd had horrible visions of them spending Christmas out in the cold, or in a shelter. Now, thanks to Nick's kindness, they were going to be celebrating Christmas in this beautiful, rambling house. Thinking of how lucky they were to be safe and warm, she stood there letting the tears fall freely.

And that's how Nick found her.

Her back was turned toward him and she was wearing a worn, thick flannel robe, pink with blue faded flowers and small red heart-shaped designs which, in the moon's soft spotlight, reminded him of aged paper valentines. He felt as if he could watch her forever, but when he heard her soft intake of breath and saw her wipe at a tear, he went to her, touching her lightly on the arm.

"Are you all right?"

Myla jumped at his touch, surprise widening her eyes. "Nick! What are you doing up?"

"Shredder woke me. That sneaky cat's taken a liking to me, I believe. He's also taken a liking to the foot of my bed, where I left him fast asleep."

She laughed then, but the laughter turned back to tears. "I'm sorry. I've been so emotional lately. Christmas always does that to me, but this year…well, I have a lot to be thankful for."

Nick once again felt the sharp contrast in her world and his own. "I can't imagine what it must have been like for you, out there. You're very courageous."

She sniffed back her tears. "Hardly. When it comes to survival, you just do what you've got to do."

"You're starting over," he said, careful of how he worded his next request. "Don't you think it's time you really left the past behind? Tell me everything about your marriage, Myla."

She looked up, deciding there in the darkness she could trust him with the truth. "Yes, I think it's time to move on, and I guess talking about it would help." Then she gave him one last chance. "Are you sure you want me to burden you with the sordid details, though?"

"Burden away," he replied, his voice quiet and encouraging. "I won't be able to sleep if you don't tell me what's made you so sad.''

She took a deep breath, then brought a hand up to play with one of the buttons on the front of her robe. ''My husband deceived all of us. Sonny was a big fake, in complete control. And he had me trained as his robot. He even had the children trained, too. Only I didn't see it until it was too late.''

''Tell me why.''

She leaned back against the counter, her eyes shining. ''I wish I knew why. Why I let him do the things he did, why I let him make me feel so small and helpless. Looking back, I think it was my need to please—my family, his family, our friends, him. I wanted to be a good wife, a good mother. That was my only ambition in life, because that's all Sonny wanted me to be. He'd convinced me that I wasn't very good at anything, but I thought at least I could be good at that. As it turned out, I didn't do such a hot job.''

Nick took one of her hands. ''Hey, who's doubting now? I can't believe you'd let anyone make you doubt yourself like that. You seem so capable, so strong.''

''I wasn't always so surefooted,'' she said in a whisper. ''I did have doubts, and I'm so ashamed of what I let happen.''

He shook his head. ''It can't be that bad.''

Pulling away, she headed to the refrigerator to pour two glasses of juice. Then she found the cookie jar and placed two fresh oatmeal cookies on a napkin for Nick. ''It's so bad, I'm still ashamed to talk about it. Nick, Sonny embezzled funds from the bank he managed, and when the authorities found out…he committed suicide in his fancy car.''

Nick could only stand there staring at her. The background check had only listed her as a bankrupt widow, just as she'd told him. ''Myla, I had no idea.''

''No, how could you? No one did. We went to church every Sunday, we had a nice ranch house in the country. We had everything. But it was all a sham. Sonny only played at being a Christian. He used church for networking and finding new clients. And when that didn't bring in enough money, he turned to crime.

''He had this obsessive need to always have more. More money, more power, all of the latest things—cellular phones, computers, any kind of gadget that would make him look successful. He never spent much time with the children—he had very little patience with them—but then he'd buy them all sorts of expensive toys to win their affection after he'd treated them badly. And I...I was so blind, so convinced that I had to work harder, try harder to be the perfect little wife, I didn't see that he was suffering, until it was too late. I never wanted more money or things. I wanted more of him, emotionally. But he couldn't give me that. And I didn't do anything to save him.''

"But it's not your fault—''

"Yes,'' she said, bobbing her head. "Yes, it is. And I've been running ever since. From my family, because they blame me. From my so-called friends, because they can't be seen with me anymore. From myself, because I can't stand to look in the mirror each day. I had to protect my children, and that's the only thing that kept me going, until that night when I realized I wasn't alone.'' Looking up at him, she said, "Then, not too long after that night, I found you.''

He turned to stand beside her as they both stared out into the bleak winter night. "So you've been struggling with this, all this time?''

She took a sip of juice, then set the glass down. "I kept thinking I should have done something to help Sonny.''

"Help him? What could you have done?''

She turned, both hands braced on the counter. "I should have followed my instincts when I suspected something was wrong. But Sonny was hard to deal with even on a good day. He'd threaten me by telling me that I wasn't a good wife, and that it was my fault he felt so much pressure. Then he'd tell me he'd leave and take the children. I...I began to doubt my own Christianity. I mean, here I'd lived with this man for years and I'd believed he truly felt the same way I did, but he didn't. He put up this big front, but it was all an act. And I was too afraid to do anything about it, so I did what I had to, to protect my children.''

"Why did you marry him?''

"I loved him, and I wanted a family. Sonny promised me we'd have a good life. He came from a wealthy family—his parents always overindulged him—and I'd never had very much. It seemed like a dream. And turned into a nightmare. After he...after he died,

I found out there was no money, no insurance, and most of the expensive things he'd bought got repossessed, right along with my house.''

She faced him squarely now, her pride gone right along with all the fancy possessions and high hopes she'd once had. ''I will always remember the day they came and locked up my house. The bank officer had been a friend of ours. He kept telling me how sorry he was, but he didn't really offer to make things any better. He was just doing his job.''

''You don't forget that feeling, you don't forget the scorn and pity you see on people's faces. Ever. That's why, this time I intend to do things my way, with the help of the Lord. I won't ever let anyone make me doubt myself or my faith again.''

Nick leaned close, his gaze sweeping her face. Unable to see his expression completely in the muted light, Myla waited, wondering if he, too, would turn away in disgust. But he didn't. Instead, he placed his hands on her face, his touch as soft as the moonlight, and then he kissed her.

The touch of his lips on hers was gentle, yet powerful. No one had reached out to her like this in a very long time. A soft, secure warmth spread through her, blocking out the cold night and the bad memories. As much as she needed this, Myla was still afraid to give in to the myriad feelings coursing through her system. She couldn't let herself become too dependent on this man's kindness.

Nick felt her tense up, heard the defeat in her soft sigh. Cupping his hands on her shoulders, he stared down at her. ''You don't have to doubt me, Myla. I know I was completely indifferent when we met, but I've changed a lot since then. I want to help you through this.''

She touched his face with her hand, hope warring with despair in her mind. ''I know you do. And you can, with your money, with your connections, but don't you see—that's the kind of help Sonny provided. He took care of me materially, but he was never there with me spiritually. I won't be a burden to anyone again. And I won't commit to anyone who can't go the distance with me. Right now, I'm still too battered to take things any further, Nick.''

Nick stood there holding her, wondering if he, too, was afraid to take things any further. He'd certainly done a complete turnaround.

But from the moment he'd looked into those luminous green eyes, he'd been hopelessly lost. Or maybe hopefully found.

Still struggling, still amazed, he said, "What about feelings? What about need?"

She gave him an imploring look. "Do you need me, Nick?"

"I think so," he said honestly. "But I'm moving into dangerous territory here. I've got to learn *how* to need someone."

Myla took their juice glasses to the sink, then turned to face him across the kitchen. "Maybe we both should step back and consider the consequences of our feelings. You've got everything a human could possibly need, but you've lost your faith. I've lost everything—all the comforts of home—but I've found my faith again. I won't have it stripped away, and I won't let you step in and take control the way Sonny always did."

"You think I'd do that to you?"

"No, you're not like him, but you're still fighting against your own feelings, and that could cause the same sort of resentment Sonny felt toward me. He teased me about my church work and my beliefs, then pretended he felt the same way when others were around. That hurt more than anything. I won't get into a battle of that kind with you. I won't make you choose. That has to be your own decision. And, needing me has to come from your heart, not from some sense of obligation or sympathy."

He moved across the kitchen to take her back into his arms. "I'm not so sure what I'm feeling right now, but I do know that it's not just an obligation to ease my hardened soul. I want to take care of you, but I understand how important it is for you to pull yourself out of this, both emotionally and financially. I should know—I've been doing that same thing since my father died."

"We've both been lost," Myla said, her gaze holding his.

Nick tugged her close then lifted a hand to touch her face again. "Right now, I don't feel so lost anymore." After a tender kiss, he told her, "But I do think I'm losing the battle, with you and with your mighty God."

"We have to be sure," she reminded him. "No matter how we feel about each other, there has to be a commitment to a third being in this relationship. That's the only way it can work."

Nick didn't reply. He knew she was right. She wouldn't live a lie again. This time, she wanted a commitment that meant turning control over to God, instead of letting another human being control her. It was a tall order, and one he'd have to give careful consideration and prayer.

"We'll make it work," he assured her. "We'll take it slow. I'm not a very patient man, but…I think I can learn to be."

Myla's heart soared as she gave him a chaste kiss on the cheek. "Thank you, for listening. And for not judging."

As he watched her walk down the hall, her long red hair trailing around her neck, Nick realized she might be the one without a place to live, but he was the one without a home.


"Mama, Mama, can we get up now?"

Myla rolled over, opening her eyes slowly to find her children sitting up in bed, watching her as if she knew all the secrets to life. Moaning, she sat up to wipe hair out of her eyes. "What time is it?"

"Six o'clock," Jesse said, reaching out to hug Myla tightly. "Can we please see what Santa brought?"

Christmas morning. Myla hugged Jesse against her. "Sure, honey. Just let me get the sleep out of my eyes."

As the children jumped up and down in glee, Myla thought about the Christmas Eve service they'd all attended last night, including Nick.

"It's his first time in ten years," Lydia had explained, tears in her eyes. "Oh, Myla, this is the happiest Christmas we've had in a long time."

It had been happy for Myla, too. Reverend Hillard was a wonderful, compassionate preacher and a good listener. He'd helped her deal with her past through prayer and positive discussions. Then, to relive the Christmas miracle, to see the shining faces of faith in the muted light of hundreds of candles, had only renewed her own faith and strength. She'd come so far with God's help, and now, Nick, too, seemed to be finding a new strength. Could it be possible that God had brought them together to help each other heal?

But she had to remind herself, she was still fearful of depending too much on anyone else to help her back on her feet. Especially Nick, since he still seemed so unsure himself.

After church, he'd dropped them off back at the house, then after making some excuse about putting in an obligatory appearance, had headed out to a party at Carolyn's. Myla had never felt so lonely, sitting there watching her children sleep. Was Nick still fighting his feelings? Did seeing Carolyn only reinforce his need to stay in control?

But, Myla groggily reminded herself this morning, she had no hold over Nick, and soon, she'd be moving out anyway. God had a purpose for her, but maybe that purpose wasn't for Nick and her to be together. She'd have to leave that in God's hands.

"Mom, hurry," Patrick whined from his perch at the foot of the bed, his cartoon character pajamas as bright as the glow in his eyes.

"Hold on, sweetie." As she washed her face and tugged on her clothes, Myla said a prayer for guidance.

*Help me to do Your will, and guide me in my feelings for Nick. If You want us to be together, give Nick the strength to learn to love. Show me the way, Lord, and give me the courage to walk away from him if I have to make that choice.*

"Get up, Nick!"

Lydia yanked the covers back, sending a cold rush of air into Nick's warm, sleep-covered world.

"Why do you always have to stalk into my bedroom and bother me?" he asked, groping for the blankets as he took in her bright red flannel pajamas. "And do you have to look so jolly?"

Lydia held the blankets away. "I heard the pitter-patter of little feet downstairs. You wanted to be awake and alert for the big event, remember?"

"I remember."

"Well, get moving. I want to see them when they find all that loot you bought for them."

He'd only meant to buy the children a few toys, not a truckload. "Did I go overboard?"

"That's an understatement, big brother. But I seriously doubt the local toy store is complaining. You made them go over the top in sales, I'm sure."

Nick sat up, then gave his sister a sleepy stare. "Lydia, I've been meaning to ask you—has Myla talked to you any more about her marriage?''

Lydia's usually perky face became guarded. ''What do you mean?''

''She has, hasn't she? Lydia, I want to know what's going on with her. I mean, she told me what happened, with her husband's suicide and all. But, I need to know—is she healing now? Or does she still feel guilty?''

He didn't want to scare Myla away, but he had to know if she was really feeling better about things, because his own patience was wearing thin. He wanted to nurture her and protect her, yet he held back, waiting, hoping.

''That's very personal, Nick. And you know I can't discuss that with you.'' Sitting down on the bed, she said, ''Please, don't press her on this. Women who've been through that kind of pain…it takes a while for them to trust again.'' Maneuvering him back to the task at hand, she added, ''But, at least she's been receiving counseling from Reverend Hillard. That's so important for her state of mind.'' Then, changing the subject with expert ease, she added, ''And at least she can't fault *you* in the gift-giving department. Now, hurry up!''

Nick went into the bathroom to wash his face and toss on his clothes. Minutes later, he came back, dressed in khakis and a sweater, and worried that he'd made a big mistake. ''I just wanted them to have a good Christmas. Think Myla will mind?''

Lydia extended a hand to him as he emerged. ''Only one way to find out.'' Hugging him close, she said, ''Merry Christmas, Nick.''

The sound of squealing children greeted Nick and Lydia as they entered the double doors to the den. The room was in total chaos. Wrapping paper and toys decorated its usually sedate interior.

Lydia patted her brother's neck, then pushed him into the room. ''My, my, sure looks like Santa came here.''

Patrick looked up from the gigantic toy train that whistled as it sped around the Christmas tree. ''Look, Mr. Nick. Santa brought me a train and some boots and a farm set. How'd he know we used to live on a farm, anyway?''

''Santa's very smart,'' Nick said, his eyes meeting Myla's. She stood in the corner by the window, her expression tight-lipped, her face pale.

"He gave me a mermaid doll that sings," Jesse shouted, running up to Nick and Lydia to proudly display the beautiful doll. "And a dollhouse."

Lydia fell to the floor, exploring the treasures as if she were only eight years old herself. Holding up the less expensive doll Myla had bought for Jesse, she asked, "Who's this?"

"I don't know her name," Jesse replied, her attention on the other toys surrounding her.

"She's very pretty," Lydia coaxed, her gaze flying up to meet Nick's.

He looked from her to Myla, his heart sinking. Uh-huh, he'd blown this one, big-time. What had he been thinking?

Myla pivoted to head for the kitchen. "I'll go make some coffee."

Nick followed, ready to apologize for his excessiveness. He winced as she yanked the refrigerator door open and pulled out a huge can of coffee. Taking a deep breath, he stopped her before she could bring the scoop to the filter cup. "I'm sorry, Myla."

Myla set the scoop full of coffee down with a shaking hand. "How could you, Nick? After I told you how I felt...after I told you how Sonny used to try and buy our affection."

"I...I got carried away," he tried to explain. "Christmas around here is usually so gloomy, and I wanted to do something special for the children."

Some of the anger left Myla. How could she be mad when he'd been so generous? Although she knew his motives were completely different from Sonny's, it still worried her that he had some of the same traits. "I know you meant well, Nick, but I can't have them thinking this is the way it's going to be from now on. A lot of expensive toys can't prepare them for the tough time we've got ahead of us. I want them to be children, to enjoy the wonder of Christmas morning, but I also want them to understand that Christmas is about more than getting toys."

"Of course," he agreed, helping her to finish making the coffee. "And I truly wasn't thinking. I never meant to overshadow what you'd already bought for them."

Myla turned on the oven and shoved in the coffee cake she'd made the day before. "I'm very grateful to you," she admitted, "but you have to understand how important this is to me."

"I do understand," he said, following her to the cabinet. "But it's important that you understand me, too. I'm trying to change, Myla. I've…I've been bitter and self-centered, and so preoccupied with work since my father's death, and you know how I am. I'm used to taking charge and telling everyone what to do."

At her knowing I-couldn't-agree-with-you-more glance, he hurried on. "This was a big step for me, to celebrate Christmas in any way at all. And to be able to give to someone, freely and with sincerity…well, it's been a long time since I've felt like this. Maybe I never knew what Christmas was all about myself, until now."

Myla had to swallow the lump in her throat. His admission reinforced what she already knew about him. Behind that indifferent exterior lay a heart of gold. A hurting heart. He had so much to give, much more than a pile of money. And he was trying hard to show her that, even if he had gone about it too excessively.

She stopped her busywork and turned to stare up at him, her eyes wide. "Oh, Nick, it was wonderful, watching their eyes light up when they ran into that room. What you did…it was so sweet, and I shouldn't be mad. But what am I supposed to do with all those wonderful gifts when we move into Magnolia House?"

"You've got awhile," he said, not wanting to think about that. "And you can let them keep their things here and come back here anytime to play with the stuff until you get settled in your own place."

She placed her hand on his. "Christmas is here, Nick. In a few days, Henny will be back from Arkansas. We're on the list to move into the shelter. Lydia says we can move in soon, and after a few months, I should be able to find a low-income house with Lydia's help. I've still got a lot of hard work ahead of me."

He lowered his head, then held her hand tight against his. He couldn't tell her that he had no intention of letting her move into a homeless shelter. "I know—we agreed from the beginning this situation couldn't last. I guess I'd just conveniently forgotten about it."

No, that wasn't exactly true. He'd thought of nothing else, but he had to tread lightly here.

"Yes, we agreed this was only a temporary arrangement," she reminded him. "Don't make it any harder for me, please?"

He saw the pain in her eyes, saw the plea to let her go peacefully, without a big fuss. How could he do that now, when she'd opened up his heart and staked a claim on him? But her firm resolve told him he didn't have any control here, none at all. "If you need any advice—"

She pulled her hand away, trying to ignore the little sensations coursing through her body. "Sonny always advised me. It's time I did things on my own."

That angered him. His voice deepening with each word, he said, "I'm not Sonny."

Lydia peeked in the swinging doors before Myla could reply. "Hey, everything all right in here?"

"Fine," Nick said, waving her away. "We'll be back in soon with some coffee cake."

That reminded Myla of the hot oven. With a wail, she hurried to check the cake. Smoke poured from the stove as she pulled the door open. "Oh, I forgot about it. It's ruined!"

Lydia stepped inside the kitchen, her eyes wide with disbelief. "Have you ever noticed when you two get together in the kitchen, something always goes wrong?"

Myla pulled the charred cake out of the oven, then rolled her eyes. "Too many cooks spoil the broth."

Patrick and Jesse came running. Patrick held up a bright green laser gun and aimed straight for the blackened cake, firing a noisy round of pretend lasers. "Got it," he said with a grin. "Gee, Mom, you used to know how to cook."

Myla looked at Nick, a smile twitching at the corner of her mouth in spite of her earlier concerns. He laughed, too, relaxing as the tension between them eased.

"Anyone for pizza?" Lydia asked, her eyes lifting skyward.

"Dinner was wonderful."

Nick's eyes met Myla's across the expanse of the Queen Anne dining table. He liked this. He liked having Lydia and the children here to share a big Christmas dinner. He didn't know when exactly he'd started liking it, but his mood was more in line with the holiday spirit because of Myla and her two children. Now if he could just convince her to stay here, with him.

"Thank you," Myla said in a hushed tone. Her mind kept going back to what Nick had said in the kitchen. He was changing. She could tell that. He'd even said grace before he carved the turkey for dinner. Still, she was reluctant to trust him completely. Yet when she sat here, looking at him, exchanging warm smiles at some cute comment from one of the children or just noticing how handsome he looked in his sweater and casual slacks, she knew it wouldn't take much for her to fall for him. Oh, this was so hard!

Lydia cleared her throat loudly, bringing Myla's head up. "And the dressing…I love oyster dressing, don't you, Nick?"

"Yes, love it."

"Can I have a piece of pecan pie?" Patrick asked.

"You've barely touched your meal," Myla said, her eyes still on the man at the head of the table. "Considering we had a light breakfast, I'd say you'd better eat as much as you can."

"I did eat," Patrick whined. "I'm ready for pie."

"In a few minutes, Patrick."

Jesse tried. "I'm ready for pie, too, Mama."

Myla's gaze shifted from one child to the other. She couldn't help but smile. Jesse was almost completely well from her cold, and her children were well fed and warm. In many ways, this Christmas had been one of their best together. "Oh, all right. I guess you can have dessert now." Looking down the table, she saw Nick's grinning expression. "I suppose you want some pie, too?"

"Yes, Mom," he said, bursting out in laughter, then quickly clearing his throat to look serious. "If that's all right with you?"

Myla rose to get the requested goodies. "Of course. I didn't bake it for it to just sit there looking pretty."

After the children hopped up to follow their mother, Lydia gave her brother a curious look. "What's going on?"

"Nothing. Everything's great." He changed the subject. "Remember when you mentioned taking the children to see the Christmas lights at the American Rose Center?" At her confused nod, he added, "I think tonight would be a perfect time."

"What are you up to, big brother?"

He leaned forward with a conspiring look. "I want to give Myla her Christmas present, is all. Oh, and take Shredder with you. I don't want any children, dogs, cats, old girlfriends, or sisters around when I do it."

Myla sat on Henny's bed, reading a how-to book on opening a small business that Lydia had given her for Christmas. A cup of lemon-mint tea steamed nearby, while Shredder snoozed in a curled ball at her feet. Dusk played across the back gardens, coloring them in a golden brilliance that reminded her of the paper Jesse's mermaid doll had been wrapped in. Shaking her head, she wondered if Nick had wrapped it himself, or paid a department store a pretty penny to do the job.

Placing the book on a nearby table, she rose to watch the cold December dusk entice the waning sun behind the trees. It had been a good Christmas, but it was almost over. This would soon only be a memory. Nick would soon be a memory. Would he think about her after she'd moved on with her life?

She sighed, then settled into a wing chair to read some more of her new book. This quiet time was much needed and appreciated. Lydia was such a help with the children and they loved her. They'd miss that attention when they had to leave.

Where was Nick? He'd mysteriously disappeared right after the meal. Was he at Carolyn's house, begging her to understand why he'd been late yet again?

A tapping on the partially opened door caused Myla to glance up. Nick poked his head in, a hesitant smile cresting his features. "May I come in?"

She slapped the book shut, rising up out of the chair to greet him. At the sight of him in a tuxedo with his dark hair glistening, she had to hold her breath. How she envied Carolyn right now.

"Going out?"

He walked into the room, stopping inches from her. "No, I'm dining in tonight."

"But I...after our late dinner, I thought—" She tried to hurry around him. "I'll go warm things up right now."

"Myla, you don't have to rush into the kitchen and cook."

The look in his eyes caught her, holding her with its secretive warmth. It was a look of knowing, a look of wonderment, a look of pure pleasure.

"Okay. What's going on?"

"We're going to spend some time alone," he explained. "And I've instructed Lydia to take good care of the children, so don't worry."

Wary of his motives, she asked, "Is this some sort of scheme to make up for your extravagance?"

"Are you still mad about that?"

"No, I'm not so mad now."

"Good. I want you to put everything out of your mind. Don't worry about the children, or this house, or the future. Can you do that for a little while, Myla?"

"But Nick—"

"No questions. Trust me."

He reached out a hand, and she took it, the beat of her heart following his lead. Trust. That was the one thing standing between them. She hadn't quite learned how to trust again.

As if sensing her reluctance, Nick smiled down at her. "Come on, Myla. It's Christmas. Let's enjoy it together."

Christmas. A time of love and miracles. Was it so selfish to want a little of the joy for herself?

The sight that greeted her was indeed full of magic.

Nick took her to the glass-enclosed sunroom off the den, where a table was set for two, complete with candlelight and two steaming mugs of hot chocolate. And all around the room were roses, dozens and dozens of yellow roses, sitting amid the scented candles and the ficus trees. She'd never seen so many shades of the color yellow. The fat, buttery petals ranged in shades from pale cream to deep, bright lemon, and the fragrance reminded her of her own long-lost rose garden.

Tears misted her eyes as one word escaped her throat. "How?"

He looked pleased as punch. "My secret. But before we eat, I've got a few other surprises for you."

She couldn't speak. When she held back, he said, "Trust me, remember?"

Then he handed her a basket full of scented soaps and colorful bottles of bubble bath, along with her mug of hot chocolate.

"Thank you," she said, pleased with his thoughtfulness. "It's been a very long time since I've indulged in a bubble bath."

"And this," he added, handing her a large, colorfully wrapped box.

Gushing, she set her other goodies down, then opened the box to find a full-skirted, round-necked dress with long, tight-fitting sleeves. The fabric was a flowing, vivid Christmas green brocade. "Oh, Nick, it's beautiful, but I can't accept this."

"Yes, you can. I want you to go back to your room and enjoy your soaps and bubbles, soak for as long as you want. Then put on your new frock. We'll eat when you're ready."

Surprised, she shook her head. "I can't. The children, the kitchen needs cleaning. I've got a million things to do."

"Not right now. Now, go. I'm still the boss around here, remember?"

She saw the teasing light in his eyes and sighed. "You're spoiling me just as much as you tried to spoil my children."

"Let me, for just a little while?" he asked in a quiet tone. A request, not an order, Myla noticed.

She looked up at him, seeing the need in his eyes. He wanted to do this, needed to be able to give. But this was more than showering her with gifts, this was a gift from his heart. Her own heart answered, beating tightly against her chest.

She turned to go, but stopped at the door to glance back. "How did you know, about the roses?"

He lifted a finger to his lips and smiled. "My secret."

She went into her room and ran a long, bubbly bath and enjoyed reliving each of his gifts. A bubble bath. A new dress. Yellow roses.

Then suddenly it hit her how he'd figured it all out.

The children! Now she knew. Her children had told him her fondest desires. Overcome with joy, she tried not to cry. Not now. Maybe tomorrow, or the next week, when she was alone and struggling again, but not now. But she wouldn't cry tears of pity; her tears would be full of joy for a man who'd tried to make her dreams come true, for a man who'd seemed so distant until he'd touched her, physically and spiritually. A man she'd fallen in love with.

*I love him,* she thought. Maybe she'd loved him from the first time she'd seen him there on the road. But would she ever be able to admit to that love?

*Trust me,* he'd said. Could she?

"Just for tonight, Nick," she whispered as she relaxed in the scented bubbles. "Just for tonight."

# Chapter Six

A little while later, Myla entered the sunroom with an expectant feeling of hope, her eyes meeting Nick's in shy anticipation.

Nick swallowed hard, then extended his hand, his heart beating against the tucking of his shirt. He'd wanted everything to be perfect, but he'd never dreamed a woman could look so lovely, so radiant. "You look wonderful. The dress becomes you."

She patted her upswept red hair and lowered her head. "You did a great job of guessing my size."

"The children helped out there."

"Ah, would that be the same children who told you about my silly daydreams?"

"The very same. Did I leave anything out?"

She took the glass of mineral water he offered her. "No, not a thing." Then reaching out to touch one of the roses, she said, "Thank you for the flowers. It means a lot to me."

He guided her toward the table. "Well, if I have it my way, you'll never be without yellow roses again."

His firm declaration touched Myla, making her love him even more. "Sonny hated them," she said quietly.

"I could never hate anything that made you happy," he replied steadily. Then, "Hungry?" He lifted the top off a silver server.

Myla relaxed then, bursting out in a fit of laughter. "Turkey sandwiches?"

He grinned. "My specialty. I'm not as proficient in the kitchen as you. I did, however, bring a bag of chips and the rest of the pecan pie.''

"Oh, that reminds me," she said, sitting down, "I've got a surprise for you. I'll give it to you after we eat.''

Nick helped her with her chair. "I thought I was the one full of surprises.''

She watched him sit down. "You certainly are, and I really appreciate all of this.''

Reaching out, she took his hand to say grace. "Thank You, for bringing Nick and me together to heal each other. Thank You for finding me a place to feel safe when there was no room in the inn. In the same way You protected Your Son, Jesus Christ, on the night of His birth, I ask You to now protect us on this holiest of holidays. Amen.''

Nick looked up at her, his hand still holding hers. "I want to tell you something.''

"All right.''

"I saw Carolyn on Christmas Eve.''

Myla's heart sank. Had he done all of this just to let her down easily? Swallowing her pride, she said, "I know. You don't have to explain.''

"Yes, I do. I told her I can't see her anymore. We both knew it wasn't going anywhere. Carolyn has a lot of things she needs to work through, but I'm not the one she needs to make her happy. I'd rather be here, with you.''

Myla's eyes brimmed with fresh tears. "Do you mean that?''

"Yes, I certainly do. I understand we also have a lot to deal with, a lot of things to get cleared up between us. But I'm willing to try. I'm willing to work toward that commitment you need.''

"Meaning, you're ready to make a commitment to Christ?''

He nodded, then bowed his head. "Yes, I am. But I'll need your help.''

"I'll be here.''

Lifting his head, he said, "What about Magnolia House? What about finding your own place?''

"I can do all that, and we can still get to know each other. It can work, Nick. All I ask for is some time.''

It wasn't the answer he'd hoped for, but he didn't intend to give up. Not at all. "Okay. I've been told patience is a virtue. Eat your sandwich."

He smiled, content for now to sit and watch the play of candlelight on her face. Later, he'd figure out how to keep her by his side.

Myla smiled back, then lowered her head, the action causing a tendril of hair to slip over her brow in a looping curl.

Nick Rudolph, ruthless oil millionaire and man of action, was left breathless and speechless—immobilized by an endearing smile and a wayward curl.

Myla Howell, the no-nonsense, pragmatic woman, felt like a princess—captivated by a set of golden brown eyes and the scent of yellow roses.

The meal was wonderful, Myla decided. She could see the change in Nick, from the glow in his dark eyes to the sincerity of his smile. And she loved him because he'd been willing to change, for her. Tonight, she refused to think about her doubts or how she'd ever be able to leave this lovely house—and this lovable man.

They finished the meal, then Nick held out his hand to her to dance to the soft Christmas music playing from the stereo. Bing Crosby sang about being home for Christmas.

Confused, Myla sank into his arms. "I...I haven't danced in a very long time."

Nick snuggled closer to her. "You should dance. You should enjoy life to the fullest."

"Sonny didn't like dancing."

He frowned, then spoke into her ear. "Well, I do."

His nearness left her feeling lightweight and listless. Breathless. "You're very good at it, too."

He lifted his head, his gaze slipping over her face like brown velvet. "It helps to have a lovely woman in my arms."

"Nick, I—"

He held a finger to her parted lips. "No doubts. Not tonight, Myla, remember. It's Christmas."

"So it is," she said, her face inches from his, her eyes shining.

He lowered his head to hers, kissing her with all the warmth he felt in his heart. She accepted his touch, his need, as her own. His gentleness moved her beyond doubt.

And so, they danced, slowly, quietly, softly, while the winter wind lifted up to the glowing stars outside.

When the song ended, Myla took him by the hand, pulling him into the kitchen. "Want your surprise now?"

Not wanting the moment to end, Nick held back. "Hey, I set the rules. Who said you could start bringing out surprises?"

"How about, together we make a new set of rules?"

"Sounds good to me. My father taught me the old set, and I don't think they worked so very good."

"Sit down," she instructed, shoving him into a chair, "and close your eyes."

"I like this game," he teased, his eyes tightly shut.

The smell of pound cake wafted through the warm kitchen. "Ah, now I know this has been the best Christmas ever."

"Okay, open your eyes."

The cake sat whole and fat before him, waiting for him to take the first slice. He didn't remember having ever received a better present.

"You carve, and I'll make coffee," she called over her shoulder.

"Hey, just a minute." He stood up to pull her into his arms. Giving her a thorough kiss, he said, "Merry Christmas, Myla."

"Merry Christmas, Nick."

"Now, let's eat some of that cake before something happens to destroy it!"


Three a.m. Nick stood by the fireplace in his bedroom, watching the dying embers with unseeing eyes.

It had started out innocently enough. All he'd wanted to do was show Myla a good time. Give her something special for Christmas. An evening she'd always remember.

Instead, she'd given him an evening he'd never be able to forget. She'd looked so very beautiful in her new dress that was the exact shade of her exotic green eyes.

Nick had realized two things this Christmas evening. One, he'd been lost in this big house, and he'd been lost in life. He wanted to be found. And two, he had fallen in love with Myla Howell, maybe from the first time he'd seen her. It didn't matter. What did matter was that he loved her and wanted to make a life with her.

Now, he had to be very sure and very careful. Wisely, she'd seen things in him he hadn't even seen himself. He wanted to take care of her, to love her and cherish her. But in order to do that, he might have to make one of the hardest choices in his life. He might have to let her go, in order to gain her love.

And, he'd never been very good at letting go.

Thinking about her need to be independent and self-sufficient, he said a prayer for courage and patience. Then it occurred to him, his father had neglected to teach him the most important rule of all.

Follow your heart.

Myla groaned, stopping on the busy street corner to rest for a minute, her thoughts rushing by like the lunch-time traffic. The last few days since she, Nick and the children had spent a quiet New Year's Eve together had been busy and tiring. With the new year had come the realization that she needed to hunt for a new job, and prepare herself for the move into Magnolia House. This morning, she'd driven into the city to do just that, but something had happened that had left her shaken and confused, and more determined than ever to improve her standard of living.

Checking the digital clock on a nearby bank building, she reasoned she'd have enough time to meet Lydia and Nick for lunch and make it by Magnolia House to fill out some forms, before it was time for the children to get home from school. Even as she stood there, her empty stomach rumbled an urgent message, and her head felt light from lack of sustenance.

The sign over her head announced the Milam Street Coffeehouse. Lydia had said to meet them here. Pushing the dark-tinted heavy door open, Myla looked up to find a familiar face watching her from the other side.

Nick. He looked as wonderful as the coffee smelled. She didn't know if her stomach lurched from hunger, or from the sight of him waiting there for her. Every bit the successful business tycoon, he was dressed in a dark wool suit and cream-colored shirt, the browns and blues in his tie picking up on his dark good looks.

Myla's heart thudded, causing her next words to rumble much like her empty stomach. "Well, hello there. Where's Lydia?"

Nick grinned, then stood to greet her. "She got tied up with a phone call. Sent me on ahead to meet you.'' Glancing around with disapproval, he added, ''Although this place wouldn't have been my first choice.'' Guiding her to a chair, he said, ''You look tired.''

She couldn't yet bring herself to tell him what had happened to her today, so she just said, ''Job hunting is hard work.''

He waved to a nearby waiter. ''You'll feel better after you eat something. And, I have a bit of good news, I think.''

''Oh, and what's that?''

''Lydia said something about knowing the man who owns this restaurant. He's looking for help, and that's why she wanted you to meet us here.''

Myla glanced around at the eclectic style of the new eatery, her eyes scanning the paintings by local artists and the other forms of artwork decorating the two-storied open-air building. ''It's different, but I like it.''

Nick didn't look so sure. ''Well, I don't. This place doesn't look as classy as Lydia described. Hope the food is good, at least.''

''Hope I get hired,'' Myla said in a weary voice.

Nick didn't like the idea of her working in an eclectic restaurant centered in a run-down building, but he didn't think she'd listen to him. ''Are you interested?''

Her eyes lit up. ''Of course. I got really down this morning, kind of depressed.'' Shrugging, she decided not to tell him just how down she'd been. ''But I'm better now.''

''Good.'' Taking her hand, Nick waited while she told the waiter she'd have a chicken salad sandwich, then he reluctantly ordered himself a hamburger. ''You know, even though Henny's due back any day now, you don't have to move out immediately, and you don't have to take the first job that comes along.''

''Thanks,'' she said, taking a sip of much-needed coffee. Her empty stomach rejected it, though, so she pushed it away. ''But I don't want to miss my spot on the list at Magnolia House. It's hard to get in, with so many people needing temporary shelter.''

He tapped his fingers on the glass-topped bistro table. ''Well, don't overdo things. Lydia tells me you've already enrolled in a business class and a cake-decorating course for the spring.''

''Yes, I need both to get me started and give me some experience.''

Finally, his patience sorely tried, Nick said, "Look, you don't have to move into the shelter at all. I have guest rooms. You can stay as long as you want."

Both hands on her coffee cup, Myla said, "Nick, we agreed that I'd leave after Christmas. I'm not your responsibility, and technically, it wouldn't be right."

"But I feel responsible...I want to be responsible for you, and technically, we wouldn't be doing anything wrong. I'd be a perfect gentleman."

Touched by his thoughtfulness, she said, "That means a lot to me, because I know you are a gentleman, and if I get in a pinch, I'll call you. But I need this time, if for nothing else, to prove to myself that I'm capable. I depended on Sonny for so much...it's time I learned how to deal with things on my own."

He ran a hand through his hair, frustrated with her stubborn determination. "Yes, and I promised I'd give you some time to do just that. I'm sorry."

Sitting back in her chair, she said, "I'm going to Magnolia House after we eat. You're welcome to come along and see the place for yourself."

"I just might," he replied. "Lydia's been after me to take a tour ever since the place opened. Of course, I'll probably take one look at it and tell you not to leave me."

The way he'd said that spoke much more than mere words. They sat looking at each other for a minute, then Myla said, "I'm not leaving you, Nick. I'm just doing what I have to do. We can still see each other."

"Right. You think you have to do this, to prove something to yourself and the world. I'm trying very hard to accept that and understand."

"And I appreciate your efforts. If we still...feel the same about our relationship after a few months, we'll see what happens next."

He continued tapping on the glass tabletop. "I know, I know. Patience is a virtue."

She shot him a broad smile. "Hebrews, chapter 10, verse 36— 'For ye have need of patience, that, after ye have done the will of God, ye might receive the promise.'"

Nick shook his head. "That's all great, but what about my will?"

"You have to give that over to Him, for now."

"It's hard."

"But you'll receive the promise."

"Which is?"

"A good life, the life you desire."

When she looked up, Nick's eyes were centered on her. "I hope the life I desire turns out to be with you."

His reply overwhelmed her. What was he saying? Had he really come to care for her as much as she cared for him? Afraid she'd cave in, she asked, "Have you heard from Henny?"

He leaned back in his chair to loosen his tie a notch. "Only to say she'd be here any day now. She sounded odd, not herself, kind of distant and tired. I'm worried about her," he added with concern. "Her health isn't good at all these days but she's far too stubborn to let anyone know if she's not feeling well."

"Maybe she misses fussing over you. And me, I've got to continue this job search. I'll talk to the owner here, to see what he has to offer, then fill out a few more applications."

Nick did not want her to work in this fledgling establishment. It was just like Lydia to go for the underdog, even in her choice of restaurants, but that didn't mean Myla had to work here.

"Can you type?" he asked, his tone light and hopeful.

"Barely. I haven't since high school."

"I don't suppose you've ever worked on an oil rig?"

Myla looked skeptical until she saw the laugh crinkles surrounding his eyes. "No, but thanks for the offer. So far, I've been turned away at six restaurants, two offices, three fast-food joints, and a half-dozen retail stores. I've offered to cook, clean, type and file, and just about anything else I can think of. The job market is slim for a woman without a college degree who's fast approaching her thirties. But I'm not the only one." She looked down at the marble design on their table. "Today, I saw several people worse off than me."

Nick stopped his tapping. "I can't imagine not having a job. My grandfather did all the scraping and clawing in my family."

His words reminded Myla of Sonny. "You know, Sonny's parents gave him everything. They spoiled him, then when he got out on his own, he couldn't handle the responsibility." She glanced up at Nick, a deep sorrow filling her soul. "Money really can't solve our problems, no matter how much we think it can. So just be glad you've done a good, honest job of holding on to what your grandfather built."

He looked sheepish. "I'm not so proud. I'm an overachiever, and unlike Sonny, I am responsible—my parents taught both of us that lesson—and a lot of people depend on me."

Myla knew he was right there. Nick had a strong sense of responsibility. And now, he had taken her on as his own responsibility, too. "Does it get to you, knowing people's livelihoods depend on your daily decisions?"

"Sometimes, yes, but I've never had time to dwell on it too much. My father had bad timing." A dark look twisted his features. "He died right in the middle of the oil crisis, and I've been trying to keep my head above water ever since. So far, I've done a passable job…Rudolph Oil is still intact."

"But what about its leader? It's important to take care of your spiritual side, too." Sensing his need to talk, she said, "Tell me about your father."

Running a finger over his coffee mug, Nick looked away. "He died of a broken heart. He loved his company and my mother. Watching her die from cancer wasn't easy for any of us, and then when he thought he was going to lose Rudolph Oil, too…" He shrugged, then turned quiet again.

Myla saw him in a new light, understanding why he'd tried so hard to stay detached and distant. Pain did that to people. Touching his hand, she said, "Haven't you done enough scraping and clawing yourself? You do work hard, but you need to work on that chip on your shoulder, too."

"I can't be weak," he said, telling her his worst fear. "I can't become the man my father became. You talk about living a sham—he did. He thought he was so in control, then he crumbled right before my eyes. I can't let that happen to me."

"God won't let that happen, Nick. Not if you use Him as your strength and your guidance. He won't leave you. If you crumble, He will be there to catch you."

"Maybe. That still doesn't explain my mother's death and my father's heartbreak."

Now she understood completely. He blamed God for making his life miserable. "No, God didn't want you or your parents to suffer. But he can't stop a person from dying when that person's time has come. Sure, the circumstances aren't always pleasant, but that's part of life. God is our guide, but it's up to us to make the first steps toward our journey. That's called free will."

"Free will. The will to make our own choices. But you just quoted me scripture about doing God's will."

"God's will, yes, but based on the right choices," she explained. "We can't blame God for all the bad, and then turn around and expect Him to take care of all the good we want in life. We have to trust in Him, pray for His guidance, then go out and make our own choices, based on an educated, gospel-backed decision. We use the scriptures, past traditions, our own experiences, and our own reasoning, to decide what to do. And sometimes, we have to face great grief and bitter sadness, but we go on, using God's love as our strength."

All around them, the restaurant flowed and ebbed with people. The sound of the cash register computing tabs blended with the burr of a coffee grinder, while the laughter and whispered words of the few patrons filtered up to the high ceilings.

"Life goes on," Nick said, his gaze settling on hers. "How'd you get to be so wise?"

"Not me, the Bible," she replied, hoping she'd helped him feel better about things. And herself as well.

Just then a tall man with sandy blond hair and horn-rimmed glasses brought their food to the table. Nick immediately gave the grinning man a get-lost look.

But the lanky man continued to stare. "Hey, I'm Grant Lewis. I own this place. Lydia told me to look for you today—she described a tall woman with long red hair and uh…an uptight executive."

Myla giggled while Nick frowned. "That's us," she said.

Nick had no choice but to shake the man's hand, then watch with jealous politeness as Grant smiled down on Myla.

"So, this must be the great cook Lydia's been hounding me to hire."

Myla shook his hand, then asked, "Do you need someone?"

"Sure do," Grant replied as he pushed at his glasses, his blue eyes bright with hope. "One of my best waitresses quit last week. She's a college student and her course load was too heavy. Said she had to crack the books or lose her scholarship."

Myla nodded her understanding, then said, "Well, I can start right away, but only part-time for now."

Nick shot her a warning look. "Don't be so hasty. You don't even know what he's paying."

"Minimum wage plus tips," Grant replied, his hands on his hips. "We're not in the black yet, but we're getting there, so hopefully I'll be able to offer you better pay one day."

"One day? She needs a stable job right now," Nick said, his scowl deepening. "And she has one, with me."

Myla watched Nick's brow furrow. So much for being patient. "Nick, I need a *permanent* job," she reminded him gently.

Grant obviously hadn't missed the friction between them. "Is there a problem?"

"Yes," Nick retorted.

"No," Myla insisted. Giving Nick a meaningful glare, she added, "Mr. Rudolph is afraid of letting me make my own choices, but I'd be happy to work for you, Grant. After all, we did agree that I'd need to find another job soon, right, Nick?"

Nick shrugged, frowned, then sighed long and hard. Just to show Grant that he wasn't as uptight as his sister had implied, he said, "Oh, all right. It's your decision."

Myla smiled appreciatively. "I can start today, if you need me. But until I can find adequate child care, I can only work the early shifts—I have two children. And right now, I have to fill in for Nick's housekeeper, but she's due home any day now."

Grant waved both arms. "That sure would help. As you can see, we stay pretty busy with the lunch crowd. Lydia tells me you can cook, but do you have a problem with waiting tables?"

"No, of course not," Myla replied. "I'll do whatever needs to be done. I really need a job. I'll be moving into Magnolia House in a few days."

Grant adjusted the salt and pepper shakers, then shook her hand again. "Lydia explained your situation, and I understand completely. When you're done with your meal, come to the counter and fill out some paperwork. I've got to get back to the kitchen."

After Grant left, Myla looked over at Nick. He didn't look as happy about this as she felt. Wanting reassurance, and wanting him to know that she appreciated his help, she said, "What do you think?"

"I think I'm going to be very jealous of Grant Lewis," he admitted. "You'll be working closely with him every day."

"Nick—that's very flattering, but I'll be fine. I only have eyes for men who buy me yellow roses."

That made him smile. "I'll keep you in a fresh supply to remind you—and him."

Lydia fluttered onto a chair just then, collapsing in an elegant pile against the table. "Nourishment, please?"

Grant was back, Nick noticed. Johnny on the spot.

"Hey, Lydia." Grant said, beaming like a street lamp.

There went that puppy-dog grin again.

"Grant!" Lydia sat straight up, causing her silk floral print scarf to do a fast float. "Nice to see you again." Smiling over at her brother and Myla, she said, "Did Grant tell you he writes poetry? He's a very good writer," she added emphatically.

Grant looked sheepish, then lifted a hand in explanation. "We have open mike night sometimes. People can share their work."

Not liking the way Grant was ogling his sister, Nick said, "How very generous of you."

Myla caught Nick's blazing gaze, her look warning him to back off. It was obvious Grant was smitten with Lydia. And vice versa.

Leaning close while Grant and Lydia flirted tactfully with each other, she said, "Well, at least you don't have to be jealous of Grant with *me*. Not with Lydia around."

Nick glared at the man who'd just ruined his day completely. "No, I just have to worry about some smooth-talking artistic type hoodwinking my baby sister."

"He's not trying to hoodwink anybody," Myla whispered as Lydia's sharp ears perked up. "Now, be nice."

"I don't want to be nice. And I intend to have a private conversation with Lydia later. She's far too gullible and naive when it comes to these matters." Concentrating on Myla again, he said, "You haven't eaten much."

Myla's stomach did a revolt as she eyed her half-eaten sandwich.

"I guess I'm too keyed up to eat." She stood up, turning to Grant. "Could you give me that application? I can fill it out while we finish."

Grant managed to tear his eyes away from Lydia. "Sure, just come on back to the kitchen." Then to Lydia he said, "Stay here. I'll be right back."

Whirling around, Myla started to follow Grant. The room began to spin, making her feel as if she were being sucked into a huge black vortex.

"Myla?" Nick saw her go pale, watched as she stumbled, then crumpled into a heap. He reached out to catch her as she went limp.

Grant came rushing over to pull her chair out, while Lydia took her hand. "She doesn't look too great," he said, his eyes meeting Nick's.

"Myla, can you hear me?" Nick asked softly, concern evident in his words. "What's wrong?"

"Blood," she managed to whisper.

"Blood?" Nick looked down, searching for any signs of red. "Did you hurt yourself?"

She raised an arm to show him the wide bandage running across the fold inside her elbow joint. "I gave blood this morning. It always makes me queasy."

Lydia's worried gaze flew to Nick's face. "We need to get her home."

Grant took her arm, then shook his head. "Ah, man, they do it all the time."

"Do what?" Nick screamed, all sorts of horrible thoughts rushing through his head.

"Homeless people," Grant explained. "They give plasma to get money. It doesn't pay much, but when you're out of work, it will buy food."

Shocked, Nick looked down at the woman in his arms. "Myla, do you need money that badly?"

Slowly, Myla opened her eyes to focus on his face. "No, I don't need money too much now, thanks to you. But...someone I met today did. So I gave some blood. I had to do it, Nick. Please try to understand."

# Chapter Seven

"You're right, Lydia. I don't understand."

Nick paced the length of the kitchen, his eyes dark with a rage he couldn't even begin to contain. "Giving plasma for money! I've never heard of such a thing. I give blood...I donate regularly at the Red Cross, but she did it out of some sort of desperation. And she didn't even take the time to eat properly before or after she did it. She's barely above the required weight, to begin with!"

"Nick, calm down," Lydia said, her gaze shifting to the array of voices coming from the den. "Myla will be back in here soon. It won't do for her to see you so upset."

"Oh, she knows I'm upset."

He glanced toward the den where Jesse and Patrick were playing with Shredder and their Christmas toys. Myla was in Henny's room, washing her face.

"Yes, I imagine she does, since you practically carried her all the way to your car—after causing a scene with your ranting. Thank goodness Grant was able to stay calm, at least."

Pulling his hands through his hair, Nick grimaced. Now he was being compared to a poet! "Yes, Grant Lewis is a very understanding man. He did settle me down. And he got Myla to nibble on a cracker and drink some juice."

Lydia smiled slightly, relief washing over her youthful face. "Yeah, Grant is so sweet. I've gotten to know him better since approaching him about this job for Myla. In fact, we have a date tonight."

Nick looked at his little sister as if she'd lost her head. "A date? You hardly know the man!"

"I'm getting to know him," Lydia stated. "And don't you start with me. You never approve of anybody I date."

Nick cringed at that accusation. "That's not true. I liked Ralph Pimperton."

"Ralph Pimperton is a pompous…snob."

"Well, yes, he is that, but he really liked you, and he comes from a fine family."

"I didn't like *him*, Nick. Now, please promise me you won't try to intimidate Grant. He's really shy, you know."

Nick glowered at her. "This day is going from bad to worse. First Myla takes a job that I think is unsuitable, then she faints, and now you're telling me you're smitten with a coffeehouse poet."

Lydia stood nose to nose with her brother. "He's more than that. He's a good, decent man and I'm glad to know him. And his place of business is very suitable."

Nick gave his sister a quizzical look, his protective instincts surfacing all over again. "Well, get to know him even a little more before you get all mushy about him."

Lydia stuck her tongue out at him, contradicting her words. "I'm a grown woman, Nick. I know how to handle my own social life, thank you very much. And Myla knows how to find a job. You'd better just stay out of all of this."

Heaving a heavy sigh, Nick tried to relax a little as he listened to the noise coming from the den. He didn't like having to second-guess women. He did, however, like the noise that children could make, he decided. He especially liked knowing they were all here, safe and happy. And he guessed his sister deserved to be happy, too. But what was so wrong with wanting to protect the people he cared about?

But Lydia was right. He couldn't control her life forever. And he certainly couldn't control Myla's, not when he'd promised her he wouldn't interfere.

"Oh, all right. Invite him over for dinner sometime," he suggested, defeat pulling him down. "That way, *I* can get to know him, too."

Lydia grabbed him by the head, then gave him a wet, sisterly kiss. "That's the spirit. I think you'll be pleasantly surprised."

"Well, I've had enough surprises for one day," he said in a low growl.

The sound of a door shutting brought his head up. Myla came in, her walk not nearly as wobbly as it'd been earlier. Nick gave his sister an imploring look.

"I'll go play with the other kids," Lydia said, winking at her brother.

Nick shot her a mock nasty glare, then turned to the auburn-haired woman who'd caused him no small amount of worry, and joy, over the last few weeks. "Are you all right?"

"Much better," she said quietly. "I'll start dinner."

He reached out a hand to stop her. "Forget dinner. Lydia's taking care of that. We need to talk."

Myla placed both hands on the sparkling clean counter, avoiding the accusation in his eyes. She really didn't want to talk about her reasons for doing what she'd done. In spite of her calm front, she was still shaken.

Nick stood across from her, his own hands braced tightly against the same counter. "Myla, if you need more money—"

"I don't. That's not why I gave the plasma."

"Then, please, explain it to me."

She brought her hands together, then clasped them in front of her, closing her eyes for a minute. "I was out job hunting, walking the streets from door to door, and I passed a plasma center. I was tired, worried, frustrated, and there was this line of people blocking my way. Then I saw the sign that said the center would pay for plasma. I looked around at the people—they were waiting to give blood."

She stopped, taking a long swallow as tears welled in her eyes. "That's when I saw this old man, dressed in ragged clothes, sitting on the curb. He looked so gaunt and frail, and when he saw me coming, he held up a hand and asked me if I had a few dollars so he could buy food. He explained that he wanted to give plasma, to get some money. But he wasn't in very good shape. The nurses had turned him away."

She looked up at Nick, her expression grim. "So I offered to go in and give my own plasma. When I came out, I gave him the fifteen dollars I'd earned. It upset me so badly, I gave him the money, then I ran away, down the street.'' Lowering her head, she covered her face with both hands. ''I didn't want to wind up like that, but I had this horrible vision of my children standing in the street begging for food. I sat on a bench and...after a few minutes, I was okay. Just a moment of self-pity. I was so ashamed of how I'd reacted, I tried to forget all about it. But I can't get that old man's face out of my mind.''

She looked up, seeing the compassion in Nick's eyes, hoping he could understand how profound seeing the homeless man had been for her, that she'd had no choice but to help him in some way.

''Myla.'' He came around the counter to take her in his arms. ''You're not so very tough, after all, are you?''

Myla leaned against him, allowing herself this simple luxury. ''No, I'm not tough. I'm scared to death of being a failure. I can't let my children down, though.''

Nick patted her back, then lifted her chin so he could see her face. ''You won't let them down. I know that in my heart. What you did was a sweet and noble thing, but you don't have to worry. I won't allow that to happen to you and your children.''

''But what about that old man? What about all the children lost out there in the cold and the dark? Somebody has to do something. We can't just keep running away from people who need our help.''

He couldn't answer that. ''I know they're out there. And we can try to help, but we can't save all of them.''

She looked up then, a new light of hope cresting in her eyes. ''But you will help me, right? You'll help me to find a way to save some of these people. I have to do it, Nick. I know how they feel.''

A strange thudding began deep inside Nick's chest. Was this his calling then, to help those who couldn't help themselves? Was this a way to bring him closer to God, and his beloved Myla? Was this a way to redeem himself at last?

''We'll do it,'' he said. ''Whatever we can, we'll do it, together. I promise.''

Myla hugged him close, a new warmth flowing through her tired body. ''That was worth fainting over,'' she said, her worry turning to happiness.

He stroked her hair, then said, "Well, just promise me you'll take care of yourself. You gave me a bad scare back there."

"I'll be fine now."

The back doorbell rang, bringing Patrick bounding through the kitchen. "Pizza man's here. He sure got here quick."

Nick took Myla by the hand to head for the door. "He knows the address well," he said dryly.

"Another week." Myla's attention shifted from Nick's worried expression to Lydia's pleased one. "I'm next on the list. I can move into Magnolia House this weekend. With my new job, and now this, my life is beginning to take shape again. I won't have to resort to welfare."

Nick wished he could be as happy about this as the two women sitting across from him in his kitchen. Lydia was positively giddy over the poet fellow, the noble Mr. Grant Lewis, and now Myla was happily working two jobs and in sheer joy about moving into a homeless shelter of all places. He really, truly, would never understand women.

Glancing up from his apple strudel, he gave Myla an encouraging look in spite of his mixed feelings about her leaving. "How long will you be able to stay there?"

Seeing the worry in his eyes, she tried to reassure him. "We can stay up to a year, but I don't intend to let it drag out that long. I'm saving as much money as I can to find a low-rent place."

Still concerned, Nick said, "Now explain how this place works to me again. I want to understand the whole process."

Lydia piped up. "I've been explaining it to you, but you never listen." At her brother's wince of disapproval, she said, "Grant was interested, so I gave him a tour. He's more than willing to help out with the homeless situation in this city."

"Very honorable," Nick said. "Is there anything the wonderful Grant Lewis isn't willing to do for you—or to you—for that matter?"

"Nick!" Hurt, Lydia implored Myla. "Will you please ask my overbearing brother if he could possibly put a little faith and trust in me."

Myla glanced at Nick, her brows lifting in a question. When Nick only pouted, she said, "Look, I work with Grant every day. He's a very nice man."

"His company isn't very stable," Nick argued. "The restaurant business is fickle and unpredictable. He might have to shut down any day now."

"You know that for a fact?" Lydia asked, anger slicing through her words.

Nick looked smug. "No, but I know enough about business to predict such things."

"We're getting rave reviews," Myla stated. "In fact...Grant and I are considering opening up a catering business just as soon as I can get back on my feet."

"What?" Nick gave her a surprised look. "Myla, don't overextend yourself."

"I won't," she said, a wary tone in her words. "Grant's already allowed me to do some extra cooking. We're trying out new recipes on the customers. And just as soon as Henny's able to come back to work, I intend to expand on that."

Nick threw up his hands. "Can we concentrate on one change at a time? Let's get back to talking about Magnolia House. If I hear one more word of praise for Grant Lewis, I think I'll lose my lunch."

"Poor Nick, he never handled change very well," Lydia explained to Myla, before launching into a thorough speech on how the homeless shelter was set up. "Magnolia House is a transitional place, not just a homeless shelter. It's more like an apartment building, and since this is a new program to help the homeless, it's in high demand. It's always full—a sign that this problem is growing."

Myla offered Nick some more strudel, hoping to soothe his temper and his concern, but put the lid back on the pan when he silently refused with a shake of his head. Taking a bite of her own dessert, she said, "Which is why I'm anxious to learn all I can about it and help others."

"We're behind you all the way. Grant's willing to help and we know big brother wants in on the action. Right, Nick?" Lydia gave her brooding brother a hearty shake.

Nick moaned, then sighed long and hard before glancing over at Myla. "Don't you just love eternally perky people?"

Myla gave him a serious glance. "Do you want to help us with this, or not?"

Turning serious himself, he nodded. "Absolutely. I'm already looking into it. I've talked to several other prominent businessmen in the area, and they've pledged their support, too."

"Thank you." Myla started clearing the dessert dishes away. "I'll bring home some more information next time I go in."

The phone rang nearby, and Lydia hopped up to get it, giving Nick an opportunity to talk to Myla alone. "I guess this is it, then. You'll be leaving soon."

"Yes," she said, her heart fluttering at the thought of having to leave the safety of this wonderful old house. "I don't want you to worry about me, though. I'm tough and I have a strong sense that this is what the Lord wants me to do."

Nick wanted to tell her he had his own strong sense about what she needed to do, but he held back. "You and my baby sister," he said, shaking his head in wonder. "You both seem so sure, so confident. Me, I'm still floundering around, afraid."

Myla smiled at his endearing self-doubt. "Lydia will be all right, Nick. Grant is really a decent man."

Nick nodded, his eyes on his sister. "I guess I hadn't realized she's all grown-up."

"And very capable of taking care of herself," Myla reminded him. "You should be very proud of her."

Lydia's concerned call to Nick stopped his reply.

"It's Henny's daughter. They had to rush Henny to the hospital. Nick, they think it's her heart."

Myla heard the fear in Lydia's voice and saw that same fear shooting through Nick's dark eyes. She listened as Nick took the phone, then placed her arm around Lydia's shaking shoulders.

"I see," he said into the receiver. "Keep us posted. Call day or night, collect. And we'll be on the first plane up there—I don't care what Henny says—I'm coming."

Hanging up the phone, he turned in shock to his sister. She fell into his arms, her muffled cries absorbed into his shirt.

"It'll be okay, honey," he said, kissing Lydia's fluffy bob. "We'll go up there to be with her, make sure she takes care of herself.'' He looked over her head at Myla, his expression dark and grim.

The pain Myla saw in his eyes ripped her heart apart. She'd seen Nick struggle to downplay his emotions, but this pain was too fresh and too much of a shock to hide.

''Nick, what can I do?'' she asked, wanting to comfort him.

Gently extracting Lydia from his arms, Nick handed his sister a tissue.

Lydia rushed away, a new batch of tears welling in her usually bright eyes. ''I'll go call the airline and book us a flight.''

Nick waited until his sister had left the room, then turned back to Myla. ''Lydia's been warning me about Henny's health. But I was always too busy, too absorbed in myself, to notice.''

Myla knew he was telling the truth. And she also knew he'd changed a great deal in the last month. She watched as he tried to shut himself down, as he struggled against the old pains and resentments. Giving him some time alone, she began clearing the dinner dishes away, but Nick's hand on her arm stopped her.

With a gentle tug, he pulled her close, burying his face against her hair. ''Stay. Stay here. I need you to be here when I get back, in case…''

He left the statement hanging, but Myla understood what he was asking. If she stayed, though, she'd risk losing her spot at Magnolia House and a chance at a fresh start. But she knew in her heart she couldn't desert him now.

''Of course I'll stay, Nick. Henny might need help once she gets back.''

He lifted his head then, to look into her eyes. ''If she doesn't make it back—''

''We have to pray that that doesn't happen,'' she gently reminded him. ''But if it does, we'll get through it, together.''

''Together,'' he repeated, his eyes dark and somber. ''God sent you to me just in time, didn't He, Myla?''

She patted his cheek. ''Go check on your sister.''

A few days later, Myla answered the phone at the coffeehouse, expecting it to be an order for a late lunch.

''Myla?''

Nick's voice cut across her midafternoon tiredness, making her snap to attention. She'd been waiting to hear about Henny's condition since Nick and Lydia had left for Little Rock. "Nick, how is she?"

"She made it through the bypass surgery," he said over the wire, his tone hopeful. "The doctors assure us she'll have a full recovery."

Relief flooded through Myla. "That's wonderful. When will she be able to come home?"

He hesitated, then plunged right in. "That's the other reason I'm calling. Her daughter wants her to recuperate here in Little Rock, with her family and the doctors nearby."

"Well, that's understandable." She waited as silence echoed through the line. "Do you want me to stay awhile longer, to help out?"

He let out a long sigh. "You know I'd like nothing better than that, but you'll lose your spot on the list at Magnolia House. I can't ask you to do that, but on the other hand, there's really no need for you to rush now."

Giving up her place at the shelter wouldn't be half as hard if it didn't involve living under the same roof with him, she reasoned. Sending up a prayer for strength and guidance, she swallowed back her concerns. She could do this. She had to do it, for Henny's sake, and to show Nick that she believed in him. She wouldn't run out on him when he needed her the most.

"I'll be here, Nick."

That simple statement seemed to reassure him. "Thank you. I know how much I'm asking, Myla, but I won't forget this. I'll make it up to you, somehow."

Hanging up, Myla looked up from the order pad she'd been doodling on to find Carolyn Parker coming toward her. What on earth was the tall blonde doing here? And why now, of all times, when Myla's doubts were foaming over like the cappuccino she watched Grant mix for a customer.

"Hello," Carolyn said as she dropped down on a stool at the long lunch counter. "How are you, Myla?"

Myla didn't like the appraising look the other woman was giving her, but she managed a polite smile. "I'm fine. It's good to see you again, Carolyn. I'm sorry about what happened with my children and the cat.''

''No problem.'' Carolyn tossed her long hair away from her face and placed her black leather purse on the counter in front of her. ''Guess you're wondering what I'm doing here.''

''Well, yes, I am,'' Myla admitted. ''Would you like something to drink?''

''Oh, no. I just wanted to talk to you, about Nick.''

''I see.''

Carolyn's luminous eyes softened then. ''He's changed so much, I guess I'm just trying to understand what's happened to him.''

Confused, Myla studied the other woman's face. She looked sincere, and sad. ''I don't know if I can help you out, Carolyn. I don't understand Nick too well myself.''

''Oh, but you do,'' Carolyn insisted. ''He's different since he met you. And I've been stewing about it for weeks now. You see, I had this silly idea that Nick would ask me to marry him. We've been kind of dating for so long, but I guess in my heart I knew it was more of a convenience than anything else. Still, I never gave up. Until you came along.''

''I'm sorry,'' Myla said, embarrassed at the woman's directness. ''I didn't mean to come between you and Nick.''

''Maybe not,'' Carolyn replied, her eyes cool. ''But I can't compete with you and your Bible.''

That statement left Myla unsettled. She didn't like the implications of the other woman's words. ''What do you mean?''

''I mean, I've seen a lot of come-on lines in my time, but spouting Bible verses is a new one. You have Nick's attention now, but I don't know if you can hold him with that demure little self-righteous act for long.''

Shocked, Myla lifted her chin, then gave Carolyn a direct look. ''It's not an act. My beliefs are sincere, but I'd never use them to try to win a man. I care about Nick because he took the time to care about me. Maybe you never got any closer to him because you can't see beyond his money or his status.''

Carolyn snorted. ''And you can?''

Myla bristled, but stood her ground. ''Yes, I've seen Nick's gentle side, his caring, giving side. He's a good man, and I'm glad he's changing for the better. You should be, too.''

Carolyn rose, her eyes now full of hostility. "Not if it means I have to give him up.''

Myla felt sorry for the beautiful blonde. "Maybe you never really had him to begin with.''

That caused Carolyn to pause. "Maybe not. But it's not over yet. You're just a housekeeper, after all. He feels sorry for you. He'll get tired of playing this new game and he'll come back to me. He always does.''

Hiding the pain of the put-down and Carolyn's smug assumption behind a serene smile, Myla could only hope that didn't happen. But she wouldn't give Carolyn the satisfaction of seeing her doubt. "If you really love Nick,'' she said as Carolyn turned to leave, "you'll be glad that he's finally getting over his bitterness and pain. Or were you even aware that he's been suffering all these years?''

Carolyn rolled her eyes and laughed. "Funny, he always seemed happy when he was with me.''

"Then you really don't know him at all,'' Myla said softly.

Carolyn lifted her arched brows. "I know him well enough to warn him away from you. You're living in his house. How does that fit in with your holier-than-thou attitude? Or had you stopped to think what any hint of scandal could do to Nick's reputation and his business?''

With that, Carolyn lowered her head and walked out the door, leaving Myla blushing and angry.

Grant came to stand beside Myla, his eyes on the woman leaving the restaurant. "Wow, who was that?''

"A friend of Nick's,'' Myla said absently, trying to hide the embarrassment Carolyn's words had inflicted. "And a very lonely woman, apparently.''

"That's a shame,'' Grant replied, his mind already back on business as he greeted a customer across the room.

"Yes, it certainly is,'' Myla said to herself, her own doubts working their way through her mind in the same steady pace as the lunch crowd had worked its way through the diner earlier. "She's worried about competing with me, but I know I don't stand a chance against her. Especially if she decides to make trouble for Nick.''

Just one more thing to add to her list of worries.

Grant came back then. Tapping Myla on the arm, he said, "Hey, where'd you go?"

"Sorry, boss. Just woolgathering. Did you need to talk to me?"

Grant lowered his head, his shy eyes studying the counter. "About our catering business—"

"Don't tell me you've changed your mind?"

"Oh, no." He shook his head. "I want to start it, right away. It will mean lots of long hours, though."

"I can handle it."

"What about your children?"

Myla traced an invisible pattern on the rich mahogany of the counter. "Well, Lydia has offered to help out. And once I move into Magnolia House, I'll have trained counselors there to help with the children."

"A built-in day care?"

"Something like that." She swallowed the dread back. "I don't have much choice. I have to work. And, I am very interested in this, Grant."

"Enough to form a partnership?"

Surprised, Myla looked over at him, her smile beaming. "Partners? I just thought I'd be working for you."

"I think partners would be better," Grant said. "You have a lot of fresh ideas, and hey, the customers keep coming back for your muffins and cookies."

"They seem to like them," she agreed. Extending a hand to him, she said, "Thank you, Grant. This is like a dream come true."

"Well, don't get too dreamy," he replied. "First, we have to work out a plan and set some goals."

"I'm ready," Myla said. Somehow, she'd make it all work. For her children's sake. She had to remember that their needs would always come first. Even if that meant giving up being with Nick.


Myla's new routine kept her busy, which kept her mind off Carolyn's dire warnings about Nick. She worked the breakfast and lunch shifts at the coffeehouse, then rushed home to do her work at the mansion while waiting for the children to come home on the school bus. She was tired, but content. With two jobs, she was steadily saving money. Of course, when Henny recovered, one of her jobs would end.

Myla was almost glad Nick had been called away. It would be much easier to leave his home, to leave him, now that she'd had a few days without him in her life. But he was never far from her thoughts. She'd missed him terribly.

Right now, she remembered Nick's knock on her door late last night when he and Lydia returned from Little Rock. He didn't say a whole lot, but she could tell he needed to see a friendly face.

"Thank you for staying," he whispered so as not to wake the sleeping children. With that, he gave her a quick hug before heading upstairs with his tired sister. This morning, he was up and gone before she could get breakfast started. So she came to work wondering if he was really all right, and wondering if he was having second thoughts about their budding relationship.

Just to keep herself busy, she'd baked a blueberry cobbler, and smiling, was happily serving it up to the few customers who'd come in for a late lunch.

"I'll have a double helping, if you don't mind," a deep male voice said into her ear.

Whirling, Myla laughed, her heart skipping a beat as Nick grinned down at her.

"Nick! It's good to have you home."

"It's good to be home," he said, settling onto a bar stool, his expression as carefree as a schoolboy's. "We got back so late last night, we didn't really get a chance to talk. I missed you."

"I missed you, too. How's Henny?"

He took the cobbler Myla automatically scooped up for him, his eyes lighting up at the sight of it. "Doing great. She insisted I come back to check on you. She thinks we were made for each other."

"Were we?"

"I'm beginning to believe that, yes."

Remembering Carolyn's declaration that Nick would soon get bored with her, Myla turned away to finish filling the sugar containers. The sooner she could move out of his house, the better, no matter how much she cared about him. Then she'd be able to think this through and get a clear grasp on reality.

Nick stopped nibbling his cobbler, his eyes locking with hers in the mirror behind the counter. "What's wrong?"

Should she tell him? Deciding to keep things light, she only said, "I saw Carolyn the other day."

That got his attention. "Really. I haven't talked to her in a while. How's she doing?"

"She seemed confused," Myla admitted. "I think she misses you, too."

"Did she say something to you, to upset you?"

Because she cared for him, she didn't tell him about Carolyn's other threats. "No, not really. Nothing I can't deal with. Maybe you should check on her, though."

Giving her a curious look, he said, "All right. But I have to admit, I'm not accustomed to the woman in my life telling me to call my ex-girlfriend."

"I'm not like other women," she told him in a curt little tone.

"No, you're not. For one thing, you make such an incredible blueberry cobbler, that it makes me want to weep with sheer joy."

She smiled in spite of herself.

He leaned over the counter, his hand touching her face. "And for another, you're much too smart to let anything my ex-girlfriend might say upset you. Right?"

"Right," she said, touched that he'd worded it in a way that didn't force her to admit to anything. "Just see about her for me, all right?"

"All right."

She sat down beside him to drink a quick cup of coffee while he finished his dessert. When he rose to leave, she said, "I'll see you at dinner. I've got a meat loaf ready to pop in the oven."

"Okay." He headed toward the door, thinking how comforting it was to have someone to come home to. He'd rounded the corner, heading the short distance back to Rudolph Oil when Myla's frantic call stopped him.

"Nick!"

Myla's shouts echoed through the skyscrapers. Nick pivoted to find her running toward him, a look of panic draining the color from her face. Hurrying to meet her, he said, "What's the matter?"

"It's Jesse. Her school called. She's got a fever and she's having trouble breathing. I've got to go and get her, but Grant borrowed my car to make a delivery. Can you give me a lift?''

''Of course.'' Taking her by the arm, he guided her across Milam Street. ''My car's parked at the office. It's just around the corner.''

''Good. I got one of the other waitresses to cover for me. I really appreciate this. I know you've got a lot of work to catch up on.''

''Don't worry about that. I don't mind. I'll call the office from the car and let my secretary know I won't be back today.''

They reached his car in record time. As Nick leaned down to unlock her door, Myla put a hand on his arm, her eyes full of gratitude. ''I owe you so much.''

Nick wanted much more than just gratitude, but he couldn't tell her that. ''Stop worrying,'' he said in a reassuring tone. ''Now, let's go take care of Jesse.''

# Chapter Eight

"It's not your fault," Nick said softly as he handed Myla the cup of icy soda. All around them, hospital personnel whizzed by, taking care of the business of healing the sick.

Myla looked around, a concerned expression darkening her face. "I've been so busy lately. I should have seen this coming. I've always been able to gauge her allergies before, but I just thought she'd caught another cold."

"You had no way of knowing it would turn into pneumonia," he told her as he urged her to sit down on the mauve floral couch in the pediatric waiting room of Schumpert Medical Center. "This stuff is very tricky."

"But I should have been more careful," Myla said, holding her head against one hand. "She's been so sick all winter, and I just kept pumping her full of medicine and sending her to school. I can't believe I didn't catch this in time."

Nick put an arm around her, then squeezed her shoulder for reassurance. "You've had a lot on your mind."

A burly, gray-haired doctor came marching up the hall from the pediatric ward. Spotting Myla and Nick, he halted in front of them. "Ms. Howell, I'm Dr. Redmond." After giving Myla a brisk handshake, he spoke to her in a hushed tone. "You've got one very sick little girl on your hands. We'll need to keep her a few days. She's very congested."

Myla put down her cup of soda with shaky hands. "Will she be all right?"

"I think we can help her," the doctor said. "We've already started administering antibiotics, but it's hard to pinpoint whether this was brought on by a bacterial infection or her allergies. We'll run tests to be sure. We've got her under oxygen until she can breath a little better on her own."

"Whatever it takes, Dr. Redmond," Nick said, his arm around Myla's waist. "I'll cover all the costs."

"Of course, Mr. Rudolph. Anything for the son of Joseph and Ruth Rudolph. Your mother was a special woman. We all miss her very much."

"Me, too," Nick replied. Then, "Just take care of Jesse for me, okay?"

"That we can do." Giving Myla another pat of assurance, the doctor said, "You can see her now, Ms. Howell."

After the doctor told them he'd check back with them later, Myla looked up at Nick. She was already feeling tremendous guilt because of Jesse's illness. Now, she had the added burden of owing Nick yet again. Maybe if she hadn't been so distracted these past few weeks, if she'd kept her mind on her children's welfare instead of obsessing about Nick, this wouldn't have happened.

Her tone firm, she said, "I can't let you pay for this. I'll use the money I've been saving."

"Myla…" Nick pulled her out of the hallway, away from prying eyes and ears. "Don't think about all of that right now. Your little girl is sick and you don't have insurance. I can help you."

In spite of his good intentions, Myla felt ashamed for having to rely on him, and even more ashamed that she'd let Jesse get so sick. "And what about the next time, and the time after that? Nick, don't you see, you're stepping in to take care of me." Her voice cracking, she added, "Which means, I can't even take care of my daughter on my own!"

The frustration in her eyes only made Nick want to protect her even more. She blamed herself for this, no doubt. And, she probably wanted to blame him, too. "Listen," he said in a gentle tone, "this isn't your fault. And I don't mind whatever comes our way. I want to take care of you."

"I've got to learn to handle things on my own," she retorted, a desperation in her words. "I've got to be more careful from now on." Giving him an imploring look, she grabbed his arm. "Nick, she's so sick."

Nick pulled her close in spite of her resistance. "All the more reason to let me help—this time. Stop worrying about being so self-reliant and concentrate on your daughter." Pushing her hair away from her temple, he looked down at her. "And would you please stop apologizing and thanking me for my generosity. I'm not a saint or a martyr, Myla, but I refuse to let you do this on your own. End of discussion."

"Why?" she had to ask, the humiliation of being needy fighting with her love for him. "Why do you insist on being my knight in shining armor?"

Hearing her ask that question, Nick wondered why himself. Maybe because he *needed* to do something. He couldn't stand by any longer and watch her struggle. Not because she was a widow with two children; not because she didn't have a decent place to live or a good job; but because…he was in love with her. The urge to tell her so hit him with the force of the wind whipping outside the hospital windows. He stared at her, wanted to tell her, but her look of dread and defeat stopped him. "Because you need me," he said.

Myla couldn't deny that. Just having him here made this easier. Sonny had always insisted Jesse didn't have allergies and that Myla was just babying the little girl. Nick hadn't even questioned it. Yes, she needed him. But she wasn't willing to admit just how much. Not yet.

"I'll pay you back, a little each week," she declared, her tone stubborn.

He reached for her, gently urging her back into his arms. "Okay. We'll work out the details later."

"I want to see my daughter now," she whispered. Then, "Nick, I am really grateful to you. Thanks, again."

Gratitude. Nick had never had much time for that kind of mushy sentiment. Now, as he stood staring out the window of Jesse's room, he thought how ironic it was that he'd fallen in love with a woman who thanked him almost daily for his generosity. He'd dated lots of women and they'd all had some sort of pedigree attached: old money, new money, star quality, socialite connections, snobbish attitudes, but never had one of them given him any gratitude.

Myla was different. Stubborn. Determined. Firm in her beliefs. And bound to show the world she could handle things on her own. Would she resent him for always rushing to her rescue?

Jesse stirred under the oxygen tent, bringing Myla up out of her chair and Nick back from the window.

"Mama?" A small hand reached out in the darkened room, and Myla was immediately there to take it.

"I'm right here, honey. It's all right. Try to go back to sleep."

She patted Jesse's hand, her eyes meeting Nick's over the bed. He seemed so distant, so far away in his thoughts as he stood there by the window, watching the sun set. Now he moved to stare down at her daughter, concern evident in his dark eyes.

"She's drifted off again," he whispered. "Want to step out and get some fresh air?"

"Maybe in a minute." She walked around the bed to join him. "She looks so tiny and helpless, lying there like that. I'm afraid to leave her."

He wrapped an arm around her waist to tug her close. "Then we'll stay."

Myla leaned against him, glad for the support. "It's so late. Why don't you go back home? You've been at one hospital with Henny, and now this with Jesse. You need to go home and get some rest."

"I don't mind. I don't want to leave you."

Touched, she asked, "Does being here make you think about your mother?"

"Yes, but it's better now." He kissed the top of her head, then said, "You know, after Mother died, my father donated a huge sum of money to help build a new cancer wing. But he never set foot in this hospital again, and neither did I, until today."

Myla lifted her head to gaze into his eyes, her heart going out to him. "Nick, why didn't you say something? You didn't have to stay."

"Yes, I did. You were right, Myla. I can't blame the doctors or God for my mother's illness. I know miracles happen everyday, but sometimes there's just no way to save someone you love. When I think of all the time I wasted, blaming others, wallowing in my misery, I wonder sometimes how I got through each day. Now, after having been around you, I'm finding it easier to accept. Why was it so hard before?''

She held her arms on his shoulders, smiling up at him. ''Maybe because your grief was getting in the way. You weren't open or willing to listen then. Now, you are.''

He threw his head back, lifting his eyes to the sky. ''It sure takes a heavy load off my back.''

''That's the beauty of having someone higher to turn to. We don't have to waste our energy worrying about things we can't change.''

''But we can concentrate on the things we can change.''

''Exactly.''

''Well, then, Ms. Howell, take some of your own advice, and stop worrying about your daughter. I predict she's going to be just fine.''

Myla shot Jesse a loving look. ''I certainly hope so.''

''Would you feel better if we said a little prayer?''

''I've been praying,'' she admitted, ''but, yes, I'd appreciate it if you'd pray along with me.''

He did, asking for Jesse's quick recovery and asking for the courage to go out and help others who might be worse off. Because, it would take courage and strength to make a visible change within himself. But he intended to do it.

Jesse's harsh cough broke into his thoughts. Myla wasted little time slipping out of his embrace to rush to her daughter's side. Nick watched helplessly as Myla soothed the little girl with a few gentle words.

The tender scene shattered his heart into a million pieces, reminding him of how his father had held his mother, trying in vain to ease her horrible pain. Had his father been weak then, or had he simply been overcome by love and grief? Maybe his love for Ruthie had been his strength. Bitterly, Nick wondered if he'd misjudged his father, after all. Was it possible to be vulnerable and still remain strong?

If this was a test, he was certainly going to try to live up to it. Walking to the bed, he leaned over Jesse. ''We're both right here, honey. Do you need anything?''

The little girl reached out her hand, taking Nick's stronger one.

He wrapped his fingers around her frail little bones, his heart bursting with such a protective warmth that he wondered how anyone ever managed to get through fatherhood at all.

"I'm scared," she whispered, her big blue-green eyes wide and misty.

Nick gripped the tiny fingers clinging to his hand. "We all get scared sometimes, Jesse. But you're going to be all right. I won't let anything bad happen to you."

Myla looked at the man holding her daughter's hand, her own tears mirroring the moisture she saw gathering in the depths of his eyes. He didn't know it, but he'd just given her the one thing all his money couldn't buy. He'd given her that part of himself he'd been hiding from the world. By admitting his own fears, Nick Rudolph had shown just exactly how much courage he had.

And, he'd given her the ability to trust again.

Later, when dawn colored the trees outside a vivid newborn pink, Myla roused Nick out of his cramped position on a nearby chair. "I'm worried about Patrick. Will you go and check on Lydia and him before he goes to school? And get some rest while you're there."

Half asleep, Nick smiled at her bossy nature, feeling warm and content with the new intimacy that had developed between them during these past few hours. "How's the patient?"

"She's breathing better."

He got up to stretch long and hard. "Ah, we made it through the night."

Myla's warm gaze touched on his face. "Yes, we did."

He shook the creaks out of his neck. "Okay, then, I'll check on our other wards, then I guess I'll see you for lunch, maybe." With that, he headed for the darkened door.

Myla handed him his coat. "Nick?"

He turned, an expectant look on his face.

"Give Patrick a kiss for me."

With that, he took the two steps to reach her. "I'll do better than that. I'll take him one from his mother."

Surprised, Myla lifted on tiptoe as he kissed her solidly on the lips. When he reluctantly let her go, she managed to say, "Well, thank you, I think."

Nick's wide grin cut through the darkened room. "Now that's the kind of thanks I can live with."

"She's much better."

Myla held her daughter's hand, rubbing her fingers back and forth over the soft skin as she waited for Dr. Redmond to give them an update. Nick sat nearby, his relief evident as he smiled over at Jesse.

After three days in the hospital, the little girl was getting restless. "Can I go home? I miss Shredder."

Dr. Redmond held his hands together, absently pivoting on his tennis shoes, his eyes fixed on Jesse. "The antibiotics have kicked in," he said, his gray brows knotted together. "She showed all the signs of having bacterial pneumonia, but based on her history with allergies…I'd say this was more an allergic reaction than a case of pneumonia. This dry heat we use to stay warm, coupled with her not being able to get out in the fresh air, probably triggered all of this. But we still need to pinpoint exactly what caused her to have such an adverse reaction."

"What should we do?" Nick asked, his own gaze centered on Jesse. "What do you think caused this?"

"Oh, could be several things." The doctor eased over to Jesse, his smile reassuring. "I'm sure regular old dust and mold contributed a lot to it. Pine straw, dry leaves, and as I said, dry heat—a humidifier would help there."

"She does have a hard time with mold," Myla said. "I always kept our house as clean as possible to avoid provoking her allergies."

"Yeah," Jesse added hoarsely. "Mama wouldn't let me play in the barn back home." Then giving Myla a sheepish look, she added, "But I did help Lydia rake pine straw the other day. Me and Patrick and Shredder played in it."

Myla shot her daughter a reprimanding look, then quickly amended her feelings to reprimand herself instead. "I'm sorry, honey. I should have told Lydia, but I never thought about all those pine trees in the backyard."

"Hey," Nick interjected, "it's okay. Now that we know, we'll all be more careful. And we'll go out and buy a humidifier right now.''

The doctor flexed his shoulders, then smiled down at Jesse. ''Who's this Shredder I keep hearing about?''

''My cat,'' Jesse piped up, beaming.

The doctor stopped smiling. ''You have a cat?''

Myla nodded. ''Yes, a stray. We kind of adopted him.'' Seeing the doctor's disapproving look, she asked, ''Do you think she's allergic to the cat?''

Carefully wording his statement so as not to upset Jesse, the doctor told them, ''No one can predict these things. She picked up a bug and her allergies collided with it. It's that simple. We'll send her home with some medicine for the symptoms, but I'd like to do a new set of allergy tests and start her on shots once we find the culprits. But even then, you'll need to keep her away from dust, and that tempting pine straw.'' Pulling Myla aside, he whispered, ''And I'd advise getting rid of the cat.''

Later, as they zoomed away from the hospital to take Jesse home, Nick turned to Myla. ''What if she's allergic to Shredder? We'll have to give him to someone else.''

''She'll be devastated,'' Myla whispered, glancing over her shoulder to make sure Jesse wasn't listening. ''But if it's dangerous to her health, we won't have a choice.''

''Of course, I can keep the cat after you move out,'' he offered, thinking the tiny animal would help ease his own loneliness. ''Maybe by the time you get a new place, we'll know one way or the other.''

''That would make Jesse feel better, I'm sure.'' Giving him a meaningful look, she added, ''Now I'm worried about moving at all. If we do go to Magnolia House...well, it's very old and not in the best of condition. I hope the move won't provoke another allergy attack.''

''That is something to consider,'' he said, feeling a wave of hope rise in his heart. ''And wouldn't it be a shame now, if you just had to go on living at my big, old house?''

Myla stared ahead, acutely aware of how Nick had talked to the doctor as if Jesse were his own child. But the reality of this was that Jesse was her responsibility. "I can't do that, Nick. And you know why."

He maneuvered the car through a busy intersection, then gave her his full attention. "Why? You'd still be my employee and we have plenty of chaperons."

"It's not that. You've been very understanding about our relationship."

"Yes, I've learned extreme patience. You know you can count on that. So, what's the problem?"

"It's just not right, Nick. I need to get my own place for my own peace of mind, as well as your standing in the community."

Taking one hand away from the steering wheel, he gave her a sharp look. "My standing? What are you talking about?"

Gritting her teeth, she plunged right in. "Carolyn could make trouble for us. She hinted at it the other day. She said people would talk if they knew we were…living together, so to speak, especially if they found out we had feelings for each other. I can't put you through that, and I certainly won't expose my children to that kind of ridicule."

Stopping for a red light, Nick banged the wheel of the car. "Well, you're right about one thing. I do need to pay Carolyn a little visit. And when I'm finished, I think she'll be straight on a lot of things."

"Don't…don't say anything you'll regret," she cautioned. "I don't want Carolyn to think I'm telling you things about her that aren't true."

"I know what to say," he assured her. "You taught me patience. And I'll sure need it with Carolyn."

True to his word, Nick did have a long talk with Carolyn Parker. But to Myla's dismay, instead of making it clear that he was ending things with Carolyn, Nick invited the blonde to serve on the grass-roots committee he was forming to help the homeless.

"If she sees that I've changed for the better and that I still care for her as a good friend, maybe she'll leave us alone," he explained to Myla. "Besides, we've done nothing wrong, so we have nothing to hide."

Myla wasn't so sure, but she did agree that they had nothing to be ashamed of. She was working for Nick, nothing more. No matter that she loved him dearly. She'd do the right thing, for her children's sake.

Tonight, she stood in the kitchen preparing a hearty dinner for the ad hoc committee Nick was heading up. The team included Nick and Lydia, a reporter from one of the television stations to bring in publicity, Carolyn because of her connections within the society of Shreveport, and Grant—because Lydia had insisted he was sensitive to the needs of the homeless.

Now, Carolyn came into the kitchen, her cool gaze slipping over Myla to settle on the pot of gumbo Myla had stewing on the stove.

"Have you heard the news?" Carolyn asked, flipping on the nearby television set. "I thought you'd like to know."

"Know what?" Myla asked warily.

To her surprise, the reporter who was due here any minute was on the early news, covering a story on Magnolia House. The sound of hammering echoed behind the smiling dark-haired newswoman as she explained how a group of local companies had banded together to donate a new heating and cooling unit to the transitional shelter.

"These men are installing the new unit while we have this mild break in the winter weather. And they're cleaning and renovating the ancient air ducts, too," the reporter, a lady named Brooke Alexander, explained.

"A new unit?" Myla's eyes widened. Thinking about the mold and dust that would be cleared away, she remembered Dr. Redmond's warning. That wouldn't be a problem for Jesse now.

"This gesture of kindness is costing a small fortune," the reporter continued, "but these companies banded together to pay all the expenses."

Suspicious, Myla leaned over the counter. A thought popped into her head, but she couldn't quite put it to words. Anxious to hear more, she turned up the volume.

"The leader of this project has asked to remain anonymous," Ms. Alexander said, "but sources tell us he runs one of the most successful oil companies in Louisiana."

No doubt who that was, Myla mused, her gaze locking with Carolyn's. "Nick did this, didn't he?"

Carolyn nodded slowly, no hostility in her eyes. "Yes, I believe he did. He'd mentioned it to me when he asked me to serve on this committee, and I guess he couldn't wait to get started on things. You must be very proud of him.''

''I am,'' Myla admitted. ''And you should be, too.''

Carolyn came around the counter to sample the gumbo. Taking a spoon, she dipped a helping, then held it away to cool for a minute. ''I am. And Myla, I want to apologize for the way I acted the other day. I've always been a sore loser.''

Myla searched Carolyn's face, then, seeing the sincerity in the other woman's eyes, went back to her task of slicing French bread. ''You're not a loser, Carolyn. You're a lovely woman and I know Nick cares about you. I'm just sorry if I've caused you any heartache.''

''You didn't. Nick did. But I'm over it now. You see, I've never seen Nick like this. He really has changed. And when he took the time to come and really talk to me, in a way we haven't talked in years…well, I knew I'd never win him back. All he could talk about was you and how he was going to form this corporation to help the homeless.''

Myla chuckled softly. ''He's pretty determined, once he sets his mind to something.''

Carolyn grabbed a slice of bread and dipped it into the gumbo for one more taste. ''Yes, and you'd better remember that.''

''Oh, I'm well aware of it,'' Myla answered. ''But thanks for the warning.''

Carolyn lifted one brow. ''You know, I thought Nick was married to his work. Maybe I was wrong. Maybe I just wasn't the right person to pry him away from Rudolph Oil. I think you might succeed, though.''

''If anything happens,'' Myla said, stressing the *if*, ''we will have to take it slow. I have to be very sure.''

''Just don't hurt him,'' Carolyn warned. ''That would devastate him at this point.''

Myla watched as Carolyn pranced out of the room. Maybe she should consider her feelings for Nick long and hard. After all, she'd spouted platitudes to him, talked to him, helped him to find his faith again. If she let him down, he might lose all the trust he'd gained over the last few weeks, and never regain it again.

Had Carolyn really been trying to understand, or was this warning just another way for her to fuel Myla's own doubts?

"Trust in God," Myla said as she absently stirred the thick gumbo. "And put a little trust in Nick, too."

Now, if she could just learn to trust herself.

# Chapter Nine

After Myla served coffee and dessert, everyone gathered around the empty dining table with pads and pens. Nick stole away and found her in the kitchen, busy loading the dishwasher. Stopping in the arched doorway, he remembered watching her like this before. How natural she looked, so domestic and womanly, so beautiful. She was the type of woman who loved having a home to call her own.

Yet she didn't have any place to call her own.

"Need some help there?" he called, lifting his shoulder off the doorway to push toward her.

Myla pivoted at the sound of his voice. Noting how attractive he looked in his old jeans and faded red polo shirt, she calmed her tap-dancing nerves to a slow waltz. "How's the planning committee going?"

"For the moment, it's going without me." Handing her a glass, he added, "We were hoping you'd join us."

She shook her head. "I…I used to serve on committees, too many of them. Sonny resented it, but he couldn't tell me to stop—all part of his carefully constructed public image. I've already told Lydia I'll be glad to work behind the scenes, but I don't want to be on the committee. It's nice to just do my job now."

She didn't tell him that since Jesse's illness, she'd made a firm commitment to sticking strictly to business—just until she could get out on her own and get a proper perspective on her feelings for Nick.

Nick didn't let her get away so easily. "But isn't this part of your job? I mean, aren't you the one who told me we had to do something, make some changes?"

She lifted her brows, stopping her busywork to stare up at him. "I intend to do something. I'll stamp and fold mail-outs. I'll make copies and run errands. I'll even cook for the volunteers."

"And stay hidden away, just like you once accused me of doing?"

"That sounds like a challenge."

"It is a challenge. None of us know what we're doing in there. But you, you've been there. You could be a big help, and I want you...because you have firsthand experience."

Placing one hand on her hip, she teased him to hide the warm feelings his words provoked. "Oh, and since you're the boss, I guess that's an order?"

He smiled when he saw the twinkle in her eyes. "Yes, I guess it is. But I'm asking, not demanding. And I'm not asking to enhance my public image, but because I care."

"You have changed."

"Okay, okay. I get the point. Are you going to help us or not?"

She turned on the dishwasher, then took one more look around the spotless kitchen. "Okay. Guess it wouldn't hurt to just sit in and listen. Let me check on the children, and then I'll be right in."

He waited for her, watching as she kissed her sleeping children, his heart helplessly opening another fraction because of the sweetness of her nurturing strength. Then when Jesse opened her eyes and called out to her mother, he stopped at the door.

"Mama, where's Shredder? I want him to sleep with me."

Myla leaned over her daughter, placing a hand on Jesse's face. "You know Shredder is off-limits in here until we're sure you're completely well, honey. He's just fine in his little bed out in the garage, and during the day he gets to roam around the rest of the house."

Jesse looked so sad, Nick couldn't help it. He stepped back into the room. "Your mother's right, sweetie. You might be allergic to that crazy cat."

Jesse sat up, her big eyes imploring Nick. "But I love Shredder. You aren't going to make us get rid of him, are you, Mr. Nick?"

Nick squatted by the bed, so he could see Jesse better. "Of course not. He just has to stay out of Henny's rooms for a while, until we're sure you're not allergic."

That seemed to calm the little girl. "Okay. That's all I was worried about. Mr. Nick, please take care of Shredder for me—after we move into the shelter."

Nick glanced up at Myla, then looked back down at Jesse. Swallowing the tightness in his throat, he said, "I will. Shredder will always have a home here."

"Even if I can't come to visit?"

"Even if you can't come to visit."

Jesse lay back down then, her voice so soft, Nick had to strain to hear her words. "'Cause Shredder was just like us, wasn't he? He didn't have any other place to go."

Myla sat down on the bed then to gather her daughter close. Her words were husky, but Nick heard the tremor in her voice. "That's right, honey. Mr. Nick took us in when we didn't have a place to stay, and I know he'll take care of Shredder for us. You don't have to worry about that."

"I promise," Nick said, his eyes on the woman holding the little girl. "Always."

Myla tucked Jessica back in, then pulled the door partly closed before turning to Nick. "Nick, I—"

"Don't say thank you, please," he whispered. "You don't owe me anything. Can't you see, you and your children have redeemed me. I was so lonely, so alone, so bitter. Now, I have something to fight for. And I will fight for you, Myla. Oh, I know you're holding off on any decisions and I know you have to do things your way, such as writing me those checks for the doctor's bill. But I won't give up. I don't give up too easily."

"I have noticed that about you," she said, stopping him in the alcove just outside the door to the dining room. "Nick, I'm really proud of what you did for Magnolia House."

Shrugging, he said, "I don't know what you're talking about."

"Yes, you do. You went in there and overhauled their heating and cooling system. It was a very unselfish thing to do."

He lowered his head, not used to being heralded for doing good deeds. "I did it for Jesse."

"I know that," she said softly, "and you helped all those other people in the process."

"That's me, just an all-around good guy."

"You are a good guy. Jesse obviously thinks you hung the moon."

He shook his head, then grinned. "No, I just hired someone to do it for me." Then turning serious, he said, "Your daughter and I have grown closer in our efforts to keep Shredder from being booted out of the house."

Myla had noticed that bond between her daughter and this man, especially tonight. It would be so hard to pull her children out of the safe environment Nick had provided for them. "It was very sweet of you to talk to her about Shredder."

"I talked to her because I care about her—and that wild cat. And like I said, I don't give up easily. Not even on a woman who thinks she has to do everything her way."

No, he wasn't one to give up, Myla thought. She had to make him see her fears, though. Make him understand that this wasn't so simple. "But *I* don't have anything to offer you, Nick. I'm so afraid I'll make the same mistake twice."

He held her, his hands firm on her arms. "Look at me, Myla. I'm not like Sonny. I'd never treat you the way he did. I'd never hurt you."

"I want to believe that," she said, hoping to make him understand. "I do. And really, it's not you I'm worried about. It's me. I don't want to let you down."

Amazed at her self-doubt, Nick said, "You haven't let me down so far. You don't give yourself enough credit, Myla."

Voicing her worst fears, she said, "But what if Carolyn is right? What if you're just intrigued with me because I'm your new cause? What if these feelings aren't strong enough to carry us through in the long run?"

He hissed a bitter laugh. "Do you think I feel sorry for you? Is that it? Do you think I'm doing all of this out of pity?"

She dropped her head. "Maybe. I don't know."

He gently tugged her close, then wrapped his arms around her waist. "Myla, Myla, sometimes I *envy* you. I envy your strength and your courage and your convictions. I've wanted to help you all along, but...I don't feel sorry for you. You don't allow that.''

She lifted her head, her eyes searching his. ''You've changed so much since that first night. I just have to be sure, Nick. Very sure.''

He touched a hand to her hair. ''Well, I am sure. I was lost the night I saw you standing in the middle of that road.'' Seeing the stubborn glint in her eyes, he plunged on. ''I'd always heard Lydia talking about Magnolia House, but I never had the time or the inclination to go to the place myself. Well, the other day, after what the doctor told us about Jesse's condition, I did go. I had to check the place out before I could bring myself to let you move in there.''

He stopped, taking a long breath, his eyes going dark. ''When I saw the other children—the ones I don't even know, living in those cramped apartments, wearing clothes donated by other people and eating food provided by someone else—I understood why Lydia does the things she does, and why you gave that old man your plasma money.

''It broke my heart to see those families, but they all had one thing in common. They were all fighting this thing together, and they seemed secure and happy. And I kept remembering that Bible verse from Proverbs about those who are rich yet have nothing, and those who are poor, yet have great riches.''

''I know the verse,'' Myla said, thinking of how many times she'd counted her blessings, even when she had nothing worldly in her possession. ''It's hard to grasp, though, when you see homeless people on the street.''

He nodded. ''Yes, especially when you live in a mansion and have a fat bank account, yet still manage to gripe your way through each day. I'm ashamed to think I never really cared about what was going on around me before.''

She patted him on the arm. ''Well, now you do care. And that's what's so important.'' If nothing else, she and Nick would have that bond to share. And she'd be remiss to turn him down now, when *he* was asking for her help. Smiling up at him, she said, ''I'll serve on your committee, Nick. I'll do whatever I can.''

He gave her a quick, reassuring kiss, then took her into the long dining room. Lifting a hand to the others at the table, he announced,

"We have a new recruit. Myla has agreed to serve with us—and not just behind the scenes."

Lydia clapped, her smile broad. "Oh, good. We've got the preliminary plans for the charity ball laid out and we've registered our incorporation papers with the state—we're calling our organization Hope, Faith and Love, Incorporated. But Myla, we need to ask you something."

Eyeing her warily, Myla said, "Sure, I think."

Brooke Alexander, the reporter who'd joined up to promote her television station's charitable image, said, "We've come into some property, a house in the old Highland District, and we're going to recruit people to remodel it for a deserving family. From everything Lydia and Nick have told us tonight, you're eligible to apply for it."

Her interest growing, Myla sat down. "I've been trying to find out more about how to qualify for one of those low-cost houses. Are you saying I could possibly get this house?"

"We think so," Grant said, tapping his ink pen on his notepad. "The house has already been donated, free and clear. All you need to do is fill out the application and wait for the board's approval. But, whether you get the house or not, we'd like you to give a speech at the charity ball—telling about your situation."

Lydia gave Grant a look of total adoration. Nick, however, didn't have time tonight to fume at his little sister's obvious infatuation. He was too busy studying Myla's reaction to the news of the house. Would she be pleased?

Too astonished to notice anything else, Myla asked, "How many people will be at this event?"

Lydia leaned forward. "If all goes as planned, about two to three hundred."

"Three hundred people!" Myla shook her head. "I couldn't possibly."

Carolyn gave her a level stare. "Nick thinks you have a story to tell."

"He would." Myla sighed, then ran a shaking hand through her long tresses. Could she really face all those people with her humiliating story? "I'll...I'll have to think about this."

Lydia jotted down some more notes. "Well, we don't have much time. We've already formed a solid board of directors, and we're setting up the bylaws now. We're shooting for mid-April for the membership kickoff, with the ball as our first fund-raiser.''

Myla shook her head. "That's only a couple of months. No, I can't. I'm not ready to talk about everything that's happened to me.''

Nick spoke softly from the doorway behind her. "Think of all the people you'll be helping.''

His dark eyes washed her with a warmth that left her mystified. This new Nick was even more intriguing than the old reserved one. And rather than making her into a charity case, he was working toward helping her in a positive way. He was willing to let her make it on her own, without any pressure about their relationship. This would be a risk, but it would also give her the freedom to make her own choices. And she'd have a home again.

"Hope, Faith and Love,'' she said, her eyes meeting Nick's. "These three.''

"And the greatest of these is love,'' he reminded her gently.

Biting her bottom lip, she nodded slowly. "I'll be so nervous, and we don't even know if I'll get the house.''

"You'll win the house and every heart at the ball,'' Nick said. And he'd see to it personally, if it would make her regain her self-confidence.

"Looks like she's already won one,'' Brooke teased, her keen eyes lighting on Nick. "Maybe that's the real story.''

"Yeah,'' Carolyn added, getting up to leave. "And if you can win ruthless Nick Rudolph over, you don't need to worry about anyone else in this town.''

Myla didn't miss the sarcasm or the hint of regret in the other woman's parting words. And apparently from the interested look in her eyes, neither did Brooke Alexander.

"I don't want to make a big deal out of this,'' Nick warned the reporter. "Let's keep my involvement low-key, okay?''

"Sure, Nick.'' The woman's smile was practiced and precise. "Just the facts, I promise.''

Myla waited until the others had left, then turned to Nick. "Did you plan this—getting me involved, I mean—just to shift the spotlight from yourself?''

He gave her a level look. "No. Actually it was Carolyn's idea to have you speak at the fund-raiser. You've managed to win her over, too. Quite a coup."

Myla looked skeptical. "Well, if I get my own place, I'll be away from you. Probably why she suggested this."

"Whoa, I hadn't thought about it that way. Carolyn's pretty crafty, but I do believe she's sincere about this. She didn't flirt with me once tonight. In fact, I think she's found a new catch—my friend from the city council. He's single and up-and-coming, just her type, and Lydia had the good sense to seat them next to each other at some stuffy social event the other night."

Myla laughed in spite of her worries, then said, "I appreciate your board's considering me for the house, and of course I understand I might not qualify. I just hope you didn't bully anybody into doing this—"

He shook his head. "I'm doing what I thought you wanted most in the world—I'm helping you to find a place to live."

Realizing he was right, she didn't argue with him any further. This had been her goal, her dream all along. This was her chance to prove herself. And maybe, this was Nick's chance to prove himself, too.

"I'll be at your fancy ball," she said at last.

He gave her a look that told her everything, yet revealed nothing. Did she see regret in his eyes, or relief, or maybe both?

"You can wear the green dress."

Gripping her hands together, Myla looked away, sweet memories of that special Christmas night coloring her mind. "Yes, that is the only elegant thing I own."

"Wear it for me," he whispered, reaching out to draw her into his arms. "And we'll come home and have a turkey sandwich and pound cake, and we'll dance underneath the stars."

"Sounds perfect," she said as she leaned into his kiss.

Except by that time, she might be living in a different home.

"I'm getting a house," Myla told Grant a few weeks later as they cleaned up after the breakfast rush at the coffeehouse.

"That's great, isn't it?" he asked, giving her a questioning look.

"I mean, this is all you've talked about since you started working here. Now you won't have to live in the homeless shelter, right?"

"Right." Myla finished making a fresh pot of French vanilla decaf. "At least I can bypass that part of the transition. I wasn't looking forward to shifting my children around."

Grant stopped stacking dishes to stare over at her. "So, things are working out for you. Then why do you look like you've just lost your best friend?"

Myla started doodling on an order pad lying by the cash register. Grant was very astute and sensitive. And right on target about her mood today. She had been down since learning that the board of directors for Hope, Faith and Love had voted for her to be the recipient of their first house.

She didn't know why she was reacting this way, but something just didn't feel right about this. Maybe it had all been too easy, and she surely wasn't used to getting things the easy way. Or maybe, the truth be told, she didn't really want to leave Nick, after all.

Deciding she could trust Grant, she said, "Oh, who am I kidding? It's because I love working for Nick, and I love cleaning that big old house of his, and cooking and pretending I'm a housewife again."

Grant nodded, his poetic eyes gazing over at her with a too knowing expression. "Oh, I see. You've found a home and you don't want to leave it, because you have feelings for the owner. Does he know how you feel?"

Embarrassed, Myla placed a bundle of clean forks in a nearby holder. "*I* don't know how I feel. On the one hand, I think I love Nick and could be completely happy with him. But on the other hand, I still don't know how he really feels about me. And I have to be sure, not only of him, but of myself. So, I figure the only way I can do that is to go ahead and move out on my own and see if we can hold on to what we think we have."

Grant rolled his eyes. "This is complicated, huh?"

"Very." Turning to a customer, Myla handed him his espresso, then took his dollar. "And I don't want to burden you with the details."

"Hey, that's what friends are for," Grant said, his gentle blue eyes touching hers. "You'll find your way, Myla. After all, you've come this far."

"Yes, I have," she reminded herself. "And I am excited about the house. It's so cute. It needs work, of course, and I'm required to put in five hundred hours of sweat equity to help fix it up, but I can't wait. I get a twenty-year, interest-free loan, so it's really going to be mine."

"That sounds fair," Grant remarked, straining as he reached for some clean coffee cups. "Need any help?"

"Yes. We rely on volunteers to help do most of the work. Nick has set this corporation up so that everything is donated, including time."

"I'll be there," Grant said, pushing his glasses up on his long nose. "Especially if it means I'll get to see Lydia more."

Smiling at last, Myla nudged him with her elbow. "How's that relationship going, Romeo?"

Grant sighed, then shook his head. "Let's just say, I know what you mean about Nick Rudolph. That man's hard to get to know." He waved his hands. "One minute he's teasing me, the next, he's glaring at me."

Myla could picture Nick doing exactly that; he'd certainly shifted moods on her enough. "So, in other words, things could be great between you and Lydia if Nick would just back off?"

"Something like that," Grant replied. "Her big brother thinks I have less than honorable intentions toward Lydia, but I really like her, you know."

"I do know," Myla said as she took the money for a customer's cookie and coffee. "Lydia has a kind heart and she's very serious about helping other people."

"She sure is," Grant agreed readily. "I'll admit I didn't believe that at first. I thought she was just some bored rich kid out to appease her sense of social duty. But now that I've spent some time with her, I can tell she's really sincere. Did you know she's thinking of going back to college to become a bona fide counselor? She wants to do more than just volunteer a few hours a week."

Surprised, Myla gave him a wide-eyed look. "Does Nick know that? No, of course, he couldn't, or I'm sure I would have heard all about it."

"No, not yet," Grant said, his voice low and worried. "She's been trying to figure out a way to spring the news on him."

"That should be interesting." Then, wanting to reassure her friend, she said, "Nick means well, Grant. It's just...he's been both Lydia's brother and surrogate parent for so long, he's forgotten how to let go. I think he's turned all his pain into some sort of overprotective focus on his sister."

"Yeah, I know," Grant replied. "And Lydia sure sees it. That's why she's afraid to tell him about her plans. She doesn't want him to lash out at me, or think I put her up to this—which he'll do, I guarantee."

"Maybe I can talk to him," Myla offered. "Smooth the way once Lydia breaks the news?"

"You've got enough to deal with."

"I can handle Nick," Myla said, although she dreaded the tirade once Nick found out about Lydia's plans. "Let me take care of him, and you concentrate on Lydia, okay?"

"Okay," Grant said, "but I can fight my own battles. I'm not afraid of Nick Rudolph."

"Very noble," Myla teased, "but...Nick's really an old softy underneath all that bluster. We both need to remember that."

Grant nodded, then patted Myla on the shoulder. "Well, now that we've discussed both our personal lives, how about we discuss something else that's been on my mind?"

"What's that?" Myla asked, confused by the intense look on his face.

"Adding more to the menu," Grant said. Waving his hand again, he added, "After all, we've made a good team so far."

Relieved, Myla grabbed the computer printout of their profits and losses. "Oh, that reminds me—"

Grant wiped his hands on his white apron, a frown marring his boyish face. "You're not going to quit on me, are you?"

"No, nothing like that." She tapped the ledger with her finger. "I got a call about a catering job—they'd like us to cater a sit-down dinner for about twenty-five people and I'm anxious to test the waters." Before he could answer, she continued, "It's going to be hectic, but I think this is a good opportunity. We'd get lots of publicity."

Grant's eyes lit up. "Are you serious?"

She gave him a playful punch on the arm. "Well, as you just pointed out, we've made great progress so far and this would give us exactly what we'd hoped for, even though it is earlier than we'd planned. We can start building a strong base for our catering company. That is—if you think we're ready?"

Rubbing a hand across his swarthy chin, Grant thought about it for about a minute. "You do have a point, and from the smell of that garlic bread baking, I'd be crazy to let our first catering customers get away without sampling it. After our first hundred thousand or so, we can branch out." Grinning, he extended his hand. "I think it's a good idea. Tell them we accept."

"What's a good idea?"

Myla looked up to find Nick staring across the counter at her, with Lydia right beside him, smiling shyly at Grant. Grant glanced over at Myla, panic in his eyes.

Lydia hopped up on a bar stool, spinning around before she stopped, breathless and giggling. "Hi, Grant."

Nick sat down in a more dignified manner, his curious look moving from Myla to Grant. "You two look as if you've just committed a felony. What's with the guilty faces?"

Before Myla could answer his question, Lydia spoke to Grant again. "How's it been going?"

"Great. It's good…uh, real good. We were just—" He shot Myla a beseeching look.

"We were just going over the books," Myla interjected to stop Grant from stuttering. "Business is picking up."

"That's wonderful," Lydia said, her eyes on Grant. "By the way, I really enjoyed that movie the other night."

Grant pushed his bifocals up on his nose. "Me, too. Uh…can I get you a cup of coffee?"

Myla glanced at Nick. He was glaring, his dark eyes flashing such a protective fire for his sister, she was surprised he didn't come across the counter to grab poor Grant by the collar.

To waylay any such action, she said, "We've been making plans to branch out, and start our catering services right here from the coffeehouse."

"Really?" Nick spoke at last, a look of disbelief plastered across his face. "Are you sure you're ready to take on more work?"

Trying not to get too defensive, Myla placed a hand on her hip. "With Grant's help, yes, and only after Henny's completely well and back home, of course." There, that should reassure him that she wouldn't slack up on her responsibilities to him. "We've been offered a small catering job, and we just now this very minute decided to go for it."

"Sure did. That's what we were doing when you two showed up." Grant handed Lydia her coffee, then managed to ramble on. "Myla's a real treasure. Since she's started working here, we're becoming famous for our cookies and pastries."

Lydia bobbed her blond head. "Yep, Nick and I have put on a few pounds ourselves since Christmas."

"Speak for yourself," Nick said, his expression relaxing as he patted his tummy. "And pass the double chocolate chip cookies and a cup of that New Orleans blend coffee, please."

Lydia grabbed a cookie as Myla held out the basket. "Grant, you've done a wonderful job with this old building. This is fast becoming one of downtown's most popular spots."

Grant lowered his head and smiled, his face flushing red. "Like I told you, I needed a place to read my incredibly bad poetry."

Lydia looked pleased as punch. "A poet *and* a smart business-man. I like that."

Grant blushed, then offered to show Lydia a new display of paintings they'd hung that very morning.

Nick rolled his eyes as his sister practically skipped away with Grant, then said under his breath, "I think my sister's about to make a conquest. She's been stringing him along for weeks now, in spite of my warnings for her to be careful. I don't think I can bear to watch this anymore."

"Well, don't worry," Myla said, hoping to calm his brotherly concern. "Grant is a good man. He goes to church every Sunday and plays his guitar with the choir at times. And his poetry is very spiritual. He wouldn't hurt a fly."

"Great. My sister falls for the Lord Byron of Coffeeshops."

Myla glanced over at Lydia and Grant. They were deep into their own conversation, both with stars in their eyes. Deciding now wasn't the best time to tell Nick about his sister's plans—in fact, it might be best to let Lydia handle that herself—she told him, "She'll be fine." Then, she added, "What brings you two in this early in the day, anyway?"

"Wrapping up plans for the benefit ball," he explained. "Can we still count on you to make that speech?"

Her stomach twisted into a bowknot, but she quickly calmed it down. "I'll be there, but I'll be busy over the next few weeks working on the house. I got a call today, telling me I passed the application process."

He sat perfectly still, his pride shining in his golden brown eyes. "I knew you would. Need help with the renovations?"

She didn't miss his smug expression. Challenging him, she said, "I expect you to be the first in line."

"You can count on it," he replied, his tone casual. "I need to do something to make up for causing you to miss your spot at Magnolia House."

"Yes, but you've already worked hard to make up for that. Setting up this corporation will help so much, Nick. You're going to make a big difference in this community."

"That's a switch," he said, a look of humility on his face. "But you're right. This is different from just writing a check. I've never worked harder."

"And I'll bet you're enjoying every minute of it."

He gave her a wide smile. "That I am."

Lydia's hands clapping together brought both Myla and Nick's heads around. "Grant has agreed to come to our benefit ball. He can sit at our table, since I just talked him into making a sizable contribution to our cause."

"Lucky Grant," Nick teased, his eyes settling on his bubbly sister. "You never stood a chance, you know," he said to Grant.

Grant's laugh was more from nerves than humor. "I can live with that."

Nick turned back to Myla, his expression blank. "Now if I only can."

"You're doing great," Myla said in an encouraging voice, thinking he was as hard to read as the abstract art hanging on the high walls around them.

He feigned a look of innocence. "Far be it from me to interfere with my sister's social life, even though she's accused me of doing just that. I've got enough problems trying to deal with my own."

Just then, a customer called to Myla. She hurried to get the man his bagel and latte, waving to Nick. "I've got work to do."

"So do I," he said, rising up off his stool. "See you at home?"

"Okay." Myla watched him leave, all the while wondering where exactly her own home was supposed to be.

*Dear Lord, show me the way. Do I belong with Nick, or should I make this move out on my own? I leave it in Your hands.*

Out on the sidewalk, Nick said a similar prayer of his own. He hoped he'd done the right thing this time. He only knew he was letting the woman he loved go in order to win her back fair and square.

The little voice inside his head reminded him that he hadn't been so fair and square.

He told the little voice to be quiet.

# Chapter Ten

"Well, it's finished."

Nick stood back to admire the cottage they'd renovated for the first recipient of the Hope, Faith and Love, Incorporated, Housing for the Homeless. "My neck aches," he added as he rubbed the sore muscles at his shoulders.

Myla saw the pride shining in his eyes. That same pride shined within her heart. "It's beautiful, Nick."

He glanced over at her, one paint-dusted hand still on his neck. "And it's yours. All yours."

Weeks had passed—long weeks of hard work and dedicated hours of remodeling the little house. All the volunteers had left after they'd celebrated with pizza and soft drinks. Jesse and Patrick were running around in the backyard, happy to be in their own home. Shredder had opted to live with Nick and Lydia at the mansion, and Jesse hadn't argued. She planned to visit the cat often. Her allergies were all clear now, but Myla was watching her closely with spring coming up.

Now, Myla walked up onto the tiny front porch, admiring the fresh coat of white paint and the blue-colored shutters. "I'm going to plant azaleas," she told him over her shoulder.

"And don't forget the yellow roses."

"Lots of them."

"I'll help you."

She whirled to lean over the new spindle railing. "You have

helped me, from the very beginning. I'll never be able to repay you, Nick.''

"You already have," he said, coming up to sit on the gray-painted wooden steps. "You gave me something I never dreamed I could find again—my faith.''

"I didn't do it," she explained, lowering herself down beside him. "God did.''

"He sent you to me.''

"He knows how to deal with ruthless executives.''

"Yes, He certainly dealt me a curveball. And not just with you—now I've got that Grant fellow to contend with, also.''

"How are things with Lydia and Grant?'' she asked, careful that she didn't put her nose into their business without being asked.

Nick gave her a knowing glance. "Don't pretend you don't know a thing about them. I know Lydia confides in you almost daily.''

Myla tossed her ponytail off her neck. "Okay, yes, I know a little. But I want to know how *you* feel.''

He fell back against a square porch column. "Like I'm losing my baby sister…like I'm losing control.''

"Or gaining a brother-in-law?''

Nick held up a hand. "Don't! I'm not ready to hear that yet.''

"She could do worse," Myla offered, taking his hand in hers. "And I'm proud of you for staying so *in control*. Lydia has to be able to make her own decisions, good or bad.''

"Oh, I'm trying hard to stay sane. Especially since she also informed me she's thinking about becoming a social worker. What's gotten into my sister?''

"How long have you known about that?'' Myla questioned, surprised that he hadn't ranted and raved about it.

"She told me last night.'' At Myla's questioning look, he added, "Don't worry. I handled it with brotherly concern and complete calm. You've taught me patience, see? And as you just pointed out, the good Lord has dealt me a whole new set of challenges.''

Myla couldn't help but love him all over again. He looked so completely, utterly confused. And so adorable. "But you took what He dealt you and did something positive. And now look.''

He lifted his head to look around the peaceful, tree-shaded neighborhood, refusing to feel guilty about her happiness. Spring was just around the corner; already the dogwoods and crape myrtles were starting to bud. He shouldn't feel so lousy—he'd only given the woman he loved the very thing she wanted most in the world.

To hide his overactive conscience, he said, "This is only the beginning. We have two other houses lined up for this summer and fall."

Myla leaned back to take a long breath of the clear, crisp air. "Everything's so beautiful today. So green and fresh. The air smells so rich."

"All is right with the world," Nick said, his tone light in spite of the great sadness coloring his heart. "My sister's changing right before my eyes. Henny's glad to be home, and she's taking things easy. You have a good job with Grant and your catering business. And I've just lost…a wonderful housekeeper."

Myla's heart shifted into an erratic beat. She wanted to thank him for keeping this light, but she didn't think she could voice the words. So instead, she said, "I left you a pound cake in the pantry."

His eyes went all warm and misty. "I'll savor each bite."

Myla sat still, the awkward silence surrounding her. This was it; this was the moment she'd dreamed about since that cold, dark night in her car. She had her own home again, but it was a bittersweet victory.

How could she say goodbye to Nick? She should be happy; she had a place to call her own, at last. Was it wrong to want to be with him?

As if sensing her doubts, Nick looked across at her, his dark eyes holding hers. "I'll miss you so much."

Now, why did he have to go and say that? Swallowing back the tears threatening her eyes, she said, "I know. But we agreed we'd see each other a lot. At church, at the HFL meetings, and you can come over for pizza anytime."

His laugh was stilted. "I'll probably be over a lot. Henny won't be able to cook those elaborate meals anymore. We're both on a low-fat diet now."

"I'll come and help out," she offered, her heart melting. She wanted to run to him and hold him in her arms forever. But…he needed time and so did she. At least, that's what she kept telling herself.

He got up to leave. "I expect you to, but not tonight. Right now, you need to enjoy your first night in your new house."

"Nick?" she called. "Your parents would be so proud of what you've done."

That statement brought his head around. "Do you really think so?"

"Yes, I do."

He came back to lift one foot up onto the steps, his gaze searching her face. "I want to tell you something—something I haven't told anyone, not even Lydia."

"Okay," she said, patting the place he'd just vacated. "I'm listening."

He sat back down, his hands clasped. "I told you my father died during the oil crisis, but I didn't tell you how he died. He loved my mother so much, but he wasn't much of a church-goer. Mother and Lydia went to church, while Father and I concentrated on the business, always the business. Anyway, when Mother was diagnosed with cancer, well…he literally fell to pieces. And it got much worse after her death.

"I couldn't deal with that—seeing him so weak, so lost. It confused me because he'd always been so strong and firm, so distant and hard to understand. I turned away from him, refusing to help him through the worst time in his life. I couldn't deal with his grief, or mine."

Myla grasped his arm. "Go on. Tell me everything."

"I caused my father's death, Myla."

She gasped, her heart filling with compassion. "What do you mean?"

He continued to look down at the shiny new steps. "We had a terrible argument. He had changed so much, I was only trying to pull him back, to snap him back to reality. I needed him to be strong again. I shouted at him, reminding him of all the things he'd taught me—show no weakness, be a man, don't let anybody get the best of you.

"I think he realized he'd created a monster. I saw the disappointment in his eyes, watched him grip his chest. He died before the paramedics could get there. A massive heart attack. But even after his death, I was still that monster. I became even more cold and uncaring. I didn't have Lydia's strength, or the ability to open my heart."

"Nick, Nick, that's just not true." She brought his head around, pulling him down on her shoulder. "Inside, you were a caring person. You were just still grieving, and no wonder. Your father taught you about business, but he didn't teach you about what's really important in life."

He buried his face in her hair, his words muffled and raw with pain. "I can't do it anymore, Myla. I can't be that person. None of us can go through life without experiencing love. And for such a long time, I was afraid to love because I didn't want to wind up hurt and broken, like my father."

Myla didn't speak. She stroked his hair, understanding he'd carried this burden for so long. He cried softly, draining all the bitterness and the coldness out of his soul, then he lifted his head to look at her.

"I didn't know how to help him. I equated love and need with weakness." Taking her face in his hands, he said, "But you taught me that it's okay to be weak sometimes. You taught me that love is our strength."

"It is, it is," she said, closing her eyes to the overwhelming love inside her heart. "God has forgiven you, Nick. And so has your father. Isn't it about time you forgive yourself?"

He wiped the single tear from her face. "Isn't it about time we both forgive ourselves?"

He was right. She'd blamed herself for Sonny's misdeeds and his death. Nick had been through a similar pain. Maybe that was why God had brought them together.

"Let's forgive each other, right here, right now," she said, tears trailing down her face.

"Amen."

Together, they asked for God's forgiveness, and together, they prayed for a new hope and a new beginning. Then they sealed it with a kiss.

And somewhere, high up in a tree, a gentle dove cooed softly, her sweet call echoing their prayer and lifting it up toward heaven.

\* \* \*

"Momma, you look so pretty," Patrick said, a baseball glove in one hand and a Popsicle in the other.

Jesse nodded her agreement, her mouth opening with a squeal of glee. "It's the dress you dreamed about!"

Myla smiled down at her children. "Yes, it certainly is."

The green brocade dress brought back all the memories she'd stored up like a hidden treasure in her mind. It was a beautiful dress, but the real treasure was in the man who'd given it to her. Yet she'd chosen to leave him.

And he'd honored her choice by biding his time, learning patience, doing things that made her more and more proud of him each day.

He'd helped her realize her dream. She now had her own home. Glancing around the white walls of her small living room, Myla again felt the pride of being here, safe and in control, self-sufficient. That she'd gotten the house on her own merit helped to ease her loneliness. Maybe that should be enough.

But lately, other dreams had been filtering into her mind. What was stopping her from rushing into Nick's arms? What was holding her back from being with the man she loved with all her heart?

Knowing Nick had suffered a pain so similar to her own had made Myla see she'd been unfair to him right from the beginning. Nick was a self-made man, fashioned after his father's skewed idea of the perfect son. When he'd realized his father's stipulations were really a sham, that there was no foundation holding up his father's firm declarations, Nick had turned bitter. But Myla had seen that bitterness melt into a warmth that promised a new beginning for Nick. He was the best of his father, and his mother.

Tonight, she'd tell Nick that she loved him. She was out here on her own now, secure and confident that she could handle any situation. Although Nick had helped her along the way, she'd earned her catering reputation with her hard work and her determination, and she'd earned this house through her own efforts and the backing of a group dedicated to helping others. She wouldn't let any of them down.

Especially Nick.

Car lights illuminated the front yard, shining through the screen door like a spotlight. A neighbor's teenage daughter, a sweet girl named Lily, came into the room with popcorn, all set to stay with the children and enjoy a movie on television.

"Looks like your date's here," Lily said, her expression dreamy. "Wow, he's nice-looking."

"Yes, he is," Myla had to agree.

"Isn't he the one that planted that big yellow rose out by the front steps?"

"The very one," Myla replied, remembering the morning she'd awakened to find the beautiful rose planted underneath her bedroom window. She'd fallen for him all over again.

Nick stepped onto the porch, his gaze settling on Myla as she opened the screen door. "You look great," he said, his eyes sweeping over her. "I'm as nervous as a teenager at his first prom."

"You don't look nervous," she said with a breathless laugh. "Black tie becomes you, Mr. Rudolph."

He tugged at his bow tie. "Thank you. Green brocade becomes you. Are you ready?"

"Ah...yes." She grabbed the small black purse she'd found at a secondhand store. Turning to the children, she said, "Behave for Lily, okay? And go to bed on time."

"I'll stay as long as you need me," Lily offered.

"Thanks," Myla said. She leaned down to kiss Patrick and then Jesse. "I love you," she whispered.

Her words tore through Nick. He wanted her to say those words to him. But he was fast losing hope. He'd watched her walk out of his home; he'd let her go, hoping against hope that she'd come back. He couldn't bear to have her out of his life, but he'd planted her a yellow rose as a symbol of her new freedom. When would she come back home to him?

He guided her down the steps, silent and serious, then helped her into the car, his heart now a hopeless mess, his mind tortured with loneliness.

Myla noticed his silence and tried to relax, but her nerves were strung tight. Thinking of how she'd changed since her first ride in this car, she looked out the window, watching the cottages and apartments give way to businesses and skyscrapers as they headed downtown to the Expo Hall located on the Red River.

"Are you all right?" Nick asked, his eyes on the road.

"Fine." She chanced a glance at him, wanting to ask him the same thing. "I just hope I don't embarrass myself or you."

"You won't. You probably gave the hardest speech of your life that night in my kitchen when you first told me about Sonny."

They reached the parking lot, which was already packed. Nick concentrated on finding a spot close to the building. Pulling the car into place, he switched off the ignition, then turned to Myla. "Before we go in, I just wanted to tell you—" With a groan, he reached for her, kissing her firmly on the lips. Then he let her go to stare at her. "Good luck."

"Thanks," she said, breathless. "I'll need a little luck to survive this speech." *Especially after that kiss.*

"Oh, you'll survive. That's what you do best."

Stopping him, she said, "Nick, I couldn't have survived these past few months, not without you."

She wanted to say more, but his continuing dark mood only added to her anxiety. Was he having doubts of his own?

As Nick helped her out of the car, then quietly and firmly guided her toward the doors of the big building, her heart sank. He seemed so distant tonight, more like the old Nick. Yet his kiss had been so real, so stirring. Maybe she was just imagining things because of her jittery nerves.

After the speech, then, she'd tell him she loved him. If it wasn't too late.

Inside, the glittering crowd of some of the city's richest patrons contrasted sharply with their purpose of being here. Lydia had estimated they'd be raising over one hundred thousand dollars to help build and remodel low-cost housing.

The minute they entered the massive hall, people began to stop Nick, shaking his hand, patting him on the back, congratulating him for being the steering force behind this ad hoc organization. He introduced Myla as they went along, but the glamorous faces started to merge in her mind.

Then the reporter who'd been in on the first committee meeting walked up to greet them. "Hello, Nick," Brooke Alexander said, her smile beaming as brightly as her simple diamond pendant.

Nick shook her hand. "Hi, Brooke, how are things at KTAS?"

"Great." Turning to Myla, the petite brunette said, "Good to see you again, Mrs. Howell. I understand you'll be giving testimony to HFL, Incorporated's good work here tonight."

Myla nodded. "Yes, as you know, I'm one of the recipients of that good work. The Rudolphs have helped me tremendously over the past few months."

Brooke stuck her microphone in Nick's face. "What do you have to say about that, Nick? You used to be called ruthless. You always wanted to remain anonymous, sort of a silent backer. Since serving on this undertaking with you, I've seen a different Nick Rudolph. Care to tell our viewers what's changed?"

Nick looked at the woman in green beside him, his eyes locking with hers. "A lot of things, but mostly, my attitude. Now, if you'll excuse us—"

With that, he urged Myla to keep moving. "I've had enough of reporters for one night."

Myla glanced back at him, thinking maybe she'd figured out the reason for his dark mood. "She's right, though, isn't she? You did want to remain anonymous before."

Nick shot her a frustrated look, tugging her close in the crowded room. "Yeah, right. Well, not anymore. I'm right here in the spotlight tonight, and involved in every aspect of this new organization."

Aggravated with his sarcasm, she said, "Well, why do you look so miserable?"

"Because I'd rather be somewhere else, alone with you." His eyes blazing, he said, "I miss you, Myla. I prayed for patience, but it isn't working."

She couldn't help her smile, and the wave of relief that washed over her. "I can tell."

"I want you back," he said just as the crowd shifted, pushing them together. He stared down at her, longing to tell her what was in his heart. But he'd promised to give her time. So he could only hold her close, taking in the fresh scent of her upswept hair, taking in the emerald green of her shining eyes as he fell in love with her all over again. "I want…to kiss you again."

Before Myla could tell him that she wanted to be back with him, and that she wanted him to kiss her again, Brooke Alexander appeared by his side. "Oh, Nick, I had one more question."

Groaning, Nick tried to be polite to the smug woman. "Look, Brooke, I don't have any comments to contribute to your newscast. I just want to enjoy this evening."

"Oh, don't be so modest," Brooke insisted. "Everyone knows you spearheaded this organization, but do they know the real story?"

"What story?" he asked warily, his gaze shifting from Myla to the jeering reporter.

The reporter leaned forward, her tone conspiring as she covered her mike. "From what my sources tell me, you had a lot more to do with Mrs. Howell getting this first house than anyone is aware of. Rumor has it your relationship with her involves more than just a neighborly concern."

Nick tried to pry Myla away, but she stood watching the reporter's face expectantly. The woman was obviously implying she knew about their relationship, Myla decided. Well, she wouldn't let Nick take the heat, and she certainly wouldn't let this woman turn their relationship into something other than what it was, just for the sake of sensationalism.

"It does involve more," she said, deciding honesty would be the best policy. She'd tell this nosy newshound the facts about what a good man Nick Rudolph really was. "It involves people caring about the community; it involves a kind, decent man helping someone in need. I think your viewers should know that, Brooke."

Sensing she had a story, Brooke Alexander pressed closer. "Anything else you'd like my viewers to know, Mrs. Howell?"

Nick tried to shove Myla away from the pesky woman. "No, she doesn't have anything else to say. As you know from serving on this committee, Mrs. Howell had to be approved by the *entire* board of directors in order to receive her house. I actually had very little to do with their decision to finance her house."

That didn't stop the reporter. "But shouldn't she know *who* donated the house she's living in?"

That stopped Myla in her tracks. "What do you mean?"

Her expression triumphant, Brooke continued, "We all know about the volunteers who've worked on remodeling the house, but we don't have the whole story on the person who actually gave the house to Hope, Faith and Love, Incorporated.''

Shoving the mike back at Myla, she asked, "Wouldn't you like to know who that person is, Mrs. Howell, so you could thank *him* personally and publicly?''

Myla's heart raced as fast as her mind. It didn't take much to figure out what the reporter was hinting at. Nick had bought her house for her. That's why this had been too easy. Why hadn't she seen it before? Maybe because she hadn't wanted to?

Before she could comment, Nick tugged her through the crowd. "Just keep walking."

"What was that all about?" she asked. "Or should I tell you? When he didn't turn around, she said, "You *gave* me that house, didn't you?"

Nick looked at her as if she'd gone daft, but she saw the truth in his eyes.

"You did. You bought me a house!" Anger spilling forth, she added, "After all that talk about the board's approval and other people being screened, you handpicked a house for me, then you just gave it to me. I didn't get it on my own, after all."

Dragging her close, Nick decided it was time to put all of his thoughts into action. "All right, yes! I bought the house—to remodel for you—because I love you."

That declaration stopped her. "Love? You love me?" Even as her heart swelled, she relived the dread that being married to Sonny had brought her. "But you deceived me, Nick. This is downright unethical, just like something Sonny would have pulled."

"I am *not* Sonny," he said, drawing a weary breath. "And for months now, I've been trying to prove that to you. I wanted you to be happy, Myla, and if that meant letting you go, then—"

"Happy?" She snapped the one word back at him. "How can I be happy knowing the man I love lied to me about something so important?"

Through his embarrassment, Nick saw a ray of hope. She'd said *the man I love.* He'd heard her, and so had half the city. He had witnesses.

All around them, people were staring and whispering, some with smiles on their faces, others with shock registered in their eyes.

"I wasn't deceitful," he insisted. "I didn't lie to you. I just never exactly spelled out the stipulations. All I did was buy a piece of run-down property. As a matter of fact, I bought several. Then I backed off and let the board decide the rest." Wanting to convince her, he said, "There were several applicants, too, but you had the best record. You had two jobs, and you were trying to find a place to live. A lot of the board members remembered you from our famous Christmas party, so they knew you were working on improving your situation.

"The other applicants, while needy, didn't seem as determined as you. One complained about having to work on the house, and the other, well, he took off to another state with some hefty donations he'd stolen from Magnolia House. I'm learning that not everyone is as trustworthy as you, Myla."

"So am I," she retorted, tapping her foot in agitation, her green eyes blazing fire.

"Just try to understand," he said lamely, wishing hard that he'd been honest with her all along. "I just wanted you to have a chance."

"*Everyone* who applied for that house deserved the same chance," she said, her anger calming to a slow boil. "But you bypassed that and gave the house to me."

"No, I did not," he said in defense of his actions. "I simply donated a house to the cause. The board picked you. And me, well…yes, I wanted to help you. I'd already cost you your place at Magnolia House, so I wanted you to have what you most desired."

"I won't live there, not knowing you practically gave it to me."

"I did not give it to you. You still have to pay off the loan," he reminded her, hoping to encourage her to be reasonable. When she kept heading for the door, he added, "I only did it because I love you, Myla. You see, I learned another lesson my father forgot to teach me—the one about having to let something go, in order to prove your love."

"You have a funny way of interpreting that," she said over her shoulder.

Determined, he called after her in a loud booming voice, "Myla, let's stop fighting. We love each other. I need you. And you need me."

Embarrassed and aware of their growing audience, she gave him a scathing look. "No, I don't."

Nick waved a hand in the air, scattering curious, elegantly dressed people left and right. "Yes, you do. I know it. You know it. And now, everyone in Shreveport knows it."

Looking across the room at him, she said, "And they also know that you're still as ruthless as ever. How could I have ever trusted you?"

"Because we love each other."

She ran out the door. Behind him, Nick heard someone clapping. The entire mob chimed in with a hearty round of applause. Turning, he saw Lydia and Grant watching him, along with everybody else in town.

"Bravo!" Lydia called out. "Glad you two finally saw the light. Now go after her. She's still got to make her speech!"

Growling at his sister's unsinkable optimism, he called back, "I think she just did!"

He caught up with her out on the steps facing the river, where a spring breeze teased at her billowing skirt. Inside, the Shreveport Symphony launched into Mozart, while Nick's head buzzed with adrenalin and aggravation.

"Leave me alone," Myla said, her hair whipping in the wind. "I need to think."

Groaning, he jabbed a hand toward her face. "Myla, think about this—buying the property was the only way I could get things started. Someone had to donate the first house to be renovated. I had the funds to do it, but I knew you'd never agree to me just handing it over to you."

"Yes, you knew!" She faced him squarely, her eyes blazing. "But you did it anyway. Can't you see, Nick, I've lived with deceit and lies and hypocrisy for so long, I just can't tolerate it, even for a good reason, even for someone I—"

"Someone you love?" Nick reached out, pulling a sprig of burnished hair away from her face. "It's scary, isn't it?"

Her eyes widened with wonder. "You're scared, too, right? You've practically told me how scared you are. But you shouldn't have lied to me, Nick. We're supposed to trust each other, remember?"

His heart soaring, he tugged her around. "Of course, I'm scared, and of course, I trust you. It's myself I couldn't trust. Why do you think it took me so long to tell you how I feel? I'm so used to taking action, I forgot to just tell you with words."

She thought about how he'd opened up to her, sitting there on the porch that day. "You told me about your father. Why didn't you tell me what you'd done with the house?"

He shrugged, then looked away, out at the churning waters of the Red River. "You wanted the house. I wanted you to be happy. I guess I'm still working on the part about putting things into God's hands. This wouldn't have backfired on me, if I'd only placed more trust in Him."

"And if I'd put more trust in you," she admitted. Searching his face, Myla took a long, shuddering breath to control her skittish emotions. "We've both been busy trying to control *my* life. I've been as bad as you, not willing to give an inch because I felt I had to show everyone I could do it."

Laughing softly, he urged her to him. "Myla, sweet Myla. I don't want to control you. I just want to spend the rest of my life with you. We can have fun working out the details."

But she still wasn't so sure. "What do you see in me?"

Cupping her face between his hands, Nick searched her eyes. "I'll tell you what I see. I see a strong, beautiful woman who's worked hard to bring herself up out of poverty. I see hope, faith, love…and my own salvation."

She started to cry, then—tears of joy, mixed with tears of pain, as her heart let go of its pride. "Oh, Nick. You planted me a rosebush. That was the sweetest thing. You planted me a rosebush at a house you managed to get for me—just so you could give me the freedom to make my own choice. There is no greater sacrifice than that."

Loving her logic, Nick said, "I had to let you go, in order to win you back. It was the hardest thing I've ever tried to do. Please tell me I didn't fail completely."

Watching his face, seeing the sincerity and fear playing through his eyes, Myla was touched in that distant, secret spot where she'd stored up her love for him. Nick had the same doubts, had known the same pain and hopelessness she'd once known. But in spite of it all, he'd stood by her and her children. She realized with a burst of joy that neither of them had had a choice in the matter.

It had been in God's hands all along.

As if reading her thoughts, Nick said, "Myla, if I didn't have a dime to offer you, I'd still want to help you, to give you anything to make you happy and secure. I'd never desert you or try to control you. I just want to love you, to spend my life with you, whether it's at my house or yours. Wherever you are—that's my home, Myla. And that's the honest truth."

With that, Myla threw herself in his arms. "We both had something to prove."

Nick hugged her close, relief washing over him. He'd never make the same mistake twice. From here on out, he'd be completely honest with her, and with himself. Starting now.

Letting her go, he bent down on one knee. With the Red River flowing by a few feet away from them, he took her hand in his. "Now that we've settled all of that, I have something to ask you."

Myla's eyes widened while her heart fluttered like the flags flapping in the wind above their heads. "Yes?"

"Okay, I was only going to ask if I could have your cheesecake at dinner."

With both hands, she playfully slapped him on the shoulders. "Oh, you!"

Lifting his head, Nick asked her the real question on his mind. "Will you marry me?"

Tears fell down her cheeks. "Will you stop doing things behind my back in the name of love?"

"Hey, I'm doing the asking here, but yes, I promise to be completely up front with you—always. Now, I repeat, will you marry me?"

"Yes, I'll marry you."

"Do you love me?"

"I do love you."

"That's good, because I love you, too. Let's have pizza at the wedding reception. And a huge, fattening pound cake."

"Okay." She waited for him to stand, then threw herself into his arms for that other kiss they had both been wanting.

Nick enjoyed the kiss, then looked at his watch. "Come on, you have a speech to make."

"Wait." She reached into her clutch purse to pull out her dog-eared copy of the speech she'd prepared. "I don't need any pointers. I know exactly what I want to say."

"And what's that?"

Myla stopped, looking up at him, her eyes filled with tenderness. "I couldn't have done it without hope, faith, and...love."

Nick looked up at the stars twinkling over their heads. "And the greatest of these is love."

"That's right," Myla said, moving up the steps toward the ballroom. "It's all a matter of knowing whom to trust."

# Epilogue

"Quite a crowd today," Nick said, his arm wrapped around his wife's slender waist.

"Yes, but we expected that with the holidays so near." Leaning against him, Myla watched as people came and went, Christmas packages tucked underneath their arms, the smell of fresh-baked bread and homemade vegetable soup wafting around them.

"Well, you should be proud. I am." Nick kissed the top of her head, then patted the soft rounding bulge just beginning to show in her stomach. "We have a lot to be thankful for this Christmas."

"Uh-huh." Myla grimaced. "If I can just get through morning sickness."

"Feel bad?"

"No, I feel marvelous, happy and in the Christmas spirit. I can handle a little nausea."

"Yeah, I believe you can handle just about anything. Guess that's why I love you so much." He gave her another peck on the cheek, then let her go. "I've got to get moving. The next group of volunteers is waiting for me to teach them how to build houses. Come on, walk me to the truck."

Myla followed him through the glass double doors of the modest brick building, squinting at the noonday sun running down Line Avenue. After eight months of marriage, she was still very much in love.

And amazed at how blessed her life was now. She'd become partners with Grant, her soon-to-be brother-in-law. Then, keeping that partnership intact, and with Nick's encouragement, she'd opened up this place.

Bread of Life was more than a restaurant, though. It was a unique place where people who didn't have money for food could eat a good hot meal, along with some of the most influential people in the city, who paid donations to keep the nonprofit restaurant open. So far, the response had been tremendous.

Homeless people found hope here, in the form of job offers or assistance with education, or medical needs.

Nick liked to tell people it offered more than a meal, it offered solutions. And he was now a vital part of those solutions, a devout advocate for homeless rights and ways of getting people off the streets and back to productive lives.

He and Myla had even toned down their own lives, remodeling the mansion to make it more childproof and homey, and putting a needy family in the house he'd originally donated for Myla.

Reaching his used work truck where Jessica and Patrick sat waiting, Nick turned now, pulling Myla into the circle of his arms. "Don't work too hard, Mrs. Rudolph. We've got a lot to celebrate this year."

Myla nuzzled his neck, savoring the warmth and security he always offered. "Yes, we certainly do."

"Hey, Mama," Patrick called through the partially open window, "are you sure you're gonna be done here by Christmas?"

"Of course she will," Jessica replied in her proper, big-sister tone. "She's just doing her job first."

Giving her children that endearing look Nick loved so much, Myla nodded to her family. "I promise, I'll be home for Christmas."

Nick looked up to the shimmering winter sky, then smiled at his wife. "This year, we'll *all* be home for Christmas."

\*   \*   \*   \*   \*

Dear Reader,

Homelessness has always been a problem the world over, yet we can never give up hope that it will eventually be solved.

I'm thrilled that Steeple Hill has included this special story in this 3-in-1 volume. This story has a lot of meaning for me because for the last few years I've been involved with a local homeless shelter called Providence House. It is much like the shelter portrayed in Myla's story. At Providence House, residents are taught how to get back on their feet. They move from having nothing to having the kind of safe, secure lives we all cherish, and they do it one day at a time, one step at a time. You see, we can't just feed someone the fish. We have to teach them how to fish for themselves.

While Myla's story is part fairy tale and part reality, I have seen other mothers with children who have accomplished going from homeless to finding a home in time for Christmas. It happens all the time, but it's a long, hard road. I believe in these women. I know they can achieve the same success that Myla found with the help of organizations such as Providence House.

It's not easy, but there is a way to break the cycle. I hope my story will inspire you to work toward helping the homeless, and in doing so, may you find nourishment for your own soul, because having a home truly is a gift. Have a blessed holiday season!

Until next time, may the angels watch over you always.

Lenora Worth

Next Month From Steeple Hill®'s

## *Love Inspired*®
# Sadie's Hero
by
## Margaret Daley

Irrepressible Sadie Spencer would do anything to help her students—including bidding on wealthy Andrew Knight at a charity auction! Soon Sadie realizes her students aren't the only ones in need of help. Andrew turned away from God after a tragic accident robbed him of his parents. Slowly, Sadie's love breaks through the walls Andrew has built around his heart, but will Andrew find the courage to finally make peace with God?

**Don't miss**
**SADIE'S HERO**

*On sale November 2002*